SHANTY GOLD

SHANTY GOLD

Daughters of Ireland

Jeanne Charters

OPEN ROAD

INTEGRATED MEDIA
NEW YORK

ISBN: 978-1-5040-8022-4

This edition published in 2023 by Open Road Integrated Media, Inc.
180 Maiden Lane
New York, NY 10038
www.openroadmedia.com

SHANTY GOLD

CHAPTER ONE

AUGUST, COUNTY CORK IRELAND

May the road rise to meet you.

Near dawn, others join me on the walk to Cobh. Silent stragglers they are—a man, a woman, and a wee boy, dragging behind them paltry gatherings from a lifetime of poverty. At first, their presence is a comfort, but the shuffling feet send dust into the air and me mouth turns to sand. I spy a pond in the distance and crawl toward it, but the water's mostly mud. Back on the road, me three companions are gone.

I fall onto the stones. You win, Ireland. Killed me like me kin, you did. 'Tis a relief to quit this hopeless effort. Time drifts by. So this is how it feels to die, is it? Not so bad.

But then there are hands, tugging under me arms and pulling me over a rough rail into a wooden cart. That gobsmacks me brain some, I'll tell you. I thought I'd left such things as splintery carts behind me. I close me eyes and fall into sacred sleep.

The sun is high in the sky now, so time has passed, but I don't know how much of it. I yearn to straighten me legs, but boxes cram every inch of space. A blacksmith's anvil digs into me spine.

3

Sweet smells of wildflowers drift into the cart. 'Tis the wondrous scent of summer in Ireland. Could I move, I'd pick some to slake the hunger gnawing me belly, but I'm too tired.

A woman speaks, "Look, Tim. The road to Cork City. We could kiss the Blarney stone." She laughs. "That'd do us well in Canada."

Canada? She hums a Gaelic song Mam used to sing. It lulls me back into sleep, but the noisy caw of herring gulls jolts me awake. Da once said, "Blast those birds. Had I a gun, I'd shoot them all out of the sky."

This day, I'd do the same.

The hands shake me awake. "Girl, who are you? Where are you headed?" He is elderly, nearly as old as me father, with at least thirty years etched on his face, so I try to give a respectful answer.

"Mary Boland, sir," I say, shocked by the rasp that is me voice. "I was walking to Cobh, but . . ."

"The blessings of St. Brigid are with you this day, Mary," the woman says in a voice soft as a lamb's coat. Her face glows with kindness, like saints on holy cards. She strokes the hair from me eyes. "That's where we're headed as well. But the Cork harbor is called Queenstown now, not Cobh. To honor Victoria's visit."

I close me eyes again. *Who's this Victoria?*

Bits of their talk mix with the sounds of the squawking gulls. "She's just a child, Tim. Why is she be traveling to Queenstown alone?"

"Let her rest, love. Lots of children have tried to get to the ships. Most don't make it. She's a lucky one."

Night darkens the sky, and rain pounds on me back. A blanket lowers over me, and I sigh in gratitude.

As the sun reddens the East again, I sit up, wincing at the soreness in me hip. Biting wooden splinters out of me hands,

I glance up and see them staring back at me. A grin feels silly on me face, but 'tis the best I can do.

"So, you're Mary Boland, are you?" the man says.

"Yes, sir."

"We're Tim and Moira Donahue," she says. "Call me Moira and him, Tim," she gestures toward the man.

It is unseemly to call someone her age by a first name, but I'll do as I'm told. I don't want to get kicked from this wagon. "Thank you, I will, Moira."

"How old are you, child?" Her voice is sweet as soda bread.

"What year is this?" I say, knowing that sounds ignorant. "No one in me village kept a calendar."

"It's 1849, girl," Tim answers.

"Well, I was born on St. Patrick's Day, 1836, but I'm no good at ciphering." I blush, knowing how stupid they must think me.

"You're thirteen-years-old then," he says.

Thirteen is it? My, I'm nearly grown.

"Where are your mother and father?" Moira asks. I brace me heart against the telling.

"Da sailed for America a while back. He said he'd send money for us to come over. We never got it, though. I think the landlord stole it."

"I wonder if he even survived the trip," Tim whispers.

Me heart stops. "You think me da's dead?"

"Nah, girl. He's probably fine." His deep tone reminds me of Da's when he held me on his lap reading from *Gulliver's Travels*.

"And your mother?" Moira asks. I don't want to remember, but must.

"Mam died a week ago, along with the baby, Ellen."

The woman's eyes are brimming when she looks at me again. "I'm so sorry," she whispers. I can tell she means it.

"What was your village?" Tim asks.

"Kinsale."

"Ah, lovely place," Moira says. "On the Great Ocean."

"Aye, 'twas lovely," I answer, as images wash over me—green rolling hills, whitecaps and white sails, salmon jumping to the nets, sheep, friends, parties, and family—most of all, family. The memories threaten me speech until hot anger rescues me tongue. "But no longer. The ships there fly British flags now."

Tim grunts. "Since that hoor's melt English Pope let Henry the Eighth invade us seven-hundred years ago."

"Hush with your blaspheme, Tim," Moira hisses, then turns to me, "How did your mother pass?"

I brace me heart against the telling. "Before he left, Da sold his fishing boat and nets and bought oats to last us till he could earn money for our passage. But our sheep died, and we had no wool to ship to England. The landlord burned our cottage."

"Most of our village was burned out this past year," Tim says, shaking his head. "All that remains there is a few pitiful huts and the landlord's grand house. We knew we'd be next." He turns to face me. "Why did you not go to the nuns?"

"Mam wouldn't hear of it. 'Bolands don't take charity,' she said, and meant it."

He shakes his head like maybe his mam was proud, too.

"When Mam made her mind up, there was no changing it. So I found us a cave." I shiver, remembering, and then hug meself so I can go on with the awful next part. "It was cold and wet in the cave. Da had given me his revolver before he left and trained me to use it. I was a good shot. I sold the gun for peat to warm the cave. But then, Mam got the dysentery. I couldn't make it stop, though I tried all the old remedies. I think it was from spoilt soup the British gave us at the soup kitchen."

Tim's murmur is harsh. "Bastards! If they can't kill us by

starving or burning us out, they poison us with their putrid gruel."

"I tried to make Mam better," I say, swallowing a moan, "but nothing helped."

Moira touches me cheek.

"When Mam's milk dried," I say, straightening me back, "the baby passed quick. Mam died soon after. I think her heart was broken." The fury of watching them die returns in a rush. Then, the anger turns to grief. Tears won't help, but that doesn't stop them. I brush them away. I never cried, not even when I took the gold cross from Mam's fingers and fastened it around me neck. Not when I dug their graves with me hands and laid them there together beneath the hawthorn tree. Not when I took the boots from Mam's feet and pulled them onto me own. Not even when I covered the two of them over with the stones.

At once, the memory flips me sadness to wrath and I nearly scream. I think of Da's words. 'Meter your temper, Mary. Me mother was an O'Brien. The O'Briens have Banshee blood. Save your rage for those who deserve it.'

These dear people do not deserve it. The cart is quiet for a time. I think we all are deep in our own memories, but then, Tim says, "You walked all the way from Kinsale? That's at least thirty miles from where you fell."

"I'd have made it the whole way but, once down, couldn't wake up. I'd have died for sure if you hadn't come upon me."

Moira climbed into the back of the cart and wrapped her arms tight around me shoulders. "Ah, love," she croons, rocking me like a báibín. The kindness of her touch nearly sets me weeping again, but I set me jaw tight as a badger trap. She taps the man on his shoulder. "Tim, give me a bit of that bread and the water jug. The child is starved to bone." When she hands me the bread, I try to chew slow. Mam said you could pick out a lady from a shanty girl by the way she ate. But the hunger makes me swallow too fast, and the bread sticks in me throat. I hiccough like a common drunkard. "Excuse me, please. I ate too quickly."

"That's all right, Mary. You're hungry. The good Lord sent us to help you," she answers. "Things will be better now." I lean back against her. Her arms feel good—almost like Mam's.

"What was your village?" I ask, and then take a swig from the water jug, careful not to let it dribble down me chin.

"Killarney," she says. "We held on through the first year, but when the potatoes came up black again, we couldn't produce our quota of grain. It was only a matter of time 'til our cottage would be ashes.

"We've booked tickets on the Sheridan, a ship headed for New York. Cost us dear, four pounds each, British sterling. It's all we had left. We sail tomorrow." She turns me around and looks deep into me eyes. It's as if she's looking for me soul itself. "What ticket did you book?" she asks. *Can I trust her with the truth? Will they put me back on the road if they know I haven't a farthing in me boot, let alone money for a ticket?*

I decide on a half lie. "I haven't a ticket yet, ma'am. I plan to buy one at the wharf."

Her face goes dark. "Are you sure you have ticket money, Mary?"

"Sure I do," I lie all the way this time. "I saved it from what me da got for the boat." She needn't know that all I have in me pocket is a toothbrush. I haven't reckoned yet how I'll get on a ship. I'll figure that out once I get to Cobh or whatever they're calling it now. What did she say? Queenstown? No matter.

She lifts me hair off me face and twirls it around her fingers. "Lord God, your hair must be lovely when it's clean. Such a pretty shade of red and so curly. You're going to be a beauty when you grow up." I feel heat rising all the way up to me scalp, likely turning me face the fiery crimson I hate. Compliments embarrass me. Da used to say I have the coloring of a Celtic goddess to make me blush. I know how I look—too tall for me frame, too scrawny, too pale, and all of it topped off with crazy red hair spiraling around me head like the Banshee herself. That's what Siobhan used to call me when she got mad at me—Banshee girl. All the blather in the world can't turn me pretty.

"Ah, that's just blarney, missus," I tell her. "Me mam was the pretty one, and the baby, too. Their hair was black as midnight and their eyes blue as the River Shannon itself. Honestly, when you touched their skin, it felt like flower petals. I'm white as that stupid goat there." I point to one in the field. "Mam and Ellen were plump and soft before the hunger wasted them. I've always been bony like a skeleton, the gránna one of me kin."

"You're wrong, Mary," she says. "You will be a great beauty."

I shake me head and fake a grin. "Nah, I'm the strong one. Da taught me to ride the horse faster and shoot a pistol straighter than any boy in Kinsale. I could out wrestle them, too.

"Mam always said to the neighbors, 'Ah, look at me Mary, will you? Láidir, she is. She has the strength of the son I never had.' She was right. I am strong and faster than any of the lads in me village. I won all the races."

Moira laughs out loud. "I wager you're right at that. You must be strong and fast. Look how far you got before you fell." I nestle me cheek against the soft flannel covering her shoulder and gaze at the sun lighting the whitecaps of the Irish Sea. I've loved this land since me birth, and grief at leaving it nearly takes me over. But this blossoming countryside is fake as a leprechaun's kiss. The glory of Ireland was fashioned by the devil's hand, not God's. So I sit up and stiffen me neck. Touching Mam's cross, I remember me pledge to her. I will get on a ship. I will find Da. I will go to a land where food grows plentiful. Ireland is a place of death, not plenty. I will not falter. "Don't be so strong you make all the boys run from you, Mary," Moira says. "Someday, you'll want to marry, you know."

"Oh, not me, Moira," I say, stammering the name even as I say it. "I'll not marry, ever. That's what I told me friend, Siobhan, before she sailed off to Australia with her family. Siobhan was always picking one lad or another to be her husband when she got grown. But when she asked me who I would marry, the answer was always the same. No one."

"You'll change your mind when the right one shows his face," Moira says. Let her think what she wants. I know what goes on between a man and wife. Our cottage was one room after all. In the dark of night, I heard what me parents did when they thought me sleeping. Nothing of that sounded like something I'd fancy. Of course, I can't say that to the Mrs. Donahue. Such talk would be a scandal.

CHAPTER TWO

A heart as black as Satan's cloak . . .

When we pull into the Queenstown harbor, me mouth hangs open at the sights and sounds of it. People swarm across the wooden dock, some laughing like eejits and others keening as if mourning their own death. And why not? Life as they know it ends this day. But if I'd ever wailed publicly like they do, Mam would've switched me for acting the culchie. Laughing or crying, all these people look the same. Thin and grey as ghosts and dressed in layers of ragged tatters. But who am I to talk—me in me gunnysack dress and muddy old boots.

Heavy scents of salt and fish invade me nose. And different smells as well. Food cooking from harbor-side restaurants and the sour reek of alcohol. I recognize that one from the mornings-after parties in Kinsale. Mam always said the men never figured when to quit with the poteen.

As Tim ties up the cart, Moira and I climb down. As soon as we light on the ground, a plump lady with fair hair piled up in a topknot rushes over to us. It's strange to see anyone with so much flesh on her body when everyone else looks to be starving. When she speaks, I understand. A British accent hums thick on her tongue.

"Moira," she says, grabbing the Missus into her arms. "I'd hoped we'd meet one more time before you sailed."

Moira hugs her back and turns to me. "Mary Boland, meet Elizabeth Bradshaw. We met in Killarney only last week. She was one of Victoria's ladies-in-waiting when the Queen visited this year." The Bradshaw woman puffs up her chest like the cocky village rooster who used to wake me up at home.

Ah, so that's who this Victoria is. I spit on her name. I make an awkward curtsy to the woman, and she pulls me up and stares me straight in the eyes. "No need to bow to me, girl. I'm not royalty, just a woman from London who got stuck in this Godforsaken country after the Queen sailed back to England without me." She cackles a harsh laugh.

London. That's where our landlord came from. He was fat, too, and his homely wife even fatter. Me lip curls as I remember the time I tried to sell him our wagon for grain, and he wouldn't budge on the niggardly bag of oats he offered. When I dangled Mam's gold cross in front of his pudgy face and asked for a shilling or two, he'd said, "Oh no, Mary. I wouldn't want no one thinking me wife's a Papist, now would I?"

I've never met a kind Brit, but I must be polite for Moira and Tim's sake. "It's good to make your acquaintance, Mrs. Bradshaw."

"It's Miss Bradshaw," she says.

I warm to her with that one, I'll tell you. A woman who has never married. I peer at Moira and cock me eyebrow.

"Mary has vowed to remain single, Elizabeth," Moira says, laughing.

The British lady turns to me. "It's not as if I remained a maiden lady by choice. Me father favored no one who asked. Everyone was running short on cash when I was a girl. Since me family was approaching poverty, too, at the time, I was not considered a prize." She bleats out a loud guffaw, one me mam would have called a belly laugh, and that's a surprise. I've never met a merry Brit.

Me da used to say, 'Those limey bastards find nothing funny.' That's what he always called them—limey bastards. But I daren't mention that here, though I grin at the memory.

"I wager you'll find plenty of suitors when you reach the age for marrying, Mary," Elizabeth says. Then, she pinches her fingers across her nose. "However, I warrant it's been a while since you've had a bath. Would you like one?"

A bath? Next to food, I can imagine nothing more heavenly. "Oh yes, Miss. I would fairly die for a bath."

Moira frowns and asks. "Where can she get a bath, Elizabeth?"

"I've a small set of rooms on Haverly Street. See, it's right over there," she points to the right.

Tim scowls. "Watch Mary carefully, Elizabeth," he says. "The harbor can be a dangerous place for a young girl. Don't let any crewmen near her."

"Don't trouble your mind about that, you silly boy," she simpers, pushing at his shoulder with her hand. "I'll watch over her like a mother hen."

"Please, Moira, let me go. I so want to be clean." I tug at her sleeve like a child.

Moira's eyes fog with what looks like concern. She starts to say something to Tim, but finally turns back to Elizabeth. "All right, if you're sure." She takes me face into her hands. "Come to the party on the dock with Elizabeth tonight, Mary. We'll say our farewells then."

"We'll be there," Miss Bradshaw answers, hooking her arm through mine and pulling. "I never miss an American wake party. We'll meet you on the wharf after you've settled in your room and Mary has cleaned herself up a bit." She turns me away. "Ta ta."

I look back at the Donahues. Moira says. "See you soon, Mary."

We walk to a big stone house. Her rooms are on the second floor, and her apartment is double the size of our mud cottage in Kinsale. Bright sun shines through lace curtains, and the place is jammed with furniture. Every sofa and chair has a piece of Irish lace on it. Then I spy it—a bathtub. She strikes a match and I can smell the sulfur as she lights the wood under a large pot of water on the stove. "Mary, don't sit on the furniture," she says. "Stand where you are until the water is hot. Then, fill the tub.

"There are dresses available at the church," she continues. "The one you're wearing is far beyond washing. I'll find you a clean dress and pantaloons for under it."

Pantaloons? I try to remember if I ever saw Mam wearing them, but I can't recall. Such a thing seems a dreadful waste of money since no one will ever see them. But how sweet she is to want to buy them for me.

After Elizabeth leaves the room, I slip the filthy grain-sack dress off me. I start to toss it to the floor, then remember it was Mam's hands that made it. I bury me face into the rough fabric. Grief hits me like an ocean wave, but I shake it away. This dress cannot be part of the future I plan. Besides, I have Mam's gold cross, and no amount of dirt can ruin that. I caress the cross and take one final look at the dress, roll it into a ball and toss it into a corner.

The water doesn't scald at all, and when I lower me backside into that tub, it feels like I've entered heaven itself. Down, down I slide until me whole head is under. I don't come up until I need air. "Ahhhh." It's the only sound I can utter, but it does describe what I'm feeling.

After a blissful time of soaking, Elizabeth's voice comes from outside the door. "Mary, I'm leaving your dress and pantaloons here. Get them when you're ready."

There's a bar of soap in a little plate at the side of the tub and a cloth hanging on the front of it. Dare I use them? Would that be an overstep? No, she wouldn't have left them there if they shouldn't be used. Surely high-born Brits know better than that.

Once I've scoured so hard me skin burns and me hair is free of grit, I dry meself and cover up with the towel. Creeping to the door, I crack it wide enough to grab the clothes lying outside it. Good, no one's there to see me.

I slip on the pantaloons and turn to the looking glass. I was right. A scandalous waste of money.

The dress, though, is a treasure. It's soft flannel and smells so clean. The hem falls all the way to the top of Mam's boots, like a proper lady's. The high neck frills with a bit of lace. The lace is yellowed some, but surely better than anything I've ever known. The sleeves fall almost to me wrists. I curse me gangly long arms. I'd like for the sleeves to cover me scabbed-up hands, but ah well, we can't shine shit, now can we?

The dress is green and has rows of yellow flowers dancing across it like faeries freed from the forest. And there are buttons down the front. Mam sewed me dresses from grain sacks that I could pull over me head. I begin to fumble at those buttons, trying to fit them into the little holes on the other side and finally, the bodice covers me. I look in the glass and catch me breath. Wouldn't Mam love to see her Mary now? Looking like gentry and not the shanty girl she really is.

I spy a brush on the table beside the looking glass and, though it fears me some to use it without permission, I run it through me hair. When I'm through, I make sure there's nothing left in the bristles, for I wouldn't want to scandalize Miss Bradshaw with red hair stuck in there.

I twirl around in front of that mirror, loving the look of me in a proper dress. Me breath catches and I'm shocked to stillness to hear a knock on the door.

Chapter Three

Put silk on a goat, and it's still a goat.

I stand frozen at the mirror, and a voice says, "Mary."

It is Miss Bradshaw.

"Yes, ma'am."

"Are you decent?"

What? Of course, I'm decent. A good Catholic girl, that's what I am. Why would she ask me such a thing? I hold me breath and don't answer.

After a moment, she says, "I mean, are you dressed?"

Feeling foolish, I answer, "Yes, Miss Bradshaw. I'm dressed." I must learn to understand these things foreigners say, lest they figure what a dúr amadá I truly am.

She opens the door and looks me up and down like she's sizing up the value of a heifer. I banish this unkind thought from me head. This woman has been good to me and is a friend of Tim and Moira's. Mam always said to give people the sunny side of me judgment. "Trust, Mary, until you have reason not to." Those were her exact words.

"You look very nice, Mary."

"Thank you, Miss Bradshaw." I puff the skirt out from me and twirl like a dervish right there in front of her, so pleased with me reflection in the glass I can't stop the spinning.

She laughs. "You may call me Elizabeth. I hope we'll be friends."

I jolt to stillness. It feels unseemly to call a Brit by her first name. Me parents would never approve, but I swallow and say, "All right, Elizabeth. I hope so, too."

"Come now. The parties are starting on the dock. We'll find Tim and Moira." Right away, I feel better knowing I'll be with the Donahues again. What an eejit I am to yearn for them after Elizabeth's been so kind to me. Why can I not warm me heart to her? Is it because she's English? I must rid meself of such bigotry. It's not Christian. And besides, once I get to America, I'll be mingling with lots of people who aren't Irish, so I'd best get used to it.

As we walk toward the harbor, there is music playing in the distance, and me heart races at the sound of it. It seems I haven't heard such instruments in forever—not since I was a child. The beat stirs me deep inside. Me da said it's the music of the fairy folk and druids that still thrive in the green hills of Ireland. He said their blood runs in me veins as sure and true as that of me human ancestors, and that's why me intuition is so keen.

The sun is setting on the horizon as we arrive on the dock. Soon, it will be gone. Immediately, I am assailed by the scent of cooking meat. A rumbling stomach reminds me that, other than the bit of bread in the wagon, I haven't eaten for days.

But me hunger is almost forgotten when we arrive on the dock. Now, the music is loud and glorious, better than any I heard in Kinsale. Fiddles and penny whistles and a bodhran pound out the steady beat of a jig. I can't stop me body from bouncing to the rhythm. I was the dancer at home. Mam sang and Da tooted on a whistle, and I danced. Best in the village, that's what they called me. As bodies swirl around me, a man jolts into me and nearly knocks me to the ground.

"Sorry, love," he says, looking at me in a funny way.

I feel skittish at the look but figure he wants to see I'm not hurt. "That's all right, sir. I'm fine."

Elizabeth grabs me by the elbow. "Come. I'll buy you a sandwich."

A sandwich? Is it something else to wear? I've never heard the word. She takes me across the harbor to what seems to be a place for food. As we get closer, the smell of the meat sets me mouth drooling. I wipe it on me sleeve.

"Lamb on brown," she says to the man behind the counter, holding up two fingers. "And a stout for me." She turns to me. "Mary, would you like a stout?"

"Isn't that beer?"

"Yes, of course, it is."

"Oh no, Elizabeth. Mam said I'll need at least five years on me before I can drink spirits."

She turns back to the man. "Just water for me young friend."

"Right you are, Bess," he says with a wink.

Strange that he'd treat a queen's lady so casual. Ah well, like I said, I've much to learn of the ways of foreigners, and it's never too soon to start.

"Here's your sandwich, lass," he says, handing me a piece of thick brown bread wrapped around meat. *So this is a sandwich?*

"Thank you, sir," I say, then cram it in me mouth before I can remember me manners. Oh! Is it as good as it seems or am I that starved? No, it's truly better than anything I've ever tasted, and I thank God for His kindness in letting me eat it. *Sandwich.* I mark the word in me brain. I hope they have sandwiches in America.

As we walk back to the dock, I notice a little girl staring at me. No, she stares at me sandwich. Her eyes are large and black. More than anything, they are hungry. I take a big bite of me sandwich and hand the rest to her. As she crams it in her mouth, she mumbles a muffled, "Thank you, miss."

"Mary," a man's voice yells. When I turn toward the sound, there's Tim waving his hand above the sea of heads. It's a good thing he's so tall or I'd never have spotted him in this crowd.

He and Moira push their way toward us. "Mary, you look so pretty," Moira says, turning me around and around to get a good look at me dress.

"Elizabeth got it for me," I say, loving the compliment. I lift me skirt a bit. "And look, Moira, pantaloons under it! Though I do think it's foolish for a skint like me to be wearing such things."

Elizabeth smiles. "She cleans up nicely, doesn't she?"

"Jaysus yes, grand," Tim says. As he gazes at me, though, a frown creeps onto his face. Maybe he doesn't like me dress at all, but probably that's me silly imagination. Mam always said I could fancy a problem where none existed. Da, though, told me I sense things others don't, like a true Celt. But why is Tim frowning? Ah, foolishness. He's probably sad that he's sailing off tomorrow morning.

He turns to Elizabeth. "You've spoken to Moira about contacts you have on the ships."

"Yes, I have many," she answers, her voice cheery as a warbler in springtime.

"You will book a safe passage for Mary then?"

"Without a doubt."

He puts his hand into his pocket. "This isn't much, but I want you to use it to get her onto a reputable ship." He hands her some coins.

She pulls open the drawstrings on her little purse and drops the money into it. "Thank you, Tim. Every little bit helps."

Moira puts her arms around her husband's neck and pulls herself up on tiptoe to give him a kiss. "Thank you, love."

"So, are you two ready for your journey?" Elizabeth says.

"We've been ready for months," Moira replies. "Though it pains me heart to think of it. The hardest part was bidding goodbye to our families." She seems close to weeping, but then stamps her foot and says, "We surely can't stay in Killarney, though." Tim wraps his arm around her shoulders and she gazes up at him, love filling her eyes. "Tim, dance this reel with Mary, won't you? I'm too tired and you so enjoy a dance."

"Mary?" he says, looking down at me.

"Ah yes, Tim. I love to dance," I answer, then run quickly to the only empty space I see on the dock.

He puts his hands on me waist and I hold him round the neck. We spin and dance around the dock until Tim can scarce catch his breath. He holds up his hand and pants, "Enough."

When we get back to the others, he gasps, "This girl could dance the feet off Lola Montez. I'm too old to keep up with her."

"Who's Lola Montez?" I ask.

"Just the most famous dancer in Ireland, that's who," he answers.

As the music starts up again, I can't stop jumping up and down to its rhythms. I wish me da were here now. He'd show Tim how an old man can keep up with me. Da was the second best dancer in Kinsale.

A tall boy with brown hair and smiling eyes appears before me and says, "Would you dance with me, please?"

I look at Moira. She smiles and nods her head.

The boy and I take off across the floor in a breakneck jig. At its finish, we're both breathing hard. I laugh up at him and see that his eyes are beautiful, blue like me mam's were. Me heart races at the way he's smiling. No boy's ever been this close to me before.

"Another?" he says.

I nod yes, but before I can raise me arms to him, I'm caught into a reel by a burly young blonde lad whose arms are so muscled I fear they'll leave bruises on me skin. But I flex me own muscles up and follow him step-by-step until the crowd of people creates a circle around us and stand clapping as we dance like furies in the center of them.

At a quick pause in the music, I catch a glimpse of Moira and Elizabeth in the crowd. Elizabeth is laughing and drinking her stout, but Moira never takes her eyes off me.

The music stops, and the blonde boy with the hard arms tells me that these parties are held on the dock every night before a ship sails off from Ireland. "They're called American wake celebrations," he says, still gasping to recover his breath, then lowers his head. "Because those who leave never return."

His words leech the merriment right out of me heart. I look around at me people and see their struggle to be jolly in spite of hearts clearly breaking. Enough of this. I cannot allow the sad side of me nature to take me over now that escape is near.

When the blue-eyed boy taps me on the shoulder and asks for another dance, I shake me head. "I must return to me friends," I tell him. "They sail tomorrow. I need to wish them Godspeed."

The boy's face crumples some, but I figure he understands what loss has done to me, what it's done to all us Irish. He turns away.

Moira kisses me cheek when I go into her arms to say farewell. I know she can hear me sigh and feel the wetness on me cheeks. "Ah hush, mo chuisle," she croons. "We're all off to a better time of it." As I cling to her, she says, "Get up on the deck as often as you can, Mary. Breathe the sea air in deep. When you're down in the hold, stay away from anyone who's coughing or vomiting. Typhus is the thing that kills on these passages."

Finally, she pries herself away and lifts her chin so me eyes stare into her own which are now brimming with tears. "Your life is only beginning, Mary. Go with God."

Elizabeth circles us both in her ample arms. "Now don't you worry your head about the girl," she says. "She'll stay with me tonight, and I'll get her on a ship on the morrow."

Isn't life a wonder? I'd figured to sleep on the street this night. Who'd have thought that I'd be staying in the rooms of an Englishwoman? Dear God, please remind me not to pass harsh judgment so quick.

"You will watch her, Elizabeth?" Moira says. I see worry pushing the tears down her cheeks. "She's just a child. These ships can be hard on a girl. Make sure she gets on a good one and not one of those awful coffin ships."

"Now, now, Moira," Elizabeth says, patting her hand. "Put your concern out of that pretty head. I'll take very good care of Mary. Now off you go to your rooms." She sweeps at the two of them as though she carries a broom in her hands. "And bon voyage on the morrow."

Tim and Moira bid me goodbye with a last embrace, and I see tears glistening even in his eyes. "Stay well, Mary Boland," are the last words he says.

He takes Moira's hand. She kisses me cheek and silently walks away.

CHAPTER FOUR

A quiet start to the morning can mean a storm before night's end.

I am deep in a dream of running on the hillside with me friend, Siobhan, the two of us chasing a goat and laughing. The vision is so beautiful I want to stay in it, but a hand shakes me shoulder and a voice says, "Time to get up, Mary." It's Elizabeth. "After you're washed and dressed, take this brush and have a go at that hair."

"Are we going somewhere?" I ask, rubbing me eyes.

"Indeed, we are. We'll get a bite of breakfast and then I have an appointment."

"An appointment?" I ask. "With who?"

In a snap, she looks mad as a goat left overnight in the rain. She's shaking so much her topknot quivers. I notice streaks of gray in it I hadn't seen before. "Do not be impertinent, Mary. Just obey me."

So, I do as she says, all the time wondering what happened. There seems to be more than one Elizabeth, and I'm not sure which is real. I've not met people whose moods change so quickly. Maybe this is how many people behave. At any rate, she's all I have, so I must make the best of things.

The sun shines bright on the ocean when we walk out of the stone house. Already, the streets are bustling with travelers. Some carry pots and straw mattresses. "They must bring their own supplies onto the ships," Elizabeth explains. She buys two scones from a street vendor and a coffee for herself. "What do you want to drink?" she asks.

"A bit of goat's milk, perhaps?"

Without a word, she turns back to the vendor and orders the milk. I thank her, grateful for another day with food in me belly. She acts different this morning. Colder. Is it me imagination? Maybe me happy dream twisted me head off kilter.

We finish our scones, and she takes me into a store on the dock and buys a length of Kelly-green ribbon that exactly matches me dress. "Here, Mary. Tie up your hair with this," she says.

"Ah, thank you, Elizabeth. It'll be good to get it off me face."

As I tie me hair up onto me head, she picks up a white bonnet. "And put this on. Some sailors feel vexed at having a red-haired woman on a ship. An old superstition; something about a Banshee."

I understand that one all right. Once the Banshee picks out an Irishman, there's naught he can do to save himself. She'll wail him to his death. I tie the bonnet firmly under me chin.

In an instant, she becomes the Elizabeth of yesterday, sweet and caring. She stands back and stares at me. "Yes, now you look quite pretty."

I catch a glimpse of meself in a store window and am surprised to see she speaks the truth. I do look nice. Like a proper colleen in a lady dress, her hair covered with a neat new bonnet. Like a girl who has a Mam who cares for her and tidies her up proper like. I know me mam would have liked to do all this for me had she the chance, but there wasn't money for fussing.

As we walk along the dock, I notice many of the men call her by that other name. "Bess," a sailor with skin like mahogany leather yells, "how're you keeping?" The women, though, are different. They turn away when they see us coming toward them. Since none of them has ever seen me before in their lives, I can think of no reason why they should shun me.

As the sun rises higher in the sky, she takes me sleeve and pulls me toward a ship anchored to the dock. It isn't like the other ships there; its paint peels on decaying wood, and I know me dad would not have approved of the way the sails are rigged on the masts. It looks like a shanty boat sitting there next to its grand neighbors. The other ships at least look sea worthy, while this one appears scarce able to sail out of the dock.

Elizabeth says, "This is it, Mary. *The Pilgrims Dandy*." She points to a name on the side of the ship that I can't read, but I nod as though I can. "I have connections here."

"Have you no connections on that ship?" I ask, pointing to the one on the right.

"That's the *Canada Adventure*, girl. It sails to Nova Scotia, not America. And it costs five pounds British sterling to board her. Can you come up with that kind of money?"

Since me pockets are empty as the cup that held me milk, I shake me head.

So I'm to be on The Pilgrims Dandy, am I? It doesn't look dandy at all to me. It is a purely awful looking tub, but as Mam said, 'Beggars can't be choosers.' If Elizabeth has connections that can get me on a ship to America without a ticket, I'll have to be grateful.

She stands next to the gangplank and shouts up toward the deck, "Seamus, come down here."

I am shocked down to me toes. Now, she doesn't sound like a high-born lady at all. She sounds like a screeching fishwife.

But what do I, ignorant Mary Boland from Kinsale, know of such things?

A bald head sticks out from a porthole on the rickety ship. "Bess Shaw," the man yells. "You're a feast for sore eyes, you old bat."

Shaw? She called herself Bradshaw. And how dare such a decrepit sailor speak to a fine lady to the queen in such a way?

But she doesn't seem offended by his words. As a matter of fact, she bellows a loud laugh and yells back up at him, "Seamus, get your fat arse down here straight away. I've a delectable young lass for you to meet."

The head pokes back into the porthole and, in a flash, he's running down the gangplank. I'm shocked to see a wooden peg in place of one leg and even more surprised at how fast he can travel on it.

I'm scarce past blushing over her bad language when he's standing in front of us.

"Well now, Bess, who is this sweet thing?" I recognize his accent as North Irish. It has the sound of Belfast to it. That means he's a Protestant and no kinder than the British.

She puts her hand on the middle of me back and pushes me forward. "Her name is Mary. What do you think of her?"

"A bit scrawny for me taste, but pretty enough."

"And young, just the way you like them, Seamus."

His sneer makes me shudder. "How old is she?"

"Never you mind that. She's old enough."

Me skin begins to prickle with goose bumps, but I force a smile. I must get on this ship.

"So, you want to go to America, girl?"

Me heart pounds in me chest. "Ah yessir, that I do—to find me father. I want that more than anything in the world."

"And what'll you do to get on this ship headed there?"

"Anything, sir. I'll clean till things are spotless, and I can cook a bit." I think as hard as I ever have in me life, trying to come up with anything that might appeal to him. "I say me prayers every night and every morning. I'm as strong as a lad and fast as a rabbit." He doesn't look impressed, so I think even harder. "Oh, and I'm a fine dancer. Best in me village. Everyone said so."

His lips draw into a grimace, revealing black stubs of teeth that look as if they haven't seen a scrubbing in all their life.

"Come on, Seamus," Elizabeth says, poking him in the ribs. "You can't afford to be fussy. After all, *The Pilgrim's Dandy* is scarce a notch above a coffin ship."

"Coffin ship, me fine Irish ass," Seamus says. "You're hardly in no position to do better, Bess. Don't go putting on tony airs with me."

Their words stop me cold as a windy night on the Irish Sea. A coffin ship? Moira had mentioned such ships and I'd heard tales in me village. We've all heard of them. Only half the people who board one ever get off on the other side. The rest are thrown to the sharks. The owners don't care. They make more from insurance if the ship sinks.

I turn to Elizabeth. "Is The *Pilgrim's Dandy* a coffin ship?"

"No, of course not," she murmurs. "But tell me, how bad do you want to get to America, girl? Standing there all gussied up doesn't change the fact you haven't a farthing in your pocket. You're lucky to have this chance; it's the only one you'll get."

I am paralyzed. This boat doesn't look fit to sail to Belfast, let alone America. But what will I do if I don't get on it? I haven't money for boarding a better ship. "Will you let me think on this a moment?" I ask them.

He scowls and Elizabeth looks madder than a leprechaun cheated of his gold. I walk to a bench and sit down. The vast ocean seems to trap me. I must cross it, and this may be me only chance. Even on coffin ships, half the people make it to America. I'm young and strong after all, so I'll be one of the ones who survive the crossing. Haven't I lived through worse?

I take in a deep breath and walk back to them. "Mr. Seamus, sir," I say, smiling at him. "If you'll get me on *The Pilgrim's Dandy*, I'll do anything you need."

Elizabeth turns to him. "So, we have an agreement then?"

He nods. "I reckon we do. Let me go in and get the payment." She smiles.

As he goes back up the gangplank, I turn to Elizabeth. "What payment does he speak of? Why would he pay you?"

She seems happy once again; the sweet Elizabeth has returned. I can't fathom this woman's moods. "Oh, don't worry your head about that, Mary," she says cheerily. "I have an arrangement with the crew on this ship. You needn't be concerned."

"Will you give him the money Tim gave you to help with me passage?"

Her smile twists to a frown in an instant. "In me own good time, girl. Now enough of your questions."

In moments, he's running back down the gangplank. He hands Elizabeth a packet of something. She shoves it in her purse, pulls its drawstrings and turns to me. "Well, Mary, goodbye and bon voyage." She turns her back and walks down the dock swaying her bustle side to side.

"Goodbye, Elizabeth. Thank you," I call after her.

She doesn't turn back.

"Okay, girlie. See you on board." Seamus says as he hobbles on his peg back up the gangplank.

I nod. Me only ticket to a better life floats before me. Turning around, I take a last look at Queenstown. People swarm across the dock looking like frantic rats trying to escape a burning prison. The herring gulls swoop down so close I fear they'll steal me bonnet off me head, and the smell of salt stings me nose.

All around me, families sob and keen as they bid each other goodbye. When they come close, I notice that most reek of poteen from the American wake party last night.

A man stands beside me wearing a homespun cap like Da used to wear. He embraces a thin, young woman.

"I'll send money for your passage, Bridget, as soon as I can earn it, I promise," he says to her. His voice croaks with anguish. The girl, all skin and bones of her, holds him as if her only hope of survival rests on his skinny chest. She sobs into his shirt like her heart might break.

Though her eyes burn like fevered black coals in her face, she struggles for a smile. "I know you will, Padraig," she says, finally. I think she's using the last bit of bravery in her soul to bid him goodbye.

She'll be dead by the time she gets that money. I shake the thought out of me head. There's no time for grieving. What does one more dying girl matter? If I cried about every Irish woman who passed during these awful troubles, I'd flood this ocean over its banks and out into the whole world. I squeeze me eyes shut and turn back toward *The Pilgrim's Dandy*.

CHAPTER FIVE

May the wind stay at your back.

Me boots feel as though they're loaded with lead as I walk up the gangplank. The wood beneath me looks so rotten I fear it'll break and dump me into the filthy water. Dead fish float around the ship, and the stink of them twists me stomach. Storm clouds gathering overhead swell a sense of unknown danger. *Ah, stop it, Mary. 'Tis foolish Irish superstition shooting dice with your brain. Think of America.*

Stiffening up me back, I put one foot in front of the other and get on with it. Decrepit or not, this ship is headed to a world where I won't starve.

The deck's rail teems with bedraggled passengers. A few look excited and happy, but others keen so loud it sounds like bagpipes playing, low and mournful. A woman at me elbow weeps piteously. Old and bent, she scarcely reaches the ship's rail, but she clutches it like a lifeline in her gnarled hands.

"Granny, why do you wail so?" I ask her.

"I'll never see me home again," she moans, her hands white from gripping. "Me husband's grave, our parents' before us and theirs' before them."

"Ah now. Go easy on yourself, Missus," I say, wrapping me arm around her shoulders." Unexpectedly, the ship heaves. I hold her close and brace us both lest she fall to the deck. "What's your name and why are you leaving if it makes you so sad?" I ask her.

"I'm Maeve Maloney. Me daughter begged me to come with her."

"Well, that's good now isn't it, Mrs. Maloney?" I say, rubbing her back. "Wouldn't you rather be with your girl than stay here keening over the graves of the dead?"

She raises tear-reddened eyes to me. "Ah, you're but a child. One your age can't imagine the pain of leaving the place your kin have lived since the beginning of time."

I turn away, lest she see me own sadness, but she tugs at me sleeve. "Where are your parents, girl?"

Lifting me chin, I say. "Gone—all gone."

Mrs. Maloney grabs me round me hips, and the nestling of her head on me chest nearly does me in. "I guess you under-stand more than I thought, little colleen."

"High tide," a sailor on the dock yells as he tugs the ropes off the bollards and then jumps onto the ship, nearly landing in the water as the ship rolls again.

Another seaman hollers, "Weigh anchor," and three men begin to turn a giant wheel as an anchor clatters up the bow of the ship. The passengers yell in excitement when the rowing barges pull us away from the wharf. With a great huff, the sails fill, and we leave the barges behind us. Passengers cram against the leeward railing and strain to watch the land recede. The wind whips me hair out of me bonnet and into me face, and it stings as though I've been slapped.

Queenstown is so beautiful now. Seagulls swooping up toward the heavens look like they could surely hook onto angel's wings.

People waving from the dock appear cheery at this distance, and I wish I could stay.

Stop it, Mary. Ireland is not the fertile place it looks to be. The green is a mask of the devil himself. This land produces naught but rot, and rot you will if you don't escape.

The anchor winches up onto the deck in a terrible clatter. Everyone jumps at the sound. "So, we're off?" an old man asks.

"Aye, Da," a woman says, wrapping her arms around her father.

"Say goodbye to your homeland then," he says, bursting into tears.

Without warning, me anger flares. Me Irish temper was a legend in Kinsale, and I must learn to tamp it down. But just like that, it's on me, and I can't control me yapper. "Stop the weeping!" I yell.

For a time, the others are startled to stillness, but then a young woman cradling a wailing baby against the wind speaks. "But we'll never see family again. How can we not grieve?"

I whirl toward her. The baby she cradles is as young as Ellen was. Pain steels me resolve. "Me family is gone. Me home is burnt. I leave Ireland gladly and forever." The words hold more force than I feel, but I need to say them lest I fall to the deck in grief.

"That's pure blather, girl," says a male voice behind me. I turn toward a red-bearded man with kind, smiling eyes. "Sure as me name is Liam Horan, I know you're hurting as much as any on this ship." Then, he clamps his hat down against the wind like Da used to do.

I turn away quickly.

"Ah! Look at those cliffs," a blonde girl standing beside me yells, pointing. I follow her finger and glimpse a most beautiful sight. Sheer rock rises out of the sea like it's reaching toward heaven itself. The majesty of the cliffs sets me mouth to gaping.

"I wager that's the Dingle Peninsula," Liam Horan says, raising his hand to shade his eyes. "I've never seen it, but me dad spoke of it often. That must be it."

The blonde girl tugs at me hand. "Lovely, isn't it?"

She's the prettiest girl I've ever seen; all blonde curls dancing in the wind and Celt blue eyes alive with merriment. "What's your name?" she asks.

"Mary Boland."

"Where's your Mam?"

"Dead."

"I'm sorry," she says squeezing me hand. "Will you be me friend for this voyage?"

A dark-haired girl standing nearby says, "Ceili, you said you'd be *me* friend."

"Oh, Agnes," Ceili says "a girl can surely have more than one, can't she?"

The girl called Agnes scowls and turns on her heel to stride away against the bluster of the wind.

"Who's that?" I ask.

"Her name is Agnes Dooley. She's fifteen. I met her a few minutes ago. She can be our friend, too, if she wants to. But I'll warn you, she's a surly one."

A friend? I haven't had one since Siobhan sailed off. "Yes, I'd love to be your friend. What's your name?"

"Ceili O'Shaughnessy," she answers, so happy she begins to jump up and down.

"And where do you come from, Ceili O'Shaughnessy?" I ask, laughing at her excitement. "And how old are you?"

"I come from Tullamore in Kings County," she says. "I'm twelve. You?"

"Kinsale," I answer. "Thirteen. Do you know where we sail to?"

"To a place called Boston," she answers clapping her hands together. "It's a beautiful village right on the edge of America. Me mam says we'll be rich as the Brits once she finds work there."

"So where's your dad?"

The joy fades from her face. "He took a boat up the Canal to Shannon to get us food from the soup kitchen, but never made it back to Tullamore. Mam figures he died somewhere along the way."

I tell her what happened to Mam and Ellen from the soup in Kinsale.

"Oh Mary, I'm sorry." She takes me hand. "At least I didn't have to watch me da die. We just figure that's what happened. Could you find no other food?"

"I dug up wildflowers and gathered seaweed and tried to make a broth of them for Mam, but nothing helped. After the baby died, Mam just gave up on living; that and Da sailing off." I pull the cross from me bodice. "This was her cross. She made me promise to find Da in America and give it to him." I look down at the shining gold. "And to tell him how much she loved him."

"Did he just leave you all in Ireland?" Ceili's curls whip against her face, and she pushes them back.

"Yes, but only to earn money for our passage."

"Where are your mam's and sister's bodies?"

"I buried them. The baby in Mam's arms." Immediately, I am assailed by the memory of them lying there. So still. So very still. The pain of the vision nearly doubles me over. I clutch at the cross.

Ceili seems to read me feelings and brushes me cheek with a kiss soft as angel's wings. She touches the cross. "It's beautiful, Mary. It'll protect both of us during our journey. That man there," she points to the red-haired man named Liam, "says this boat looks like a coffin ship." She looks around the deck. "I fear he might be right."

Recovering from the grief of me memory, I gaze at the patched-over sails, I think he's right, too. Why did Elizabeth choose such a scow? Surely, she might have had connections on something more seaworthy.

I must shake off me fear, so sticking me arms straight away from me, I start to twirl in the wind. I grab Ceili's hands into mine. "Whatever it is, pretty Ceili, we're on our way to Boston, America. That's what counts."

The two of us dance in circles around the deck. Then, a dark cloud covers the sun and a cold puffing gust trembles a chill down me back, but Ceili continues to dance, hands extended to the heavens, full of the joy of a glorious future. Her blonde braids swirl around her shoulders like golden ropes.

The other passengers circle Ceili, clapping and cheering, me the loudest of them all. Then abruptly, Seamus breaks through the crowd, nearly shoving old Maeve to her knees. He grabs me by the arm. "Girl, you have work to do."

"Wait," Ceili says, panting from her dance, "Mary, what work does he mean?"

"I'm not sure. But I got on this boat knowing I'd have to earn me keep. So, I'll do whatever they need doing."

"All right," she answers. "When your work is done, meet me back up here."

She runs against the wind again, arms reaching as if she wants to catch it in her hands.

Chapter Six

If God sends you down a stony path, He will give you strong shoes.

"Hurry yourself, girl," Seamus yells as he pulls me toward a ladder that goes down into the ship. He shoves me toward it and then follows me down. "In an hour, the bos'n's whistle will call me watch on deck."

It's dark in the fo'c'sle, and at first, I can't see anything. As me eyes adjust to the dimness, though, I make out other men lying on bunks. There are four, stacked two on two. Three look occupied. I figure the fourth must belong to Seamus.

"Well, lads, look what I've brought you. Meet Miss Mary."

I try for a curtsy and bow me head, but I've not had practice at such things and probably look like a leathcheann. "Hello, gentlemen. I'm pleased to make your acquaintance."

A large man with a hairless head rolls off his bunk and stands in front of me. He has a skull and crossbones tattoo on his right cheek and wears an anchor ear ring in his left ear. "Well now, mates, look what we've got for ourselves." His crude Belfast accent is the same as Seamus's. He wipes a greasy mouth on the back of his sleeve. "You'll call me Bart, lass." He starts to circle around me. When he's behind me back, I crane me neck to see what he's looking at, but I can only get so far. I don't like him, nor the look he's giving me. Me skin prickles.

"Is that red hair peeping out under the bonnet?" he says. "That's bad luck."

"Don't be a silly mick," Seamus says, shoving Bart's shoulder. Bart comes closer to me face.

A chill creeps up me spine. "Would you like me to clean up your quarters?" I mutter, backing away. "By the look of things, it's been a while since anyone did that, and no one scrubs cleaner than me, if I do say so meself." I pretend to pat meself on the back.

Bart stares at me as if I had grown another head, and another man lumbers from his upper bunk, laughing all the way down to the deck. "Clean? Now why would we want such a thing, girl?" He's even bigger than Bart and has a large chew of tobacco stuck in his cheek. His greasy hair is caught at the nape of his neck with a leather strip. "I'm Jack," he says, spitting a long stream of brown juice into a pot on the floor.

"Are you hungry?" I ask through spasms of nausea.

None of them answers.

Frantic for words, I stammer "I see some potatoes in the corner and here's a cook stove." I pat the old stove on its lid and giggle nervously. They stand there looking me up and down. Me eyelid begins to twitch. "If you've a bit of mutton, I could make a shepherd's pie. Mam taught me to cook. She was a good cook. I'm not as good as her, but I'll do me best."

Much as I prattle, none of them says a word. Me fear turns to desperation. Are they going to hurt me? I look around for escape, but they surround me.

Finally, Seamus speaks. "Count yourself lucky, girl. Down here, at least you'll have food and water. The ones in the hold get one gallon of water a day for all their needs. Second half of the voyage, that ration is usually cut in half."

Remembering the people topside, me heart breaks. "How can they live?"

"Not our problem," he says. "The ship owners make the rules. We just follow them. Catholics are dispensable. There are so damn many of them."

There's a sound from the other upper bunk. I turn toward it. There's a boy there. His skin is black. The whites around his eyes glare out from his face at me. The sight of him terrifies me. How can anyone be so dark?

"Get down here, nigger," Seamus says. "Meet Miss Mary Boland herself."

The boy doesn't seem to understand and stays in the bunk until Seamus yanks on his arm. Then he tumbles off it and lands in a heap on the floor. When he stands, I realize he's young like me and looks just as scared.

Seamus turns back to me. "So, Miss Mary, what did Elizabeth tell you about this voyage?"

"She said it would get me out of Ireland."

He rubs his chin and grins, again revealing the black teeth. He gestures to Bart.

Strong hands grip me wrists and pull me arms behind me back. Oh, no. God, no. Is this what I think? I struggle as hard as I can, but they hold me in a grip like a vise. "Take your hands off me!" I yell at the top of me lungs, pulling with every bit of strength in me body.

"Bart, hold her firm," Seamus says. "She's skinny but wily, I wager." Bart pulls me arms up above me head.

Seamus stands before me. He runs his hands down me body. I begin to shake uncontrollably. "Don't do that!" I scream.

"Relax. Maybe you'll like it. Bess did."

"But she was a lady to the queen," I stammer.

He roars in laughter. "You believed that? She's a corker; could bluff the spots off dice."

"I trusted her."

"No wonder you Catholics are starving to death. You're too stupid to live."

I kick him in the leg.

"Owww," he yells. "Those boots are hard." He checks his shin. "I'll have a bruise the size of me fist. You'll pay double for that, Miss Mary. Jack, grab her ankles."

Jack jumps toward me dodging me feet as I wildly thrash them. He clutches around me right ankle and pulls me off balance. Then he grabs the other ankle and lifts me off the ground.

Seamus gestures toward the deck and the two men slam me down on it, one pinning me arms and the other, me legs. "Spread her out."

The wind is knocked out of me and, gasping for air, I try to scream, "Let me go." The grip on me ankles and wrists does not loosen. I fight furiously.

"Gag her," Seamus screams. "The Captain'll hear." A rag jams into me mouth as Seamus kneels down. "Mary, this will go better if you relax," he says. He unbuttons the top button of me dress.

"God, please help me," I vomit into the gag. He slaps me face to the side and the vomit rolls down me cheek to the floor.

God does not listen.

CHAPTER SEVEN

What doesn't kill you makes you stronger.

The bos'n's whistle blows.

"Damn it," Seamus says. "Our watch."

The three of them wash themselves, laughing to each other. Bart says, "Haven't had a cherry in a month of Sundays."

Hatred envelops me so tight I cannot think of good things. No more the green hills. No more me da calling me Anu, his Celtic goddess. No more me mam and baby Ellen before the famine wasted them. Only pain and hatred exist now on God's earth. And blood. Everywhere on the floor, on my hands, on my dress. I wonder if I got the monthly Mam told me about, but I think this is just from being torn to ribbons down there.

What God would allow this?

Crawling into a corner, I bunch up me dress and sob into the green fabric. Now, when I look at it, I don't see faeries dancing out of the forest. I see only Bess, hateful and knowing exactly what was in store for me on this ship.

"Girl," Seamus says. "Clean up this floor." He tosses me a rag. "Do it before we get back here."

Painfully, I stand up, cover meself with the discarded dress, and walk, rag in hand. Then, I stop in front of Seamus and spit in his face.

"Christ, boys," he says. "We've got a little spitfire on our hands. Who wants to dampen her fire next time?"

They circle me like jackals. I drop the rag and extend me fingers toward them. "The next one who touches me will leave without eyes in his head. I swear that on the life of me mother."

I see something like fear in their eyes. I stare at each of their disgusting faces, baring me teeth, and swinging at them with nails that now look like filthy claws. "I mean it."

Seamus is the first to laugh, but there's no mirth in it. He backs away, only an inch or so, but that is enough. "Ah hell, boys," he says. "We've got to get topside. Our watch is on." He starts to climb the ladder, then turns back. "Let's keep this 'un to ourselves, mates. Don't want the Captain to hear of her."

Chapter Eight

May the devil follow them all the days of their lives.

Suicide is the most mortal of sins, but I cannot live now—not after this. I will go up on the deck and throw meself over the rail. I swear I will.

But what of me promise to Mam? That matters no longer. She would not want me as her daughter if she knew what happened to me. And Da, dearest Da. I'll never find him now.

Crawling back into the corner, I pull me knees to me chin, staring into nothingness. I beg the filthy wood of the deck to open and let the roiling sea drown me, but it stays firm. *Please God, let me die*, I pray with all me heart. *If not the water, let me catch the typhus now before they come back.*

I close me eyes and the sobs come. When I finally open them, two filthy dark feet stand before me. Recoiling from the black boy I'd seen in the upper bunk, me dirty nails coil toward him, again like claws. "Don't you touch me."

The boy kneels on the floor a safe distance away. "I not harm you," he says. "I Kamua. Call me Kam." His voice is deep, like a man's. He must be at least fifteen. He bows his head. "Before today, they use me like you. I help you. They no hurt you or me again."

"Help me?"

"Yes. Your name?" he asks.

"Mary Boland," I answer without thinking. I'll speak no more to him. I cannot trust him. I trust no one.

"Mabo," he says.

He is so dark. I've never seen anyone like him before, and he terrifies me. He gets me a wet rag and instructs me to wash meself with it. I hesitate. How do I know what this strange boy has put onto the rag. But I feel so dirty, so I do as he says. I throw the rag back at him. He discards it and returns with a second rag.

"This one sting," he says. "Use." He turns away. "Me father say keep baby away."

A baby? Fathered by a monster? I take the rag.

He turns his back as I clean meself. "I know ship," he says. "Work in galley, Captain's quarters, everywhere. We hide and get food. I save you."

Save me? I start to laugh. How can this skinny boy save me from such beasts? And do I want to be saved? For what?

"Crew come back. We hide here 'til dark—when they sleep."

"But if they . . . they'll . . ." I cannot finish.

"Not find us."

He shows me a place behind a sea chest beneath the gunwale. I crawl into the space and he pushes the chest back so tight I can scarcely breathe. For once, I'm grateful for me skinny frame.

His voice comes from somewhere in the crews' quarters. "When hear men, make no sound."

Hours pass as I crouch there, me back plastered against a beam, me legs tucked under me. Then I hear them. Feet stomp overhead. The hatch creaks on salt-grimed hinges. The crew clambers down the stairs, laughing and cursing. I do not breathe.

"Mary, oh Mary." It is Seamus. His laugh is raucous. The smell of rum drifts through the quarters. "Come on, sweet meat."

43

I close me eyes, holding me breath.

"Where the feck is she?"

Bart speaks, "I don't see her or the nigger nowhere."

"Find her," Seamus answers, sounding angry. "She must be hiding. Playing hard to get that's what she's doing."

I hear them wandering around the quarters, opening hatches and slamming them shut. Grunts of displeasure follow each sound.

They scuffle as they move things out from the wall. Oh God, don't let them move this chest. Feet walk to the front of where I'm hidden. Someone slams his hand on the chest and tries to look behind it. The darkness envelops me, and I cease to breathe at all. "Not here," Jack's voice says.

Finally, the second man says, "They must've snuck topside. Find them."

I exhale for what feels like the first time since they came in the cabin. Their feet stomp back up the ladder. The hatch slams shut.

Within seconds, I feel the chest being pulled away from me. Kam stands there. "When hear them, I push it back. When they sleep, I come for you."

I do not move.

By the time they return, grumbling and swearing, the boy has again shoved the chest tight against me. "Crazy bitch," Seamus says. "Feckin' nigger." Boots thud as the three men drop them on the deck. "I'm bushed, mates," Jack's voice says. "We'll find her tomorrow."

Soon, I hear them breathing in an ugly dissonance of snores, snorts and farts. When their breathing grows deep, lulled by the rocking of the ship, the chest moves. It is Kam.

"Come," he whispers.

We creep across the floor like vapors, careful to not kick a boot or the britches tossed there. Kam glides up the ladder, me close behind him. The hatch creaks open and, in seconds, we are topside breathing the cool night air of the sea. Wind whips me hair from me bonnet and into me face like a lash. I welcome the sting.

Kam takes me to the bowsprit, and we creep into the small space under it. I stare up at a peeling statue of a mermaid above me head, now grateful for respite from the wind. The stars shine overhead as if nothing on earth has changed, but everything has changed.

"We hide here. If wind shift, I wake," Kam whispers.

I do not trust him. I trust no one. I will not close me eyes this night and, before dawn, I will creep to the rail and hurl meself into the sea. The church says suicide is a mortal sin, but I cannot live with the pain of what happened. Yes, that's it. Tomorrow, blessed death.

But then I remember Boston, America. Da. Streets paved with gold. Sandwiches.

CHAPTER NINE

Surround this child, Lord, with the soft mantle of your smile.

I lie on me belly as far from him as I can get. In an instant, he's asleep. I don't take me eyes off him. At three bells, he wakens. His eyes look like white moons floating in the darkness. "Stay," he says.

He slithers out from our hiding place. I pull meself up, gulping in fresh air. Me eyes are so heavy they begin to close, but then I see a figure crawling and pushing something along the deck toward me. I strain to see who it is, and, in spite of me fears of him, I'm relieved to see it's Kam.

There is no sound as he crawls back into our hiding place. "Bread," he says, handing me a piece. I grab it greedily and start to chew. "Slow," he says. "Quiet." He touches his lips.

Then, I notice it was a bucket he was pushing in front of him. It's full of fresh water. "Drink," he says.

I push me face down into the pail, drinking in as much as I can. When me thirst is slaked, I lift me face from it and see him smiling. "Good?"

I nod, never taking me eyes off him. He eats his piece of bread and then extends his hands for the wooden bucket. I slide it to him, being careful not to let me hands touch his. He drinks deeply, then falls asleep again.

When me eyes drift closed, I see Seamus above me and again smell the putrid scent of his rotten teeth. Then, it's Bart, greasy with sweat, the anchor bobbing from his ear. Then Jack, juice from his chaw slathering down his chin and onto me chest. I waken with a jolt, nearly screaming. Kam sits up. He puts a finger over his mouth.

The next two nights are disturbed only by Kam's quiet movements. He speaks to me without words, and I begin to understand his every gesture. These nights, we hide under an unfurled canvas. When the wind strengthens, he touches me shoulder. I do not jump away. It is our signal to leave our hiding place and find another before the crew breaks out more sails.

I follow Kam everywhere, dependent as an infant. Finally, one night on a starless night in a dead calm ocean, I fall asleep. When I jump awake hours later, he's there, sitting far from me, as always. He smiles the gentlest smile I've ever seen. "Good," he says. "Mabo sleep."

A week passes. Kam never comes close to me in our hiding places. When I must relieve meself in the dead of night, he stands guard with his back to me. He makes sure that as he hands me food or water, our fingers never touch. In spite of me fears or because of them, I begin to realize I must trust him. There's no other choice.

As far as Seamus, Bart, and Jack can tell, Kam and I have disappeared. Often, I hear them—devil's spawn that they are— grumbling about how we vanished into air even as we hide only feet away from their hard-stomping boots. It's then I must stifle me laughter.

On the twelfth morning, Kam whispers, "Me father sangoma in village."

I peer at him. "Sangoma?"

"Witch doctor. Strong medicine." He straightens up. "Me—Kamua mean quiet warrior."

Looking now at this proud boy, I can almost see the warrior he would have become. Sadness clouds his face. "Slave ship took father to place called Louisiana," he says. "Mother and sister murdered. Me, sold to sailors."

In time, I learn the ship nearly as well as Kam knows it. I become expert at finding places for us to hide, too. Sometimes, it's under an unfurled sail or a nook where ropes are piled for rigging. He points to the heavens and explains how looking at them helps him chart our journey. When I ask him how he knows such things, he shrugs. "Stars, moon, sun."

Kam steals food and water from the galley when he knows Cookie is sleeping off his ration of rum. Kam's quick as a beetle, and I learn to move fast, too, when a crew member draws near.

One morning, as we hide only feet away from the passengers, I hear Ceili tell her mother, "I am so worried about Mary, Mam. She's me friend, and since the day we boarded, I've not seen hide nor hair of her." She starts to cry.

Her mother soothes her with crooning and soft touches. "I know, love. I can't tell you where the girl's gone. I've been worried meself."

After that, I feel an overwhelming need to see her again. "I want to go down into the hold," I tell Kam. "I want to see Ceili."

"No, Mabo," he says. "They tell crew."

"They'd never do that. The Irish take care of their own."

"Kam not Irish," he answers.

"But you're me friend."

"Kam friend?" he says.

I nod, realizing it's the truth. This strange, dark boy has become the rock I depend on. He has defended me against violence and sin. No friend could do more. "Please trust me. They won't turn you in."

As we creep down the ladder into the hold, I am assaulted by an unholy stench. Bedpans spill and slush across the rolling wooden deck. Rats hiss, their eyes glittering from every corner. Smells of vomit, urine, and shit invade me senses and when I open me mouth to breathe, I taste them all deep down into me belly. The rotting scents of tobacco, vomited whiskey, waste, and mold seep into me hair, me skin, me very soul.

Desperate, I search for light, but there is no porthole here. The place is airless and dark. I yearn to race back up the ladder to the wind, but these are me people. This is where I'll find Ceili.

Kam lights a candle. I squint as me eyes adjust to its meager light. Now I can see them. People, crammed tight together on straw-covered slabs of wood with only inches for each body. Vacant eyes stare out at us.

Ceili's the first to recognize me. "Mary, where have you been?" She tumbles from her place on the wood to the filthy deck. She appears even thinner than when we sailed. Her cheeks have lost their luster, and her eyes are huge and fearful as she stares at Kam. "And who's this?"

"He's a slave from Gabon in Africa. His name is Kam. His family is gone, too. He saved me life."

Kam extends his hand to her. "Hello, Miss Ceili," he says.

She takes his hand, then looks down at her own, mystified. "It doesn't rub off."

Kam smiles.

"What's happened to you, Mary?" Ceili's mother says. "Where've you been all this time? We were worried witless."

Though I yearn to escape this fetid place, I tell Ceili and her mother of me violation. Mrs. O'Shaughnessy holds and soothes me through the awful tale. Agnes Dooley, the surly girl who stood near Ceili that first day, sneaks close and says, "Sure and I think you asked for it, Mary, with your fancy dress and bonnet. I saw how you sashayed around in front of those sailors."

Me emotions bounce between pain and fury even as me stomach retches from the rancid odors. I open me mouth to tell Agnes what for, but Ceili's mam puts one finger on me mouth, then turns to Agnes. "Agnes, quit acting the maggot."

I tremble into the comfort of Mrs. O'Shaughnessy's embrace and watch Agnes slink off to her place on a plank, a frown plastered across her puss.

"Ah lass, what an awful thing to happen to such a báibin," Ceili's mother whispers. "We'll help you and the boy as well. He's but a child, too."

"Thank you," I mumble into her shoulder.

From this moment of comfort, I hold me breath and look more closely at the poor souls in this hell hole. At least sixty of them are jammed into a space built to hold cattle. Smells of sour milk and cow manure leech from the wooden deck and mingle with the fetor of human waste. Four wooden shelves line the walls. People are crammed onto each of them. I think of Elizabeth Bradshaw and know she would be booted out her first night here. One so fat wouldn't fit.

Much as I yearn to escape the stinking hole, Kam and I stay here this night because a gale rages and pounds the ship. Storm-tossed passengers are thrown like rag dolls to the deck. Sewage spills across them but no water can be spared for cleaning, and no one can brave the storm topside to draw up salt water.

We sleep on the floor this long, long night, and, though no light reaches down into this airless place, Kam stirs and touches me shoulder when he knows the sun cracks the sky. Then, he stands and gestures to the passengers to go topside and, one by one, filthy and sick, they crawl up the ladder and through the hatch, drawing in great gulps of clean air as they emerge from the hell below.

I crouch to blend into the crowd, and the man I remember as Liam Horan throws a towel on top of Kam's head so no crewman can see his face. We sit on the deck, caressed by wind and unspoken affection in the heart center of me people.

I hear it, then, the sound of an Irish whistle. Kam and I slink away to hide under an unfurled sail as the others rise and slowly begin to dance. It's a jig. What a wonder! No matter how dreadful things become, me beautiful, wretched countrymen hold on to their sense of joy and faith. At that moment, me pride in being Irish swells me heart nearly to bursting.

That afternoon, Ceili sneaks under the sail to hide with me and Kam. She opens her story book. "Do you want me to read you the story of *Snow White*?" she whispers.

"*Snow White*?" Kam says, his eyes alight with interest.

Excited, I nod to her. "It's a made-up story about make-believe people, Kam. What they call a fairy tale."

He nods. "A fable. Like in Gabon." He says, "Read." He puts his finger to his lips. "Soft."

When Ceili gets to the part that tells about the seven dwarfs, Kam says, "What dwarf?"

"A little person," I explain.

"Ah," he answers. "Pygmy."

I look at Ceili, and we smile. "Yes, I guess so," she says.

Ceili quickly learns our hiding places, and every day she comes to us with another of her wonderful books. As we hide in a covered lifeboat one morning, she brings jacks. After one game, Kam has collected all the jacks and declares himself jack warrior of the *The Pilgrim's Dandy*.

After two weeks of hiding and playing together, as the three of us crouch behind the rope pile, Kam asks a strange question. "What scares people in your country?"

Ceili and I look at each other with questioning eyes. "Nearly everything," she answers, finally. "The Irish are the most superstitious people anywhere."

"What superstitious?" he says.

"Scared of things," I say. "Mostly for no good reason."

"For instance," Ceili says, thinking. "If a cat licks its paws and looks at you, you might die."

"No cats on ship," he says.

How odd he is.

"A broken mirror always means bad luck," I add.

Kam shakes his head. "No good."

What's he looking for?

Ceili's face lights up. "Of course, the most frightening thing to any Irish man is the Banshee."

"What Banshee?" he says.

"Legend has it each of the five great Gaelic families were tormented by a Banshee from the beginning of time. Some had more than one. The O'Brien's Banshee was called Eevul and ruled over twenty-five other Banshees. We had O'Briens in Tullamore. Believe me, nobody crossed them."

"Me grandmother was Maeve O'Brien," I say.

"Ooooohhhh," she says, crossing herself.

"What Banshee do?"

"She chooses a man as her victim. There's no escaping her. He will die, pure and simple. Every Irishman thinks that," I say.

"How Banshee look?"

Ceili says, "Sometimes, she's a wraith of an old woman and sometimes—" she pauses, "she's young and beautiful with wild hair. Sometimes, fair, sometimes red."

Kam straightens. "Like Mabo?"

Ceili's eyes narrow. "Yes! Just like her. The Banshee picks her victim, then wails and twirls around him. She screams and points at him, and he knows he's doomed." She laughs. "Once a man in me village thought he saw the Banshee and purely peed his pants he was so scared."

Kam's eyes glisten like dark pools. "Banshee," he says. "Mabo, can you wail?"

"Me dad said when I was a báibín, me wail could wake the dead themselves."

"Good," he says.

What's he thinking now?

CHAPTER TEN

May you have a cure for all that ails you.

As Ceili crawls out from under the sail, her skirt pulls up, exposing an oozing sore on her lower leg. The thing is angry and festering. "Ceili," I say, "where'd that ugly thing come from?"

"I don't know, but it hurts me something fierce."

Kam looks at it closely. "Bad. I fix."

Ceili laughs at him. "How can you fix this? No one in the hold knows what to do about it."

He doesn't answer her, but in the dead of night, I am wakened by his soft, "Mabo."

Instantly awake, I look at him.

"I go to galley. Need to heal Ceili's wound."

"How?"

"Come with me."

We sneak across the deck and down into the galley. Cookie snores off in a corner. A goat tethered in a hay-filled pen bleats when she sees us. Kam creeps across the floor, scattering roaches in his wake, pets the goat for a moment and begins to milk her into a nearby pail.

"Can I have a taste of that milk?" I whisper.

He hands me the pail, then quickly takes it back.

He pours the milk into a bowl, and then finds a half loaf of bread on the counter. Breaking the bread into the milk, he mashes it with a wooden spoon, then quietly, so quietly, he finds a clean towel in a drawer and nods for me to follow him.

He carries the bowl and I, the towel. As the two of us creep again down into the hold, he lights a candle. Ceili's mother sits up with a start. "What?" she says.

Kam puts one finger on his lips and gestures toward Ceili. She nudges her daughter, and Ceili jumps to sitting.

"Kam!"

Again, he puts one finger over his lips. We go to where Ceili lies and Kam points toward her leg. Ceili raises her skirt to reveal the sore. It oozes more than before. Kam lifts a tiny bit of the milk-soaked bread and covers the wound. Then, he takes the towel from me and wraps it around her leg. He puts the bowl into Ceili's mother's hands.

"In morning, wash with salt water. Then, put more on and tie up again. Do until mixture is gone."

Her mother nods, her eyes wide. I can tell she trusts Kam, and I understand why. There's something about him. When he says something, you know he speaks the truth.

I haven't noticed Maeve Maloney approaching Kam until she whispers, "Boy, I am suffering from a fierce sore throat. Can you help me?"

Kam nods. "Tomorrow."

"Excuse me, please," Ceili says, crawling past her mother and disappearing behind a filthy white tablecloth hanging in the corner.

"That was me mother's tablecloth," her mother says. "We put it up so we may have a bit of privacy when tending to our personal needs."

The thought of being here with all these people while I take care of such secret things is awful to consider. I've learned to pass me waste once each day—late at night. I hang onto the rigging for dear life as I dangle me bottom off the side of the ship. That's when Kam keeps guard.

When Ceili comes out, she says. "I'll find where you're hiding in the morning. I have a story book you've not heard before." She turns to her mother. "Is that all right, Mam?"

"Sure, it's grand. Let's sleep a bit longer and then you go play with your friends."

She turns to me. "You will watch her, won't you, Mary?"

"I promise I will, Mrs. O'Shaughnessy. Always."

"Kam watch Ceili, too," he says.

CHAPTER ELEVEN

A faithful friend, more valuable than gold.

The sea is rough when Ceili arrives, and I put me arms around her shoulders and pull her into the lifeboat. She whispers to me. "I don't like this new story as much as the others, but I figure Kam will enjoy it because it's the story of a boy. It's called *Jack and the Beanstalk.*"

"How leg?" Kam asks.

"Ever so much better, I think." She lifts her skirt.

"Don't remove cloth," Kam says.

She nods and opens her book. Kam and I settle ourselves in to listen to another of Ceili's wonderful stories. When she gets to the place where Jack climbs the beanstalk, though, she stops and turns to me. "Mary, I just remembered. Me mam says I must warn you." Her eyes narrow. "Be careful of Agnes Dooley. Every time she talks of you, it's like she wants to eat the face right off you. Calls you the whore of the sailors."

"But why?" I ask. "I've done her no harm."

"Mam says it's because she's homely and jealous."

Her mam's right on one count. Agnes has a bad puss on her for sure. Though I'm no beauty, I don't have the Irish beak she has. I've heard Liam joke that if he lowered Agnes into the sea, she could catch a fish on that hook."

"I don't give a horse's hoof what Agnes thinks of me. I have you and Kam. That's plenty enough friends for me."

Ceili grins and turns back to her story. When she finishes, Kam who has listened wide-eyed to every word, says, "I find magic beans. I climb beanstalk and bring down stars for you and Mabo."

Ceili's giggle is pure mischief. "Kam, to get up a beanstalk, you'd have to do the climbing for sure. If I tried it, I'd fall off the thing like an eejit."

I laugh, too, at the thought of Ceili climbing anything. Once, when she tried to get up the rigging, she got scarce a foot off the deck before falling back onto it. She's fragile, not like me who could scale a wall if there was a scrap of bread atop it.

She closes the book. "I suppose I should get back. Mam worries about me."

"Be glad of that." In spite of meself, me voice trembles.

She's instantly contrite. "I'm sorry, Mary. I forgot about your mother. Tell me about her, won't you?"

Kam protests, "Another story."

Ceili says, "Next time. I promise, Kam. But right now, I want to learn about Mary's mother."

He shrugs and begins to study the pictures in her book.

She turns to me. "Do you look like your mam? Me da always said I'm the spittin' image of mine."

"I look nothing like her. She was a beauty." Then, I recall something. "Remember that picture of Snow White in your book?"

She nods.

"That's what she looked like. Exactly. Black hair, blue eyes. Ah, she was lovely."

"What did she do in Kinsale, Mary?"

"Lots of things. She sang like an angel—knew all the old Gaelic songs. Her voice sounded like chimes drifting across the winds. And, she birthed the babies. She was the village midwife. I helped her."

"You helped birth babies?" she exclaims.

I nod, proud.

"Oh, Mary. You are such a grand girl. I'm so glad to be your friend." She stands up. "Now, though, I think I'd best get back."

She takes the book from Kam's extended hand. "When we get to America, we will always be friends. I'll write you both every day."

I mustn't mislead her for another moment. "Ceili. I won't be able to answer."

"Why?"

"I can't read or write. Neither can Kam."

He lowers his eyes.

I look at her closely. "You knew that, didn't you?"

"I wondered a bit since neither of you ever asked to read from me books, but I wasn't sure. Don't let that trouble your heads. When we get to Boston, America, me mam'll teach you both. She's the one I learned from."

Ah, what a wonder that would be—to read. I whip me head around and look at Kam. Unspoken joy gleams in his eyes.

Ceili crawls out of the lifeboat, looks around to make sure no one sees her, and then turns away. We watch as she tiptoes carefully across the rolling deck, her blonde curls blowing in the wind. Before we lose sight of her, she smiles and waves.

Chapter Twelve

Why does Satan never sleep?

When the moon is bright overhead that night, Mrs. O'Shaughnessy comes to the lifeboat. "Where's Ceili?" she asks, her voice cracking with exhaustion. "She didn't come back to the hold."

Kam jumps to attention. "She leave before sunset."

We leap from our hiding place, for once unafraid of being caught.

"We'll find her, Mrs. O'Shaughnessy," I say.

All the passengers are now up on the deck searching for Ceili, so we blend in as best we can with the rest. Kam covers his face and head with a rag, and the darkness is a good cover for me. We search for a long time, our hearts beating faster as each moment passes. Where can she have gone? This ship isn't large enough for a girl to go missing for so long.

Then, I hear it. The hatch to the crew's quarters slowly creaks open. I'm the first to see her. Or is it her? She doesn't look at all the same. Her hair is matted. Her dress is torn off her shoulder. But it's her eyes that terrify me; her eyes are dead.

She walks trance-like to her mother who takes her face into her hands and says, "Ceili, what happened?"

She doesn't answer, just stands there with those dead eyes staring into nothingness.

Seamus, Bart, and Jack come up out of their quarters then. Liam Horan rushes them, yelling, "What'd you do to the girl?"

They overpower Liam and toss him back into the crowd of passengers.

"What happened to me child?" Mrs. O'Shaughnessy sobs into Seamus's face. "Please tell me."

He shoves her to the deck. "Let's say she's paid a just debt, for her friend, Mary who welched on a promise."

I shrink into the crowd, bending me knees so me head won't show above the others.

"I know how you micks have been hiding that red-haired whore," Seamus went on, "and the little blonde just happened to come along as we were getting off watch. Since the redhead reneged on her debt, we decided to collect from her good friend, Miss Ceili."

I crawl to where Ceili stands over her mother and pull her down to the ground with me. Others crowd around us. "Ceili," I say "did they?"

The dead blue eyes stare straight ahead.

Wildly, they come alive, but not with recognition. They flame with madness. With a strength I didn't think she had, she shoves me away from her and jumps to her feet.

As she races through the stunned crowd of passengers, she begins to keen some phrase in Gaelic. It is the screech of a maniac, inhuman and heartbreaking. She runs to the rail.

"No, Ceili," her mother screams. "Wait! No! Don't! Please don't!"

Kam, on his feet in an instant, chases her, with no regard for being caught. He reaches her as she hoists herself up onto the rail. He grabs onto her leg. But he's too late. As she jumps, her make-shift bandage comes off in his hand. He raises it to the heavens and screams, "No-o-o-o!"

The passengers race to the rail with Mrs. O'Shaughnessy in the lead. "Grab a rope," one man yells.

"Save her!" another screams.

In the chaos of finding the rope and tossing it over the side, no one sees Mrs. O'Shaughnessy hoist herself up onto the rail. We don't realize she's jumped until we see her there in the water, flapping her arms helplessly as she tries to reach Ceili.

It's the mother's flailing that attracts the first shark.

CHAPTER THIRTEEN

As bitter as gall on Christ's lips.

Kam and I do not speak as we cower under the sail, I see it all again. The two small figures in the water, the fin gliding slowly toward them, Ceili's blonde braids floating on the waves, the flailing arms, the shrieks of pain, the blood that drifts over everything like a red shroud, and then . . . nothing.

"It's me fault," I finally whisper. "I promised Ceili's mam I'd watch out for her."

"I promised, too," he answers. His eyes glisten like dark liquid spheres. I see a tear spill from one of them. He clears his throat. "No time for grief. Time for vengeance."

We hear the Captain shouting to the crew to man the sales. The night is dark and they scurry like terrified lizards around the deck, giving us freedom from their attention. We sneak down into their cabin. I follow Kam without a word. He creeps around, gathering strange objects. He picks up a feather from the floor, straw from each of their bunks, a comb filled with hair, a smelly pair of under pants, and then a cracked drawing of an unrecognizable woman. His hands move so quickly I can't see all he grabs. But I see the last thing. It is the sheet from Seamus's bunk.

When he's finished and we're safe back under our sail, he tells me, "I make voodoo doll."

Dully, I ask him what voodoo means.

"Black magic."

With scraps of the crew's clothing, hair from the comb, and straw from each of their bunks, he twists an ugly little thing into shape. I watch as he weaves the straw around bits of fabric and hair while chanting a mix of African and English words, most of which I cannot understand. But I do catch the name "Seamus" entwined constantly with a word that sounds like sterf. When the little doll is finished, I ask what sterf means.

"Mean die," he answers, and then falls into an exhausted sleep.

We remain hidden the entire next day, neither of us uttering a word. Finally, a full moon rises from a calm sea. The wind is slack now and the water still. We know the crew will be fully pissed from too much rum. We stare at each other silently as they stumble and laugh their way to their bunks. After the last of them has gone down, Kam turns to me and says, "Now, Mabo become Banshee."

We slither like ship rats on the rope ladder leading down to the galley. Kam goes first. He clenches a lit candle in his teeth. The sea roils and the ladder swings under me clammy hands and feet. I almost fall from it, but Kam grabs onto me leg. "Hold tight, Mabo," he whispers.

In the faint glow of the candle, I notice again that the galley is as filthy as the rest of the ship. Roaches scurry across the wooden deck. The sight of them makes me shudder, though I wonder if, in time, hunger will make them palatable.

Kam dashes soundlessly toward a shelf. Rats run to corners I cannot see, but the sound of them scratching there sets me quivering. Kam holds up a bag. "Flour from America," he says.

He pours a small amount into a cloth bag and stuffs it into his ragged trousers.

A crate holds two chickens, and Kam reaches into it carefully. With a triumphant look, he pulls his hand back. Two eggs are nestled in it. He hands them to me. "Do not break."

He goes into a tiny room. "Root cellar," he says. He brings from it a red thing that looks like a turnip. "Beet," he says, and tucks it into his sleeve.

Hidden again behind our sail, I ponder, *Where does his resolve come from when mine is mired deep in the sea with Ceili?* I sit numb beside him as he begins a strange ritual.

He breaks the eggs, carefully putting the whites into a cup. "Drink yellow part," he says, extending one shell to me as he tilts the other into his mouth. It tastes slime going down, and me stomach threatens to toss it back up to me throat, but I breathe deep until the nausea subsides.

He begins to whip the whites in the cup with a stick until they are frothy, then reaches down into a bucket of sea water. He mixes it into the eggs and stirs some more. Then, he holds it out to me. "Put in hair, Mabo."

As if hypnotized, I remove me bonnet and untie the ribbon. Taking the cup from his hands, I pour the thick mixture into me hair. He helps me work it into every strand. "Bend," he says. "Let hair dry upside down." A sudden, stiff wind dries me hair quickly and I right meself to look at him.

"Good," he says.

He pulls the flour from his trousers, mixes in some sea water, and pats the paste on me face and neck until I feel caked with it. When he's done, he narrows his eyes and looks at me again. "Good," he says again.

A lump of coal materializes in his hand, and he spits on it. Holding it up in front of me eyes, he studies me face, and then begins to draw. "Close eyes," he orders, I obey. He scrawls the coal around me eyes and down me cheeks and neck.

I drift back to when Mam would paint me up for All Hallows Eve. I remember our All Hallows dinner of potato, cabbage and raw onions followed by Barnbrack cake. Once, I got the coin in me piece of cake. "Ah, Mary," me dad said. "That means you'll be rich." That was before the troubles started.

"Open eyes," Kam orders, startling me from me memories.

I do as he says and see him cutting the beet with a folding knife he took from Jack's bunk. When it's in pieces, he says, "Open mouth." I do as instructed and he rubs the beet on me teeth and lips. "Eat," he says, giving me half the beet. It tastes delicious.

"Stand," he says and hands me a grime white piece of muslin. "Sheet from Seamus's bed," he says. "He drunk. Not see gone." He wraps the sheet around me and ties it onto me shoulders and around each of me ankles.

"Done," he says. "Mabo, Banshee."

I feel purely the fool standing there until he holds a tiny mirror up to me face and lifts the lamp so I can see meself.

"Oh sweet Jesus," I say, then cross meself against the blaspheme. The image in the mirror scares even me, though it's me, meself, I'm looking at. Me face, neck and hands are a ghostly white. Kam has drawn black lines of coal down the sides of me mouth and around me eyes. Me teeth are red as me lips. They look as if I've drunk a cup of blood.

Me hair stands away from me head by a foot, and that's no Irish exaggeration. The curls are stiff as crimson worms trying to flee me scalp. "I am the Banshee," I say in a low wail which dissolves into hysterical laughter.

"No laugh." His voice is deep, no longer that of a boy. "Mean it."

His eyes burn into mine and ignite me fury in an instant.

He's right. After what Seamus and his crew did to Ceili and her mother, only rage will do this night.

The full moon rides high in the sky. The passengers are up on the deck, trying to get a last gasp of fresh air before going into the fetid hold. In the first days of this voyage, there had been dancing in the cool evenings, but no more. Now, they are too sick, too hungry, and some, too weak with fever to dance.

When I stick me head out from under our sail, I see Ceili standing there with her mother. I shake me head to dispel the illusion, but she's still there, so pale that me skin goes to goose bumps. She leans on the rail and her mam puts her arm around her shoulders for steadying. Then, the two of them turn and look at me and, as God is me witness, smile.

"Kam," I whisper. "I thought I saw Ceili and her mam."

He nods.

"Did you see them?"

"Yes."

With no warning, he grabs me arm so hard that I jump under his hand. Kam, always gentle, now has the grip of a fierce animal. "Forget Ceili," he says, snarling. "You are Banshee."

I am the Banshee. I feel it in the pounding in me temples and the heat racing through me hands. The Irish believe that every day has one hour in which a wish may be granted, and I pray that this is me hour. "Dear Jesus," I pray. "Make me a Banshee this night."

It seems a peculiar thing to be asking of one so gentle as Jesus, but I figure He understands. Enough of such gobdaw musings. The deck is empty. The moon beckons. 'Tis time.

Without a word, Kam and I get to our feet and creep down the ladder.

I hear the devils snoring as we slither into their hell. The place reeks of rum and tobacco and body gas. Kam carries the kerosene lantern but will not light it until we are on the deck. He creeps to Seamus's bunk and hangs the voodoo doll with a fish hook over Seamus's pillow.

The folly of what we plan to attempt hits me like a blow from the mainsail. Have we lost what little sense we ever had? How can the two of us—one shanty Irish girl and a boy child from Africa—fool these monsters? I look back at Kam, wanting to escape. If they catch us, they'll rape us again.

He curls his hand into a fist and raises it in front of me face. All I can see is the startling white of eyes and teeth. He looks mortally fearful. He'll surely smash me in the beak if I back down now.

Narrowing me eyes, I nod to Kam, acting braver than I'll ever be.

Seamus lies there, his mouth gaping like a fish tossed on the rocks. His wooden peg hangs out the side of the bunk. A slather of drool courses down through his whiskers and drips from his ugly chin. He seems not to be breathing at all, and I wonder for an instant if he has purely died on us. But then, with a great noise he gasps in air and lets out a loud snore. I nearly jump from me skin.

I turn to Kam, lighting the lantern behind me, and feel a fear-some panic. Again, his glare rivets me. The heat of the lantern now warms me back. Kam places it on the floor and hides under the stairway. He reaches through the steps and punches me in the back. It is our signal.

I take in a huge breath of air. "A-y-e-e-e!" I wail.

Seamus jumps to sitting and tumbles out of his bunk, falling to the floor as the peg turns under him.

The other two crew members jolt up, too. "What the feckin' hell?" Jack yells.

"A-y-e-e-e!" I wail again, forcing me face down close to

Seamus's own. "I am the Banshee, come fer ye. Seamus must die." The lantern blazes brighter, and I clap me hands together and commence a crazy whirling dance around his bunk, all the time, shrieking his name.

"Banshee?" His hiss sounds like a snake.

"Banshee! Banshee! Banshee!" I shriek again and again, louder with each repetition, and never cease the whirling and clapping. "Die! Die! Die!" I point to his face and with every bit of strength me mam bragged about, pull him with both hands up onto his bunk.

At that moment, he spies the voodoo doll hanging above his face. He begins to moan and drool as he writhes there. He's caught between the doll and me and tries to recoil from both of us, though there's nowhere to go.

His fear makes me bolder, and I increase me shrieking to a level that could surely wake the dead. As I get louder and more piercing, I actually become a different creature—a being from the dark, hellish center of the earth. In me soul, I become the Banshee. All fear is gone.

Bart cowers under his blanket, his bald head all that is visible of him. Jack vomits up rum and chaw all over his bed covers. Bart starts to squall like a baby, frightened to madness by the sight of me.

I scream louder and louder, advancing nearer to Seamus's face with each shriek. "Die, pig, die! The Banshee dooms you for what you did to Ceili."

He jolts to sitting in his bunk, knocking his head against the voodoo doll. He grabs at his chest, his mouth gasping for air and his eyes rolling back into his head. "Ahhhh no," he moans, his arms, leg and peg jolting up and down. He slams back down onto his back and looks like a rock-stranded fish flopping around as it tries to reach the sea.

A final moan takes him, and he quivers to quiet, eyes staring open at the doll above him.

Is he dead? The thought of it drives me to even wilder dancing and I spin meself toward Bart, still mewling in his bunk. "Ayee!" I scream at him. "Beware the Banshee. You're next." I whirl toward Jack, and he covers himself with his vomit-soaked blanket.

Kam grabs me by the shoulder and nods toward the ladder. "Now," he says.

It's over.

CHAPTER FOURTEEN

May the rains fall soft upon you.

When Kam and I get back to the deck, a heavy downpour falls. It feels like a benediction, as though heaven blesses me with holy water in spite of me evil deed. I lift me face to receive the rain like communion wine. When I have drunk me fill, I rub me face and eyes to wash off the flour and coal. At first, the stuff sticks like glue, but I scour me skin nearly raw until it breaks free. The gunk, black mingling with white, runs down onto the deck, then into the scuppers, and out to the sea.

The rain isn't enough to cleanse the egg from me hair, so Kam finds a bucket and positions it near the sail where we will hide this night. I will use the collected rain water to wash me hair in the morning.

When we are safely hidden, Kam turns his eyes away while I take off me wet dress and wrap meself in Seamus's drenched sheet. I wring as much water as I can from the dress and stretch it out next to me under the sail. It will still be damp in the morning, but I've endured worse things than a wet dress on this Godforsaken ship.

Kam's black eyes blaze so bright I can see them even in the darkness of our haven. "Mabo do good," he says.

I lie back onto the pillow I've fashioned from me pantaloons and stare, wide eyed with disbelief over what happened. Lifting a side of the sail, I see a single star shining through a break in the clouds high above me. In God's universe, it looks as if nothing at all has changed.

But everything has changed. I, Mary Boland, shanty girl from Kinsale, have killed. Sure as the tides, Seamus lies dead there in his bunk, and his body will be the next one tossed. The passengers will probably cheer as the circling sharks pull the despised skegrat under.

Others might say it was his time and that his heart simply gave out from rum and tobacco, but I know the truth. I took his life. And, forgive me me sin, sweet Jesus, I'm not sorry.

After a time, me heart stops its wild pounding. Kam lies deep in slumber. I envy his way of falling asleep no matter the night's happening. I don't have that skill.

As I stare at the heavens, I think about Mam and baby Ellen and hope they're up there together looking down and that Mam is not horrified at what has become of her Mary.

Perhaps Ceili and her mother are with them there. I recall Ceili that first day on the ship—how she danced, so full of life and joy—and then I remember her last moments. Cold in the water with crazy, lifeless eyes. Then I hear again her screams when the shark pulled her under. How can such a delight of a girl be gone?

Sometime in the deepest part of the night, I drift into a sleep filled with nightmares and monsters.

I'm startled to waken at dawn, surprised to still be breathing. Kam goes to relieve himself, and I slip back into me damp dress. Dunking me head into the bucket, I wash the egg from me hair as best I can with a tiny piece of soap Kam took from the galley, then tuck the dripping mop back up into me bonnet just as he returns.

Hearing a ruckus on the deck toward the starboard side, we peek up from under the sail.

The passengers have circled a man and are screaming at him. The man had shoved old Maeve Maloney off her feet. She cowers on the deck beneath him. Me heart stops when I see the peg leg. Kam stares into me eyes and puts one finger to his mouth.

"He's not dead," I whisper.

As I look Seamus over, though, I can tell he's weaker. He has a fever in his eyes that wasn't there before and is unsteady in his stance. Sweat pours down his face and his mouth is pulled back from his black teeth like an animal gasping for breath.

Liam advances toward Seamus. "Coward," he says, his red beard plastered by wind against his chin. "First, you destroy Ceili and her mam and then pick on an old woman. Are you afraid to fight a man?" He puts his fists up.

The other crew men rush Liam and wrestle him down. Strong as he is, he's no match for all of them.

"A coward you call me?" Seamus snarls and brings a rope out of his pocket. "Let's have a swinging party, mates, shall we?"

Rage fills me soul. No more of me people will be hurt by this beast. I stand in the lifeboat. Kam pulls on me sleeve to get me back down, but I shake him off and step out onto the deck. I feel detached, as if it is someone else approaching the monster who took me innocence.

Liam tries to stop me, but something drives me forward—something old and primitive—something that tells me this fight must be finished now.

Seamus hears the commotion behind him and turns.

"Why did you hurt Ceili O'Shaughnessy?" I say. Me voice comes from somewhere deep in hell. It's a voice I've never heard before.

"Well, if it isn't little Mary," he snarls. "About time you showed your face again. I've been needing your services." His filthy hand reaches for me arm.

I step back, out of his reach. "Why did you hurt her?" I repeat.

"Because I felt like it," he answers. "Not that it's any of your business. But I'll be teaching you a lesson about *your* business later." He steps closer and I smell his rank breath.

The sky begins to darken, and the wind whips into a gale. It's as if I am alone on the deck with the devil himself. Seamus grins, but his smile is the strained grimace of a cadaver. "Come here, darling. Just looking at you again makes me lad twitch in me pants like a boy's."

I part me legs and take me stand firmly as the wind swells, whipping me dress tight around me body. Other passengers huddle together grasping the rail and studying the black skies.

"Look at this, mates," Seamus says to the two others flanking him. "It's little Mary and her nigger. I think I'd like a taste of her again. How 'bout you?" Kam touches me back to let me know he's there. Seamus steps toward me.

As the storm blackens the sky, hatred surges within me. It turns me bones to iron and me blood to fire. His words ring hollow—they're blather—like those of the village boys who bragged they could beat me in a race. His face looks gray as death, and he nearly falls when the boat is smacked by a giant wave.

The other two crewmen run to man the sails which look ready to rip apart from the force of the wind.

I ask Jesus to give me the strength to defeat this man before he can hurt anyone else.

I loosen the ribbon and tear the bonnet from me head. Me hair whips wild in the gale. I stalk toward Seamus and begin to scream, "I am the Banshee, you black-toothed beast and you cannot escape me. You are doomed for what you did to Ceili. Prepare to die."

His hideous face melts into a mask of fear, and his jaw goes slack with confusion. "It's you?" he says.

He believes me now, and I believe as well. Though he struggles against his superstitions, it's clear he is losing the battle. As I get closer, he backs away until his back presses against the rail. Other sailors crowd around him. The fear I see on their faces goads me to louder and louder wails.

I turn me dance toward them. "Protect him at your peril," I scream. "Protect him and you will be next."

They slink away, leaving Seamus alone before me. I snarl and dance up to him, screeching in a voice so high I don't recognize it as me own. "Die, Seamus! Die! Die! Die!"

He screams in terror. "Mates! Help me! Get her away from me!" His wooden peg gives out from under him and he falls to the deck. Scrambling like a spider, he rights himself finally and grips the rail.

No one comes to his aid.

Spittle comes down onto his chin. He looks like he's foaming at the mouth. His fear makes me stronger. He'll not escape me this time.

Standing in front of him, I place me hands on his shoulders and bring me knee up between his legs. His face contorts in a grimace of agony. Again, he falls to the deck.

At that moment, a giant wave crashes atop him. I jump away. In slow motion, he rises up onto the wave higher and higher. I hear one of them, Jack or Bart, scream, "Rogue wave, rogue wave."

There is a long moment where Seamus glares down at me, disbelieving, from the top of the water, and then he washes over the rail and into the sea.

I race to the rail and look down at him. He thrashes and screams for help.

"Grab a rope," one of the crewmen yells, but it is too late.

Already I see the sharks gathering around him. His eyes glow up at me like red fires from hell.

I turn away as he goes under the water, screaming in agony.

Liam is the first to stand beside me. He looks frightened. "Mary," he asks, "are you truly the Banshee?"

Am I? Perhaps I am. "Does it matter?"

CHAPTER FIFTEEN

May you see God's light on the path,
though the road you walk is dark.

Three days later, a pall of despair still envelops *The Pilgrim's Dandy*. So many passengers who boarded in Queenstown have since died of typhus or hunger. But Ceili was the hardest to lose. Ceili, with her golden hair and bright smile, enchanted everyone. She was the darling of the ship. Some people are like that. Their light shines on those around them, and when the light goes, darkness seems an endless midnight. I think sometimes that's what hell must be like—an absence of light. I don't believe it will be fire and burning, the way the priest in Kinsale described it.

The loss of Ceili shakes me faith even more than me rape. How could a just God have allowed such a magical creature to die so young? Kam tries to cheer me, but nothing feels happy anymore.

But there is one good thing. We no longer need to hide. We move about the ship in brazen daylight and grin as Jack and Bart pretend not to see us. We go into the galley whenever we wish and take food and water down to the passengers in the hold. Some who looked near death begin to recover the color in their faces.

Kam teaches me to count time by the rising and setting of the sun. Two full moons have risen and set since we sailed from Queenstown.

Liam Horan finds Ceili's books and jacks and gives them to us.

I am grateful, but say, "Liam, neither Kam nor I can read. Give the books to a child who can."

One day, as we play jacks on the deck, Kam says, "Mabo, I have secret."

He pulls two shiny coins from his pocket. "From Seamus's boot—ten pounds British sterling."

"You took them?" I ask, me voice louder than I'd intended.

He nods. "He not need them in hell."

I laugh for the first time since Ceili's death. "Yes, and that's where he burns this very minute." I spit on his memory. "What're you going to do with them?"

"I give them to you for Boston, America."

"To me?"

He looks at me, eyes gentle. "Yes."

"But you'll be with me there, Kam."

He lowers his eyes. "Kam slave to ship."

"No, you're me friend. You're a hero to all on this ship."

He shakes his head. "Crew own me, not let me off ship, but I not forget you. Mabo friend. Forever."

"I swear to you, on the life of Ceili O'Shaughnessy, that you will be with me in Boston."

Me words are brave, but I have no idea how to make them true.

After a few days, our games of jacks grow tedious. Without Ceili and her books to entertain us, time drags.

"Why Mabo not read?" Kam asks.

"In Kinsale, only boys went to the hedge school. The price was dear, and Mam figured I'd have a man to take care of me."

"Why need man?" Kam says. "Did father say Mabo need man?"

"Ah, Da's face scowled into a frown every time Mam said that. He told her I was smarter than any of the boys in Kinsale. He tried to teach me to read once, but the lesson didn't stick. By the time I was seven, he was gone most of the time fighting the Protestants for property rights. The land we lived on had been in the Boland name for centuries, but they didn't care. 'Those Brit bastards,'—that's not me swearing, Kam—that's me da.— 'took our land as if we were no better than the goats that roamed it.' And there was not a thing we could do about it."

I can almost see him again. Tall, broad backed. Scowling at the ships in our harbor as he circled me shoulder with his strong right arm.

"Mabo," Kam says, looking deep into me eyes. "Think good things."

I shake meself straight. He's right. If I dwell on what's past, I won't be able to breathe. If I think about the crew me first night on board, I'll go mad. The sadness is something I fight every day, but at night, when the nightmares come, the battle goes against me.

CHAPTER SIXTEEN

Remember, 'tis always darkest before the dawn.

Kam says we'll land in a matter of days. When the passengers hear him, they become excited, then the grief returns as they remember those who didn't make it this far.

Maeve Maloney's daughter was tossed yesterday. She had the fever for less than a week before it took her. By the time Maeve told Kam of her illness, it was too late to help her. Maeve keened so loud I worried her mind had left her altogether. "What will I do in America now?" she wept. "I know no one there. I'm sixty-six years old. Who will care for me?"

Liam Horan went to her and put his arm around her. "I have no mother left, Mrs. Maloney," he said. "So, you'll be me mam from now on."

The old woman looked up at the strong young man in disbelief. "Do you mean it?"

"I don't say things I don't mean," he answered. "Me cousin in Boston will take us in, for sure."

Though I know she grieves, Liam's kindness seems to have revived Maeve's will to live a bit longer. She spends every minute at his side now, and this morning I heard her humming an old

Gaelic melody. I love hearing those songs. They almost make me forget for a while the awful things that have happened on this scow which has surely earned its name of coffin ship.

One thing is gained. Now, I have faith in me instincts. They are sharp. Mary Boland is no longer the foolish girl who trusted the likes of Elizabeth Bradshaw back in Queenstown. From this day on, I'll look beneath the surface of a fancy outfit before I judge a person. Those are lessons that will serve me well in Boston, America, I think.

CHAPTER SEVENTEEN

'Twas hard to fight the wide, wide ocean.

October, 1849

A voice screams across the brisk wind, and at first I think it's the screech of a breaking mast.

Creeping from behind the sail, I stand up. Though it's autumn, the sun is so bright I can't stare directly at it. Wind fills the sails in a way that would bring delight to any seafaring man. Then, I spot him. It wasn't a snapping mast. The sailor yells again. "Land ho." He hangs from the crow's nest, shielding his eyes, and points to the West. "I see it. Boston Harbor."

The passengers race to the rail. They crane their necks in the direction he points. "I can't see anything yet," Liam says to Maeve, holding her safe beside him at the rail. "But keep your eyes peeled. If he sees it, we will, too, soon enough."

The ship hurtles forward, its sails billowing us toward land. Kam runs up to me and grabs me hand. "Mabo, Boston, America."

A young boy begins to toot on his penny whistle. It's a familiar Irish reel, and quick as you can say begorrah, the passengers start to dance in joy around the deck.

Kam pulls me to the rail. He shields his eyes with his hands and leans far out over the water. Wanting me to see, he grabs me hand again and says, "Look, Mabo. Look."

I pull me bonnet down to shade me face and narrow me eyes in the direction he's looking. "I don't see anything, Kam."

He stands behind me and twists me neck a little to the left. "There," he says. "See now?"

Is there something or is it me imagination? There's a hazy grey blur off in the distance that rises a bit above the water. "Is that it?" I ask Kam, pointing. A big grin splits his nodding face. Me spirit begins to lift in excitement. "Is it Boston, America?"

"Aye," a sailor says as he passes behind me. "And it can't come soon enough for me. I want you and that red hair off this ship. I haven't had a night's sleep since you sent Seamus to the sharks."

His words bring a grin to me face. This power to transform meself into something that creates fear has been a wonder to learn about meself. And now I know that fear based on a sham is every bit as strong as the real stuff.

Liam begins to move through the bedraggled crowd. "Gather up your things now, all of you. From the looks of it, we'll be getting off this hell ship soon."

Only thirty passengers are left. Half the people who boarded in Queenstown have not survived the voyage. I would have expected death for the old and infirm, but many of the ones tossed were children, some younger than Ceili.

People file down into the hold to bring their few possessions up on the deck. I watch as Maeve Maloney sets her ragged straw sewing basket carefully beside Liam's wooden tool box and then heads back down. Suddenly, I am gripped by terrible sadness.

Kam sees the look on me face and touches me shoulders. "Ceili?" he says.

I nod and brush at me cheeks. I *am* thinking of Ceili but also wonder what'll happen to all of us? We who have managed to stay alive during this dreadful journey? How will we survive life in this strange new world? And, most important, how will I ever get Kam ashore?

When Maeve appears again, she carries the tablecloth Mrs. O'Shaughnessy had used to shield Ceili's modesty. It is filthy and a bit tattered but made of fine Irish linen.

"Mary," she says. "Ceili's mam would want you to have this." She folds the tablecloth until it's the size of a small towel and lays it gently into me hands. I hold it to me cheek, thinking of the joy it once brought Ceili and her mother. I can almost see them dishing up stew in their cottage at Tullamore. The remembered scent of lamb mingling with carrots and potatoes is an old one, but potent.

"Thank you, Mrs. Maloney. I'll treasure it always. I'll mend it and get it clean again. Every time I lay it on me table, I'll think of Ceili and her mam."

The old woman smiles. "I knew you'd understand its value, Mary. You're a good girl, you are. Make us proud of you in Boston."

Her words stun me. How can I make me people proud of me, ignorant girl that I am? But the phrase sounds dear to these ears after thinking I was a disgrace to them.

I hear laughter behind me, but it's more the sound of a snarl than a ring of joy. Agnes Dooley stands there.

"What's funny, Agnes?" I question.

"Oh, I just heard that foolish old woman tell you you're a good girl. It's enough to make anyone laugh, all things considered." With a toss of her head, she continues on her way, carrying her mother's hat box toward the pile of her family's belongings.

I follow her. "And what might you mean by that, Agnes?" I hear the dangerous fury in me voice.

She turns to face me. Her close-set eyes narrow in disdain. "You know exactly what it means, Mary. No matter what Ceili said about you, we all know what you are. The crew's whore, that's what." Her expression is cruel as she turns away and places the box on the deck. "Isn't that how you paid for your passage?"

I grab her by the shoulder. "Take it back, Agnes."

She twirls to face me, her face flushed and ugly. "I'll never take it back. It's true."

I pull me right arm around behind me back. Before I let it go to smack her square in the puss, Kam grabs it. "No, Mabo."

"But she's hateful." I am so wound up I nearly begin to cry, but Kam takes me flailing hands in his and holds them firm.

"Think," he says. "Ceili say Agnes jealous. Not worth fight."

At the sound of Ceili's name, all the rage drains out of me. I drop me hands.

Turning to Agnes, I say, "He's right."

"Oh, I forgot," she says with a sneer. "Besides being a whore, you sleep with a nigger, don't you?"

This time, Kam isn't quick enough. I smack Agnes so hard she falls back, smashing her backside directly onto the hatbox. As the tears begin to roll down her flaming cheeks, she screams. Maureen Dooley, her mam, comes running. When she sees the flattened hatbox, the woman's mouth gapes so I think she could catch a seagull in it. She pulls the lid off the box.

"Agnes Dooley, look what you've done," she yells. "The one pretty thing I have in me life and you've ruint it." She pulls a mess of pink straw and veiling from the box, trudges to the rail and throws it into the sea. Then she stomps back to Agnes, who sits cowering on the deck, and smacks her even harder than I did. "You ugly, clumsy girl," she says. "Of all the people to take after, why'd you have to pick your father's homely sister?" Then she storms back down into the hold.

Kam and I look at each other, confounded. Finally, he walks to the sobbing Agnes and extends his hand.

Of all the lessons I've learned from Kam, perhaps the most important is forgiveness. He's crafty and smart, has been hurt bad as anyone I know, and yet, he never loses his sweetness. Yes, Kam's lessons are deep and true.

But Agnes hasn't learned such lessons. She ignores his hand, stands up, and wipes her nose on her dress. "I don't want your black to rub off on me," she says and turns her back.

He looks down at his extended hand, smiles and shrugs his shoulders. "No rub off."

At that moment, the sailor called Jack, the one who first held me down when Seamus did his dirty deed to me, grabs Kam by the arm. "Don't be thinking you're getting off this ship, boy," he says. "You belong to us. We bought you."

Kam slumps. He starts to follow Jack.

I grab him by the arm. "Oh, no," I hiss, "not while there's a breath of life left in me, they won't keep you here. We'll get you off this hell ship sure as me name is Mabo."

CHAPTER EIGHTEEN

May the face of every good news and the back of every bad news
be toward us.

I run to where Liam and Maeve bundle up their things. "Mr. Horan," I say, me voice breathless and high. "One of the sailors just said they're keeping Kam aboard; that they won't let him off the ship in Boston, America."

"Does that matter so much to you, girl?" he asks.

"Yes, it matters more than I can say. Without Kam's help, I'd be dead by now. I know I would." I stare deep into Liam's eyes. "And so would you. Remember all the food and fresh water he snuck to you and the other passengers? We can't abandon him now."

Liam starts to scratch his beard. Maeve looks up at him. "She's right, you know, Liam," she says. "Without that boy, more of us would've starved for sure."

"Let me think on this, Mary," he says, finally. "I'll talk to the other men on board and see what we can come up with."

"Thank you, Mr. Horan," I answer. "I knew I could depend on you to do the right thing."

But what if the right thing can't save Kam?

Liam begins to talk to a group of the men, pointing all the while at Kam and me. Some shake their heads, but others nod in agreement. After a time, I see they're all nodding.

Finally, he comes back to Maeve and me. "All right. We have a plan. When we begin to disembark, if anyone tries to block Kam from getting off, we'll rush him. There's more of us than them. We'll get him off this ship."

Maeve reaches up and pats Liam's cheek. "Good boy," she says.

He looks down at her fondly. "Seems to me us Irish better start sticking together, Mam. God knows what we'll face in Boston." Then he lets out a great laugh. "I guess Kam really can be called black Irish, now, can't he?"

An hour later, as the sailors lower one sail to slow our approach, all the passengers are out of the hold and standing on deck ready to disembark. I whisper to Kam, "Remember, if any sailor tries to block your exit, Liam and his boys will rush him."

He nods. "Thank you." But he doesn't look confident.

"Ah, don't be thanking me, Kam," I say in a mock scolding voice. "We're friends, right?"

"Mabo and Kam—friends forever."

We sail to sighting distance of the harbor, and the crew strikes down all the sails and drops the anchor.

"What's this?" Liam says to a crewman who rushes past him.

"Ya can't go into Boston Harbor direct, you foolish mick. First, they've gotta examine everyone to see who's got the typhus. Them that might'll be quarantined on Deer Island."

Maeve grabs onto Liam's sleeve. "Quarantined?" she says. "They won't let us off yet?"

"Don't trouble yourself, Mam," he says, gentling her. "We'll get to Boston soon enough."

The passengers grumble at this new delay. The land is so near, and I understand how they yearn to get to it. All of us huddle together on the deck, confusion and hunger clearly battling for attention in each head. This voyage has lasted eleven weeks. The feel of solid earth under our feet is a desperate need.

Small boats pull up beside *The Pilgrim's Dandy*. Men climb up the anchor chain and onto the deck. Masks cover their mouths. "Line up," one of them yells.

Some of the men have sheets of paper in their hands. "Who of you can write?" he yells again.

Only a few hands go up. Liam's is one of them. I am shocked that so many of the passengers are like me. How will we all survive in this new land not being able to read or write?

"All of you with your hands up step forward," the man calls out.

When they comply with his order, he says, "I'm the Customs Officer. Sign your name and Irish county in this space." He points to a line on the paper. "If you have family in Boston, name them here." He moves his finger down the page. "They'll be informed that you're landing and to come meet you."

When all who can write are finished, he yells, "All right, now the rest of you line up."

"Kam, stay close beside me," I whisper. "The minute I get to him, I'll shove you in front of me." He looks scared but does as I say. Liam and the others surround us.

When I stand before the man with the tablet, I push Kam ahead of me. At that moment, Jack rushes up and grabs Kam by the shoulders, his greasy hair escaping the leather thong that holds it. He struggles to wrest Kam from his place in line. "This boy is property of *The Dandy*," he says to the officer. "He has no business being on your list."

Liam and five other men get behind Kam's back.

The Customs Officer lifts his pencil from the paper. "What did you say?"

"I said this nigger is our slave. He can't get off this ship, sure as me name is Jack McQuiggen."

The Customs Officer smiles a peculiar smile. I've no idea what it means, and I'm shaking in me boots he'll say Kam must stay on board. This new land of Boston, America surely has laws that must be obeyed.

But then the Customs Officer speaks, "Well, Jack McQuiggen, it appears your luck has run out this day. I happen to be the nephew of William Garrison. Ever hear of him?"

Jack shakes his head, his jaw so slack tobacco juice runs down his chin.

"He's the leader of the abolition movement here in Boston."

"Abolition?" Jack says.

"Yeh, a tough group of lads and ladies who don't think it's fitting for anyone to be owned as a slave. In fact, the state of Massachusetts outlawed slavery almost seventy years ago. So, you see, Jack McQuiggen, this boy *will* be getting off this godforsaken scow today."

Jack starts to speak. "You can't do—"

"Ah, but I can, Jack. And you and you scurvy ship can go to hell if you think different."

Jack tries a charge, but Liam and the others block his way. "Mates," Jack calls to the crew. "Get your arses over here."

"I'll waste no more time on you, Jack McQuiggen," the Customs Officer says. "I want your Captain."

A pale, slender man passes by me. I smell whiskey, strong and recent. He wears a dark blue uniform with some tattered gold braid hanging from his shoulders. "I'm Captain James Barlow," he says quietly to the Customs Officer. I realize this is the first time I've laid eyes on the man during this long sail.

The Customs Officer scowls. "Just how many passengers boarded this ship in Ireland? From the looks of this meager crowd, I'd say you've lost quite a few. Is this a coffin ship?"

The Captain darts his eyes around as if wishing he were anywhere else but standing here being interrogated. McQuiggen opens his yap and stammers, "He can't talk to you like that, Sir. You're the Captain of *The Pilgrims Dandy*. Stand yer ground."

The Captain straightens his shoulders, then slumps into a posture of abject defeat. "Don't rile the man, Jack. He's the law. We can't afford a scrap with the law."

Jack's bald head turns red as me hair, and he screws up his ugly face. He storms away in disgust and defeat "Oh, the feck with ya all."

The Captain says. "We did lose more passengers this voyage than usual. It was the typhus."

Liam snorts in disgust. "And no food and water," he snarls, a scowl covering his usually cheery face.

The Captain turns back to the Customs Officer. "Look, sir, I don't want any trouble. This is my last voyage. I plan to stay here in Boston."

"Oh, wonderful," the man answers. "Just what we need. Another waterfront drunk." He shakes his head and turns back toward the passengers. "Next."

I exhale the biggest sigh I've ever breathed. "Your turn, Kam."

Before me very eyes, Kam straightens into the quiet warrior, Kamua. He grows taller and has a dignity like none I've witnessed before. He stands before the man, head high and shoulders square.

"Your name?"

"Kamua Okafor."

His voice, boy like before, sounds deeper.

"Age?"

"Fifteen years."

"From where?"

"Gabon, West Africa."

"Have you any family here, Kamua?"

Kam slumps. "Father in Louisiana, but no one here."

I speak up. "He's me brother, sir."

"Your brother?"

Seconds pass.

Liam yells out, "Mine, too."

"And mine," another man shouts.

The customs man smiles. "Pass on, young man."

Kam rushes to Liam and shakes his hand.

Now it's me turn.

"Your name?"

"Mary Boland."

"Can you spell that?"

I shake me head.

"Age?"

"Thirteen."

"From?" he continues.

"County Cork, Ireland."

"Village?"

"Kinsale."

As I speak, he writes on the lines. When he's finished, he looks up and says, "Well, Mary Boland. I must say, you don't look much like your brother here, now do you?"

"No sir, I suppose not."

He laughs. "Pass on."

Kam grasps me hand. "Mabo. Kam not slave?"

"No, Kam, never again."

When every person has their name and place recorded, men

in white coats approach. "Those are the doctors," Liam whispers. "They must examine us before we can stay in Boston."

I stand before the doctor. He examines me arms. "No rash," he says. Then, he tells me to stick out me tongue. When I obey, he puts a glass stick in me mouth. "Under your tongue," he orders.

After a time of standing there with the thing sticking out of me face, he takes it from me mouth and looks at it. "She's healthy—filthy but fit."

"What is that thing, sir?" I ask.

"A thermometer, girl. Have you never seen one?"

I shake me head.

"It measures if you have a fever," he says.

What a wonder this Boston, America is. Where they can stick glass tubes in your mouth to see if you have the typhus. I think I'll like it here.

CHAPTER NINETEEN

Keep us safe and free from sin.

There are only four small boats headed for Boston. So many passengers died on the journey, and nearly as many were sent to quarantine. When the doctor told Maeve Maloney she needed to go to Deer Island, Liam Horan stepped up and took her arm. "I'll go there with her."

"But you're healthy. You needn't be quarantined," the doctor said.

"She's the closest thing I have to a mother, sir," Liam said. "I can't leave her now."

"But you might contract typhus there."

Liam did not respond to the warning, just followed Maeve to one of the boats departing for Deer Island. As I watched them pull away, I tried mightily for a cheery smile. Maeve never looked up at me, but Liam waved once and then turned away. Though his frame was gaunt, his back looked straight as a Viking warrior's. Watching his red hair disappear into the sea's mist, I turned away lest me soul wither from the pain of seeing them go.

Sitting down on the deck, I buried me face in me hands as

three more rowboats departed for Deer Island. I knew in me very soul I'd never see these people again.

There are six in our little row boat taking us to Boston, America: two oarsmen, Kam, me, Agnes and her mother. Wouldn't you know those two would land in the same boat as me? Sometimes, God's sense of humor sure has a touch of the devil in it.

The two of them sit as far from me and Kam as they can scoot themselves. Much as I want to hate Agnes, the outline of her mother's hand still scrawled across her face pulls me heart toward pity.

What a sad thing, to have your mother think you ugly and say so in front of others. Me mam would never have done such a thing, So at least in that regard, I count meself a lucky girl indeed. I'm not sure which is worse, to lose a mother who thinks you hung the moon or to still have one who thinks you're dirt.

But I shan't ponder such things now, not with Boston there in the distance. The burly oarsman facing me and Kam is a friendly sort. When we tell him our names, he says, "I'm Stanislav. Call me Stash. Come here from Russia fifteen years ago. I'm a Jew. Russians hate Jews."

I never met a Jew before. He doesn't look much different than men in Ireland. Why would the Russians hate him? Didn't they know our Savior Himself was a Jew?

"Is Boston, America the largest city here?" I ask.

"Nah, not even close. New York biggest. Most immigrants land there." He lifts his oars from the water and whispers to me. "You should know it's Boston, Massachusetts. Not Boston, America."

"Why is that?"

"Because this is United States of America. Massachusetts is Boston's state, best state in union."

"How many states are there here?"

He resumes his rowing. "Don't know. Mexico takes some. America gets some back. Can't keep track of who owns what no more. But thing for you to know is you're going to be landing in Boston, Massachusetts."

Boston, Massachusetts. It has a nice ring to it. "And what county?"

"Suffolk County. Not important."

Not important? You could knock me over with a shamrock, that's how strange such a thing seems to me. One more thing to get used to. "Kam, did you get what he was saying?"

Kam nods. "Boston, city. Massachusetts, state."

Mrs. Dooley cranes her head around the oarsman and yells, "Can't you shut your yaps for a minute? It's enough to rattle a saint." Agnes's mournful expression turns smug.

"Some saint," I mutter under me breath, then shut me yap.

But the thing that really quiets me is I can see Boston now, and I don't want to miss a bit of it. Huge ships with tall sails circle the entire harbor. There must be a hundred of them. Men crawl over them scraping paint and climbing masts. Some nets look big enough to catch a whale. Ah, Da would have loved to see this. Seagulls swoop down into the water, probably hoping to nab a crumb of food thrown off the ships.

As we pull still closer, I see that the land behind the buildings is covered with trees. The leaves are red and gold and brown and every shade in between. I never saw such trees in Ireland; the British had scalped her so to get wood for ship building. The glory of all these trees waving in the wind fairly takes me breath from me.

Our rowboat lurches to the right, and a magnificent vessel sweeps into view. I can't stay quiet another second. "What's that?" I ask, pointing to the huge ship.

Stash turns to look. He smiles. "That U.S.S. Constitution. Old Ironsides. British couldn't knock a hole in her hull with any of their cannons. Now she travels the world like good-will ambassador. You lucky she's in port today. Beautiful lady, huh?"

"Oh, yes," I whisper. She had a hand in defeating the Brits. "Good girl," I whisper and extend me hand toward her like she's a new friend who lives in me new home, Boston, em, Massachusetts.

I tear me eyes from Old Ironsides and start to scan the wharf, now so close I could throw a rock and hit it. Stores line the street, all built tight next to each other for block after block. Some wares are displayed right out on the street; racks of clothing of every shape and color. Tallow makers light candles, and then snuff them out. Weavers work feverishly at looms. Women shove each other aside as they hustle shoppers to buy their pottery. Men hammer at horseshoes still red from the fire. Fancy horses and carriages bounce over the cobbled streets, and a small boy holds up a big piece of paper as he yells, "Map of Massachusetts, cheapest in Boston."

The sights and sounds dizzy me, and Kam's mouth hangs agape. Pulling closer, I catch the glorious smell of baking bread. Kam closes his eyes and inhales the scent. "Stash," I say, pointing toward the store where the aroma comes from. "What's that store?"

"Bakery," he answers. "Best bread in Boston." I mark the place in me memory as I wipe the drool on me sleeve.

But then me attention is jolted by a loud, deep voice. A man standing on the dock yells, "Cod fresh from the sea! Come and get it! Penny a pound!" He waves a huge white fish over his head. Its gills are opening and closing and its eyes look ready to pop from its head. A small girl stands beside him with a heavy mallet. The man slams the fish onto the wooden deck, takes the mallet from the girl, and smashes the fish's head. The gills flutter still.

Women attired in peacock finery scurry toward the fishmonger. "They must be fierce wealthy," I say to Stash. "Look at how they're dressed."

"Those aren't the wealthy ones," he says. "They servants. Work on Beacon Hill for rich people. Down here shopping for dinner."

"Beacon Hill?"

"Richest people in world," he answers. "Lodges and Adams and Lowells."

"How did they get so rich?" I ask him.

"Shipping, factories, iron, railroads. All respectable."

If the servants dress so fine, I can't even imagine how the ladies who live on Beacon Hill must look.

I'm so busy gawking that it startles me when our rowboat bumps against the dock. The other oarsman leaps out and ties ropes to the bollards. Stash pulls himself up onto the dock and reaches his hands down to help us up. When I finally stand on the boards, me legs wobble around like a drunkard. I nearly fall to the wood. Stash laughs. "Sea legs," he says. "Happens every time."

The dock is packed with men, milling around, unloading other ships, carting boxes up gangplanks. When I have me mooring, I begin to scan each one of them. Perhaps me da is here. I run to a man hoisting a huge carton over his head. He wears a cap like Da's. I tap him on the shoulder.

When he turns, I look into a pair of eyes covered by spectacles. "Yes, miss," he says.

"Never mind, sir. I mistook you for someone else." Me heart sinks in disappointment.

Mrs. Dooley grabs onto Agnes's hand and pulls her away

from us, toward a smiling man holding the bridle of a horse. She says, "Good thing you're here, Padraig. If you hadn't shown up, I'd have prayed for severe punishment to fall on your family."

The man's smile fades, and he shakes his head as he helps her into his wagon. "Welcome, Cousin Maureen. I see your journey hasn't changed your temper any."

Agnes follows her mother up into the wagon, and as they pull away, she turns to Kam and me and sticks out her tongue.

For no reason I can fathom, and perhaps it's the excitement of being on land, her nastiness sets me giggling like an eejit. What's so funny is a puzzle for sure, but I purely fear I'll pee me pants at the sight of her.

I laugh until I notice a man leaning up against a lamppost. He stares at me as if I'm a piece of meat and he's a hungry hound. The look of him stops me laughter in an instant. He's dressed all in black, is thin as a sabre, and has a black moustache waxed up on each side of his mouth. He wears a shiny black top hat. What I notice most, though, is a ragged purple scar that reaches from his eye to his jaw, dragging the entire left side of his face into a hideous scowl. Though his countenance is frightening, I can't take me eyes off him.

I tug on Stash's sleeve. "Who's that man?" I nod toward the lamppost.

Stash looks, but then jerks his head back to me. "Shiv McGraw."

"Shiv?"

"That's how he kills, with a shiv. Always in his pocket. Mob boss of South Boston. Bad, bad man."

With me attention riveted to Shiv, I haven't noticed the six burly men coming near us until one of them bumps me shoulder. They encircle us in a tight, mean trap. When I try to break through their arms, they push me back.

"What's a white girl like you doing with that nigger?" one of them hisses.

Again that word, nigger. I push at his shoulders, trying to crack the circle, but am quickly shoved back into it. Stash stiffens beside me. "Come on, mates. You've no fight with these kids."

They close in on us, so tight I can smell their sweat. Then, a shrill whistle splits the air. I twist toward the sound and realize it came from the man called Shiv McGraw. He's staring at me again.

With grunts of displeasure, the snare around us loosens. The six of them go to the man with the scar, grumbling and cursing.

"What was that about?" I ask Stash.

"People talk abolition in Boston, but hate still here." He turns to Kam. "Be careful, colored boy." He starts to walk away from us, then turns back. "Where you two sleep tonight?"

I look at Kam and raise me eyebrows. Where indeed? Neither of us had thought about that. We never figured we'd get this far. Of course, we'll need a place to sleep; this street is not a safe place.

Kam speaks up. "We have relative."

Stash scratches his chin and looks at us as if our heads have sprouted into cabbages. "One person related to both of you?"

Kam nods and looks Stash straight in the eye. Then he turns back to me and whispers, "I take care of you." He jingles the silver coins in his pocket.

CHAPTER TWENTY

And this is good old Boston, home of the bean and the cod,
Where the Lowells talk only to Cabots, and the Cabots
talk only to God.

"Okay then. good luck," Stash says as he begins to take his leave.

"Wait, Stash, I must ask you a question," I say.

He turns back.

"Do you know a man called Sean Boland?"

He shakes his head and turns away again.

I'm scared witless. I look around this wild new town in panic, not knowing where to land me eyes. Here we are, an Irish girl and a colored boy, both filthy and tattered, neither able to read or write. God, help us, I pray silently. And then I remember Ceili and wonder again if there is such a thing as God.

"Rooms to let," a voice calls out.

Kam grins at me and holds up one of the silver coins from Seamus's boot. He walks to the man. "Two rooms," he says to the man, holding up two fingers.

"Bath or not?" the man asks.

"Bath. How much?"

"Two bits a night," the man answers.

"Two bits?" Kam asks.

The man's face curls in disgust. "That's twenty-five cents, boy. A quarter. You're lucky I rent to niggers. Most don't."

Cents, a quarter? I glance at Kam and see he is as confounded as me. Stash is still visible off in the distance, and I tug on Kam's sleeve and point toward him. We run toward the broad back until we stand before his face. "What are cents?" I ask.

"Pennies," he answers. His eyes soften. He pulls the two of us to a bench and gestures for us to sit down, and then takes a place between us. "Okay," he says. "Listen. Different money system here. One-hundred pennies, or cents, to dollar."

Kam speaks up. "Pennies and cents same thing?"

Stash nods.

"Is two bits, twenty-five pennies for two rooms good price?" Kam says.

Stash throws back his head and laughs. "Good for a fool, boy. Who offer you that deal?"

Kam points toward the man letting the rooms.

Stash scowls, and then takes each of us by an arm and marches us to the man. "What you doing, crook?" he says. "Chisel kids? They pay you a half dime a night for two rooms with bath, not a penny more. Deal?"

The man looks up at the big oarsman and seems to shrink down into his own shoulders. Finally, he nods.

As the landlord gestures for us to follow him, Kam turns to Stash. "What half dime?"

Stash rubs his forehead. "You have much to learn. Get rooms and then we get food, okay? Me lunch break."

"I want a sandwich," I shout. I'm embarrassed at how loud I sound, but I can't help it. Me belly feels hollow as a bodhran, and I've dreamed all through our crossing about the sandwich I had at Queenstown.

"Sandwich it be," Stash answers, a chuckle easing the creases in his forehead. "But first, you get rooms."

The rooms are scarce large enough to turn around in, but there's a bed in each of them and a bathtub behind a curtain down the hall. A stove stands near the curtain, and a bucket of water is nearby. I lift the bucket onto the stove and light the coal.

Stash pays the landlord five pennies for the night. "Time for food," he says.

"I pay you back five pennies, um, half dime," Kam says.

Me hunger is battling the sure knowledge of me own stink, and the nastiness of the smell wins out. "I want a bath before we eat."

They look at me as if I've grown two heads. "Mabo not hungry?" Kam says.

"Starved," I answer, "but the food'll taste finer if I can't smell meself. The water's warm. I'll be quick."

"We wait outside," Stash says. "Hurry."

As we walk through Boston, I never cease looking for me da. He's somewhere here. He has to be. Soon, though, I'm distracted with all the wares offered along the road. There are shoes for human feet and horse's hooves, carriage blankets, lamps for kerosene and whale oil, golden numbers to put on a front door, dresses and bonnets and capes of a thousand colors, and chamber pots so fancy they look like soup urns. Horses pull wagons, and one with a man on its back rears right in front of Kam's face. I jump away. I've felt the landing of a horse's hooves on me back and have a healthy respect for the animals. Kam, though, doesn't flinch and whispers to me, "What that animal?"

"A horse," I answer. "Have you never seen one?"

He shakes his head.

Up ahead, a large group of men stands in the middle of the street. I yearn to ask if they've heard of me da, but their screams are so loud and their faces so red and blotchy, I'm afraid to speak to them.

In the middle of a rope ring, two roosters glare at each other.

"Cock fight," Stash says. The roosters have leather bracelets around their feet. Two-inch silver spurs are attached by leather thongs to their heels. At first, each circles the other in the ring, never taking his eyes from its opponent. Violently, one flies up into the air and lands in a heap of feathers and screeching on the neck of the other. The attacked bird squeals and tries to wrest its foe from his back until they are both again on the ground. Now, though, there is blood in the ring. The fight goes on for three minutes or so as, again and again, they drive the spurs into each other's bodies and eyes.

"A dime on Hercules," one man yells. A gold tooth shines from his mouth.

"And another dime he loses," a second man, bare from the waist up, screams.

I am horrified but drawn as if hypnotized to the bloody spectacle of the cock fight. Finally, one of the roosters forces the other onto its back and then balancing on one foot, it drives the spur into the downed bird's eyes. Blood runs in rivulets across the cobble stones. The vanquished bird's movements flutter to a stop as he emits one last, pitiful squawk. The man with the gold tooth screams, "Victory," as he goes around the crowd collecting coins, and then grabs the victorious rooster and marches off with him. The bare-chested man picks up the dead bird. "I'll get Hilda to cook up a stew with this old toughie tonight."

I look at Kam, trying to gauge his reactions, but his dark face betrays nothing.

Stash tugs on me sleeve and pulls me out of me trance. I

follow him mindlessly. We turn down a side street and he says, "Here for food. Cohen's."

The spectacle of the cock fight had almost destroyed me appetite, but it is restored when I get a whiff of the cooking aromas coming from Cohen's. The place looks no different than a pub in Ireland, but it smells like heaven should. The scents are rich and spicy, and though I don't recognize any of them, they set me mouth watering. There's a large bar with stools around it and little wooden tables set by the windows. We settle at one of the tables. Looking around, I am saddened that, though the place is crowded with men, none of them are me father.

A girl in a long skirt and a blouse that reveals more of her breasts than God ever intended a decent woman to show comes to our table. "Take your order, Stash?" Her accent is so broken I can scarce understand her.

"This Darya," Stash says. "She from Russia like me, but her English not so good yet." He smiles up at her and she bends to give him a better look at her bosom. "Darya, this Mary and Kam from Ireland."

Her eyes widen. "You from Ireland?" she says to Kam.

"Sort of," he answers.

Now, her eyes travel me up and down. "How old you, girl?"

"Thirteen."

She smiles and seems relieved for some reason. "What I get you? We got knishes, latkes, chopped liver."

"A sandwich," I say.

"What kind?"

"Meat."

She looks perturbed. "Kosher corned beef, pastrami, chopped liver?"

The choices muddle me head. I've never heard of this food, but I know me rumbling stomach wants a sandwich fast. Mam said the swells in Dublin used to cook corned beef with cabbage and potatoes, so that settles it for me.

"Corned beef," I answer.

She nods and takes the others' orders. Stash asks for a pastrami on rye bread with kraut and mustard. What are all these things?

"I have same as him," Kam says.

When she leaves the table, Stash turns to Kam. "You have any money, boy?"

Kam reaches into his pocket and pulls out the two silver coins.

"That ten pounds sterling," Stash says, his mouth opening in a big circle.

"Yes," Kam says. "I take from dead sailor. He not need no more."

Stash chuckles. "That lot of money. Worth fifty American dollars. You not want to walk streets of Boston with that in pocket."

Kam's eyes widen. "What I do with it?"

"Open bank account. Right around corner."

Kam nods.

"Now," Stash continues. "This how money works here. Like I said, dollar has one-hundred cents or pennies. They made of copper." He reaches in his pocket and pulls out some brown-colored coins. "But there other coins." He puts two silver coins on the table. "This one," he says, picking up the biggest one. "is quarter. Worth twenty-five cents. People call it two bits." Next, he picks up a smaller coin. "This one half dime—worth five cents." He picks up the last coin. "This dime—worth ten cents."

Kam grabs the dime. "Why this smaller than cent if worth more?"

Stash lifts his hands up in the air and laughs. "Beats me, boy.

But I think you smart about money." He takes some colored paper from his pocket. "This money, too. Dollar. Number on top tells you how many dollars. One—five—ten. Understand?"

Kam stares at the paper money and nods his head.

Darya returns with plates piled with sandwiches and fried potatoes. She puts a dark beer down in front of Stash and sets glasses of water in front of Kam and me.

"Could I have milk?" I ask.

"Not with meat," she answers, shaking her head.

This sandwich is different than the one I had in Ireland. The meat is of a lighter color and tastes saltier. "It's delicious," I say, fearing I have offended her by asking for milk.

I gobble down the sandwich before Kam and Stash finish theirs. The potatoes are different than in Ireland, but I make short work of them as well. As I drain the glass of water, I sit back and rub me stomach in a most perfect feeling of satisfaction. "Aaahhh," I moan.

Stash laughs and says, "No feed you Irish on those ships?"

Kam's face turns serious as death. "No, not feed. Now, let's put money in bank. But first, I pay for food."

Stash moves to stop Kam, but without warning, the quiet warrior materializes before me eyes. "I pay," he repeats and hands one of his silver coins to Darya.

She looks shocked as if he had pulled a goat out of his jacket. "So much. Don't know can change," she says. She hurries away to the man standing behind the bar. After much conversation in a language I don't understand, the man goes upstairs and comes down with a fist full of bills and coins.

"Here," Darya says, shoving the money into Kam's hands. "Change."

CHAPTER TWENTY-ONE

A fool's money is not long in his pocket.

Kam keeps his hand is in his pocket, protecting the folded bills and piles of coins he'd gotten from Darya. "So much paper," he whispers to me. "Two silver coins not so big."

When Darya handed him his change, Kam had immediately removed one coin. He extended it to Stash. "Here, half dime for room. Thank you."

Stash smiled. "Welcome." As he stuffed the coin into his pocket, he said, "I come with you to bank. Want watch teller's face when he see you. He not give you guff with me there."

When I ask Stash what guff means, he answers, "Trouble. Boston good town for coloreds, but some people weasels."

I guess he means Kam's a colored. I'd not heard that word before, but then I'd never seen anyone like Kam before either.

This big bank opens up a world of grandeur like nothing I've ever seen before. Shiny, dark wood covers the floor and half way up the walls. The ceilings rise so high I think we could have sailed *The Pilgrim's Dandy* right into the place. Plush red velvet seats tufted with buttons ring three sides. On the far wall, there are little cages with men inside them. All of them seem busy writing in books or counting bills. I like the look of their starched collars, gartered arms, and bow ties. Best of all are the little peaked hats that stretch on elastic bands around their heads. Most of the men wear glasses, and with their little caps and bobbing heads, they put me in the mind of chickens. I start to laugh.

Kam nudges me with his elbow, "Mabo, no." When I see how serious he is, I laugh even harder. Why must men act so severe, I wonder? Do they think it fools people into believing they are smarter than girls? Such silliness!

Mam always said, 'When you wed, pretend you think he's smarter than you, Mary. Use your blarney because 'twill make him happy. But never forget, in all truth, he's probably not thick as a stump about the things that count.'

I compose meself as the three of us approach one of the cages. I can scarce imagine what an odd trio we appear to the little man behind the bars. A young girl and colored boy in tattered, filthy clothes and a big Russian oarsman with sweat marks under the arms of his homespun shirt.

Stash speaks first. "Young colored gentleman want to open bank account, sir."

The bespectacled man looks us up and down as if we are the last people on earth he wants standing before his cage. Then, his eyebrows arch up nearly to the peak on his cap. "He would?" nodding toward Kam.

Kam says, "Yes, sir. I have five pounds British sterling and this American money." He pulls the one British coin and all the bills and coins from his pocket. "Put dollars, half dimes, and pennies in bank, please. Also, two bits."

I admire the way Kam speaks to the man, as if he knows what he's doing, though I'm fair sure he's as gob-smacked as I am about all this. But what if this bespectacled man refuses Kam?

Kam is proud, and if a fight breaks out, I'm pretty sure I'll land smack in the middle of it.

Stash whispers something to Kam that I can't hear. Kam turns to me, "Stash says I should keep five dollars in pocket."

The man behind the bars lifts his spectacles, pauses for a long time, and then asks Kam to slide the money through the space under the bars. He tilts his cap down over his eyes, rubs his fingers over each piece of paper and puts a small glass object in his eye and looks closely at every one of them.

"What's he doing?" I whisper to Stash.

"Using his loupe. Wants to be sure they not fake."

Fake money? Who'd ever think of such a thing? And how do they make it?

The man removes the loupe from his eye and then picks up the money and begins to count, licking one finger as he flicks through the paper bills. He goes on—lick, flip—lick, flip—lick, flip, until the last of the bills is counted. I wonder what he'd think if he knew this money came from the boot of a dead sailor. I sneak a sideways glance at Kam and see his eyelid twitching. I grin. Bet he's thinking the same thing.

Finally, the man lowers his glasses again and looks up. "This comes to forty-four dollars and seventy-three cents."

Kam looks at Stash who nods.

"Open bank account," Kam says.

"Under what name?" the man asks.

"Me name," Kam answers. His eyelid twitches faster.

"And that would be?"

"Kamua Okafor." He stands so straight he looks like he has a steel rod up his spine. His eyelid has stopped twitching, and if I didn't know him so well, I'd believe he did this kind of thing every day.

The man behind the cage takes out a paper and a small black

book. He scrawls on the paper, opens the book and writes in it. Then, he hands the opened book out to Kam. "I'll need your signature here." He points to a line.

Kam's eyes widen. His gaze darts wildly from me to Stash. Stash takes the book and says, "I help you, Kam." He turns to the man, he says, "Be back."

"I'll stay here—for just a minute." I say, turning back to the man behind the bars. "Have you heard of a man named Sean Boland, sir? He's me father."

The shake of his head sends me heart back into me stomach. Then, I thank him and go to where Stash and Kam stand at a counter in the center of the bank. Stash is fitting a pen into Kam's hand. He slowly guides Kam's fingers across the line. When they're done, Kam looks up at him. "That me name?"

Stash nods.

"Mabo, look," he says, holding out the book for me to see. "Me name."

Me heart fills to bursting with pride for Kam. Mist springs to me eyes, but I smile through it. "That's your name, Kam." I wonder what me name would look like in writing. When we take the book back to the man in the cage, he says, "When you want money, bring that book in here and we'll give you what you need until the account is empty." He puts the paper he was writing on into his drawer and for the first time, smiles. "Wait'll I tell the manager about this," he says to Stash. "First account for a colored person since I've worked here."

"That so?" Stash says.

"Will I sign name again?" Kam asks the man.

"Yes, whenever you withdraw or deposit cash, that will be necessary," he answers.

Kam squares his shoulders again. "I practice every day."

The man behind the bars smiles.

We walk out of the bank into bright sunshine. Stash says, "Congratulations, Kam. You have bank account. I wish you success." They shake hands.

"Now, buy clothes," Stash says to both of us. "Use the five dollars for them and rent and food for week. Bank account should last few months, but you need jobs. To get jobs, need to look respectable. What job you fit for?"

I stand there, flummoxed, but Kam speaks right up. "I good with potions, tonics."

"Well, Sam Mendel might be looking to hire delivery boy." He points down the street. "That Mendel's Apothecary. Tell Sam Stash send you."

A sudden wind picks up and chills me. "Oooh, that's cold," I say.

"Mary, it cold here. And much snow. Buy warm coats and snow boots. Go to Miller's Mercantile. It on Fourth Street. Fair price."

"Snow?" I say. I'd heard of snow falling in Dublin, but never saw it in Kinsale.

Kam says, "I not know snow."

Stash laughs. "Soon enough, boy. It white as you black. And cold as witch's tit."

I feel meself blushing at that remark and figure I'd better toughen me ears up a bit. There'll likely be many embarrassing remarks to hear in Boston.

We walk toward our rooming house, and I begin to ponder about what kind of work I'll get. Perhaps I can wait tables in a restaurant like Darya. Yes, that would be a grand job. Strolling along, I notice the same sign on many windows. I can't read it, but it seems to be everywhere.

"Stash," I say, tugging on his arm and pointing to one of the signs. "What does that mean?"

"N.I.N.A. No Irish Need Apply." He looks ashamed to say it. "Sorry."

"What's wrong with us?" I ask him.

"Nothing. But too many of you come here."

If that isn't a pile of bollocks, I don't know what is. It sets me fumin' like the Banshee I sometimes conjure up. First, the Brits starve us out of our country and now Americans don't want to hire us in this one? Irish people work harder than anyone. If I'd stayed in Ireland, perhaps I'd have a job as a washer woman in Dublin by now. Even as I think the thought, a nagging doubt creeps in. If I'd lived long enough to get to Dublin.

If I lived back in Ireland, though, I could visit the place I buried me mother and baby sister. The memory of them, under the dirt, untended and forgotten, eats at me heart and pesters me soul. Me mam was a sainted lady. She deserved a better fate, and I'll always regret I couldn't give her that.

The more I ponder all this injustice, the madder I get. N.I.N.A. indeed! To hell with America. If they don't want me, I don't want them. I'll ask Kam for passage money home. He'll try to argue me out of it, but he'll give it to me.

But soon as I determine to leave, I remember the ship. Even with money for the journey, I'd have to stay in the hold with all its stink. I think of me little bed in the rooming house and the bathtub and begin to reconsider.

Mary Boland is not a quitter. I haven't come this far to turn around and go back. They're not going to drive me out. I'll have to figure out how to get a job.

Finally, it comes to me. "Stash, is the working situation the same for Scots here in Boston?"

"No, people hire Scots."

That's it. If I don't get a job quickly, I'll practice me Scottish burr. Mam always said I could imitate a Scot better than anyone in Kinsale.

CHAPTER TWENTY-TWO

May you have time and health to wear it.

Stash leads us to Miller's Mercantile and then says, "I go to boats. Another ship dock. Need oarsmen."

He takes me and Kam each by a shoulder and looks down at us. "Watch out for weasels and no step in horse dung on street." He points to a pile of it.

"That another horse?" Kam says, pointing to one as it trots past us carrying a wagon.

"Yes," I answer. "I can't believe you've never seen a horse before."

He shakes his head. "I want one and thing behind it."

"That's a wagon," I say. "What would you do with a horse and wagon?"

"Get work," he answers.

I'll not tell him the dear cost of oats.

"Thank you, Stash," I say, hugging him awkwardly. "You've been a good friend."

When he leaves, Kam and I stare hard into each other's eyes, straighten up, and open the door to Miller's Mercantile.

The size of the place makes me dizzy. Shelves line every wall.

The ones on the right hold women's clothes and the distant ones on the left, look to hold men's. On the right, dirndls are stacked high on one shelf and skirts on another. Shoes and boots are in the back. Smack in the center of everything is a counter with an elegant woman standing behind it. When someone hands her a piece of clothing, she reads its ticket, accepts their money and puts the dollars in a little box she removes from under the counter. Then, she locks the box and stashes it back in its place. Next, she writes something on a piece of paper and hands it back to the customer. I am stunned with how calmly she does all these complicated things.

Flustered at how I must appear in me filthy, tattered dress, I approach the lady "What is that?" I ask. "That piece of paper you gave back."

"It's the receipt. They need to show it to their employers." Her cold face makes me think she's fierce angry with me for being so thick.

Receipt—another new word. Will I never stop hearing words that make no sense? I must mind not to anger people with questions. But how else will I learn?

Kam walks to the left, and every one of the fancy shoppers steps away. They whisper behind gloved hands. We have agreed to meet back at this counter when we're finished. As he heads toward the men's clothing, each person he passes turns and stares at him, but no one says a word.

On the right side of the store, I take a white blouse from a shelf and hold it up to me. It's pretty, I think, but probably far too fine for a culchie like me. A woman's voice behind me says, "May I help you?" I jump; that's how nervous I am. When I turn to see her, she looks prim as a nun.

"What would you do for me?" I ask.

"Measure you for size," she answers. "I'm the fitting mistress."

These things come in different sizes? Oh, sweet Saint Brigid, how will I ever find something to wear with all these racks before me?

The fitting mistress takes me behind a curtain where she pulls a tape measure from her pocket and puts it around me waist and bosom. Next, she takes the tape and pulls it from the top of me head down to me feet. "You're tall but very slender," she says. "Let me see what I have."

She begins to lift things from the shelves; puts the blouse I had in me hands back. "This would be too large. Will you need underclothes as well?" she asks.

"I have pantaloons. With a good washing, they'll do."

As she pulls more things from the piles, I marvel at the softness of the clothing. Who'd have dreamed such fabrics existed?

She shows me into a place she calls the dressing room. There's a mirror there and a little chair for me to sit on. Then, she closes the door behind her. The blouse and skirt fit as if Mam had made them, knowing me shape perfectly. This fitting mistress knows her stuff all right.

She says the items cost fifteen cents each. I've scant understanding of how much this is compared to the five dollars Kam still has in his pocket. When I ask her if there's anything cheaper, she says, "These are the least expensive we carry, miss. It's a fair price."

"I'll take them then. Could you show me where the cloaks are—oh, and also the boots?"

I find a warm knitted cloak in a pretty shade of blue that costs another thirty cents. The boots are a dollar—a frightfully expensive amount, I think, but the lady says that's the cost of all the leather boots in the store and I might as well get good ones as they'll last for years.

"You'll be needing gloves and a woolen bonnet, too, within

the next month," the lady says. She chooses them for me. They cost ten cents each. "A dime," I exclaim. See that? I'm learning!

"Now you need underwear," she says. "Perhaps a corset?"

When she shows me the contraption, I study the hooks and stays carefully. "Let me help you into it," the lady says. I shield me breasts with me hands as she tugs the thing tight around me and fastens it up.

"I don't think I could ever get into this thing without your help," I say. "And if I did, I'd never take another breath and would die before they could get it off me."

She shows her first smile. "Well, a slim figure like yours doesn't really require a corset, but you will definitely need a shift for under your clothing. Anything less would not be decent."

"What's a shift?"

She brings out a white, straight dress that has no sleeves. It reminds me of the gunny sack dresses Mam used to make for me, but the cloth has no roughness to it. "This is what you wear under your blouse and skirt," she says.

"And how much is that?"

"Seven cents."

"All right. I'll take it. Thank you for helping me. God will bless you for your kindness this day."

As I turn away with me purchases, she whispers, "May the road rise to meet you and the wind be at your back, miss." Her cultured tones carry the lilt of a Kerry brogue.

"Ma'am," I say, fingering the cross at me neck. "Have you heard of a man called Sean Boland?"

"No, miss. Can't say I have. Why do you ask?"

"He's me father. I need to find him."

"I'm sorry, dear. I don't know him."

As I wait for Kam at the counter with the money box, I look around at all the ladies browsing through the shelves. They're all dressed fine, so I wonder why they need to buy more. Do they have more than one set of clothes?

Kam strides out of the men's area, and I nearly drop me teeth at the sight of him. He's wearing a white shirt, black pants and shiny black boots. But the thing that startles me stiff is sitting on his head. It's a gigantic top hat.

"Kam, that hat is enormous," I say, giggling. "Don't you want something that will cover your ears? Stash said it gets cold here."

He shakes his head. "When people see this hat, they not forget me."

He pays the lady with the cash box for me clothes and his, and I notice how her eyes dart around as she looks at the two of us. "Are you two friends?" she asks.

"Mabo me sister," he answers.

Her mouth flies open, and I do admire her restraint as she clamps it shut and answers, "I see."

I carry me green dress in a bag under me arm. With a bit of scrubbing and mending, it'll be a second outfit for me to wear when I need to wash me new blouse and skirt. "Kam, one last thing. Will you buy me a needle and some thread? I must mend me old dress and the tablecloth."

We purchase me mending things for a half dime, and I record the amount in me brain. I will keep track of every single shilling, I mean cent, I cost Kam.

"I buy horse and wagon now."

I don't argue with him. When he has his mind set on something, there's no point in it. If he wants a horse and wagon, we'll find them. I point to a shop with a horseshoe hanging outside it. We walk in. "Sell horse and wagon here?" Kam asks.

The man's eyes narrow. "Do you have the money for such things, colored boy?" His voice is flat with suspicion.

Kam removes his top hat and bows. He pulls his bank book

out of the pocket of his pants and shows the man. "Is this enough?"

As the man scans the bank book, he barks out a laugh. He answers with a high, soft voice. "Yes indeed, young man. That'll do just fine. I figure you'll need about half that amount for a good horse and wagon."

He takes us to a stable behind the store. There are five horses there. One is a beautiful chestnut stallion that stands a full hand above the others. "This one I want," Kam says.

"That one's a handful, boy," the man says. "He's thrown the past four men who tried to get on his back."

"I want him," Kam repeats. He walks up to the stallion and stares into its eyes. "You Kirabo." He angles toward me, "Mean gift from God." He turns back to the dark eyes of the animal. "You me horse." The horse stares back into Kam's unblinking eyes and lowers its head.

When Kam springs up onto its bare back, though, the horse's submissive attitude evaporates into rage. Kirabo's nostrils flare as he rears and whinnies and tries to throw this awful burden off him. But Kam grabs onto its mane and grips its flanks with thighs that seem made of steel. Kirabo rears again and again, his front feet pawing the air. After a mighty struggle that lasts a full ten minutes, the horse settles, panting, his massive flanks heaving in exhaustion. Kam lays his head down on the horse's neck and says, "Good, Kirabo. You me horse." He strokes the horse's neck gently, leaps off its back and takes the bit and bridle from the astonished owner. "Show me how to do," he says.

"I'll do that," I say, taking the bit. "Any Irish girl knows how to bridle a horse."

Kirabo bares his teeth at me as I slip the bit into his mouth. I give him a soft slap to the jaw and attach the bridle, "Behave yourself, Kirabo." Then, I turn to Kam. "How'd you stay on him? You've never ridden before."

"Animals like Kam."

I guess so. Some of the best riders in Kinsale, meself among them, would have quit before breaking this mighty brute.

Kam gives the owner one dollar. "Be back with rest of money tomorrow."

As we walk away, he whispers, "Must practice writing name and go to bank in morning."

"Kam," I say, "you have to find a place to stable Kirabo, you know. And there'll be money for feed as well. You must be mindful of these things."

"Mabo," he answers, looking magnificent in his new clothes and top hat. "I know. You not worry."

So, I won't.

CHAPTER TWENTY-THREE

Jealousy—the enemy of friendship.

This riles me some to admit, but Kam gets a job the very next morning. I'm with him when he walks into Mendel's Apothecary and introduces himself to the owner, Mr. Mendel. "I want to learn to mix medicines. Stash send me. Start as delivery boy. Try me one week, no pay."

No pay? Why'd he say that? Perhaps it comes from having been a slave. Well, Mary Boland will ne'er behave in such a way. I'll get a proper job before the week is out. And they'll pay me. Of course, I will. Just watch me.

Mr. Mendel wears a small cap on the back of his head. He scratches his long beard. "A week for free?"

Kam nods.

"That's some hat you're wearing, boy." He circles us.

Again, Kam nods.

Mr. Mendel glances at me and says, "Who's the shiksa?"

Kam's eyes question me. I lift me shoulders. "What shiksa?"

"A white girl—not Jewish."

This man's a Jew, like Stash. I like him. He seems crafty, but kind.

"She Mary, me sister. We met on ship. She Irish."

"How'd you get off the ship into Boston?"

"Customs officer not believe in slavery."

Mr. Mendel raises his eyebrows, then with a shrug, walks to his front window and looks outside. "Whose wagon?" he asks.

"Mine," Kam replies.

"You own that horse and wagon?"

Kam nods.

Mr. Mendel laughs out loud.

"Let me think on this a minute." Mr. Mendel goes behind the counter of his store and scribbles some figures on a piece of paper. He scratches his beard again, studies Kam, and then returns to us.

"I'm gonna be honest with you, boy. I've been trying to get more business up on Beacon Hill." He looks at the horse and wagon outside and then touches Kam's top hat. "Silk," he says.

Kam nods again.

"I have a feeling you'll impress the Lowells and Cabots and the rest of them up there. They love to play at being abolitionists. Makes them feel modern. And they've sure never seen a colored like you around here."

Kam's stare never wavers. "Yessir."

"Are you ready to defend yourself if some bully gets nasty?"

Kam puts up his fists. "I strong. Not start fight. But finish if have to."

Mr. Mendel grins, lowers Kam's fist and shakes his hand. "You're hired."

The next day, fancied up in me new clothes, I begin the search for me own job. If a colored boy can get work, so can I, Irish or not. I am determined not to live off Kam's kindness a minute longer than I must.

I start on G Street, where Kam and I have lodging. It's a long street, but looking down it, I vow to visit all its businesses before they close tonight. Half way down the block, a crowd assembles in a circle around two men who appear to be trying to kill each other. I scan each face, but don't see me father. Then, I spy a grinning girl standing near the front. I think the fight is about her. She looks proud to be a trophy worth fighting over.

The two men are bare fisted, and the gang around them screams and tosses coins on the cobblestones. "Kill him, Pat. Kick him in the feckin' clackers," one of them yells. I get as far away from them as I can and press meself against the buildings as I pass, trying to make meself invisible.

Safely past the battle, I spot what looks to be a laundry. Sheets hang from the front of the building right across to the other side of the street. There is no N.I.N.A. on the window. Going inside, I see tubs and scrubbing boards all around the room. A girl bends over every tub scrubbing at clothing or linens. One of them, a girl close to me age, looks up, her face red and scowling.

Scanning the place, I see a woman hanging clothes over lines stretched the length of the store. She is older than the others, so I figure she's the boss. I walk up behind her and clear me throat, not wanting to startle her. She turns and stares at me. "Ma'am, me name is Mary Boland. Are you hiring?"

Her look is long and hard. She is stout with hair pulled so tight up in a bun I'd expect it might give her a headache. "Have you experience?" she says.

"Not in a place like this, but I scrubbed plenty on me mam's board back in Ireland."

She throws another sheet up on the hanging line. "Seems you missed your chance. I just hired Millie there," she points to the girl who frowned at me. "I have no more tubs." She sneers. "And the Irish are supposed to be lucky."

Me heart sinks at her refusal, but I'd best steel it. I might get lots of no's before I get a yes. As I pass her to leave, the girl called Millie, spits on me boot. I'm shocked to me very soul by such behavior. I reach up and grab a towel off the line and slowly wipe her spittle off me boot, never breaking me stare. I toss the towel at her feet.

Millie screams, "That bitch dirtied a clean towel."

With a grin. I walk out the door, calling back, "Next time, mind whose boot you sully, you silly cow."

I harangue meself once out of the laundry, though. I forgot to ask if anyone there knew me father. I shake me head. Me da would not associate with such trash as them.

The colorful leaves I spied as we pulled into Boston Harbor now cover the street. I relish the feel of them crunching under me boots, and their scent is headier than flowers. 'Tis a friendly feeling they give me.

A chicken blasts out in front of me, its feet scattering the leaves around it. A young girl, chasing after it, catches it with a whoop of satisfaction. One quick twist of her wrist, and its neck snaps in a loud pop. The sound sends shivers down me spine, but I figure it'll make her family a lovely dinner this night. Me mouth waters at the thought. Before the troubles, me mam cooked a chicken once, and the memory of its taste remains—succulent and crisp. The memory of her lying there in the dirt kicks me in the belly like a mule. I shake it off.

The next business I visit looks to be a butcher shop. There are big slabs of meat hanging all around it. And considering how I love meat, this would be a perfect place for me to work. A pig sits in front tied to a stake, never guessing that he'll probably be somebody's meal before the day is over. Inside, standing before a wooden block is a man in a bloodied apron. He has a huge cleaver in his hand. He raises the cleaver and brings it down onto a piece of meat. Blood spatters up onto his face.

"Sir," I say, wanting to speak before he raises the cleaver yet again. "Are you hiring?"

He looks up at me. "What you know about meat?"

"Not much," I say, figuring truth is best in this situation. "But I like the taste of it."

He holds up the bloody mess he was cutting. "What this?"

"Lamb?" I answer, crossing me fingers.

He grunts in disgust. "Get out of me shop. Stupid mick, you don't know beef from lamb." He comes toward me waving the cleaver, and I turn and run back to the street before I even get the chance to ask him about Da.

Me boots are dragging a bit after that one, but I have vowed to visit each business on this street today, so I straighten up and swear on me mother's memory that I'll keep that promise. Besides, the more I walk these streets, the better the chances I have of seeing me father.

Up ahead, I spy a striped pole. I wonder what kind of business this is but shrink back at the N.I.N.A. sign in the window. Quit it, Mary. Shrinking is not going to get you work. I put the steel into me spine and walk in. There are three chairs sitting in front of a long mirror. A man sits in each chair with shaving foam all over his face, and a man stands behind him, a razor at the ready. As if some loud voice had announced me entrance, they all turn to stare at me.

One of the men holding a razor walks up to me. "Miss?"

"Yessir. I'm looking for work this day. Have you any?"

He turns to the others. "Hear that brogue?" He laughs. "Are you blind, girl? Did you not see the sign?"

"I saw the sign, sir, but promised meself to stop in every shop on this street today—sign or not. I always keep me promises."

His smiling face transforms into an ugly scowl. "You're bold, girl. When you see the sign, it means stay out."

Tears smart me eyes and anger fills me heart, but I say, "Thank you for your time, sir," and turn to leave.

I hear him as I walk out the door. "Ignorant shanty girl probably can't even read the sign." Their laughter follows me onto the street.

Me banshee anger rises and I whirl and scream at the man. "If God can't turn your heart, let him turn your ankle."

All the men in the shop laugh out loud, sputtering shaving cream into the air.

How can it be that a slave boy like Kam got work his first try? He was hired *because* he's colored, not in spite of it. For the first time, I feel resentment toward Kam. Him and his fancy hat and wagon. Stop it, Mary. Without Kam, you'd be dead now. And without you, he'd still be on that ship. Jealousy must not come between us.

But why won't someone give me a chance? I want nothing more than to go back to me room and bury me face under the covers on me bed. But I can't break a promise made on me mother's name. I stomp me boot and trudge forward.

Me next stop is at a rooming house with no N.I.N.A. sign posted. A whiskered man stands behind a counter. "Sir, have you need of a cleaning girl here?" I ask him.

He looks me up and down. "This is a house for sailors on the beach."

That confuses me since I don't know what difference it makes to the need for cleaning. "So, do your rooms need cleaning?"

"Well, little miss. Are you planning on bringing your chaperone?"

"I need no chaperone, sir. But let me ask you, please—have you heard of a man named Sean Boland? He's me father."

"Never heard of him." He shakes his head and then shoves

his hands into his pockets. "Do you know what sailors ashore want, girl?"

I'm confused by the question at first. But then, the face of Seamus flashes into me mind, and I fathom his meaning. "Good day, sir," I say, turning on me heel to leave.

"You could make a finer living serving these boys than you ever will cleaning."

I whirl back to him, me face hot with fury. "I'd rather die." I slam the door so hard the latch breaks.

"Shit," I hear him scream through the open hinges.

Good, I think to meself as I swing onto the sidewalk and smack face to face with Jack, the sailor from *The Dandy*.

"Well, look at you, Miss Mary. All fancied up like a lady."

I slam me knee up between his legs. "May the worms eat your bod," I say as he bends in two, howling in agony. Walking away, I wonder how I recalled that vulgar Irish word for the male member.

I start to laugh, God forgive me, and me step grows light with pleasure. But then a slop bucket tossed from an upstairs window lands at me feet, its contents of garbage and dung nearly splashing onto me skirt. When I look up at the chamber maid, she says, "Watch out where you're walking if you know what's good for you."

In spite of me good spirits of a minute ago, me mood plummets. Why is everyone so mean here? Perhaps Boston is not the place for me. The people are all cruel—so cruel. Is this how I want to be treated? Even as I think the thought, though, I determine that I must keep me pledge and visit each store on this street today.

The final place I stop is a green grocer. The door slams in me face with a closed sign as I walk up to it.

I sit down on a small bench, so hungry, tired and defeated I want to weep. The setting sun brings a chill to the air as cold as the feeling in me heart. I'll never find work. It's punishment for me sins with the crew. Perhaps I'm doomed to trudge these streets of Boston for the rest of me days. This despair is an old enemy by now—I felt it first when I fell on the road to Queenstown, but it returns often now.

I pull meself to me feet and a brisk wind nearly sends me to me knees. Shivering, I begin to walk toward our rooming house but notice a small church on the corner. There's a statue of the Virgin Mary in front of it. It must be Catholic. Perhaps this is where me father attends Mass.

CHAPTER TWENTY-FOUR

May God hold you in the palm of His hand.

It's warm inside. Candles blaze before the altar of the savior, and the smell of incense warms me memories of family Masses. I kneel in the back pew and begin to pray. "Dear God and Blessed Virgin Mary, I am a sinner and shouldn't be here, but I need you so much. I was named for the Blessed Mother, but I did terrible things on the devil ship. They were against me will, I swear to you. Please grant me absolution and bring back me faith. I miss it so."

I don't realize that tears are streaming down me face until I feel a soft tap on me shoulder. I look up. He's dressed all in black and has a white collar. He must be a priest. His face is kind.

"Young lady, why are you crying?" he asks.

"Because I'm being punished for me sins. That's why I can't find work."

He smiles and asks me to stand. "What's your name, girl?"

"It's Mary. Named for the Blessed Mother, but now I think more for the Magdalene."

"Come to the confessional, Mary. I'm no saint and won't judge you, and God wants nothing more than to forgive you."

The little door in the dark confessional slides to the side. I can hear him breathing behind the curtain. "Bless me, father, for I have sinned."

I can't say how long it's been since me last confession. I honestly don't remember. I take in a deep breath and confess I wasn't able to save Mam's life or me baby sister's. I tell him about the Donahues and Elizabeth Bradshaw and that I believe the devil sent her into me life. I tell him what happened in the crew's quarters and about Ceili and how I didn't watch out for her the way I promised. I pause for a breath and then admit me worst sin. "Father, I'm not sure I still believe in God at all. He's done some hateful things." I finish with, "For these and all me sins, I am heartily sorry."

I realize I'm sobbing loud, slurpy tears that dampen the front of me new white blouse. I'll have to iron it tonight before I go searching for work tomorrow. Strangely, me tears don't appear to bother him at all.

When I'm quiet for a few moments, he speaks. "Did anything good happen on that ship?"

"Oh yes, Father. I met Kamua, a slave boy. We saved each other on the ship. He's me soul brother now."

"Well then, perhaps you should thank that God you don't believe in for sending him to you." I hear his knees creak. "It seems the things that happened to you were beyond your control, miss. I don't call them sins. I call them misfortunes. For your penance," he says "say a sincere act of contrition and three Hail Marys. That should take care of it."

The guilt flies off me straight up to heaven.

The priest insists on walking me home. "This neighborhood can be dangerous for a young girl at night."

"What's your name, Father?" I ask him as we stroll towards me rooming house.

"Father Frank Ruzzo," he answers.

"Is that. . . ?"

"Italian," he says with a laugh. "I don't suppose you've met many Italians, have you, Mary?"

"Never, Father. But I thought Italians were dark skinned. You're blonde and fair."

"Me parents came to Boston from Milano before I was born. That's in the North of Italy, near Switzerland. They'd heard America needed good Italian cooking." Now, his laugh is louder.

"Father, have you ever heard the name, Sean Boland?"

He stops abruptly and turns to me. "Sean Boland?"

"He's me da, and I must find him and show him me mother's cross." I take it up from the collar of me blouse.

He crosses himself. "I'm sorry, Mary, but all I know of Sean Boland is locked inside me by the seal of the confessional."

"Then you have heard of him?"

"Yes, but that's all I can say."

"But Father . . ."

"Please, Mary. Don't pursue this. There's no answer I can give you."

Disappointed and yet relieved at his words, I unlock the door to me rooming house. If he's heard of me da, others living here must have, too. I won't ask him to break the seal of confession.

"Father, I think I'm going to have to tell a lie to get a job. Is it a mortal or venial sin if I pretend to be Scottish?"

He fingers his white collar, then smiles. "Oh, I think God will understand that."

CHAPTER TWENTY-FIVE

As true as the gospel . . .

Twelve days pass, each one no better than the last. It's November now, and the air is frigid, and I still have no job. Trudging the streets of South Boston, going in every establishment, and always ending the day the same—without work and without an inkling of where me father might be in this vast city. When Kam meets me each night for supper, his eyes bright with hope, I shake me head.

No one will hire me, Scottish burr or not. It is so disheartening. But one weight has lifted off me shoulders. The confession of me sins and Father Ruzzo's kindness restored me belief in what is good—perhaps even in God Himself. But what is the secret about Da that the priest cannot tell me?

And why will no one hire me?

Wednesday mid-morning, I stand in front of a place that looks like a pub I once visited in Cork City. Da took me there after he'd finished one of his meetings. I look for the dreaded sign in the window and, not seeing it, take a deep breath and walk in.

It smells of tobacco and whiskey and is dark in spite of the two windows that skirt the street in front of it. The floor is rough wood, and the walls are painted a deep green. It is filled with wood tables, each topped with four overturned chairs. At the far left is a bar with at least twenty stools. The stools stand on three wooden legs and have button-tufted leather seats and backs. Three oil lamps hang from the ceiling, but they're not lit this morning. I see a piano in the back, along with a fiddle and a bodhran. There's a good feeling here—a familiar one.

A door swings open from a back room and a woman bustles in; her stride is long and purposeful. I should say she invades the space, that's how imposing she is. Though I'm considered a tall girl, she beats me by half a hand at least. I'd guess her to be at least forty, even older than me parents. Her sleeves are rolled up to her elbows, and her calico print dress is covered by a long white apron. Her hair falls down her back nearly to her waist in brown waves. Before she spots me, she tucks it up into a net on top of her head.

Then she sees me. "Whoo," she gasps. "Ya scared the life right out of me. How'd ya get in here?"

I point to the front door.

She roars a great laugh. "Ah, I forgot I'd unlocked it." She comes closer and tips me chin up to meet her eyes. "Who are ya?"

"Verra happy tay make yer acquaintance, ma'am. Ma name is Mary Boland, from Glasgow."

"Glasgow is it?"

"Yay."

"Do ya know the name of this establishment, Miss Boland?"

I look around as if a sign would tell me something. "Nay, ma'am. Din't notice it."

"It's O'Halloran's Pub. That's an Irish name."

"Irish is it?"

"Yes, and I've a feeling you're as Irish as I am." She extends a large hand. "Kathleen O'Halloran, that's me. From Dublin more than twenty years ago. When did you get off the boat?"

"Just two weeks ago, ma'am, from Kinsale. I'm sorry to have tried to fool you about being Scottish."

She howls with laughter. "Fool me? Girl, that's the worst burr I've ever heard in me life."

"But me mam said . . ."

"Yeah, and mine said I was delicate." Then, she grins. It's a smile to melt the devil's heart. I like her so much I nearly offer to work for free, the thing I vowed I'd never do after I heard Kam say it to Mr. Mendel. I bite me tongue.

She comes close to me and lifts the corner of me lip. "How'd you keep those beautiful choppers?" she asks.

Though the question startles me, I'm not totally surprised. Often, back in Kinsale, old people would comment on me white, strong teeth. "Me mam was a stickler about tooth brushing. Even when there'd been no food through me mouth for days, she'd say, 'Mary, did you brush your teeth this day?'"

"And what did ya use for brushing them?"

"Birch branches until Da traded a salmon for a toothbrush from a British sailor. Said it was the best deal he ever got from a Brit."

"Good man," she says. "Few of us Irish have our own teeth anymore. Me mam was the same. These are mine, too." She opens her mouth wide and shows me a perfect row of teeth.

"They're grand," I say, then decide to get down to business. "So, Mrs. O'Halloran. You do hire Irish?"

Again, the laugh. "What else would I hire for an Irish pub, girl? Did you see a N.I.N.A. sign in this window?"

"No, but others without the sign have refused me."

She takes me hand and leads me to one of the tables, then lifts two chairs to the floor. "Sit yourself down," she says.

"I've tried to get work all over South Boston, but no one will hire me because I'm Irish." I make sure the words don't sound whiny. No one wants to hire a whiner.

"Were you quarantined?"

"No, the doctors found me healthy."

"That's good. Most who go to Deer Island never get to Boston. If they don't have the fever before quarantine, they get it there."

I look down in me lap, thinking about Liam and Maeve. And what if me father was quarantined? No, he was so strong. He would've survived the journey healthy.

"Where are you staying?"

"Me friend, Kam—he's a black slave boy who saved me life on that hell ship—has some money. He booked two rooms for us."

"And has Kam found work?"

"Yes, ma'am. He's been working as a delivery boy for Mendel's Apothecary soon as we arrived." I laugh a bit at the memory of that day. "Kam bought himself a horse and wagon, and the biggest top hat you ever saw. It sits on his ears some, but he reckons he'll grow into it. Says it gets people's attention."

"I saw him yesterday. Folks here in the neighborhood are flapping their yaps about that colored boy. He's bold for sure, walking around Boston in that top hat. People say that if he weren't so polite, they'd call him uppity. And uppity's not a word a colored boy wants to be called in this town." She leans back in her chair. "I've known Sam Mendel for years. He's a good man. Is Kam smart?"

"Yes, ma'am. He's the smartest person in the world. He knows things I've never heard of even. His father was a witch doctor, and Kam has powers other people don't."

Her eyes narrow. "Is he more than a friend to you?"

I ponder her question. When understanding hits me thick skull, I answer quickly. "No, ma'am. He's a brother to me."

She looks me up and down and then asks the strangest question. "Can he read?"

Her words stun me. I falter, scarce able to speak. I must tell this Kathleen O'Halloran the truth. She'd know quick as Irish rain if I tried to lie. "No, ma'am. And to be honest, neither can I. I hope you won't let that stop you from hiring me. I learn quick and have been studying how to make change."

She puts her chin onto her hand and looks me deep in the eyes. "Are you a good girl, Mary? I mean, can you be trusted not to carouse with the sailors who come through this door?" She points to the front door of the pub. "That's been a worry to me about hiring young girls here."

I lean forward, returning her stare. "Oh yes, ma'am. I am a good girl. I had some troubles with the sailors on the ship. They hurt me so bad I wanted to die. But I confessed me sins to Father Ruzzo and feel ever so much better now. As a matter of fact, I plan to remain pure for the rest of me life."

She slams back in her chair. "Whoo! You needn't go that far, girl. When you're older, you'll love a man and marry him. Then, your purity won't seem such a prize to you or to him. But I am glad to hear you practice the faith."

Me purity is not a subject I want to discuss, even with this big, friendly woman. "So, Mrs. O'Halloran . . ."

She interrupts me. "Call me Kathleen."

"Are you sure that's fitting?"

"Yes, I'm sure, Mary. If you're going to become our new waitress, it's best we not be so formal, don't you think?

"Your new waitress?"

"Yes, your timing is good. Let's call it the luck of the Irish. I do all the cooking and waiting tables by meself, plus taking care of me two girls, Shannon and Molly. Shannon is seven and Molly, five. Girls," she yells, "get down here."

CHAPTER TWENTY-SIX

'Tis easy to halve the potato where there is love.

Two little girls run down the stairs. I'm shocked that a woman her age has such young children. The smallest is a spitting image of her mother, but the older one, Shannon, I guess it is, staggers me with her resemblance to Ceili. All blonde curls and sparkling sweetness she is. When she looks up at me with her excited blue eyes, me heart melts in remembrance. Molly hides behind her mother's legs, but Shannon walks right up to me. "Hello," she says, "what's your name?"

"I'm Mary Boland, and you?"

"Shannon O'Halloran. I'm seven years old." She reaches behind Kathleen and grabs Molly's hand. "Molly, come here and meet Mary."

Molly is nearly the size of her big sister and, though pretending shyness, has a twinkle of mischief in her eyes that promises fun to come. Finally, she says, "Hello, Miss Boland."

"Call me Mary, won't you?"

Without another word, Molly starts singing, "Mary, Mary, quite contrary, how does your garden grow?" and dances into the center of the pub. She's a handful, this Molly. Reminds me of me as a child.

Shannon speaks up. "She's pretty silly, but she's only five."

"Almost six," Molly yells, doubling up a fist.

"Almost six," Shannon says and then turns to me. "When she's a big girl like me, her manners will be better."

I kneel down and put me arm around the beautiful child. "Yes, darling, I'm sure her manners will be brilliant in a couple of years. But remember, it's never a bad thing to sing and dance if you're happy."

"She's right, Shannon," Kathleen says. Then she turns to me. ""Shannon's the shy one. We've been practicing friendliness. It's good you tell her to express herself like Molly does. They're good girls, but I'm worn to a frazzle minding them and this pub. Looks like you're good with children."

"I do like them."

"Your pay will be twenty cents a week with room and board included. I'll put straw and a cot in the basement room. There's a stove down there for the winter and it's cool in summer. I'll make it cozy for you. Is that agreeable?"

Agreeable? I have a job. I fear I'll burble with excitement and make her change her mind. Kathleen begins to stand, but I touch her arm. It's time for the question I've asked every person I've met in Boston. "Mrs. O', er, I mean Kathleen."

"Yes, Mary?" She sits back down.

"Did you ever hear the name Sean Boland? He's me father." I caress the cross at me throat.

Her brow furrows for a moment 'til she finally answers. "Sounds familiar, but I can't place it. Is he here in Boston?"

I nod. Then, I hear a booming voice. "Kathleen, who's that?"

"Tommy," she trills. "Come meet our new waitress, Miss Mary Boland from Kinsale."

The voice rises to a roar. "You hired a girl without consulting me?"

I pull the little girls closer, wishing I could disappear. But Kathleen's on her feet in a second, rushing him as he strides behind the bar. She towers over him, but he's broad as a barrel and scarlet with rage.

All the laughter is gone from her voice. "Yes, you pig-headed mick. If I'd asked you about it, you'd have stalled me until next Saint Patrick's Day, and you know it. So, I made the decision."

He sputters obscenities and draws himself a draught from a tap.

"Oh, that's the ticket, mister," she continues. "Start drinking up our profits before it's even lunch time."

His face remains crimson, but he pushes the tap back up and slugs down the inch of stout in his glass.

Now, Kathleen transforms herself again. "Tommy, love," she coos. "You know how worn I've been lately, what with the cooking and serving and caring for the girls, too."

He squints, suspicious.

Little Molly pokes me in the ribs, a grin spreading over her freckled face.

"We're making a good living here, and business is growing," Kathleen says. "We can afford a bit of help, now can't we?"

As he starts to wash his glass, she looks back at me and winks. "The thing is, darlin'," she continues. "I've been so tired at night I feel I'm neglecting you. And you know that's not something I'd ever want to chance. If I don't take care of me wifely duties, some hussy could come along and take away me big, beautiful man."

He smiles and grabs her close for a hug.

Molly whispers, "See, I knew she'd win."

He grabs at her backside, but Kathleen pushes him away, laughing. "Mary," she says. "Come on over here and meet himself—Mr. Tommy O'Halloran."

* * *

That night when Kam looks at me with hope in his eyes, I nod yes. "I got a job, Kam," I'm so excited to tell him that I just ramble. "At O'Halloran's Pub. My boss is Kathleen O'Halloran, and I love her. She has two little girls, and I'll help out with them and the cooking and the serving and everything. There's a cozy room in the basement where I'll live, and oh, Kam, I'm so happy."

"So, you leave me?"

"I'll never leave you, Kam. You're family. And you'll be family to Kathleen, too. I just know it, but I will be moving out of the rooming house tomorrow."

For a moment, I think his beautiful, dark eyes fill with tears, but then he jumps in the air and shouts joyfully, "Mabo! Boston is ours. And now let's have the biggest sandwich we can find."

CHAPTER TWENTY-SEVEN

A cabin with plenty of food is better than a hungry castle.

November 1, 1849

When I waken, I discover blood on me sheets. At first, I am fearful that what the sailors did to me is still a trouble. I go upstairs to wash the blood out in the kitchen, and Kathleen comes in. "What's that, Mary?"

"I'm not sure." My eyes fill with tears. "Maybe it's from the sailors."

She comes to where I'm pumping water and wraps me in her big arms. "Ah no, love. It's just your time, the curse of being a woman." She brings me clean rags and tells me how to use them and to wash them out each night, all the while gentling me as if I were her very own daughter. Maybe there is a God after all. I don't understand why He'd let those sailors hurt me so bad, but this woman surely comes from heaven.

The following day is me first work day at O'Halloran's Pub. I rise before dawn and light the coal stove in the kitchen. The heat is welcome as the weather is quite chilly. Kathleen first puts the big beef roast Kathleen purchased yesterday at Quincy Market into the stove.

"Rump roast," she says. "That makes the best sandwiches."

I clean the pub until the meat is cooked and has cooled enough to handle. The scent of it has me drooling into the dust cloth.

At Kathleen's direction, I then tear the meat into shreds and skim the fat off the juices. "Go ahead, girl. Take a bite. I know you're dying to taste it." She's right. It's delicious, salty and dripping with juice. She tells me to put the torn meat back into the broth and that later we'll warm it for O'Halloran's famous scrappy beef sandwiches.

The beef bone from the roasting pan simmers in a large pot with water, salt and vegetables. We mix noodles from egg yolks, flour, and salt and after rolling it thin, hang the dough in sheets in the pantry to dry. "Thirty minutes before serving time, we'll cut and add them to the soup," Kathleen says.

Ten loaves of bread were kneaded the night before and left near the stove embers to rise. I punch them down and set each in its pan to rise one last time before baking.

Next, the ham goes into the stove. As it cooks, I make fillings for ten pies while Kathleen rolls crusts. The pies, along with the bread, will be placed in the oven soon as the ham comes out. We make only apple and custard at this time of year.

"Cherries won't come till summer," Kathleen says.

As she takes the first batch of pies, hot and bubbling from the stove, she talks of the day she met Tommy. "Knew the minute I laid eyes on the ruddy bloke he was the one for me. Built like a barn he was—sturdy and square. And oh, how he chattered his mouth with jokes." She bellows a laugh. "Some so dirty I pretended to be embarrassed. The lads lapped up his stories quick as they sucked down his stout." She puts a pie on the counter to cool. "Took me eight years to get the ring on me finger; he's an Irishman, you know. They think they can stay bachelors forever." She straightens up and wipes the flour from her face. "But once he tasted me pie, the Banns were posted within a month." Again, her great laugh rings through the kitchen. "Remember, Mary, the bedroom may be what they think they want, but it's the kitchen that often makes the match."

I lower me head in embarrassment. I can't fathom the kind of love Tommy and Kathleen share, nor do I ever want to know it. What happened on the ship still wakes me weeping at night. How can a woman *want* to bed a man? I tremble at the thought.

"That's why himself finally married me," she laughs. "He knew a good draw for his pub the first time he tasted me pie."

We finish everything minutes before lunch customers—hungry sailors and red-faced iron workers—arrive demanding soup, sandwiches and stout. When they grab at me, I push their hands away and laugh I've no need for me anger now, not with Kathleen around. She grabbed an iron worker by the ear earlier today and booted him out the front door. She didn't like the way he was looking at me.

Most of them finish their meals with a piece of pie. "The best pie in Boston," they call it. Kathleen agrees. "Truth is truth, after all," she says with no hint of modesty. Her mother taught her crust making back in the old country, and no one, me included, knows her secret for making crust so flaky. "People come here from as far away as Cambridge to get a slice of me pie," she says.

As I clear the tables, Tommy approaches me. "Mary," he says, "twenty cents a week is a dear price for a waitress. Do ya think maybe we could make it fifteen?"

Though startled, I am ready to agree. I'd agree to anything to keep this arrangement.

I don't realize that Kathleen, coming in from the kitchen with Shannon and Molly, has overheard him until she yells. "Don't you dare try to chisel that girl, Mr. O'Halloran. I promised twenty cents, and twenty t'will be. And I'll not hear another word from you about it."

The girls run to me side. I cower between them at the front door, wishing nothing more than to disappear.

"Love," he says, trying to grab her hand. "It's just good business to try to get the best deal for the dollar, don't you know?"

She smacks his hand away. "The day you turn this place into a sweatshop, that's the day I leave it," she hisses. "We're a fair business, and fair we'll remain."

He tries to nuzzle her neck, but her back turns into a rod of steel and she shrugs him off. "How dare you go behind me back and try to swindle our first employee? What about your own daughters? Will you want them chiseled, too, when they grow up?"

She's hit the soft spot in him. "Of course not. I just thought . . ."

"You weren't thinking with your head, Mr. O'Halloran. You were thinking with your pocketbook. You'll confess this to Father Ruzzo next Saturday."

He groans. "Ah no, Kathleen, not confession."

Molly nudges me in the ribs with her elbow and says, "Watch this."

"If you intend to take communion at St. Augustine's Chapel on Christmas Day, you'll go to confession, Mister." She moves in on him, topping him by a good half foot. "And if you don't receive, all in the congregation will wonder what mortal sin Tommy O'Halloran's been up to that's keeping him from the rail. See how *that* helps business."

"But Saturday's our busiest day," he whines.

"We'll close from four to five. That'll give you time to get to confession."

"Kathleen, be reasonable. Think of the money we'll lose in that hour on a Saturday."

"Consider it as your penance."

That closes the subject. She turns her head and tosses me and the girls a wicked grin. "Now come here, Tommy love," she says, putting her arms around his shoulders and cradling his head to her bosom. "I've an idea for tonight that'll make you frisky as a colt on Kerry races day." She whispers something into his ear, and he smacks her a light tap on the buttocks. He shakes his head wearing the biggest grin you ever saw in your life.

At night, the beer and whiskey flow freely. Tommy stands behind the bar, beaming from one ear to the other. He trades tales and drinks and piles the dollars into his cash box. And I think no one on earth likes his work better than Tommy O'Halloran.

Some of Tommy's jokes make Kathleen cover Shannon's and Molly's ears with her hands. Tonight, though, he told a good one.

"This very afternoon, a Frenchman, an Italian, and an Irishman come in me bar. A fly lands in the Bishop's collar on each of their stouts. The Frog pushes it back toward me for a new one. The Dago just picks it out and drinks the beer. But the Mick picks it up by its wings and shakes it fiercely, yelling, "Spit it out, ye wee bastard. Spit it out!"

"The lads have all heard that one a thousand times," Kathleen says to me, shaking her head, "but the fools still laugh each time he tells it."

When supper is finished, Kathleen mixes the bread for the night's rising and I set the meat purchased that afternoon out into the cold New England night. Finally, I clean the kitchen to gleaming.

At 8:00 o'clock, Kathleen, the girls and I have our family rosary in the upstairs parlor. Tommy's still busy in the bar. When we've finished the last Our Father, Kathleen yawns, kisses us all, and picks up her books. How I envy her. Every night, she lights her candle and reads herself to sleep. By week's end, she's finished three or four new novels. Someday that will be me, I tell meself.

By nine, I am into the sleep of the exhausted, but I waken in the deepest part of the night to a nightmare about the ship. I smell Seamus's rank breath and see again me blood on the floor staining the dirt. Though I'm safe now, fear still grabs me at the darkest of the witching hour. All that dispels me terror is thinking of Da. He's bound to come into this pub eventually. He'll find me and protect me forever.

CHAPTER TWENTY-EIGHT

May the entrails and mansion of pleasure of this worm fall out.

Kathleen says that the worst day of each month is its third Tuesday. That's when Shiv McGraw visits the pub. She's warning me because that will occur next week. "Run down to the basement when he gets here, Mary. Stay there till I call you up."

Shiv McGraw? I remember that name. "I saw him the day we arrived in Boston. What happened to his face?" I ask.

"I'm not sure," Kathleen answers. "He was quite the pretty boy in the old days. Pranced around Boston dressed like a dandy. No one knows who disfigured him. But it's fitting; now his face matches the evil of his heart."

On the following Tuesday, Shiv stalks in with two of his goons plastered to his side. Instead of running to me room as instructed, I crouch and hide in a corner to watch. Shiv's cigar belches smoke, and our toughest customers slink to tables in the back. The tension he brings into O'Halloran's could color the air black. After Kathleen hands him a packet, Shiv finally leaves, and Tommy starts swearing in a loud voice and slamming his bar rag on the tables and chairs.

I ask Kathleen what she gave Shiv, but her mouth sets in a tight line and she shakes her head. "Not for you to worry about. Stay away from that man, Mary. His is the face of evil." She trembles as she says this, and I can't believe this strong woman allows any man to cow her.

Two weeks later, I collect me first wages and invite Kam to supper at O'Halloran's—me treat. Kathleen knows he's coming. She's anxious to meet him.

I'm thrilled when I see Kirabo pull the wagon up and run outside to greet him. Kam ties up the horse and hugs me.

When we walk into the pub, three men are at the bar—ironworkers from the South Boston Iron Works. Even sober, these three are a tough crew. And they're far from sober this day, judging from the blear of their eyes. They turn as they hear us enter and when they spot me with Kam, I can almost see the hair rise on the back of their necks. Their snarling grumbles raise goose bumps on me arms.

They pull themselves to their feet and lumber toward us. "What're you doin', lass, bringing a colored in here?" the biggest one says.

"He's like a brother to me, sir," I say, standing in front of Kam.

"Brother, me arse," he answers. "He's black as a Newgate's knocker."

"He was a slave boy from Africa and he saved me life on the ship from Ireland," I say, trying to block their way to Kam. But they knock me aside, and one of them wrenches Kam's arm up behind his back and tries to march him to the front door. Kam lowers his head. He doesn't fight back.

Then Tommy jumps over the bar and places himself in front of the three of them. "I make the rules for this establishment, boys," he says, "and I've no ban on coloreds."

"I leave, sir," Kam whispers. "Not make trouble." The one holding Kam releases his arm.

"I own this pub. Me rules stand," Tommy says, standing there broad as an ox and bold as brass.

The three of them waver before Tommy as if they're trying to make up their minds what to do. The mouth of the one who spoke now hangs agape like a mailbox waiting for a letter. Finally, he shrugs and says, "Okay, Tommy. If you want niggers in here, I guess it's your right. Just don't let 'em stand near me." He turns to his two friends. "Let's have one more and then head for home, boys." They shuffle back to the bar.

"So, lads, did I tell you the one about the nun and the donkey?" Tommy says, returning back behind his bar and pulling down the tap for another pint.

Kathleen walks behind him, and I see her give his fanny a squeeze. "Hush, Thomas," she says. "No more of your jokes in mixed company." She gestures toward me and Kam. When he stops his joke, she bends down and kisses him on top his head.

She strides toward us. "So, who's this fine young gentleman?" She extends her hand to Kam.

"Kathleen," I say, "meet me friend, Kamua Okafor."

Kam had removed his top hat the minute he walked into the pub. He bows from the waist before Kathleen as if she's royalty. "Me pleasure, Mrs. O'Halloran. Thank you for be friend to Mabo."

"Mabo?"

"Her nickname from ship."

"I see," she says. "So, tell me, how goes it at the apothecary?"

His white teeth flash. "Good," he says, "Mr. Mendel teach me to mix some medicines already."

Kathleen smiles. "The swells up on Beacon Hill think you're the best delivery boy he's ever had. They say they always get their orders the same day their maids place them."

Again, Kam grins. "Yes, important to do that."

He and Kathleen take a seat at one of the tables. I go into the kitchen to fix our plates. "Kathleen, do you want some food?" I ask.

She shakes her head.

I pile his plate high with the scrappy beef we made this morning. Though I've arranged payment to Kam of a nickel a week until me debt is paid, I will always feel beholden to him. He didn't want to take the money, but I insisted. Neither a lender nor a debtor be. That's what Da used to tell me. I drop five cents on the bar for Tommy.

When I return, Kathleen and Kam's heads are close together in deep conversation. I put the plate down in front of Kam.

His eyes dance with excitement when he looks up at me. "Mabo," he says, "Kathleen say she teach us read and write."

"What?"

Kathleen nods. "I've been thinking about it, Mary. I teach Molly and Shannon every Sunday afternoon anyway. Why shouldn't you two sit in on the lessons?"

I begin to stammer like an eejit. "But Kathleen, are you sure? We don't want to be such trouble to you."

She cocks her head. "Mary, the nuns at the Ursuline Academe trained me to be a teacher. That was before the devil Protestants burned the Academe to the ground sixteen years ago. I owe those sweet women the use of me education."

"Burned?" Kam says, his eyebrows two black arches.

"Yes, the wealthy men didn't want Irish girls educated. Figured it would rob them of their maids and prostitutes. The poor sisters could never afford to rebuild the school."

Kam shakes his head.

"And you could teach us?" I say.

"Quick as a penny whistle, girl. You're both smart, I can tell that. Won't be any trouble a'tal."

I feel I am holding the winning ticket to the biggest lottery on earth. Stunned beyond speech, I stand mute.

Kam looks at me and says, "Mabo?"

"Absolutely," I stammer. "I don't know how we can pay you, Kathleen."

"Did I ask for payment?"

"No," I answer, "but this is our life's dream. We need to repay you."

"Just keep up the work the way you're doing it now, Mary. You're a whirling dervish around here." She turns to Kam. "You do the same, Kam. Make me and Sam Mendel proud of you."

He is nodding so fast I fear his head will jerk off his neck.

"We'll begin our lessons the Sunday before Thanksgiving. Oh, and Kam, tell Sam I think he's made a fine, fine hire."

CHAPTER TWENTY-NINE

Learning, the gate to destiny.

Each Sunday, O'Halloran's is closed, as is fitting for a Christian establishment. Tommy's usually sleeping off a late Saturday night, while Kathleen, the girls and I attend Mass at St. Augustine's. Father Ruzzo never fails to call me by me first name. That makes me feel grand; that I belong here.

On the Sunday before Thanksgiving, when we get back from church, Kam's horse and wagon are tethered there. He stands at the front door, his breath curling from his mouth in white vapors.

"Kam," Kathleen says, "you'll catch your death in this weather. Come in here this instant." She unlocks the door to the pub and he follows us in.

"Thank you, Mrs. O'Halloran," he says, a huge smile wreathing his face. He is dressed in his crisp white shirt and black pants and, of course, the top hat which he removes as soon as he enters the room. "Need coat," he says, "buy tomorrow."

"While you're at it, get a muffler and some gloves, too."

"Must save money," he answers. "Kirabo need oats."

Kathleen shakes her head. "I can't believe you've weathered Boston this long without a coat."

Kam catches me eye and grins. We both know how much the other has endured. A bit of cold will not be the undoing of either of us.

"Time for lesson?" he asks.

When Kathleen brings out her old McGuffey Reader, Kam opens it and looks happy as a deer freed back into the forest. After a matter of minutes, his eyebrows go up and his eyes widen. It is that wonderful expression I've come to recognize, the look of understanding "Ah, twenty-six letters in alphabet," he says.

"Right," Kathleen answers.

"And reading is just putting the letters together?" I ask.

"Yes, love, that's all there is to it," she says with a smile. "Let's start with 'A.'"

We turn to the first page.

Kam quickly emerges as the star pupil in our little class. If Kathleen says something once, he doesn't forget it. His mind is like quicksilver. I'm pretty fast meself, but must struggle to keep up with him. Which I do, for I don't like coming in second. Although Shannon is nearly two years older than Molly, it's soon clear that Molly's as smart as her sister is pretty.

After nearly a year of lessons, Kathleen says, "I must say this arrangement is mighty good for me girls. Until you two came into the class, they were little lazybones. Not anymore. Shannon is learning much quicker than before."

"What about me, Mama?" Molly says.

"You're me little genius, love," she says, taking the child onto her lap.

Shannon pouts, then runs to nestle herself into me arms. "I want to be a genius, too," she whispers.

"You will be, Shannon. You just need to find your destiny."

"What's a destiny?" she asks me, her blue eyes wide and shiny.

"The thing you're here for. The reason you were born."

"To be a mama?" she asks.

"Perhaps, but maybe there's more."

Her beautiful forehead creases. And then, she asks. "What's your destiny, Mary?"

Her question wrinkles me brain for a long while. Besides finding Da, what is me destiny? I love working at O'Halloran's, but I can do more. Kathleen says the world is changing for women. She gives me books written by Catharine Beecher and Mary Shelley. She speaks often of a woman called Susan B. Anthony who says that someday women will be allowed to vote. I don't think I could write a book, but I surely would love having the right to vote. It's only a matter of time. At least, that's what Kathleen says, and Kathleen knows everything.

CHAPTER THIRTY

Wisdom is sometimes bitter at the end.

Early on, Kathleen asked Kam his birthday, but he didn't know it, so she declared, "All right, we'll make it November 1. That's easy to remember."

So, just like last year, on November 1, 1851, Kathleen makes a big cake, and his eyes glow brighter than its seventeen candles. She and Tommy give him *Robinson Crusoe* as a gift. Kathleen has become a mother to me. Without her, I surely would expire of loneliness. I think Kam feels the same way.

The next afternoon, I'm passing a table and overhear a woman say, "They treated us Irish like slaves in New Orleans."

I turn back. "Excuse me, ma'am. Did you say you were in Louisiana?"

"Aye, spent three years there cutting sugar cane with the Africans. The Irish were treated as bad as the darkies, but we could escape."

Me heart quickens. That's where Kam's father was sent. He said so on the ship.

"It was heinous," she continues. "Hot as hades with flies and mosquitoes buzzing round me head day and night. We cut that cane from dawn to dark, whatever the weather. Look at these hands."

I gently take her hands in mine. The scars are deep and will last this woman her lifetime.

"Me sister sent money, and I finally got on a ship up here last week. Best day of me life."

I take in a deep breath and ask the question. "Did you know a man called Okafor?"

She jumps in her seat, nearly spilling her stout. "Know him? He was a saint, he was. Doc Okafor saved more Irish than any of those voodoo doctors with their spells. See, he knew things about herbs and medicines that cured the malaria. He saved me baby boy, he did. I thought little Jamie was a goner, for sure. That fever nearly burned him up, but Doc Okafor never gave up on him; the man was tireless."

"Is Doc Okafor still there?"

Her eyes turn sad. "Nah, he exhausted himself and caught the illness. Wouldn't be surprised, though, if a voodoo doc cast an evil spell on him. They were jealous of Doc because his medicine worked, and he wouldn't do their evil practices like they wanted him to. We tried to save him, Irish and Africans together, but he was so frail from working day and night he couldn't fight the fever. He passed about a year ago. We buried him in a Christian ceremony in the fields. A saint he was."

When Kam arrives later that day with a delivery, Kathleen, Tommy, and I ask him to sit down. Looking at our faces, his eyes turn suspicious. "What is it?" he asks.

"Kam, today a woman came in from Louisiana," I say.

He jerks to attention. "Did she know me father?"

"Yes, love, she did," Kathleen answers.

"And. . . ."

I can scarce say the next part but know I must. "She said your father was a hero, that he saved many Irish people from malaria there; saved her own baby. He did what the plantation doctors could not do."

"*Was* a hero?"

"Yes, Kam. He caught the disease and died a year ago."

For the first time since we met, I see Kamua Okafor weep. Tears pour from his eyes and down over the white shirt. Kathleen takes him into her arms, cooing and rocking him.

For a time, he lets her hold him. Then, he straightens. "I must go home now."

"But Kam," Tommy says. "stay here with us tonight. We're your family."

"Thank you," he says, "but no. Tonight, I stay on Joy Street."

"I'll go with you, Kam," I say, taking off me apron. "I don't want you to be alone tonight."

Kathleen gasps. "Mary, no."

He turns back to me, crossing his arms over his chest. "No, Mabo. You can't come to Joy Street."

"We need to be together now, Kam."

"You cannot go there."

"Kam. I'm your friend. You're accepted here. Why would it be different for me on Joy Street?" Even as I say the words, I know their folly. Kathleen is shaking her head sadly.

He gives a quick, disgusted snort. "Because it *is* different. I've never seen a white person on Joy Street. I can't just show up with you there. People wouldn't understand."

I step forward and put me hand on his arm. "Kam, please. I need to be with you tonight. Kam and Mabo—brother and sister forever—remember?"

He shakes me hand away, angrily. "But I don't want to be with you," he snarls. "I want to be with me own people. Men who look like me, like my father." He rises and walks toward the door. "I must honor me father's name in America. Before I die, the name of Okafor will have meaning in this country . . . and power." Kam thunders out of the pub.

I run outside and watch as he brings the reins down on Kirabo's back and rides away. Me heart is broken. If I learned that Da was gone, I'd want Kam with me. How can he not feel the same? He is me best friend, me savior. I would do anything for him, and he for me. I thought we were brother and sister.

But I am not his color, and nothing I can do will change that. The one person alive I called kin has turned his back on me. Me grief flares into anger, and rage replaces devotion. I have no family and don't need one. I need no one. I'm laidir.

I shake me fist at his back and scream. "Go ahead then, back where you belong—to nigger hill."

He doesn't turn, but Kathleen grabs me raised fist and whirls me to face her. "Are you crazy, Mary? You're talking about Kam."

"I don't care. I don't care if I ever see him again."

CHAPTER THIRTY-ONE

There's no language like Irish for soothing and comforting.

As I lay on me cot in the basement, the anger fades and reason returns. Did he hear me? He's me rock, me savior, me brother, and I said the cruelest words in the world to him. Have I lost Kam? Must I lose everyone I love? Like I lost me mother? Once again, I see her lying there before I covered her with stones. The image is as vivid as if it happened yesterday. I curl into a little ball on me side and let go to the grief. Soon, I am sobbing me heart out.

I don't know if Kathleen hears me or if she has some sixth sense that others lack, but oddly I feel her cradling me back and wiping the tears away with a soft handkerchief. "Cry, Mary. Go on, cry. It's your right."

Me body tenses. I'm embarrassed that she caught me in such a state. "Ah, Kathleen, don't worry about me. I was just missing me mam. I've got to get over that."

She sits cross-legged on the cot and pulls me up to face her. "Tell me, love. Talk to me about your mother."

I shake me head.

She tucks her finger under me chin and raises me face to meet her eyes. "Talk to me, Mary. I want to know about her."

I sit staring into her eyes for the longest time and then me tongue takes over what me brain has fought all these years. "She was beautiful and kind, Mam was. Black, black hair, pink skin, and eyes so blue you could see through them."

"Ahhh, lovely," Kathleen murmurs, closing her eyes.

"And she could sing like an angel. Everyone said so. She always looked so happy when she sang." I gulp in air. "The only time I saw her happier than singing was when she birthed a baby. She was our village midwife, you see. She always said that birthing a baby was the closest to God she'd ever be."

"A midwife?" Kathleen says, her eyes flying open.

I nod me head and find I don't want to stop talking. "Yes, and she loved me da with all her heart—and me and baby Ellen. She loved so much." Me sob catches again until I gulp it down. "All she wanted was to live out her life in Ireland and take care of us and her village. I don't know what makes someone a saint, but she was as close to that as anyone I ever knew. And I couldn't save her."

Kathleen is wiping me cheeks again. I didn't even know the tears were still there. She doesn't say words now, just sounds, soothing, comforting sounds, some in Gaelic, as she rubs me shoulders and kisses where the tears used to be.

"That's why what happened to me on the ship was so awful."

She's still for several seconds. "What did happen, Mary? You've never spoken of it."

Can I tell her? Can I tell anyone? Will she think me trash and call me whore? But without warning, the words are rushing, out of control. "Three men in the crew cabin had their way with me. Three of them. And they smelled so bad and hurt so much, and I begged them to stop and cried out for God, but He never came. He didn't stop them. All that stopped them was the whistle. By the time the whistle blared, I was ruined. Me mother would've been so ashamed. She was so good." The tears come now in great gulping gushes—from me eyes, me nose, me soul itself. "She would curse the day I was born if she knew how I was ruined."

For the first time, I don't try to stop the tears. I let them come and come until I doubt there's another tear left in me body. Kathleen doesn't speak, except for the comforting sounds and soft caresses.

Finally, spent, I look into her eyes.

"Better?" she says.

I nod. Yes, it is better. "Kam saved me life on that ship. And now, he's gone."

"Aaah, love, Kam will come back. I think you saved his life as well. He won't forget that."

Yes, I did in many ways. And without me, he'd still be a slave on that ship abused by those brutes. Me breathing calms.

"All right then," she says. "Mary, I'm going to tell you something no one else on earth knows."

From the tense set of her jaw, I know this is true. She is trembling.

She takes a deep breath. "Me family in Ireland was privileged. Owned several shops in Dublin. I was their only child, and they had great hopes for me future. Figured I'd take over running the shops for them. But I disappointed them. I was sixteen and thought I was in love. The baby was born still—a girl. Me family booked passage on the first ship they could get out. Left everything behind. They couldn't live there after that—not with the scandal of what I had done.

"It was years before I loved again, years before I'd let another man touch me. But Tommy broke me down. He doesn't know about the other baby. I've never told him. He wondered why there was no blood the first time. I lied, told him I'd punctured meself from all the horse riding. I don't know if he believed me. It really doesn't matter anymore."

She pauses, and now I see tears in her eyes. "But the thing is, Mary. I've never stopped missing that baby girl. She had red peach fuzz on her head and was long and thin, and I bet she might have looked like you had she lived. I thought that the first time I laid eyes on you. That's why I hired you. That's why I've taught you. That's why I love you, because you are that daughter to me."

Me eyes feel raw from crying, but me heart is full. "And you are the dearest mother I will ever again know. I love you, Kathleen."

And I meant it.

CHAPTER THIRTY-TWO

A Serpent in the Pew...

Though I now feel truly part of the O'Halloran family, I am troubled. We don't hear from Kam for many weeks. He doesn't come to our Sunday classes or stop by on his delivery route. I try to tell meself it doesn't matter, but in truth, me aching heart yearns for him. Even Tommy misses him, and Kathleen is bereft.

Now, though, I join her and the girls every evening upstairs. She reads us fairy stories back-to-back with writings of a woman named Elizabeth Cady Stanton. Kathleen had known Mrs. Stanton for a brief period when she lived in Boston.

Mrs. Stanton's opinions are unlike any I've ever heard. The woman helped organize the first Women's Rights Convention back in 1848 and swears that men and women are equal and should have equal rights.

Kathleen says Mrs. Stanton was one of the first abolitionists in Boston. She says Mrs. Stanton giggled to her one day that she and her sisters used to sit in the back of their Episcopal Church with a black male slave from her childhood home. His name was Peter Teabout. That makes me miss Kam even more. I would sit proudly with Kamua Okafor anywhere, but

I wonder how the people at St. Augustine's would react to him.

I'm about to find out.

One week before Christmas he sends a note to Kathleen, asking if he can join us at Christmas Mass, that he's sorry for his neglect and that he would like to resume his place in our Sunday lessons. I think I breathe deeply for the first time since the day we told him about his father. At least, me chest feels like that's true.

Kathleen reads us all the note and then gets some paper and her pen and ink well. She writes a quick note and takes it to Mr. Mendel. "It'll be good to have a man along for Christmas Mass," she tells us. "If I hold me breath waiting for Tommy to come with us, me soul will be in purgatory before I can exhale."

I pretend it doesn't matter. But in truth, I can't wait to see Kam again. I so regret me final words to him.

He pulls the wagon up Christmas morning and comes into the pub, arms loaded with gifts. Snow drips from his top hat. Tommy slaps him on the back, and the girls jump into his arms as soon as he puts the packages under the tree. I hang back, worried he's still angry with me.

But in time, in his good time, he comes to me, takes me hand, and says, "Mabo, I'm sorry if I hurt you, but I don't think you'd be safe where I live."

I lower me head, then look him square in the eyes. "Did you hear what I yelled after you that night?"

"I heard."

I incline me head once more. "I'm very sorry," I whisper.

He laughs, which startles me upright. "If I'm not used to that Irish temper of yours by now, I guess I'm pretty stupid. And we both know I'm not stupid."

I grab him into me embrace. "I do love you, Kam. I've missed you so much."

"And I love you back, my sister. I just needed some time alone to mourn in me own way, and to figure a way to honor me father's name."

"And have you?"

"I think I have."

St. Augustine's smells of pine needles and incense. Candles glow on tree branches and from the altar.

Every head in the church turns to stare at us when we walk in. Kam's is the only colored face in a sea of white. We stand in the back inhaling the wonderful sights and sounds of Christmas. Then I hear mumbling in the pews as people turn around and see us with Kam. I was fearful this would happen. Kathleen pulls herself to her full height and glares at the grousers, but I feel Kam stiffen beside me. He's bracing for a fight. There've been many of those since we arrived in Boston, most of which he won't speak about to anyone.

But then Father Ruzzo spies us. He strides up the aisle, a smile creasing his face. When he gets to us, he shakes Kam's hand, greets the rest of us, and shows us to an empty pew. He pats Kam on the shoulder as we sit down. The murmurs quiet.

As I explain the missal to Kam before Mass, some noise to the right causes me to look down the aisle. Me body stiffens.

Kathleen whispers, "What is it, Mary?"

I nod toward the front and murmur under me breath, "Agnes Dooley."

Kam catches me whisper and sees her. He sits ramrod straight and opens the missal I'd given him.

Agnes cranes her head around looking for us. Her body freezes as her mouth flies open. She leaps to her feet and flounces toward us. Me mam would've grabbed her by the ear and marched her out if she could see the low-necked scarlet dress and showy high-heeled shoes Agnes is wearing.

"Pretty trashy for church," Kathleen whispers as me old nemesis draws near.

"Well, if it isn't Mary Boland and her slave friend." Her laugh is filled with malice. "What are you doing with yourself, Mary? Working the streets?"

I nearly charge at her, but Kathleen puts her hand down on me thigh—hard. Then, I remember I'm in church. What I want to do cannot happen here.

Breathing deeply, I tamp down me Banshee nature and say, "Agnes, this is me employer, Mrs. Kathleen O'Halloran, owner of O'Halloran's pub on Second Street."

Ignoring the introduction, she crowds toward me. "So you're a barmaid? I suppose that's the best I could expect from you."

Kam closes his missal. "Are you working, Agnes?"

She pulls herself up to her tallest height. "In the house of Thomas Duncan." She waits for a reaction. "On Beacon Hill," she continues. "It's one of the finest homes in Boston." She pulls her white gloves higher up on her arms. "I'm the personal maid to Mrs. Duncan. The family is rich as Croesus."

Kathleen whispers to me, "And snobs to the core."

"That sounds like a good place, Agnes. How did you get your job?" Kam says.

"Me cousin, Padraic, is their butler." She sticks her nose up in the air, and I notice its size is not so noticeable with all the makeup on her face. She is powdered and rouged like a girl from the stage.

"Well now, isn't that fortunate for you?" Kathleen says, opening her missal.

"Yes indeed. Otherwise, I might have to be a barmaid, too. And that's such a common job."

Kathleen's body coils beside me. This time, I press me hand hard on her thigh. She looks at me, cocks one corner of her mouth, and bows her head. "No job is common, Agnes, if it's done right," she says quietly. "And no one does her work better than Mary."

Smirking, Agnes turns on her heel and saunters back to her pew as Father Ruzzo appears on the altar.

"I don't like that lady," Molly says.

"But her dress is so pretty," Shannon whispers.

I truly hate Agnes. I catch meself at the thought. It's unchristian to have such a thought on Christmas in church. Well, at least it'll give me something to tell Father Ruzzo in confession next Saturday. Me sins are usually so boring.

It's a cold March night two days after me fifteenth birthday, and as I untie me apron for the night, a pair of rough hands grab me around the waist. "Come here, little colleen," a drunken male voice slurs in me ear.

He's not one of our regulars. I struggle to get his hands off me, but he pulls me in closer to his foul mouth and tries to kiss me, missing me mouth by an inch. His blubbery lips land sloppily on me cheek.

"Let me go," I yell, pushing hard, but he won't release his hold.

Out of the corner of me eye, I spot Tommy. He springs over the bar in a way that is astounding for a man of his girth. In seconds, he has one arm pinned behind the man's back. "Release her. She's only fifteen years old, for Christ's sake."

But the drunk holds me fast. Tommy tugs his wrist high up his back. "Owww," he screams. "You're breaking me feckin' arm."

He finally lets loose of me. Kathleen has run back down from upstairs to see what the ruckus is about. She starts to go for the fellow's throat, but Tommy pushes her back. "Stay out of this, Kathleen."

Two more men now stand behind the man who grabbed me. One thing I've learned in this time at O'Halloran's is what mean drunks look like, and these are as nasty as they come. They advance toward Tommy. One of them pulls a billy club from his pocket.

Kathleen runs to her husband's side. "I told you to stay out of this, Kathleen," he says, shoving her away again.

The three of them crowd in toward Tommy. He raises his fists.

"They'll murder him," Kathleen screams. "He can't take three at a time." She runs to the kitchen and returns with her rolling pin flailing over her head.

I jump into the fight only to get tossed on me belly. I see a billy club rise into the air. *They'll kill him.*

From me place belly down on the floor, I hear a snap. A voice screams in agony. "You've popped me shoulder out."

When I look up, I see a strange young boy. He's big as a giant and looks stronger than Samson before the shearing. He grasps the hand holding the billy club.

"You shouldn't be carrying one of those things around Boston, you know," the boy says quietly. "The law wouldn't like it."

He towers over the drunks, and they shrink back looking up at him. He releases his hold on the hand with the billy club and says calmly, "So, is this fight finished then?"

Without a word, the troublemakers slink back to their table. One picks up the coat belonging to the man whose arm hangs limp from his shoulder. "Here Jamie. Let me put this across your back," he says, draping the coat over him. "Let's go to Bertha's. She'll pop that back in for you."

As the three walk out, the fiddler puts his bow to his violin and begins to play *The Gypsy Rover*. All the customers settle down with their drinks.

"I'd have taken them meself," Tommy says, "but thanks, lad, for yer help."

Kathleen runs to the boy. "Where'd you come from? We didn't see you here earlier."

"No, ma'am," he answers. "Kam Okafor asked me to meet him here after work. I was waiting outside and heard the ruckus. Figured you might need some help."

His hair is black as midnight, and he looks at me with eyes the color of Mam's. But the eyes are bold, too, and do not waver from me face. "Are you all right, miss?"

I nod like a dumb ox, too shocked to speak.

At that moment, Kam walks through the door and says, "Daniel!"

The boy turns, "Kam."

Kathleen says, "How do you two know each other?"

"More than know each other," Kam answers. "This is Daniel Kelly. He saved me life just after Christmas. I was cornered by two of Boston's finest. They planned to hijack me to Mississippi. You read about the Fugitive Slave Act that got passed a while back?"

Tommy answers, "Heard about it, yes. Didn't think anyone in Boston would allow such a thing, though."

Daniel shrugs. "When there's money on your head, people will surprise you—even coppers."

"So what happened?" Kathleen says.

"I was making me last delivery near the train station. Two policemen with a bloodhound cornered me. I talked to the dog, and it backed off. The cops wouldn't listen."

"Who were the policemen?" Tommy asks.

"I've no idea—never saw either of them before. They just said, 'Got ourselves a prime young nigger buck. He'll bring a pretty penny.'"

I fear me dinner will soon be on the floor. "Kam," I say, "they almost kidnapped you?"

"Wouldn't have been almost, Mabo, if Daniel hadn't come along. I knew if I fought them, I'd swing for sure. They were drunk and itching for a lynching. But just before they threw me on the train, he showed up. I think the sheer size of him scared them."

"I don't like bullies," Daniel says, turning to Tommy, "and Boston has more than its share of them."

"That's a sure thing," Tommy says.

"Could you be related to John Kelly?" Kathleen asks.

The boy nods. "He was me father."

"Ah, lad," she says. "I was so sorry to hear of his passing. He was a fine man."

Daniel nods. "The finest." He turns to Kam. "See you on the Charles tomorrow?"

"Two o'clock," Kam answers. "Daniel's going to teach me to row. We're borrowing a boat. This warm spell has thawed the river just enough."

"Two it is. Well, I'll be on me way then," Daniel says, turning to leave.

"Not on your life, boy," Tommy says. "How old are you?"

"Seventeen, sir."

"Old enough for a Jamesons. If ever I owed someone a free drink, this is the night. Have a seat."

Daniel shoots me one last glance and sits down at the bar with Kam. His look is frightening, but exciting. It sends a jolt of electricity down to me toes. I know I should thank him for saving Kam but need to escape those blue eyes quickly. I run down to me room.

"Good night, Mary Boland," he yells after me. "I'll be seeing you again. That's for sure."

CHAPTER THIRTY-THREE

The serpent with a seed in her belly.

Since that night, I find meself thinking often of Daniel Kelly. I look for him at church and wonder if he'll ever come into the pub again. South Boston isn't that big a territory, so I'm sure I'll see him eventually. On this glorious summer day, as I walk to market, I almost hope to run into him. Such foolishness. I must forget about him. Me reverie is startled by a male voice. When I turn and see Kam, I'm a little disappointed it's not Daniel. *Stop that, girl.*

"Mary, want a ride?" Kam calls out.

I hold up me shopping basket. "Absolutely."

As he pulls his wagon up to the curb, his smile stretches the full width of his face. It strikes me that he is handsomer each time I see him. Almost as handsome as Daniel. He'll be eighteen this November, and I hear he's very popular with the young ladies of Joy Street.

"How are you keeping?" he asks. His English is now better than mine and has a distinct elegance to it. He sounds like he came from London rather than the West Coast of Africa.

I run to his wagon and climb up beside him, putting me shopping basket on the floor. "I'm lovely, Kam. You?"

"Wonderful," he says. "I'll drive you to Quincy Market and then back to O'Halloran's."

"That would be grand," I say, laughing. "The vegetables at Quincy Market are much better than here in the neighborhood." Though me stomach tightens some for fear of trouble every time Kam and I are out in public now that we're older, I cannot let him know that. Our friendship is stronger than any bigotry Boston can slam up against us.

Grabbing up potatoes and carrots from one of the vendors, I ask, "How's your work coming, Kam?"

"Excellent. Mr. Mendel is teaching me to mix tonics. He's glad for the chance. He's getting up in years and wants to slow down some."

"That's marvelous," I answer. "Who'd have believed you'd be doing such things when we met on *The Dandy*."

His smile fades. "Please, Mabo, don't remind me of that ship. I was planning to throw meself over the rail the night they brought you into their quarters." He looks deep into me eyes. "But when I saw what those devils did to you, I couldn't." As he turns away, I see the corners of his lips curl up in a grin. "Didn't know what a good a team we'd make."

"Remember the Banshee?" I say, giggling. "Never thought we'd get away with such a wicked naff. Still can't believe they fell for it."

He swivels toward me and laughs. "I can. You're scary when you want to be."

"Me? Scary? Nah. I'm just Mabo." But then I remember the tales about me Grandmother O'Brien and jump at him with a loud, "Boo." I do have Banshee blood in me after all. He jumps, shocked, and I double over in laughter.

Righting meself and giggling like an eejit, I whirl to grab an apple and slam straight into Daniel Kelly.

"Easy, Mary," he says securing me balance by both elbows. He holds me there for a long moment, staring down into me eyes. For a time, all the noise and commotion of Quincy Market hushes and there's no one there but the two of us. Kam's voice comes from behind me somewhere.

"Hey, Daniel," he says. "I'd forgotten you said you'd be here today."

I find meself speechless but glare at Kam who raises his eyebrows in feigned innocence. His act doesn't fool me. This is surely a setup.

"Do you mind if I walk with you two for a minute?" Daniel asks.

"Of course not," Kam says.

So, around the market we stroll, like friends who've known each other for years. But one of us—me—is unable to speak a word. The boys chatter aimlessly, while I try to ignore the tight feeling in me chest and the tingling running from me belly to me toes.

"Ice cream, Mary?" Daniel asks, gesturing toward a vendor turning a noisy crank.

I shake me head.

Kam laughs. "Mary Boland refusing food? I don't believe it." He turns to the handsome giant who stands close to me, much too close. "The strawberries look beautiful."

I look again at the man cranking ice cream, then ladling it into fresh waffles. Me mouth begins to water. "Yes, but I'll pay for it."

Daniel bends down to me. "Trust me, Mary, a man buying a girl ice cream does not constitute a promise of any sort." Grinning, he holds up three fingers to the vendor.

And so we walk on, the two of them chatting comfortably and me silent, except for the sound of me tongue slurping up the ice cream followed by a slight crunching sound as I finish the waffle. Me ten cents is still safe in me pocket.

Under different circumstances, this would be a treat to remember. Even under these uncomfortable circumstances, I shan't soon forget it.

"I need to get back, Kam," I say soon as we finish our shopping.

Again, Daniel bends down and whispers in me ear. "Could we take a walk later?"

I shake me head. "I have to work." As we pull off in Kam's wagon, I look back. He stands there still wearing the devilish grin that turns me stomach to mush. He is surely the most beautiful man I've ever laid eyes on.

"Don't you like him?" Kam asks.

"There's nothing to dislike," I answer. "I'm just not interested in any man. You know that."

Shaking his head, Kam prods the horse into a trot. I'm grateful he doesn't discuss this further. Me mind is a tumble of confusion at this moment. I lie when I say I'm not interested in Daniel. I am interested, but I can't take the chance of having him around. I fear what could happen between us. But I can't share that, not even with Kam.

As we ride back toward the pub, a strangely familiar figure catches me eye. I squint me eyes toward her. Is it? I'm not certain. "Look, Kam," I say, pointing ahead. "I think that's Agnes Dooley."

It takes him a moment to remember the name. When he does, he scowls. "Are you sure?"

"I don't know, but I think so." It's been nearly two years since we saw her at St. Augustine's and she looks different now. Her shoulders are slumped and the hair hanging out of her bonnet is oily. As our wagon pulls closer, in spite of the changes in her, I know it's Agnes—that nose.

We pull up to her side, and I see what's changed. It's her stomach. Sticking out much too far to be just a gaining of weight. I whisper to Kam, "Stop the wagon, please."

I jump down as Kam pulls Kirabo to a halt at the curb. "Agnes, is that you?" I call out.

She turns to see who spoke her name. When she spies me, her face falls into a puddle of frowns. She is bloated and dirty. Her skin is pasty as a old woman's. Her eyes drop down as if she's studying her scuffed shoes.

"Yes, it's me. Who else would it be, Mary?"

I stammer in confusion. "It's just that I haven't seen you for such a long time." I struggle for words. Her swollen belly makes small talk difficult. "How's your mother?"

She laughs, though it's more a cackle than a sound of mirth. "I wouldn't know how the old crow is. Haven't seen her in four months."

Tears well up in her eyes, and much as I once hated this girl, I pity her now. "Agnes, do you need help?"

Kam materializes beside us. I don't know what second sight told him to come at this very moment, but I'm grateful. "Come, get in the wagon, Agnes," he says gently. "We'll find a quiet place to talk."

With some difficulty, she climbs up into the wagon. She can't be more than seventeen, but she moves like one of the old ladies who attend every funeral at St. Augustine's.

"Where will we go?" I turn to Kam.

"Back to O'Halloran's. Kathleen will know what to do."

And she does, of course. At first, she seems startled, but after she looks at Agnes's stomach, she says, "Well, come in here, girl, and sit down. I'll get you a cup of tea."

I thank me lucky stars that the place is fairly empty, only two men are at the bar. We sit near the back of the tavern.

Kathleen sits beside Agnes. Kam and I are across the table. After Agnes has taken a few sips of tea, her hands trembling, Kathleen says, "Are you in trouble, Agnes?"

With that, you'd think the Charles River had broken across its banks and flooded the room. That's how many tears spurt out of Agnes. Finally, she takes a ragged breath and whispers, "Yes."

"How far along?"

"About six months, I think."

I look at Kam and, dark as he is, a flush of embarrassment stains his cheeks.

"Will the father take care of you?" Kathleen asks, her voice gentle as a lullaby.

The sobs turn loud enough that the two men at the bar swivel and stare at us. Kathleen puts her hand on Agnes's back. "Hush, girl. There's no sense in turning your trouble into a public scandal."

Agnes stares into Kathleen's kind face and whispers, "It's already a scandal." She gulps in air. "Me mother has disowned me. Me cousin, Padraig, never wants to see me face again. Me life is over."

"What about the father?" Kathleen asks.

Agnes pushes her tea to the side and puts her face into her hands.

"Agnes," I say. "We want to help you. Please tell Kathleen who the father is."

She lifts her face and, with a twisted grimace, snarls, "Old man Duncan himself, that's who. He told me I was beautiful, that he'd divorce the old bat. But once *this* happened," she thumps her stomach hard, "he forgot I was alive. Now what can you do to help that?"

Kathleen remains calm. "Does the old bat, uhh, I mean, wife know?"

Agnes snorts a laugh harsh as a crow's caw. "Oh yes, she knows. But not that he's the one what done this to me." She smacks her stomach again. "She thinks I'm a whore and have lain with all the men at the house." She grabs for Kathleen's hand. "As God is me witness, that's a lie. The wrinkled old prune is the first I let into me bed."

Kathleen raises her eyebrows at me and Kam, then turns back to Agnes.

"The old bitch packed me bag herself the first day I started to show and put me on the street," Agnes continues. "I've been there ever since. I sleep under the bridge. To feed meself, I have become what she said of me." She pounds on her protruding belly, and the action sickens me at what the wee one inside might feel. "But now that this *thing* has gotten so big, I can't even do that. The men don't want me."

"Well now," Kathleen says, "stop pounding at it. Don't worry. We'll just have to see what we can do about this."

CHAPTER THIRTY-FOUR

Odd bedfellows . . .

Agnes, Kam, and I sit quietly at the table as Kathleen whispers into Tommy's ear.

He throws the bar rag down. "You want to do what?" he bellows. "Are you daft, woman?"

"Lower your voice, Mr. Halloran, or mine will go up, and you know me shriek is louder than anything you can belch out of your trap."

As Kathleen and Tommy face off, the two men sitting at the bar jump to their feet and jam caps onto their heads. "We'll be on our way now." They scurry out the front door.

"Now see what you've done," Tommy says in a lower, but still fierce tone. "Those are two of me best customers."

"Sots is more like it." Kathleen marches forward until they are chin to nose. She punches her finger into his chest. "Disgraceful it is that you're fattening your coffers with money their wives need to feed their children."

Agnes whispers, "She's a rough one, aye?"

Kam grins. "Rough as goose feathers I'd say. Kathleen O'Halloran is one of the finest ladies in Boston."

"Just watch and listen, Agnes," I say. "You'll learn a lesson in how to handle an unruly man. If ever I were to marry—which I won't—I'd pattern me wifely behavior after no one but her." I don't add that she's become the mother I'd want to be, too.

Tommy is weakening. We can all see she's hit his soft spot talking of children. He's watched many an angry wife drag her husband out of his pub. "But Kathleen . . ." he whimpers.

"Don't you go whining to me, sir. That girl there," she points to Agnes, "is in dire trouble due to one of your kind. She's a good Catholic girl," at this, Agnes crosses herself, "and has no one to help her. As God is me witness, you'll not be turning her away from your door like old Duncan did."

"But . . ." Tommy looks so confused I almost pity him.

"No buts about it. The Irish help their own, and she's as Irish as you are, or more so since you came over from bloody Belfast, that hell hole of Orangemen."

Tommy lowers his head and shakes it side to side. "So, what is it you want, woman?" She has him, and he knows it. He doesn't want his customers to think he's an Orangeman.

"To buy a cot and put it down in Mary's room. We'll keep the girl out of sight until the child comes and then take it to the nuns. Then, *you'll* find her a position with one of your cronies' companies."

"*I'll* find her a position?"

"*You'll* find her a position. Perhaps it'll make up for all the Sunday mornings you won't lift your fat rump out of our bed to come to St. Augustine's. Even Kam is a better Catholic than you, Muslim though he is."

And so it is I get Agnes Dooley as a roommate. Life is peculiar sometimes. Fate passes by all the girls in the world I'd like to share a room with, girls like Ceili or even Shannon or Molly who live under this very roof, and I end up with Agnes.

Oh well, at least she takes me mind off Daniel Kelly.

Chapter Thirty-Five

God turned His head when He made birthing.

After nearly three months living with her, I wish I could say we have become fast friends, but that would be a lie as big as Satan tells sinners. She's not easy, this Agnes. One of her many complaints is that she has to live in a basement.

"Agnes," I tell her, "this is the coolest place in hot weather and the warmest in cold. Besides, Kathleen allows you her bed during the day and early evening." Though this is true, she sniffs off me words as though I'm a shanty fool and she's a lace-curtain lady. Which I learn is far from the truth. In the dark of night, she tells me stories that make me blush right through me nightie.

"Some fools like to be tied up, Mary," she says.

"You told Kathleen Mr. Duncan was the only one."

She laughs. "Did you believe that? What a culchie you are. Old Duncan wanted things simple, missionary style. But others . . ."

In spite of meself, I am curious. "Others?"

"Yes, lots of others. When I had time off from the Duncan house, I'd moonlight at Shiv McGraw's house. That's where the real money is."

"Shiv's?"

"Sure, he has the classiest girls in the city working for him. That's where I learned all about men and how disgusting they are." She begins a litany of outrageous acts that men have asked her for. They involve licking, biting, flicking, tying up, smacking, and feathers. She laughs. "If only they knew I'm gagging most of the time, they'd be surprised. But I figure, if they pay the price, there's nothing I won't do to pleasure the fools."

Sometimes, I put the pillow over me head to shut out her words. But sometimes, God help me, I encourage her to tell me more. Once, I asked her, "Agnes, do you ever see men from St. Augustine's at Shiv's?"

"Oh, yes! It's hilarious. There they are at the communion rail on Sunday and the next Saturday night, they're in me bed at Shiv's."

"But why? They have wives."

"Here's what I figure. Catholic men want to marry nice girls, virgins even. But then, their sweet little wives turn out boring in the bedroom. That's when they go to Shiv's. They'll pay top dollar for me mouth. They don't consider that infidelity."

Though her stories disgust me, I figure education is good in whatever form it takes. And to be perfectly honest, the stories are fascinating.

One night, I need to escape Agnes. So, just before sleep, I creep up to Kathleen's room. Tommy's still tending bar and I love the comfort of climbing into their big bed and being held in Kathleen's arms for a wee chat. "How are you doing with Agnes?" she asks. I'm tempted to tell her what a wicked naif she's taken in, but hold me tongue.

"Not well, Kathleen. The only person in this house Agnes likes is Shannon. She's willing to be her slave when I lose patience with the job. Molly's too smart to play the victim and runs whenever Agnes calls her."

Kathleen chuckles. "Oh yes, Molly's nobody's fool, for sure."

One night, Agnes asks me if I've noticed how Shannon resembles Ceili O'Shaughnessy. I snap "Of course I've noticed. Do you think I'm blind?" I know me tone is mean, but I don't care. Sometimes, it fairly breaks me heart to look at beautiful ten-year-old Shannon. She looks like Ceili more as each year passes, with her golden curls and cheery blue eyes.

At that moment, Shannon comes down to kiss us good night. I grab her into me arms and hold on tight. I close me eyes and remember. If I'd protected her, things would be different. I was bigger, stronger. I should have taken better care of her.

Shannon, startled by me grasp breaks loose. "Mary, are you all right?"

"Ah yes, Shannon. I'm fine." I lie, but in me heart, I vow to God I'll guard this girl with me life if need be. I'll never make the same mistake again.

Agnes grows fatter by the week. "Agnes," I tell her, "eating so much may not be good for your baby."

"Who cares?" she says, giving her belly a good thumping. "I want the little bastard to die." She lights a cigarette, a habit she acquired from a French sailor at Shiv's. Every week, she gets a new supply of them shipped directly from Paris.

"Ah, Agnes, don't say that. God will hear. You don't mean it."

"Yes, I do. When it's born, I'll be done with it. You and Kathleen can take it to the nuns."

Looking at her swollen belly, I bless the wee child inside. *You won't have an easy time of life, baby,* I say silently. *Having a mother who hates you.* Then I remember Agnes's mam and figure no one ever taught her any different.

On October 25, 1851, she wakes me from a dead sleep. "Mary, this hurts," she says in a voice tinged with panic. "Help me."

I light the kerosene lamp between our cots. Her eyes are wide with dread. Her face is drenched with sweat, and when I lift her sheet and blankets, I see the stain of blood on her nightie. "Be calm, Agnes, it's time. I see your show. Mam said that's a sure sign birth is near."

I've thought of all the things Mam taught me in Ireland and have made preparations for this moment. The clean rags are ready in the kitchen, and I run up to start water heating on the wood stove.

When I return to Agnes, I bring with me the sharpest knife we have in the kitchen. I'd held it in boiling water before returning down the stairs. Back in the basement, I turn the knife, cutting side toward the door to hold the devil at bay until the child is safely brought. Mam always did that.

"Agnes, walk around the room with me. Hold onto me waist."

"What?" she hisses. "You want me on me feet with this thing coming out of me?"

"Yes, it'll go easier for you."

Grumbling, she pulls herself to standing. "Stupid, stupid!" she mumbles. I wrap me arm around her, but she falls to the floor. I struggle to right her, while all the while she swears at me for being clumsy.

After two hours of walking, pausing every minute or so to let the tide of pain ebb away, I say, "Now, squat down and pant."

"Squat?" she screams. "I'm not an animal."

"It'll help get the baby in place." I'm pretty sure that's what Mam did with birthing mothers in Ireland, at least I hope so.

She squats down as instructed, moaning and cursing all the while. "Goddam you, Mary Boland. I swear, if I find out you're wrong on this, I'll kill you."

Two more hours pass. By now, the pain has taken her mind.

Wailing, she throws herself onto the towel-covered cot, twisting and screaming like a woman possessed.

Kathleen comes into the room. "I heard her from upstairs. How can I help, Mary?"

"Get me lard."

"Do you know what you're doing?" Kathleen asks as she heads back up the stairs.

"I think so."

"Mary, I can't stand it no more," Agnes screams. "Me back will surely break."

I fake a confidence I do not feel. "Agnes, you're doing fine. Just breathe deep like we practiced." She'd hated the breathing practices, but I felt it would bide her well during this time. Mam always did this with her mothers.

"No, no, this can't be normal. I'm going to die."

"You will not die, Agnes. Breathe. It *is* normal." I hope I'm telling the truth as she lets out a deep, growling grunt like an animal. She is starting to push.

"Now tuck your chin down." I instruct, bending her knees up so that her feet are next to her hips. I lift her gown and apply the lard. "Kathleen, go up to her head and talk to her. Don't let her hold her breath." That's what Mam had me do at birthings.

"Push," I order.

"I can't!" she screams.

"You can! Push!" I scream louder.

Kathleen has her mouth close to Agnes's ear. "Don't stop pushing, Agnes." Finally, Agnes gets into the rhythm of Kathleen's words and pushes like animals have since time began. She pushes five or six more times, as Kathleen continues soothing her. Agnes never stops screaming, but she keeps on pushing. "Good girl," Kathleen encourages.

Then, I see it. The top of a round head covered with brown fuzz.

"Agnes, I see the baby's head." I am so thrilled I nearly weep. Kathleen rushes to me side. "I'll get the blanket I have warming in the kitchen."

I nod to her as the baby's head slides out of Agnes. It's already screaming—a healthy sign. I wrestle the shoulders and the rest of it out, excited beyond anything I've ever felt. I hold it up in front of her face so she can see it before I flop it onto her belly. "It's a boy, Agnes! It's a boy!"

Kathleen runs beside me as we wait for the afterbirth. When it comes, I tie the cord in two places with twine and cut it between the ties with the sharp knife I have ready. Silently, I thank me mam for all the times I helped her do this. I knot the cord near the baby's belly.

Kathleen picks him up and takes him to me cot where she washes him with warm, wet rags. I laugh in joy at the squalling of the healthy infant. When he's clean, Kathleen brings him back to me. I put him to Agnes's breast and try to push her nipple into his mouth.

"Take him away," she says and turns her face to the wall.

"Agnes, he needs you."

"Take him away."

Kathleen's eyes turn sadder than I've ever seen them, but she nods and carries the infant upstairs. "I'll warm some milk up in the kitchen. I still have bottles left from Molly. If that doesn't work, I'll call in a wet nurse."

I give Agnes a basin of water and some cloths to clean herself, and then take a fresh nightgown out of me chest of drawers and lay it at her feet. Taking the bloody towels and sheets from the cot, I carry them to the kitchen to soak. Kathleen is feeding the infant by the fire.

"What'll I do with the afterbirth?" I ask her. "The ground is frozen. I can't bury it."

"Just throw it out in the back," Kathleen answers. "The pigs are hungry. They'll make short work of it."

Kathleen is smiling down at the baby. "I'll take him into our bed to keep warm," she says. "I'll take care of him 'til the poor wee one goes to the nuns."

I go to them and put me arms around Kathleen. "Thank you for your help, Mam."

She melts in me arms. "You called me Mam?"

"That's what you are to me, Kathleen."

"And I'm beyond proud of me oldest girl, Mary. You were brilliant down there. You're a natural midwife."

Am I? I know I loved it more than anything I've ever done. And in spite of Agnes, it did turn out well, now didn't it?

I sleep later than usual the next morning. When I go into the kitchen, Kathleen sits there with the infant swaddled in her lap. She doesn't even see me. She coos as she feeds him a bottle of milk. "Such a pretty boy you are. Yes, you will be a heartbreaker, you will." When I look over her shoulder, she grins up at me. "I'd swear he's smiling, though I know that's not possible. But isn't he a love, Mary?"

"Indeed he is," I agree.

When Tommy comes down for breakfast, Kathleen puts the baby onto his lap as she pours him coffee. He looks confused at first but soon begins rocking him back and forth in his burly arms.

"Tommy, we should keep him," Kathleen says. "You've always wanted a boy."

He rises and hands the baby to me. Then he turns gently to Kathleen and wraps her into his embrace. "That girl could take him back any time she wanted, Kathleen. 'Twould break your heart and mine, too. No, let someone have him legal-like, and she'll never know where he is."

This is one fight Kathleen can't win. I think she knows Tommy's right, but sadness etches deep lines between her eyes, and she doesn't speak at all for three days. He then puts the infant in the back of his wagon and drives him to the convent.

Tommy arranges interviews with his friends for Agnes, but she never keeps one of the appointments. Nine days after the delivery, she gathers up her things. "Shiv McGraw told me to contact him soon as I got me figger back." She pirouettes, arms extended like a dancer's. "He sent this over for me. Look at me."

I have to admit she has regained her girlish shape quickly. As a matter of fact, when she does her hair in certain ways, you hardly even notice her nose. She's rather pretty.

"I'll bring a fine price in Shiv's and have all I want to eat and drink," she says. "Kathleen's insisting I not drink whiskey while carrying the little bastard taught me a good lesson."

"What's that, Agnes?" I ask.

"That I like whiskey."

"But, Agnes, will you not find yourself in the same situation again? I mean with a baby in your stomach?"

"Shiv provides his girls with protection made from animal intestines. If it did happen again, he knows people who'll get rid of it. He has connections, you know."

Shannon comes down to the basement and circles around Agnes with adoring eyes. "That dress is so beautiful," she says. "You look like a princess."

Agnes grabs her in for a hug. "And I'll live like a princess, too. Come visit me in me grand palace."

"I will, I promise."

Agnes actually kisses Shannon goodbye. The rest of us she leaves without a word of thanks or a backward glance.

CHAPTER THIRTY-SIX

Guinness in time of need . . .

"Mary, where's Kam?" Kathleen asks. "It's six-fifteen. He's never late, especially for his birthday dinner." His cake sits in the middle of the dining room table, eighteen candles ready to be lighted.

I'd been busy scrubbing potatoes and hadn't noticed the time. Her words stop me in me tracks. She's right. Kam is always prompt. A prickle creeps up me spine. A colored man was killed on the wharf two weeks ago. *Stop it, Mary. Don't go to the dark side of things for no reason.* "If he doesn't arrive in the next few minutes, may I take the wagon to the Apothecary and check with Mr. Mendel?"

"Sure," Tommy answers, "Go now."

Mr. Mendel is locking his front door when I arrive. His breath freezes as it hits the cold February air. Me heart lodged in me throat, I say, "Did Kam have a late delivery?" Me voice is wobbly.

"No, his last was to the Peabody's house. He wanted to get there early. He said he was expected at your place for dinner at six." He pulls on his beard. "Did he not show up?"

The prickle on me spine intensifies. "Not yet. I have to find him."

"I'll come with you. I just want to get something in me store." He goes inside.

When he returns, we race Tommy's wagon to the home of Elizabeth Peabody. "I'll find out if he's been here," he says, heading up the stairs to the front door.

"I'm coming, too." I follow him carefully. The stairs are coated with ice. He rings the bell, and we wait. He drums his gloved fingers nervously on the railing. Me heart feels ready to burst from me chest. It seems ages before the door opens.

A maid stands before us in a long black dress covered by a white apron. "Yes, sir and miss," she says, smiling.

"I'm Mr. Mendel from Mendel's Apothecary," he says. "Do you know if me delivery boy, Kamua Okafor, brought Mrs. Peabody's tonic yet?"

"Oh, yes, sir. He left here over an hour ago. Such a nice young man he is, so polite."

"Did he leave in his wagon?"

"Yes, sir. It was tied up right there where yours is." She points to the tethering pole in front of the house. "I saw him climb in it meself."

"Thank you," Mr. Mendel says over his shoulder as we rush down the stairs.

"Is there a problem?" she says from the front door.

"I certainly hope not," he calls back to her.

It is dark now, and the snowy roads are nearly deserted as we hurtle back toward South Boston. The ride takes nearly an hour. Mr. Mendel knows Kam's routes, so we follow the streets he'd likely have taken. When we arrive at O'Halloran's, me heart sinks. Kam's horse and wagon are nowhere in sight.

"I have a feeling he's somewhere near the docks," Mr. Mendel mutters as if he's talking to himself.

"Why the docks?" I ask, cracking the whip.

"Because that's where they found the body two weeks ago."

It seems to take an eternity, but finally we pull into an alley just before the wharf, What I see freezes me blood colder than the frigid night. Kam sits astride Kirabo, under a large maple tree. His back is toward us, The wagon lies on its side. The back of Kam's shirt is shredded and bloodied. He has obviously been whipped. A rope is tied to the lowest branch of a maple tree. Its other end is knotted around Kam's throat.

Three men stand there laughing and dancing around to stay warm. They are big men, all wearing pea coats and knitted hats. All of them are white, and all are customers at O'Halloran's.

Mr. Mendel draws a pistol from his cloak. "You have a gun?" I gasp.

"In me business, I need protection."

"Are you a good shot?"

He lowers his head. "I've never fired it. It was always enough if I just drew it on a thief."

"Let me have it," I say to Mr. Mendel. "I can shoot straight."

He hands it to me without a word.

One of the men raises the whip and lashes it against Kirabo's flanks. Kam whispers something to the horse. Kirabo whinnies but does not move.

"Come on, you dumb bugger," the man says, whipping Kirabo again.

"That stupid horse won't run, Jamie," one of them says. He takes out a revolver, walks to Kirabo's face and points it between his eyes. "If he falls, the nigger'll swing."

I jump from the wagon and raise the revolver in me hands. "Stop," I scream, cocking the hammer.

When they see me coming at them with the revolver, they pause for only a moment, then the one with the gun repositions it between Kirabo's eyes. "It's just the girl from the pub," he says.

With trembling hands, I focus me sight on the gun that is pointing at Kirabo. The explosion nearly knocks me off me feet, but me aim is true as Da taught it to be so many years ago. The gun flies from the man's hands, and he yelps in surprise, tucking his bruised hand under his arm.

Kirabo's whinny becomes a scream as he rears. His hoofs catch his assailant's side and knocks him to the ground. Kam grips the horse's flanks with his legs, grasps the mane, and settles the horse back to earth.

Mr. Mendel runs to pick up the pistol that flew from the man's hand. I cock me hammer again, holding the revolver with both hands and waving it from one face to another as I move in. "What have you done to this man?"

"Not enough," one of them answers. "This nigger tried something with me sister."

Kam hangs his head. It is shaking side to side.

"He wouldn't do such a thing. I've known him for years," I snarl, moving closer. "He's not that kind of person."

"I did nothing," Kam says softly.

"Like hell. That uppity nigger pranced down K Street, tipping that black hat to me sister."

"Something that I do every day," Mr. Mendel says. "Kam's a gentleman. That's how gentlemen behave. Of course, *you'd* have no way of knowing that."

"Not coloreds," the man answers. "Not with white women. Next thing you know, he'll be dragging her into an alley. You can't trust niggers. And this one's just so grand and cocky."

The O'Brien Banshee takes hold of me. It's almost like happened with Seamus. The blood of me great grandmother pulses in me veins. I squint me eyes and point the gun, determined to blow their heads off, one after the other.

Then, Kam speaks. "Mary, no. There's a better way."

I twist me neck and look in his eyes. Though sweat and blood stain his face and body and his teeth are gritted in pain, his eyes are gentle. "Think of a better way."

The Banshee grip loosens. He's right. I don't want to end up in prison if there's another way. I think hard, and it comes to me. I lower the gun and saunter toward the men, swaying me hips slightly as I used to see Agnes do. "Haven't I seen you at the pub, boys?" Me mind races in search of a plan.

They all nod their heads, dumb with confusion.

"Well," I stop in front of them, determined to turn their minds with something. Then, it comes to me. There's only one thing these beasts love more than violence. Beer!

I smile. "I bet if I tell Tommy you decided this was all just a misunderstanding, I could coax him into a free Guinness for each of you." I want to scream, but continue to smile.

They stand frozen, then start mumbling to each other. "A full pint?" the one with the sister asks.

It sickens me to bargain with these brutes, and bile rises up into me mouth. Then, I look again at Kam and swallow me feelings. "Absolutely, maybe even two."

Again, they mumble between them. Finally, they turn back to me. "It's a deal," the first one says, extending his hand for a shake. I take the hand, hoping he doesn't feel how mine trembles. They turn away and right the wagon.

"Also, I think you owe Kam an apology," I say.

"I don't apologize to niggers," one says.

"Tommy would insist that you do that," I answer.

Slowly, the three walk to Kam and mumble, "Sorry, mate."

Mr. Mendel unties Kam and helps him down off the horse. Kam falls to the snowy ground. His back is torn to ribbons. Blood oozes from the wounds. "He's lost a lot of blood, Mary. I'll get him into his wagon. Attach Kirabo to it, then take him to Kathleen."

I nod, me heart aching for me proud, devastated friend.

"I'll walk back to me store and get medicine and ointments and bring them to O'Halloran's." Mr. Mendel says.

Kam moans with each rut as I race back to the pub. When we finally arrive, I run inside to get Tommy and Kathleen. Tommy ties Kam's wagon up in the side yard and pumps Kirabo some. Kathleen face becomes ashen when she sees Kam. "Who could've done such a thing?" she asks me as she helps him down from the wagon.

"They're probably inside right now," I answer. "I promised them pints."

Although she gives me an evil eye that would chill the devil himself, she doesn't ask questions. At least, not yet.

"Tommy, please take Kam down to me cot," I say. "Make sure the stove is lit. Mr. Mendel is bringing medicines and salves. Kathleen and I will get him cleaned up and bandaged. I'll sleep with Molly until he's better."

And so it is. Three days later, when Kam is ready to go home, Mr. Mendel joins us for dinner and to check Kam's back one last time. He declares Kam on the mend and says he can go home tonight. We eat the birthday cake now gone stale.

As the two of them leave the pub, I notice the old man hands Kam the revolver he took from the thugs who accosted him. "Wherever you venture, promise me you'll carry this with you."

Kam nods and takes the revolver.

CHAPTER THIRTY-SEVEN

'Beannachtam na Feile Padraig!'

March 17, 1852

Today is me sixteenth birthday and tonight, befitting a young lady of me station, I will attend me first Saint Patrick's Day dance. But me excitement is tarnished some by dejection that me father is not here to see me grown. Though I've asked near every person in Boston if they've heard of Sean Boland, the answer is always no. Da seems to have just disappeared somewhere in the mists of New England.

But I will not dwell on what has been lost lest sadness take me over. Not on St. Patrick's Day. Not with Kathleen so excited.

When I told her I could wear me old green dress to the dance, she protested. "Are you daft, Mary? That rag is inches short on you now. Throw it out. It's not fit for a witch's shroud. Get rid of it."

At her words, Elizabeth Bradshaw flashed before me eyes and a searing rage burned me face. I hadn't allowed meself to think of that she-demon, but now I remembered. Tossing the raggedy thing into the waste can, I said, "Good riddance to bad memories," and stomped the dress and all thoughts of Elizabeth deeper down into the trash with me foot.

Kathleen makes me a beautiful new dress. It's bright kelly-green calico with the widest skirt I've ever seen. Its flounces are stiffened with horsehair braid. The bodice comes to a point in the front and the back. The magazine pictures have low necks with too much bosom exposed, but mine is more gently scooped. Kathleen says, "How could ya ever wear it to church with your flesh hanging out like that?"

As she pins me up, she says, "Your waist is the smallest I've ever seen." She pulls out her tape measure. "Nineteen inches. Mine wasn't this small, even when I was six years old."

"Da was tall and skinny, too," I answer. "I guess that's who I take after."

Kathleen chuckles and nearly swallows the pins in her mouth. "When I think of all the maids up on the hill trying to pull their ladies' corsets to this size, it makes me laugh." She straightens up and stares me directly in the eyes. "Beauty doesn't boil the pot, girl, but sure and be grateful for it while it's yours."

Beauty? Me? Looking in the mirror, I don't see any beauty, just the same pale girl I've always seen. I pull back me unruly red curls. "Kathleen, do you think I should cut this off? It gets in me way in the kitchen."

"Are you crazed? When people speak of crowning glories," she lifts a strand of hair out of me hands, "this is what they're talking about." She snorts in frustration.

Tommy comes up the stairs coughing like he swallowed a dragon. "You'll have to stay home, Kathleen," he says. "I can't handle the St. Patrick's day business alone with this grippe."

Kathleen's eyes narrow as she walks to him. "I must go to the dance, love. It's me religious duty, almost like a Holy Day of Obligation. Plus, it's Mary's sixteenth birthday. It's time she's introduced. And I won't let her go unaccompanied."

He rolls his eyes.

"I've got it," she continues. "Kam will help out." As she turns away, he swats her backside with his bar rag.

Kam agrees, and Shannon and Molly will wait the tables. I've trained them well if I do say so meself. Shannon's a whiz at serving, while Molly keeps everyone laughing with her wit, just like her dad.

At seven o'clock. Kam stands behind the bar in a white shirt, black pants and a big green bow tie. When a new customer comes in, he says, "Faith and begorrah, and a happy St. Patrick's Day to you, sir," in an Irish brogue so thick you'd guess he lived in Dublin. Kathleen and I giggle as we climb into the wagon he's lent us.

"Do you think Daniel Kelly will be here, Mary?" she asks.

Though I've wondered the same thing, I shrug as if I don't care. "Doesn't matter to me."

She gives me a knowing glance.

There are at least twenty horses and wagons tied in front of the hall, and music drifts from inside. Gentlemen in fine suits and ladies wearing feathers in their hair climb the steps to the front door. I can smell their perfume all the way down to the street. We tie Kirabo up to a post, and he gobbles the carrot Kathleen puts under his muzzle.

We remove our snow rubbers, and Kathleen hangs our cloaks on the row of pegs in the vestibule. Looking around at the other girls, I notice many are wearing pretty dancing shoes. Me everyday boots look heavy and dark. But there wasn't money for fancy shoes.

I hear a jig playing inside the hall, and the shoes don't matter anymore. It's been so long since I've danced, and the music makes me feet itch to move.

CHAPTER THIRTY-EIGHT

Dance like the devil's at your heels.

Kathleen orders a glass of stout. "Just one—that's all I'll have, Mary. But on St. Patrick's Day, it's fitting. What would you like?"

"Sarsaparilla, please," I answer. I've never tasted beer or whiskey, and the smell of alcohol on grizzled men in the pub has not made me eager to try them.

We take our seats with the other ladies lined up in chairs on the left side. Kathleen greets one of them, "Bridget O'Hara, how're you keeping? The old man still giving you fits?"

The woman hoots. "That devil'll be the end of me, Kathleen. He spends more time with your husband than with me and his children."

Kathleen shakes her head. "I'm sorry, Bridget. I'll speak to Tommy and make him kick the blackguard out before nine each night."

Bridget looks alarmed. "Ah no, Kathleen. If ya do that, I'll be carrying another baby in me belly before the month is out. Leave it be."

The hall is decked in paper shamrocks and garlands painted

kelly green. There are even green carnations on the tables. "Where'd they get flowers at this time of year, Kathleen?" I ask.

"Probably New York. You can get anything in New York." She grabs me by the shoulders. "You stay far away from there, Mary. It's a cesspool of sin."

Then, I spy a scene across the room: a table covered with bottles and glasses and five people sitting round it. I laugh. "Looks like we've got our own little cesspool of sin right in this hall, Kathleen." Two people catch me attention at the table— Agnes Dooley and Shiv McGraw, his black patent shoes propped up onto the white cloth. Another couple also sits at the table, but the fifth person is the one who shocks me. It's Daniel Kelly, Kam's friend. "Kathleen, look," I whisper.

"I see them. Look at herself sitting there brazen as brass with the biggest blackguard in Boston, and her wee babe gone to strangers." She huffs and turns away.

"But isn't that Daniel Kelly sitting with them?"

"'Tis," she answers. "I'd heard he works for Shiv."

Me heart plummets into me stomach. How can that be? Kam wouldn't associate with a mobster, and Kathleen said his father was one of the finest men in Boston. "Why would he do that?"

"I don't know," Kathleen answers. "But he's John Kelly's son, so perhaps he has his reasons." But her face is crumpled with disappointment.

"There are no reasons good enough," I say, as the band strikes up a waltz. I look down and see the shiny patent leather slippers standing in front of me. "'Tis time for *our* dance, Miss Boland."

I've always obeyed Kathleen's orders and run to the basement when Shiv arrives at the pub. So, I'd forgotten what he looks like. Now, the image of him up close startles me. The scar is purple as a grape, and his face drags down to the left like butter left to melt in the sun. Dance with him? I cringe at the thought, but he stands firm before me. I stand up and stare straight into his snaky eyes. "Certainly, Mr. McGraw." I won't let him see me repulsion. I hear Kathleen gasp.

"It's just a dance," I whisper to her.

Evil doesn't make for a bad dancer, I must say. As he whirls me expertly around the hall, heads swivel to follow our every turn. Though his hand is firm on me waist, he doesn't try to pull me in too close. If he did that, I could protest, but as it is, this can only be considered a fine dance with a skilled leader.

When the music slows a bit, I say, "Mr. McGraw, I have a question."

He cocks his eyebrow at me, straining his deformed face even more. "Yes?"

"Did you ever hear of a man named Sean Boland?"

Though other dancers swirl around us, he stops and stares at me. I want to keep moving. His gaze makes me uncomfortable, and his scar looks like it's pulsing with blood, but he doesn't take a step. "I might have. Why?"

"He's me father, and I ask everyone I meet. I thought perhaps . . ."

"And if I did know him?"

Me heart stops. It's the first time anyone but Father Ruzzo has hinted they ever heard of me da. "Did you?"

He scratches his chin. "Think he sailed back to Ireland over two years ago. No word of him since."

Two years? That could have been near the time I arrived in Boston Could our ships have passed each other on their journeys across the ocean. *Ah, Da, how could we have missed each other so closely?* I shake off the rising tears and square me shoulders. "Thank you, Mr. McGraw. Was there anything else?"

His mouth curls into an evil grin. "A hothead he was, Sean Boland. Probably joined up with the rebels over there. Not many of them buggers survived."

I step away and lift me chin. "Me da would survive, sir. I'll write him in Kinsale."

Precipitously, Agnes is beside Shiv, pulling at his sleeve. "Come on, Shiv. Cheri's getting pissed about you dawdling with this shanty girl." Her grin is malicious. I grin back, realizing I'm past being hurt by the likes of Agnes Dooley. Her words only amuse me.

Shiv pulls away from her. "I'll be there *after* I escort Miss Boland back to her chair." Agnes shrugs, pouts, and pulls her dress down further on her bosom.

Back at the chairs, Shiv says, "How're ye faring, Kathleen?"

"Good to grand, sir." Her voice is cold as the snow on the trees outside.

"Fine," he answers. "Give me best to Tommy. Tell him I'll see him Tuesday. Have the package ready." He turns and walks away, his back undulating like a panther's under the black jacket. When he sits down, a blonde girl with a painted-doll face puts her arm around his shoulders and pulls him in for a kiss. How can she kiss that face? Agnes reclines beside a fat, bald man. The sweat on the man's forehead shines from across the room. Daniel Kelly is no longer sitting there.

"Kathleen, he knew me da."

Her eyebrows raise. "He said that?"

"Yes. He said Da sailed back to Ireland over two years ago."

"And you believe him?"

"I must believe, Kathleen. I must. It's the first news I've heard of Da since Father Ruzzo."

"All right, Mary. Believe if you must, but I wouldn't trust that scoundrel's word for a second."

"True or not, it's all I've got. I'll write Da every week. I'll put Sean Boland, Kinsale, Ireland on the envelope. Perhaps someone will get me letters to him."

Me spirit is light with hope, until I look up and see Daniel Kelly standing before me.

"Dance, Mary?" he says.

Me heart nearly stops. Just the sight of him sets me shaking. The thought of being in his arms scares me beyond reason. "No," I stammer, "but thank you."

Kathleen kicks me under the table. "She's kidding, Daniel. Of course, she'll dance with you." She pushes me.

I glare at her but pull meself up and put me arms into the air, never looking at his face.

The touch of his hands on me back sends shivers through me, but I steady meself and begin to follow him around the floor. Between Agnes's childbirth and Kam's near lynching, I'd been able to put him out of me mind. But now, here he is, big and close and dressed in his Sunday suit, and it's almost more than I can bear.

He doesn't try to pull me close, but some depravity in me wishes he would. Me body yearns to curve into his arms, but the distance between us remains respectable. Then, I catch his scent. There is a whiff of soap and shaving cream and, if I didn't know better, the musky smell of a peat fire in the old country. The scents pull me toward him, even as I stiffen away.

He looks down at me, his eyes blue and confused. "Do you dislike me, Mary?"

"Of course not. I dislike no one."

"Then why do you dance so far from me?"

"Because this is the way I want to dance." I stiffen me back even more. "Besides, I didn't know you were part of Shiv McGraw's gang. A mobster." I shudder. "Now please excuse me. I need to return to Kathleen."

"Mary, please. I'm a bodyguard, only a bodyguard. Just one more dance? There're things you don't understand."

I look up into his eyes and feel me resolve melting away. But I steel me spine. "And things I don't want to understand." Me voice is cold, but I cannot remain in his arms for another moment.

His face burns red as fire, and he wheels on his heel, leaving me standing alone in the center of the floor. I walk alone to me chair.

"Mary," Kathleen hisses. "What's wrong with you? That was quite a scene. He's a dear man and handsome as Apollo. Are you crazy?"

"I want no part of Daniel Kelly or any other man."

"But you danced longer with Shiv McGraw."

"He doesn't make me feel the way that one does." I don't explain that each time I see Daniel Kelly at church, me nightmares grow more terrifying, that the ghastly feel of the sailors' hands on me body becomes so real I sometimes retch in me chamber pot, and that Daniel Kelly is the face I see over me. I don't tell her that.

We leave quickly. Kathleen is mad at me. That is a burden, but how can I explain to her things I don't understand meself? As she unties Kirabo from the post out front, I notice a form huddled by the gate. A moaning voice from under its blanket sounds familiar.

I walk nearer to it. "Can I help you?"

The blanket lifts from the face. It is female but swollen and red with scabs. Unseeing, film-covered eyes stare up at me. The look of her horrifies me until she speaks. "Please ducks, a little money to help me through this night?"

It is the voice of Elizabeth Bradshaw.

Kathleen grabs me elbow. "Come on, Mary. Get away from her. It's the syph."

"A second, Kathleen," I say. Fumbling in me purse, I take out a coin and put it in the claw-like hand.

I don't tell Kathleen who the woman is as she berates me all the way home. "She'll just drink that money away, girl." That's what Kathleen says, and I figure she's right.

But evil as Elizabeth was to me, no one deserves a fate like this.

CHAPTER THIRTY-NINE

A snake in the grass can strike as clean as in the kitchen.

The next morning, Kathleen tells Tommy I short-shifted Daniel on the dance floor, and you'd think I'd rejected President Franklin Pierce himself. "He's a fine lad, Mary," he bellows, his grippe obviously gone. "Why would you treat him poorly after he saved me arse right here in this pub?"

"He was sitting with Shiv McGraw, Tommy. He's a mobster," I answer.

"I don't believe that for a minute."

"Believe it or not, Shiv said to tell you he'll be stopping by Tuesday to conduct your regular business."

"Feck him and the whore that bore him," he yells.

"Tommy," Kathleen says, putting her finger to her lips.

"Sorry, Kathleen, but that son-of-a-bitch is bleeding me and every other honest merchant in South Boston dry as bone." He slaps his hand onto the bar. "He calls it protection money, but Shiv's the one we need protection from."

"How does he protect you?" I ask.

"From fire, robbery and the like. The thing is his goons are the ones who do the torching and stealing. He's the mob boss of South Boston. He's got us all by the ba . . ." He glances at Kathleen. "By the short hairs."

Molly runs up to him. "You wanted to say he has you by the balls, didn't you Dad?" She giggles, and he swoops her up into his arms for a hug.

"Listen here, missy," he says, planting a loud kiss on her cheek. "Don't you be imitating the way your father talks. You're a girl. Talk like your mam." He looks at Kathleen and frowns. "Truth be told, her mouth ain't so great either. Talk like Mary."

On the Tuesday Shiv arrives, O'Halloran's is packed with customers, When he walks in, I don't see him right away, so I can't get to the basement. Two men flank him. One of them is Daniel Kelly. His presence next to Shiv sickens me. How can he work for such a skegrat?

As always, Shiv's dressed in black. Daniel wears a rough workman's shirt, sleeves rolled up over muscular arms. The other man is smaller, but resembles a rat with beady eyes darting around every corner of the tavern.

"G'day, Tommy," Shiv says.

Tommy continues drying glasses.

Shiv looks in me direction and smiles, revealing a row of yellow teeth under the black moustache. "Ah, there's Mary Boland."

Kathleen comes to stand behind me. She puts her hand on me shoulder, but I move away. This man will not see fear in me. "Good day, Mr. McGraw." I say.

"Cracker of a lass, ain't she, boys?" he says.

Daniel's expression does not change. The other man looks me up and down, his eyes glittering.

Tommy comes from behind the bar. "Never mind Mary, Shiv. Your business is with me."

Shannon stands beside her father.

"Coo, and look at this wee one," Shiv says. "She'll be a class piece in a couple of years herself."

Tommy's face flares to crimson, and he lumbers toward Shiv, his fists up. The rat-faced man jumps in front of Shiv. Kathleen pulls Tommy back. Daniel makes no movement. "Shannon, go upstairs," she orders. "You, too, Molly." When the girls are gone, Tommy turns back to Shiv. "Don't you *ever* again make a crack about me daughters, Shiv. Like I said, yer business is with me."

Kathleen and I go upstairs pretending to check on the girls, but then sneak back to the landing where we can hear.

"Tommy, lad, bad news, I fear," Shiv says. "The price of protection is rising like the moon over Galway Bay. The Southies are lampin' up the action more each day."

Tommy and Shiv sit down at a table with Daniel and rat face standing nearby. Tommy's face is still scarlet, and I fear he may blow up before this conversation is finished. This is not a man who takes rough knuckling from anyone. But he clamps his mouth shut, though it's clear that Shiv expects a response.

Finally, Shiv breaks the silence. "So, the honest-to-god truth is I must double the cost of your protection."

Kathleen grips me shoulder. Tommy's clenched hands come down hard on the table. "Protection, me arse," he snarls. "Quit your faffin' around with me. All the peelers in Boston are on your take and everyone knows it."

Shiv looks down at his knuckles and rat face moves closer to the table. "I do wish you had na said that, Tommy. You've always been one of me favorite customers."

"Do ya think I came up the Charles in a bubble?" Tommy says. "You have no favorites. You hate your customers as much than they do you."

Shiv stands up, snaps his fingers, and puts on his hat. "I'll expect that payment tomorrow. If I don't get it, I can't guarantee this place will be standing tomorrow night." He leaves without another word. Rat face follows him. Daniel darts me a quick look and walks out.

I run to where Tommy sits, his head in his hands.

"What'll he do, Tommy?" I ask.

He shakes his head.

Kathleen comes down and sits opposite her husband. "Ya must call the police, love."

"Are ya clackers, Kathleen?" he says. "Shiv has the entire force in his pocket." He slams his fist on the table. "I'll have to bend over and take it up me arse from the bastard. There's naught else I can do."

"Let me come with you, Tommy," I say the next day as Tommy rigs his wagon.

Kathleen shakes her head. "No, Mary. I forbid it."

"Mam," Shannon calls, "we need help in here."

Kathleen gets close up to me face. "I mean it, Mary. You're not to go there. It's a bordello." She turns on her heel and heads back into the pub.

Tommy's bushy eyebrows rise and he jams on his cap. He starts to climb into the rig and says, "She's right, Mary."

I love Kathleen, but this time she's wrong. He must not go alone. He'll lose his temper and get hurt, maybe killed. Me disobedience will make Kathleen furious, but I will not follow her orders this time. I am going. "Ah come on, Tommy. I've always wanted to see where Shiv lives. It's up on the hill, isn't it?"

He nods.

"I've never been in a Beacon Hill house before. Kam tells me they're grand. Please let me see for meself." Me voice borders on a whine, and I bat me eyes at him, looking pitiful and needy. "Kathleen'll understand when I explain it to her." I cross me fingers behind me back. "And if there's any trouble at all, I promise I'll high tail it out of there before you can say Erin Go Bragh."

I'm wearing him down, just like Kathleen does. He sighs and looks around one last time, no doubt to make sure she's out of hearing distance, then shrugs his shoulders and says, "All right. If you're hide-bound to come along, climb in."

So it is I will see me first brothel, and me old nemesis who lives in it—Agnes Dooley. And maybe, just maybe, Daniel Kelly.

CHAPTER FORTY

You can't shine shit.

The balmy air would fool some that this harsh winter is done with us, but I've learnt Boston's lesson well: never trust such teasing from Mother Nature. The spring-like street we ride along today might well be covered in snow before daybreak tomorrow. I never knew such weather in Ireland.

Tommy ties up the horse in front of a tall brownstone. I bite me lips, pinch me cheeks, and fluff out me hair. I want to look attractive for this visit. Much as Shiv McGraw disgusts me, I sense me power with him. I will use that power to protect Tommy and, perhaps, to find out more about me father, and there's always that chance of running into Daniel.

A girl wearing a black dress and white cap answers our knock and curtsies. "Good day, sir." She turns to me, "Miss."

"Would ya tell Shiv that Tommy O'Halloran is here to see him?"

"Right away, sir. Please wait here." She gestures toward a gold tufted bench on the porch.

I touch her sleeve. "And that Mary Boland is with Mr. O'Halloran."

As she disappears through the door in a swirl of black bombazine, Tommy scowls and says. "You keep your mouth shut, Mary. We'll get our business done and be on our way."

"Of course, Tommy." I look down at me shoes in prim agreement.

In seconds, the girl is back at the door and opens it wide to us. "Come in, please. Mr. McGraw awaits you in the drawing room."

"Feckin' fore flusher," Tommy mutters under his breath. "Drawing room, me arse."

As we enter, I look around the foyer. It has a skinty look to it. The walls shine with gold; I know gilt for I saw a picture of it in *Godey's Lady Book*. In the magazine, the effect was beautiful, but here it's gaudy. Everywhere, mirrors reflect the walls. Gold flashes back and forth across the place 'til me eyes blur from the sight of it. A deep scrolled purple rug winds up a long staircase, and all the woodwork, including the winding banister, is painted a shiny black.

If the foyer is gaudy, the drawing room can be described as nothing but shanty-Irish brash. Here, the walls have black satin fabric on them, and fake alabaster columns circle them. The windows are covered with so much white chiffon you can scarce see out any of them. I can almost hear Da's voice in me ears, "Ya can't shine shit, Mary. Class is inborn; can't be bought."

Now I understand what he meant.

"Mary, glad to have ya see me place," Shiv says, rising from a tufted red-velvet chair and taking me hand. He bends deep and touches it with his lips. The ridiculous gesture brings bile to me throat.

"Shiv," Tommy says, pulling a pile of bills from his pocket, "here's yer blood money."

"Glad yer brains finally match your beard, Tom. For sure I'd hate to see something bad befall ya," he turns toward me, "especially with this bonnie lass under yer roof." I smell the whiskey on his breath.

Tommy's arm stiffens beside me, and I grab onto the back of his vest and pull, hard. He exhales and I feel his arm relax as he throws the money on the table. He turns to leave.

"Won't ya stay for a spot of tea?" Shiv says.

The British affectation completes the foolishness of this charade and would make me grin if I were not so repulsed by it, and him.

"Nah, we'll be on our way," Tommy says.

"Well then, let Mary stay. I'll bring her home later."

Tommy plants his feet in the way that means he's ready for a fight. "She comes with me."

"Ah, bein' a hard ass, are you?"

"Better than an ass hole," Tommy slurs under his breath and pulls me toward the door.

Shiv follows us and, as we approach the hall, I whisper, "Can you tell me anymore about me father, Shiv?"

He stops me with a hand on me shoulder. "Nay, I canna. I'm grieved to have been the one to tell you of your dad's leaving Boston. I hope he answers your letters." His face slumps into a look of concern.

"He will someday. I'll write him every week." I shrink away, wanting to be away from this vile creature.

Without warning, he grabs me sleeve and pulls me closer and whispers, "Don't ye be a stranger now, Mary. You and I could be great friends. Perhaps we could meet for a meal next week?"

I'd like to kick his shins at such presumption but see Tommy's neck redden. I must get him out of here before his fists go up. It's clear what Shiv wants from me, but only a fool needlessly pokes a stick at a snake. "Thank you, Mr. McGraw," I nearly choke on me words. "I'll think about it."

Tommy takes me other arm and pulls. "Mary. Let's go."

Shiv shows us out of the drawing room with one last leer and a grand sweep of his arm. The door closes behind us silently.

As we hasten toward the front door, a familiar voice stops us in our tracks. "Mary and Tommy, hello." Agnes runs down the staircase, holding her long skirts up from her ankles. Her hair is piled in a huge, hennaed top knot on her head. I see her glance toward Shiv's closed door. As she comes close, I'm struck by her musky scent. She smells like stale sex, I'd bet, though I've never known that scent before. Then, she whispers to Tommy. "Have ya any idea what happened to the wee one?"

"No, Agnes," Tommy says. "The sisters never tell."

She fluffs her full skirt back out around her. "Oh well, that all worked out for the best, now didn't it?" Her laugh has no mirth. "For me and for the little bastard."

With so many men coming through this house, perhaps she knows something about me dad. "Tommy, give us a minute, please. I'll be right out." I take her off to the side of the hall where no one can hear. "Agnes," I say, trying to sound friendly, "are you treated well here?"

"Good as gold," she answers. "Look at this fine dress." She does a pirouette. Her blue dress reflects in a thousand images around the foyer. "I've all I can eat and more to drink than I should, so there's nothing to complain over. Some of the men stink, but I just clamp me nose and count the minutes 'til the deed is done."

Even as I recoil, I remember me quest. "Since living here, have you ever heard anything of me dad, Sean Boland?"

Her chin lifts as her eyes dart toward Shiv's closed door again.

"Maybe," she says, a smirk curling her lip.

"Shiv says he went back to Ireland about the same time we arrived in Boston."

She snorts a laugh. "Yes, that is what he'd say, I s'pose."

CHAPTER FORTY-ONE

Sometimes, a wee nip will unleash the heart.

Our ride back to O'Halloran's is silent. I believe Agnes knows something about me father. But what is it? And do I trust her to tell the truth?

At the pub, Kam's wagon is tied up out front. I run inside, eager to tell him about Agnes, but jolt to a halt. He's sitting at a table with Daniel Kelly. I haven't seen him since the St. Patrick's Day dance. I paste a smile on me face and go over and sit down.

Daniel looks up and stares into me eyes. "How're you keeping, Mary?"

I break his gaze. "I'm well, and you, Daniel?" Me hands fumble around, arranging the salt and pepper shakers on the table and straightening the small vase of shamrocks. Finally, me fussing done, I have no choice. I look up at him.

"Good." His face crinkles into a small smile.

"Excuse me," Kam says. "Do you think you two could take your eyes off each other for a minute and listen to me?" He crosses his arms and waits silently.

I tear me eyes away from Daniel. "I'm sorry, Kam. By the way, did you know that your friend here has a very prestigious position—as a henchman for Shiv McGraw?"

Kam raises his eyebrows. "Henchman?"

"Bodyguard. I told you me reason," Daniel says.

A light of understanding dawns in Kam's eyes. "Oh, yes."

I feel excluded, as if the two of them are in on something and leaving me out.

"Mary, things are not always as simple as you would like them to be," Daniel says.

I shake me head.

Kam grabs me jaw gently and brings me shaking still. "I said I have news," Kam continues, "big news. Something I've been planning for the past year, but haven't mentioned—in case it didn't work out."

"In case what didn't work out?" Daniel asks.

Kam inhales a deep breath. "Mr. Mendel is giving me the chance to make me fortune. He's backing me financially and will take a share of me profits." His words are hurried and make no sense.

"What profits?" I ask, confounded.

His eyes shine with excitement as he begins to explain. "I've been working on a tonic for two years. Now it's finished. Me father invented it in Africa. I've replicated it exactly as he explained it to me and will sell it across New England. I'll use me wagon and horse." His words race faster. "I have one thousand bottles stockpiled in the apothecary. When I run out, I'll come back and make more."

I've heard of men doing such things and generating great amounts of money. They call them medicine men. I shouldn't be shocked that Kam would want to do the same, but all the medicine men who come through Boston are white. I figure I needn't point that out to Kam. I'm sure he's researched every step of this project.

He continues, getting more excited with each word. "When I've saved five-thousand dollars, I'll start the Neo Okafor

Foundation at the bank to support good causes here in Boston. Neo was me father's first name."

"That's wonderful, Kam. Where'd you get the idea for a foundation?"

"From Benjamin Franklin, actually, and do you remember when Jenny Lind toured America last year? The Swedish Nightingale?"

"Yes, I read about her in the Globe."

"She donated every penny she earned to a foundation for free schools back in Sweden. The bank is willing to cooperate."

"But how long will you be gone?"

"It'll take many months, Mabo, maybe years."

Years? Me heart sinks.

As if he's read me mind, Daniel speaks. "But we'll see you when you come back to restock?"

"Of course, and I'll write you letters each week telling you of me progress."

I admire his ambition. And I'm certain if Kam wants to set up a foundation, he'll do it. Then, something occurs to me, something I didn't ask before. Something that's quite important. "What kind of tonic is it?"

"Before I tell you, have a taste." He holds up a small bottle.

"Will it hurt me?" I ask.

"Would I give it to you if it could?" He squeezes me shoulder and smiles.

Of course he wouldn't, so I go to the bar and get two small glasses, then return to the table and sit down. Pulling the cork from the bottle, Kam pours an inch of the amber-colored liquid into each glass.

It is very sweet, sort of like liquid taffy. "That's good, Kam," I say, "give me a bit more."

"Yes, it's delicious," Daniel says. "I'll have more, too."

As he drains the second glass, Daniel asks, "What's in it?"

"Oh, quinine and honey and a touch of laudanum . . ."

"Laudanum?" I question him. "Isn't that bad?"

"I said a touch, Mary. Not enough to hurt you. But that's not the important ingredient."

"What is?" I ask.

"An herb made from the bark of the yohimbe tree. I finally got a supply of it shipped to Boston. With money from Mr. Mendel, me cousin bought a farm in Gabon. He and his children grow the trees, harvest and dry the bark, and then ship it here. It's the same herb me father used during matchmaking or when married people were having problems."

"Married people? What kind of problems?"

Kam grins and shrugs his shoulders.

I pick up the bottle and look at it. "What's the name of this tonic?"

"It will be called Dr. Okafor's African Love Potion."

"Love potion? And you gave it to me?" I say, angrily.

"And me?" Daniel echoes. But I notice he's grinning.

Kam sits back in his chair. "And you both asked for seconds."

Me head snaps around to look at Daniel. A red flush creeps up his neck all the way to his black, black hair. His square jaw clenches. The pink tongue licks his full lips. His eyes are the color of the beautiful Shannon River on a cloudless day.

Then, I realize those eyes are looking down. He is staring at me bosom. Embarrassed, I cross me arms. But then I notice the black hair in the V of his flannel shirt. It curls downward. I have an overwhelming desire to rest me cheek there. *Stop it, Mary.* What is wrong with me to have impure thoughts like these?

Frightened beyond reason and knowing me face is on fire, I force meself to look away from him and then bury me head in me hands.

"Looks like it works," Kam says, laughing like an eejit.

CHAPTER FORTY-TWO

Tread softly lest you tread on me dreams.

Me nightmares of the men on the ship are now all of Daniel, and they're not nightmares at all. I blush each morning when I remember them. With all the dreaming, I sometimes forget to ask people if they know anything of me father. Kathleen had cautioned me to stop interrogating every new customer lest I drive them away from O'Halloran's, but I couldn't help meself—until now.

To keep me mind occupied, I help Kathleen make signs for Kam's wagon and labels for his tonic bottles. One of the designs Kathleen came up with was positively sinful, with naked satyrs leering at reclining maidens. I talked her out of that one, so now the bottles look properly medicinal. She insisted on leaving Cupid on the label, though. The signs on his wagon reflect the look of the label and say, *Dr. Okafor's African Love Potion—one dollar a bottle.* That seems a frightful price to me, but Kam's certain it will sell once people see the results they get. I wonder if me sinful dreaming is a result of the glasses I drank that day.

Or is there another reason—the pure fact that I am infatuated with Daniel Kelly. Dare I say, perhaps even falling in love with him? No, I am sworn never to fall in love. And he's a mobster, too. But I can't deny me dreams. I must fight these feelings.

On the day Kam embarks on his great adventure, we pack him a basket full of salted meats, apples, bread and cheese. The wagon is loaded. Kirabo is tethered, and Daniel and Mr. Mendel are at O'Halloran's to send him off properly.

"Make me proud, Kam," Mr. Mendel says. Daniel gives Kam that awkward embrace men manage so poorly.

"See you soon, Mabo," Kam mumbles and lowers his eyes. I think he's embarrassed at the sadness he feels at leaving us.

Tears burn in me eyes as he brings the reins down on Kirabo's back and pulls away. Memories of where we both started wash over me, and I am so proud of how far he has come, but so sad he is leaving.

He turns and waves to us all, but I know his gesture is mostly intended for me. His eyes meet mine in a private farewell. Then, he is gone.

"I wish him Godspeed," Tommy says, wiping his eyes on his sleeve, "but the boy must be daft—a colored going off to be a medicine man."

"His father was a medicine man in Africa, Tommy," I remind him.

He nods, swivels and goes back inside the pub.

Mr. Mendel comes to stand by me and pats me arm. "Kam's not daft, Mary," he says, looking into me brimming eyes. "I'm very careful with me money. That boy knows exactly what he's doing. I predict someday he'll be a very wealthy man. This tonic is a well-devised formula."

Remembering the day Daniel Kelly and I drank some of it, I feel a blush deviling the base of me throat.

Smiling down at the little man, I say, "From your lips to God's ears, Mr. Mendel."

"Indeed," he says. "Well, I must get back to me shop. I've hired a temporary delivery boy, but without Kam to help me mix medicines, I'll have no time for dawdling."

Daniel Kelly doesn't leave. He stands there, arms crossed over his chest, staring at me, his eyes never wavering.

"Would you like a sandwich, Daniel, or a piece of pie?" Kathleen asks.

He smiles and ducks his head in her direction. "A piece of your pie is something I'd ne'er refuse, Mrs. O'Halloran."

"Ach, boy, call me Kathleen. Ya make me feel like a granny with your Mrs."

I hurry into the kitchen, needing to put space between me and this man. Kathleen follows and says, "Mary, serve him this pie?" She holds up a double size piece of apple pie with a quarter pound slice of cheddar cheese atop it.

"I'm slicing the beef into the broth, Kathleen. It needs to warm. It's nearly noon, you know."

"Do this first." Her voice is firm as she holds up the plate of pie and cheese. "I'll mind the beef."

I hesitate, but no battle with Kathleen is one I can win, so I take the saucer from her hand. "What'll I charge him for all this? It's nearly half a pie?"

"You won't charge him, girl. Tell him it's on the house, and that I said so." Her tone is final.

When I put the plate down on the table in front of him, he wraps his hand around me wrist. "Won't you stay a minute, Mary?"

"I can't, Daniel. There's work to do in the kitchen. Kathleen'll have me head if I don't get back in there."

But at that very instant, Kathleen sticks her head out of the kitchen. "Well, things are ready for lunch, Mary. Sit yourself down and keep this dear lad company while he eats me pie."

I have no choice but to obey her, which puts me in the dreadful position of trying to avoid his eyes and the dark hair showing at the neck of his shirt.

"Would you like a bite?" he says, grinning as he holds up pie and cheese on his fork.

I shake me head. "Nah, I get all the pie I can eat just finishing up what's not served here. Though not much is ever left I must say. Kathleen's pie is a real draw at O'Halloran's. People come from far away as Chelsea. Last week, I even served it to a family traveling through from New Hampshire. Imagine, New Hampshire people sitting right here in this pub." Why can't I stop prattling on? Is it to keep me from staring at his chest?

His lip twitches like he's trying not to smile. When I finally stop to breathe, he puts his fork down. "Mary, would you come out riding with me on Saturday?"

"Riding?"

"Yes, I have a horse and can borrow another from me brother. Do you ride?"

Do I ride? Now he's the fool. Of course I ride. I'm Irish.

"Yes, I ride."

"We could pack a picnic and ride to the West a bit. There's places there with hills and grass that look just like Ireland. 'Tis lovely."

Me skin feels all sweaty though it's mid April now and not hot. "Ah, I don't think I could do that, Daniel. I'm so busy here what with working and tending the girls." I begin to give him chapter and verse of every chore I do every day of every week. I prattle. "Besides, I don't go riding with mobsters."

"I'm not a mobster. I'm a bodyguard."

"Not much difference that I can see."

He lowers his eyes, but not before I see the sadness in them. "I understand if you don't want to see me," he says. "A girl like you could have her pick of any lad in this town, I suppose."

It pains me to see him looking cheerless so I begin to chatter once again. "It's not about me having a pick of boys, Daniel. It's just that—it's just that I want no boy at all." I look down and study the checkered tablecloth like it's a map of the world where I can chart a course for me escape. "Not ever?" he asks.

His eyes have turned dark. They seem to be peering right into me soul. I must not continue to look into them. Squaring me shoulders, I say, "Not ever. I want to steer me own ship without a captain giving me orders."

Just then, Kathleen comes to our table. "Daniel, how was me pie?"

"The best I've ever tasted, Kathleen, and that's no blarney."

She beams. Each new compliment for her pie is a reason for pleasure. With a smile stretching her lips, she sits down with us. "Daniel, now that Kam's gone, I wonder if you'd be willing to accompany Mary and the girls on their errands sometimes." I jerk me head up to her. "Accompany me? I need no escort."

He begins to shift in his chair. "I could do that, but I don't know if Mary . . ."

"Sure, and I know Mary thinks she has everything in hand," she turns to me, narrowing her eyes, "but it's not proper for you to take Shannon and Molly out alone, dear. Why, anything could happen to any one of you. Boston is a rough town."

"Kathleen, you know I watch out for them."

"Sure you do. I just feel better if you have a man along to help."

I can't believe me ears. Kathleen, a woman whom I know believes no man on earth is as capable as a smart woman, playing helpless on me.

"Kathleen, that's not the problem. I asked Mary to go riding with me Saturday, on me brother's horse, but she refused. I'd be happy to escort her and the girls, but . . ."

She whirls and stares me straight to the floor. "You refused?"

I strain for an explanation that will satisfy her. Finally, I stammer, "I haven't riding clothes. Plus, I don't want to leave you alone here, with Saturday our busiest day and all."

"I won't be alone. Shannon and Molly are quite capable of helping out. As to clothes, we can put together something suitable for riding."

A long silence follows until Daniel says, "So, Mary?"

I jump to me feet. "Oh, very well. Be here at noon."

"Do you ride side saddle or astride?"

"I've never ridden with any saddle."

He smiles. "I'll borrow an Eastern saddle then. Side saddle could get you killed if we need to jump."

In the best huff I can muster, I run to the basement stairs. I must admit, though, that inside all me bluster, there is a wee tingle of excitement.

CHAPTER FORTY-THREE

Some people welcome a good shunning.

Saturday . . .

I haven't spoken to Kathleen this entire morning, and I don't think it bothers her in the slightest. She just goes on cooking and baking and humming her head off as if I'm not in the same room with her. That makes me even madder.

Finally, I can take no more. "Kathleen, why do you insist on throwing me and Daniel Kelly together?"

She thrusts her rolling pin in the air and faces me. "Because it's time you had a gentleman caller. You're sixteen years old after all. It's clear as Waterford crystal you need a matchmaker."

"I want no matchmaker. I want no man. Why must you interfere? And besides, he works for Shiv."

"As a bodyguard." She smiles and turns back to her crust making. If I didn't love her so, I swear I'd take a butcher knife and murder the woman.

She finishes the crust and puts her rolling pin down on the counter. "So, now we have to figure what you can wear."

Just like that. She thinks she can make me life exactly how she wants it. Would me Ireland mam have been so pushy, I wonder? Probably.

She picks up her copy of *Godey's* and thumbs through the magazine. "Amelia Bloomer says women should be wearing these." She points to a picture.

Though I'm still miffed with her, I burst into laughter. It's a woman wearing huge harem-like pants with a billowing knee-length skirt over them. "That's the ugliest thing I've ever seen."

Kathleen studies the picture again. She bellows. "You're right. It is hideous, isn't it?"

"What's wrong with what I'm wearing?" I ask, holding out me long, navy skirt.

"Perhaps nothing, but you need a crinoline under that skirt if you're riding astride the horse."

"Why?"

"What if it flies up? Do you want Daniel seeing your pantaloons?"

Hmmmm. "How much does a crinoline cost?"

"Thirty cents or so."

"All right, I'll get one at Miller's tomorrow."

She studies me closely. "You need a jacket with a nipped-in waist. I have one, but it would swim on you." She ponders another moment. "I wonder if Shannon's Easter jacket would fit you." She runs upstairs, then returns carrying a pink jacket. "Put this on."

I struggle to fasten the twenty buttons down the front and then shrug me constricted shoulders. "The sleeves are much too short."

"That's all right. Pull your blouse down so that little ruffle covers your wrists. It'll be fashionable. You can wear me bonnet with the feather. It looks like a riding hat. That's the only thing of mine that'd fit you."

I wonder what Daniel will wear, not that it matters. Though he doesn't seem to care a fig about how he looks, he just naturally fits into any attire as if born to wear it. *Daniel does have a perfect male physique. Stop it, Mary.* Male physiques are not proper things for a girl to ponder. It's probably a sin.

I distract me mind with duties and prayers. Not that I'm much good with prayers. So, I just think, "God, if this is a sin I'm committing, I'm sorry. Fix me mind so I don't think about him further." But God doesn't listen; God must be a man, though I so wish he him woman, or at least that he'd take more counsel from the Blessed Mother on behalf of girls like me.

I pray meself to sleep Friday night and when I awaken at dawn on Saturday, me belly feels full of butterflies.

CHAPTER FORTY-FOUR

Galloping horses, galloping hearts . . .

The basket is jammed with beef sandwiches, jugs of water, oranges, and two slices of Kathleen's pie.

"Now don't be losing any of me plates or silverware, Mary," Kathleen says.

"I won't."

"And I slipped two linen napkins into that basket. Be sure you bring those back, too."

I nod, and then realize that Kathleen seems as nervous as I feel.

"Are you all right, Kathleen?"

"Of course I am. This just takes me back to the first time Tommy and I went out together." She is smiling, then frowns as she seems to remember something. "The bloke tried to kiss me, he did." She stares into me eyes. "Don't you let Daniel Kelly get away with any mischief, girl. Remember, men don't buy the cow if they can get the milk for free."

"That's one thing you needn't trouble yourself about, Kathleen. I'm only going for this ride because you bullied me into it. I want no man. How often must I tell you that?"

"If you can resist this one, Mary, I wager you'll get your wish."

He arrives at noon. I'm dressed and ready at the front door, attended by Shannon and Molly who dance around him like fireflies near a flame.

His grin is dazzling.

"Leave him alone, girls," Kathleen shouts, then proceeds to cozy up to Daniel herself. "Remember, lad, it's been some time since Mary has been on a horse. Look after her."

"You have me word, Kathleen."

His horse is a large chestnut. "His name is Riley," he says.

"And this one is mine?" I ask, pointing to a bay a hand shorter.

"Yes, she's a pony. Her name is Maisie. I wanted you to have the gentler animal."

I circle the animal, huffing that he thinks me unskilled.

"Me brother bought her right off the boat last year. She's a sweetheart."

I rub Maisie's snout. Kathleen hands me a carrot. "So, this is an Eastern saddle, is it?"

"'Tis." He cups his hands for me to mount. "I'll help you up on her."

"Not necessary," I say, swinging meself up on her back. The saddle is comfortable, much softer than bareback. "What're these things?"

"Stirrups," he answers. Put your feet in them."

I won't admit it to him, not with Kathleen, Tommy, and the girls all standing there grinning like eejits, but this saddle business is a vast improvement over what I'm used to. I pick up the reins.

"Here, Mary, let me take that basket," he says. He places each item into saddle bags on either side of his saddle. The pie goes on top. "Here, Kathleen. You can keep the basket."

"Now, don't break me plates, Daniel. And bring back those napkins."

"'Tis a promise," he says, grinning.

We walk the horses through the streets of Boston and, as we get to the countryside, coax them into a gentle cantor. Daniel rides ahead of me. I look away when he shifts his buttocks side to side in the saddle. He does have a fine buttocks. If I were ever to be interested in a man, I could do worse than this one . . . but I'm not.

"Where'd you get the hat, Daniel?" I yell out.

"From Kam. It's a bowler."

As we ride further west, the land becomes verdant and green. Gentle hills turn steeper. Maisie turns out to be fast as the wind, and I gently bring her to a full gallop. The wind in me face brings back wonderful memories of riding in Ireland with me da. Up ahead, a farm with a thicket fence beckons. It's more temptation than I can stand, so I kick me boots into Maisie's side and head toward it.

"Easy, Mary," Daniel calls out.

I ignore him. He is yelling behind me, but I pretend not to hear. This pony is quick. Faster and faster we gallop. When I get to the fence, I lay me hands on her neck, stand in the stirrups and adjust me hips forward for a jump. Her head rises up as her legs extend front to back. It is as if she is flying, and we sail over the fence without a bit of it brushing her belly.

I pull on the reins and bring her to a trot, stroking her neck. "Good girl." I lay me head down and nuzzle beside her ear.

Daniel rides up beside me. "Well, that was quite a show."

"I told you I can ride."

"Yes, but you didn't say you could jump."

"We had a horse before the troubles. Jumping hedge rows was me favorite sport."

"You never fail to amaze me, Mary Boland."

I look into his laughing eyes, and me skin turns to goose

bumps. "Well, that's all well and good, isn't it? But now, I'm hungry. That tree over there looks like a good place for our picnic."

We cantor over, jump down and tie the horses to the tree. Daniel spreads out a blanket and then begins to take things from his saddle bags. He hands the plates to me and I arrange them on the blanket. When the bags are emptied, we sit down opposite each other and begin to eat.

The wonder of the sandwich has never worn thin for me. Each time I eat one, I think back to the first time in Queenstown. I make short work of mine and reach for an orange.

"I like a girl with a healthy appetite," Daniel says, grinning.

I feel a blush. Does he think me a glutton?

"Don't be embarrassed, Mary. I mean that. Some girls try to be too dainty with their appetites. Food is meant to be enjoyed, and I like the way you relish it. Love is meant to be enjoyed, too."

I ignore that last part, but for some reason, it makes me feel better, so I give him the biggest piece of pie, though I want it for meself.

"So, you say you'll never be with a man?" His question is abrupt, and I nearly choke on me pie.

"That's right."

"Do you mind if I ask why?"

Without warning, me temper flares. "Indeed I do. One reason is that I don't want to have to answer impertinent questions like you just asked. That's me business and no one else's."

Now, it's his turn to blush. "I'm sorry, Mary," he stammers. "It's just that . . ."

"It's just that, nothing. What I told you is true, Daniel. For you to think otherwise is foolhardy."

We eat the rest of our meal in silence. Daniel asks no more questions of me. In some secret corner of me soul, I regret me meanness. This temper of mine continues to get me into trouble. And, to tell the truth, when Kathleen told me Tommy tried to kiss her the first time they were together, I wondered if that would be the case this day. Not that I'd have allowed it.

That night after the girls are asleep, Kathleen creeps down the stairs for her nightly visit. I put down me book, and she crawls in under the blanket with me. "So, tell me. How was Daniel?" Her eyes glow in the candlelight.

I knew she'd be here. She's taken to visiting me nearly every night. "Just checking in on you," she says. "To make sure you're all right."

"He was fine," I answer, lying back beside her. "We had a good ride. I jumped a fence and could tell he was impressed."

She chuckles. "Was he a good rider, too?"

"Oh, yes, Kathleen. A beautiful rider."

"Did he, um, try anything?"

"You mean a kiss?"

She nods.

I decide to tell her the truth. "I think he would have, but I picked a fight."

She shakes her head. "Oh, Mary, what am I going to do with you?"

"Why does it matter?" I think I know the answer but still want to hear her say it.

She rolls down to her back and puts her hands behind her head, staring up at the ceiling. "To tell the truth, I'm torn about me feelings. I believe Daniel's your true love. Feel it in me bones. I know you're too young now, but before I die, I'd like to know you're going to be with someone who loves you as much as I do."

"Die?" I roll toward her. "What are you talking about? You're young and healthy. Don't talk like that. I can't bear it."

"I know. I know." She pats me hand soothingly. "Lie back."

I do as she asks.

"The thing is I was so old when I had Shannon and Molly. I'd love to see at least one of you happily settled. And I think you're me only chance at that."

"Kathleen," I punch her with me pillow, "you'll outlive us all."

She smiles, kisses me on the cheek, picks up her candle and goes back up the stairs murmuring, "Bet your arse I will."

CHAPTER FORTY-FIVE

Magic is the return of a good friend.

I guess I've cooked me goose with Daniel. I don't hear a word from him. Why do I care? I so wish Kam were here to talk to about this. In me letter after that day in the country with him, I wrote, *"I went out riding with Daniel Kelly and think I offended him. He asked why I never wanted to marry, and I got me Irish up."*

Kam's response was, *"I get letters from Daniel often. He's busy building that house I told you about. Also, he's trying to get to the bottom of what happened to his father. Next time you see him, keep the Banshee buried, girl. Daniel's stubborn, too. He'll come back when he's ready."*

When *he's* ready? What about when *I'm* ready? And if Daniel does want to see me again, will I agree? Kathleen quizzes me about him often. 'Do you care for him, Mary?' she asks. 'Do you want him to come back?' I honestly don't know the answers to her questions, or to me own.

Two months pass. One afternoon, when Tommy sees me come in the front door, basket in hand, he trumpets, "Mary, letter from Kam." He waves a white envelope up in the air. "Go ahead downstairs and read it," Tommy says. "We'll all read it later." I appreciate his consideration in always letting me read Kam's letters first. Tommy knows how much they mean to me. We all miss Kam, but for me, it's family. Me world isn't complete when he's away.

I grab the letter from Tommy's fingers and run downstairs. It's mid-afternoon at the pub, not a busy time. I light me lamp and lie back on the cot, then carefully open the envelope. I don't want to miss a bit of it.

Everywhere I go, I sell out of me tonic. Word has spread that it really does work. But I don't guess I need to tell you that. Hmmm. How am I going to explain that to Kathleen? The letter continues. *Already, I'm up to four hundred and seventy dollars of me goal. The money is secured under the belly of the wagon.*

I'll be back in ten days to deposit the money in the foundation account and compound more tonic.

There have been problems along the way. I've been called nigger at least a hundred times a day since I began this journey, and this gets harder and harder to hear. But people keep buying me tonic, so I just let it roll off me back—for the most part." What does he mean by *'for the most part?'*

"I miss everyone and you, me sister, most of all. Life on the road is lonely."

The day finally arrives for Kam's return. Kathleen and I are preparing a big party. We deck O'Halloran's with "Welcome Home" signs and cook extra portions of beef and ham. There's a turkey dripping with buttery juice, Kam's favorite food since his first Thanksgiving at the O'Hallorans. Since Mr. Mendel will be here, we also prepare our first kosher corned beef and noodle kugel. Kosher as we could make it in this Irish pub.

When it's time to clean for the party, Kathleen says, "We'll just give it a lick and a promise this time. That's good enough."

I'm startled at her words. Kathleen is always one for deep cleaning before a party. But lately, she's been tired. When I asked Mr. Mendel for an opinion on her, he mentioned something called hypertension, a condition where the blood pumps too quickly. Doctors don't really understand it, but it seems to plague overweight women, and Kathleen has grown quite stout.

After we put the final pie into the oven, Kathleen sits me down. "Mary, I have to tell you something."

"What is it?" Her tone has me prepared for bad news.

We sit opposite each other at the table, and she puts her head in her hands.

I wait.

Finally, she looks up and I see exhaustion. "I think I'm with child."

Me heart drops. Kathleen's past forty-six; childbirth at her age could be dangerous. I take her hand in mine and stumble me words as I try to figure what to say. "Did you not use protection?" I ask gently.

"I talked to Father Ruzzo about that, and he said the church forbids such things. Besides, me monthly doesn't come regular anymore, so I figured . . ." She puts her face back into her hands and I see tears roll down onto the wooden table. I put on me most confident face. There's nothing else to do after all. Besides, me mother delivered other women near her age safely. Kathleen is so strong, surely she'll be all right. She has to be all right.

I lift her chin and gaze into red-rimmed eyes. "I'll help you through this, Kathleen. Things will go splendidly. And who knows? Maybe you'll have that boy Tommy's always wanted."

Her face brightens. "A boy? Ah Mary, wouldn't that be grand? A little baby boy." She's smiling now, though tears still streak her cheeks. "If it's a boy, I want to name him Sean. I've always loved that name, and maybe it'll make you feel better about not hearing from your dad yet."

"Sean O'Halloran," I say. "Now doesn't that have a fine ring to it?"

"Sean Thomas O'Halloran," she says. "Tommy'd never let me get away without putting him in there somewhere. He'd want the Thomas first, but I'll just tell him that would be too confusing."

When we stand, I hug her for a good, long time, telling meself that me words of confidence are true. They have to be true.

CHAPTER FORTY-SIX

Bigotry begins in a cradle surrounded by bigots.

By seven o'clock, O'Halloran's is packed with people eager to welcome Kam home. Tommy invited Kam's Joy Street neighbors, ignoring the grumbles from his regulars.

When the coloreds walk into the pub, they appear frightened. Each woman carries a plate of food: cornbread, greens cooked with fatback, a sweet potato pie. Tommy and Kathleen greet them with open arms and big smiles.

But when eight-year-old Joey O'Neill spies them, he says, "What's those niggers doing here?"

The pub hushes to an uncomfortable silence and Joey's mother's chin drops to her chest and she sputters in embarrassment.

Kathleen walks over to Joey, takes his hand, and says very gently, but loud enough for all to hear, "Joey, that's not a nice word to call our friends. They're the same as we are. They're just chocolate and we're vanilla. Come and meet them."

Joey protests, but it's not about being introduced to the coloreds. "I want to be chocolate, too," he yells. "I don't like vanilla."

Though the moment causes only temporary relief of the

tension, after a glass of Tommy's special brew, the coloreds begin to laugh along with the whites. You'd think they've all been neighbors for years. Which, of course, they have.

At that moment of merriment, Daniel Kelly walks in the front door. He wears a navy-blue pea coat and the color of the jacket makes his eyes look the exact color of the ocean. I've been pouring a pitcher of stout into Joey's father's mug and don't notice it's full until Bill O'Neill says, "Whoa, Nellie. I don't want to lap it off the table."

I know me face has turned crimson, but I force a laugh. As I offer the pitcher to others, I hear Daniel ask if Kam's arrived yet, and Kathleen says no. He doesn't speak to me, but I find meself conscious of his every movement as he moves around the crowd, shaking hands and slapping backs. I try to stop looking for him, but each time I catch his glance, he is staring back at me.

The tall-case wooden clock in the corner strikes five. "Kam's last letter said he was leaving Worcester this morning and that he'd be here around four o'clock. I hope he hasn't encountered trouble." I say this to no one in particular but hope Daniel hears me.

A moment later, a murmur of excitement rumbles through the pub. People point at the street. When I run out the door, here comes Kirabo trotting toward us, the wagon bouncing along behind him. Kam sits high on the driver's seat in his top hat. As he draws near, I nearly start to cry. I've missed him so.

When Kam jumps down from the wagon, Daniel ties up the horse. I hadn't seen him come out to the porch. That's how worried I was about me brother. Kam grabs me into his arms and we hold each other close and long. I realize he's missed me, too.

"You look different," I say, studying his face. "I don't know what it is."

He throws back his head and laughs out loud. "Remember when I told you about troubles on the road?"

I nod.

"Some fools in Chicopee beat me up. Me nose was plastered clean across my face."

I gasp, and he takes me by the shoulders. "I went to the best student doctor at Harvard. We'd become friends when I traveled through Cambridge and helped him with his lady love. By the time he finished with me, me nose turned out like this." He bends down so I can take a close look, then turns side to side. He's right. His nose is beautiful—straight, with a tiny bump at the bridge. The change is slight, but striking.

"Me doctor took tissue from me backside and used it to reconstruct me nose," he continues. "It's brand new surgery." He turns to Daniel. "I want no jokes about that from you, me friend."

Quickly, Kam is swept away by a group of girls from Joy Street. He stands smiling in the center of these beautiful, brown women. The most beautiful of them stays at a distance until Kam goes to her and kisses her on the cheek. Her skin is the color of creamed coffee and looks soft as velvet. She carries herself like the Queen of Sheba.

Kam grabs her hand and brings her over to me. "Imani," he says, "I want you to meet me sister, Mary. I've told you about her."

The girl looks me straight in the eyes. Hers are dark, intelligent, and framed with long, curly lashes. "Hello, Miss Boland," she says, her voice like warm honey.

I reach for her hands and caress both of them in mine. "Do call me Mary, Imani. I'm happy to meet you." I look up at Kam who beams with pride.

Then, the two of them are swept back into their crowd of

friends. I watch Kam and Imani, wondering what exists between them. It's easy to follow them since they are the tallest of the coloreds. And certainly, the most beautiful people in the pub.

Except for Daniel. I feel a familiar current beside me, turn and there he stands. Me heart stops. "Hello, Daniel. How have you been?" I finally say, hearing the tremor in me voice. "I haven't seen you for a long time—not since . . ." I do not finish.

"I know. There's a reason for that, Mary."

Me first thought turns me stomach to jelly. He's met someone. Half the girls at St. Augustine's have a crush on him. The others are married, and I wonder what some of them would do if he looked their way twice. I hold me breath. "And that reason?" I hate it that his answer matters so much.

"I believe a man must offer his woman something valuable to deserve her, particularly a very special woman."

I wrap me arms around me belly, afraid to say more, but I must know.

"And you've met a special woman, Daniel?"

"Ah yes, I surely have."

Who is she? Maybe it's not church at all. Perhaps some trollop he met at Shiv's. Well, good for them. They deserve each other.

"Is she fair?" *Why do I care?*

"The fairest I've ever seen, that's the truth."

I turn away. He mustn't see the tears I know are coming. With great effort, I swallow me feelings and say, "I'm happy for you, Daniel—and for her." I start to walk away.

He grabs me arm and twirls me to face him. "Wait, Mary. Why do you run from me?"

"I need to help Kathleen with the serving." I pull meself from his grasp and run toward the kitchen.

Kam catches me just before I get there. "Mabo, what's wrong?" His eyes look deep into mine.

"I'm fine, Kam. Just fine."

"Did Daniel speak to you?"

"Indeed he did."

Kam looks confused and stammers something I can't understand with all the noise around us. Then, he straightens to his full height and says, "Mabo, I want time with you alone. Tomorrow?"

"That would be lovely, Kam. Can you come for lunch?"

"I'll be here at three for tea. Is that all right?"

I nod agreement and run into the kitchen. Kathleen takes one look and knows something is wrong. "What is it?" she asks.

"Nothing. Kam is coming here tomorrow at three for tea," I say, bringing more dishes down from the cabinet. "Isn't that grand?"

"Of course it is." She looks confused.

The rest of the evening, I focus on keeping plates and glasses filled. I fake a smile all through it.

Kam says his tonic is selling out everywhere he goes. People love it. "I think I've saved half the marriages in New England," he jokes.

"What're ya doing with all your profits, Kam?" Tommy asks, ever the businessman.

"Banking them. I need five thousand dollars to start my father's foundation. I've a long way to go. While I'm here, I'll compound a supply of new tonic. Then I'm heading to New York. I hear there's a fortune to be made there. I figure I may as well make it." Kam walks to where Kathleen is sitting and kneels before her.

"Kathleen, as a gift to the woman who made it all possible for me and Mary, I've commissioned a painter to do your portrait." He had told me about this in a letter I hid from the family. We're both excited to be able to honor our Boston mother in this way.

Kathleen frowns. "Why would anyone want a portrait of me?"

"Because you're the finest woman in Boston, that's why," Kam says.

"Who's this painter?" Tommy asks.

"James Whistler," I answer excitedly. "He's studying painting in France now, but will be back visiting his mother in Lowell next week and has agreed to paint Kathleen while he's here. Kam met him in Cambridge just after he washed out of West Point."

"Why'd he wash out?" Tommy asks.

"He's a painter, not a soldier. There's something about his sketches of women that are almost magical." I answer. "I saw them once at a book store and told Kam about him."

I notice the platter of beef is almost empty, so I rush to the kitchen to refill it. When I return, I look everywhere for Daniel, but he is gone—without another word to me. *Who is she?*

CHAPTER FORTY-SEVEN

Achieving destiny begins with one tiny step a day.

"Mmmm," Kam says as he bites into a scone covered with strawberry jam. "I've missed your cooking, Mabo. Life on the road is hard on the digestion." He pats his flat middle.

"It seems to agree with you, Kam. But tell me, please, about the troubles you've mentioned in your letters."

He nods and wipes his mouth with his napkin. "There are lots of men out there who hate what I'm doing. Think I'm uppity."

"Yes," I answer.

"Well, one of them got drunk a week ago and came out to find me. I was parked and sleeping under a bridge."

I hold me breath, waiting.

"By the time Kirabo whinnied, he'd found the cash I'd hidden under the wagon and was standing over me with a knife raised. It was so dark I could barely make him out."

"What happened?"

"I pulled out the revolver Sam Mendel gave me. I'd never used it before, but I knew it was me only chance." I don't speak, and he lowers his eyes. When he raises them again, they're filled with anguish. "I killed him, Mabo. Shot him right between the eyes. His brains splattered all over the ground when he fell back."

I put me hand over his. He's trembling. "You had no choice."

Nodding, he answers. "I know that. It helps. But all I could think of then was getting me money back from his dead hand and getting away. I left him there, under the bridge. You know what they'd do to a colored if they caught me."

Of course I know. "But they didn't catch you."

"No."

Thank God. "Who else knows this, Kam?"

"Only Daniel."

"Good. Let's keep it that way."

He nods and clears his throat. I can tell he needed to tell me this; that he is now a murderer, too, like I was with Seamus. For some unexplainable reason, that gives me comfort. "So tell me, Mary, are you all right? Are you happy?"

For a second, Daniel Kelly's face clouds me memory. Then, I chase the image away. "Yes, very happy, and I'm so glad you're here. You did what you had to do to survive, me brother. And there's something I've needed to discuss with you."

"What is it?"

"Kam, I'm worried about this. But you must keep it secret."

He crosses his heart.

"Kathleen is expecting again."

His mouth opens, then closes, then opens again. "Isn't she a little old?"

"Yes, and she wants me to deliver her baby safely. That only gives me about six months."

He looks confused. "Six months to do what?"

"Become experienced."

He still doesn't understand.

"Remember when I birthed Agnes's baby?"

245

"I remember."

"I was good at it. I really was."

He looks interested. "So . . ."

"So, I've been thinking perhaps me destiny is to become a midwife. Kathleen says I'm a natural at it, and she was there at Agnes's delivery. I think I was born to birth babies. One thing about it troubles me, though."

"What's that?"

"The pain women experience. Agnes did. I'd want to help them."

"Have you heard about anesthetic?"

"I've read about chloroform, but it frightens me. It catches fire so easily."

"What about ether?"

"I don't know it."

"Just a whiff on a cloth might help women." He takes a book from his satchel. "This is for you, Mabo. The doctor friend who fixed me nose got me a copy. It's *Quain's Elements of Anatome*, a textbook used at Harvard."

As I take the book from his hands, I'm as excited as when Kathleen offered to teach us to read. This book holds the key to the mysteries of the human body. "Oh Kam, thank you so much. Starting tonight, me novel-reading days are behind me. I'll study this book 'til I have it memorized. It's a treasure."

"And, believe it or not, Dr. Quain was born in Ireland," he says, laughing.

Though I yearn to begin reading, I put the book aside and decide to ask the question that's plagued me since last evening. "Are you and Imani *good* friends?"

He sits back and crosses his legs. "I'd say that's true." His brow furrows. "Much more than good friends, actually. She'd like to be married, but I can't do that now, not with the traveling I need to do."

"Better be careful, Kam. She's a beautiful girl, much too beautiful to put up with neglect."

He takes me hand. "As are you, me sister. But now I must make me fortune and start me foundation. A new shipment of herbs will arrive tomorrow from Africa. I plan to compound fifty thousand bottles. I've bought a warehouse on South Street to store them. Mr. Mendel will manage the inventory and ship a new supply to me when I run low." He laughs. "He says I'm his retirement security."

"A warehouse?"

He nods excitedly. "Yes, and I've hired a company in New York to build me a larger wagon. Kirabo's worked hard. He deserves a pasture break. I'll buy two horses in New York." He reaches into his satchel again and brings out a newspaper—thicker even than the Boston Globe. "This is the New York Times. It's a fairly new paper but is now the biggest one in America. I've contracted with them to run an ad each week to tell people where I'll be traveling around the City of New York." He folds the paper and puts it away. "I'll sell out me supply in a little over a year."

Reality hits me. "You're going to be wealthy."

"Yes, that's my intention."

CHAPTER FORTY-EIGHT

Dreams are like stars, if you follow them,
they'll lead to your destiny.

I ponder and pray about becoming a midwife for a solid week and then make an appointment to see Father Ruzzo. We are the only ones inside the Chapel.

"Kathleen thinks I can help women with me skills in midwifery," I blurt out before I can stop meself.

"Have you been schooled in midwifery?"

"I've never been schooled in anything, Father. Except for Kathleen's home teaching." Me words make me feel instantly stupid. "But me mother was a midwife in Ireland, and I worked at her side from the time I could talk."

"Would you be a good midwife, Mary?"

Silently, I pray for wisdom. I don't realize how hard I'm biting me lip until it hurts. "When I birthed Agnes's baby, I did a good job of it, if I do say so meself. And Kathleen thinks I was splendid. I constantly study an anatome book Kam brought me from Harvard. I've read it twice so far." I pause for only a second. "Yes, Father, I would be a good midwife." It's a relief to say the words and know that they are true.

He picks up his prayer book. As he settles on a page, his lips move silently. Then he closes the book and looks at me. "There is a terrible need in this community for safer childbirth. Often, neither the mother nor the baby survives." He sits back. "Yes, I think this is a fine idea. Help those women and children. God will be pleased."

The following Sunday, Father Ruzzo makes an announcement from the pulpit that I'll help with deliveries of babies in exchange for produce and meats if money is scarce. "Though Mary is young, I believe her experience both in Ireland and here in Boston, will tide her well," he says. "Me prayers will be with her every day."

The exchange of services for produce and meat was Tommy's idea. "If ye're going to take time away from here, Mary, ya must contribute to the kitchen."

Within a day of Father Ruzzo's announcement, three couples come to O'Halloran's. Each woman is in a different stage of expectancy. I agree to go to each of their homes for an examination. Before I keep that appointment, I visit Mr. Mendel.

We sit down in the back of his store. "I've decided to begin a career as a midwife and I need your advice."

He smiles. "I'm not surprised. Kathleen has bragged to everyone about your skill at a delivery in her basement." I think he'd like to ask the identity of the woman, but he does not.

"So, as a businessman and chemist, what do you recommend I do?" I take out the notebook I brought along.

"Keep good records, Mary," he says. "If the woman can write, ask her for a letter about her experience. That will help you get new patients. Also, it will console you to look at those letters when things turn bad for a patient, which they will, eventually."

I write his comments.

"The most important thing is to keep the birth site as clean as possible," he continues. "Childbed fever is an epidemic in Boston. Dr. Oliver Wendell Holmes says it's more criminal than crime. There's a Dr. Semmelweis in Austria who blames it on the doctors themselves. He says doctors go from doing an autopsy directly to a birthing mother without cleaning themselves or their instruments. He urges doctors to scrub with chlorine, but most physicians don't believe the problem could be theirs." He leaves the room and comes back with a bottle of chlorine. "Also, use very hot water and good soap to clean both the mother and all that touches her."

"Should it be lye soap?"

He goes again to the back of his store and brings back a few bars of soap. "I'd recommend this." He holds out a bar. "This is Biechele soap, made by two brothers in Ohio. It's available only to chemists." He holds it to his nose. "It's much gentler than lye, but just as effective. None of the medical doctors here use it."

I lift the bar to me nose and inhale its mild scent.

"Kam mentioned ether," I say.

"I prefer it over chloroform. Think it's safer."

He reaches to a shelf behind him and holds up a peculiar looking instrument. "This is called a stethoscope." The thing looks just like the ear trumpets some of our hard-of-hearing customers use.

"How can this help me with birthing?" I examine it from one end to the other.

"Put the wide part of the horn over the woman's heart and listen closely. See if the heartbeat is regular and strong. Count the heartbeats. When the mother is calm and resting, her heart should beat sixty to eighty times a minute. That will increase when she's in labor."

"What if her heart is beating too fast?" I think for a moment. "Or too slow?"

He tugs at his beard. "That would be an emergency. Find a medical doctor who will come to the home and help if you feel the mother is in any kind of distress."

"However will I ever find such a doctor?"

"I know just the man," he answers with a smile.

So it is I meet Dr. James Burroughs. He has just graduated from the Massachusetts Medical College of Harvard University and is not a member of the Boston Medical Association. He is young and seems very smart. After I explain me passion for helping mothers and the mortality rate of mothers in South Boston, he agrees to work with me.

After one month, the constant carriages and wagons pulling up in front of the pub become a nuisance to the O'Hallorans. They can't get a decent night's sleep. Mrs. Moriarty, the lady who washes and irons the altar linens at St. Augustine's, decides to move in with her daughter, Annie. She wants to sell off some of her furniture, I barter a long sofa in exchange for me services. Annie will come to term in about five months.

The sofa is a red brocade with a soft seat, button back, and carved wooden arms. I position it inside the pub's front door. It makes a fine resting place for wives tapping their feet waiting for their husbands to finish one last draught and doubles as me sleeping quarters after we close. I miss me little basement room, but the slightest tap on the front door sets me on me feet, grabbing me medical bag and making me way out the door. Inside the bag are a scalpel, scissors, me stethoscope, small bottles of ether and chlorine, the Biechele soap, and plenty of gauze and cloths.

When me ladies approach their time of delivery, I tell them to make sure there's fresh lard in their kitchen, I sleep fully dressed, so no time is wasted. 'Tis a workable solution and lets the O'Halloran's live a normal life.

CHAPTER FORTY-NINE

There's no need to fear the wind, if your haystacks are tied down.

During the next four months, I deliver as many as five babies each week. Word spreads that I have no mortalities. The Lying-in Hospital begins to charge cash in advance, and then the demand for me service explodes.

I don't see Daniel at all. I've listened every Sunday to Banns of Matrimony and must admit to relief when I don't hear his name. I asked Kam about him, and his letter said, *Daniel's building a house. That, plus an investigation he's doing take up all his time. He's busy as you are, Mabo. And as I am. Believe it or not, I'm near me goal to start me foundation. Please know how proud I am of you and the way you're helping women in Boston. Kathleen will be in good hands.*

Some of the physicians in Boston start to raise a ruckus, saying I'm not qualified. This riles me since, by now, I've safely brought almost seventy infants into this world, with not one incidence of childbed fever.

A letter arrives from Rufus Putnam, M.D., Director of the Boston Medical Society, requesting me presence at a meeting, I gather together all the letters me mothers have written about their birth experiences into me satchel and go to Miller's Mercantile for a new blouse, skirt, and bonnet.

Dressed in me best and armed with the satchel full of letters, I climb the steps to the stately building. It is a Friday afternoon, November 15, 1852. I am sixteen years old and, though the very thought of confronting these hostile men frightens me, I have been coached by Mr. Mendel and Kathleen and feel prepared.

The room is enveloped in a haze of smoke. I'm used to this from the pub, but this room is smaller and the stink of their cigars and pipes nearly sickens me. There are five men seated at a long table. I take a seat opposite them. They stare at me as if I'm the one with the bad odor and I know that's not true. I bathed this morning—a day before me regular bath.

"Miss Boland," Dr. Putnam begins, "is it true you have been delivering babies for the past several months?"

"Yes, Dr. Putnam. That is true."

"What are your qualifications?"

"I was trained by me mother in midwifery in Ireland. From the time I was six, I birthed sheep and horses in me village of Kinsale. The women I help are too poor to afford the services of a physician, though I have an agreement with Dr. James Burroughs to assist me if a case becomes something I cannot handle."

"What kind of cases do you consider beyond your capabilities?"

"Where the baby is too large to be delivered through the birth canal or if the mother is older or I detect an irregularity in her heartbeat. Sometimes the baby is in a breech position, and if I have trouble turning it, Dr. Burroughs assists me."

"How many infants have you brought?"

"Nearly seventy, so far. And their survival rate is well above the ones I've seen posted in your annual publication. I believe that's because I'm a stickler for cleanliness, and me mothers do not develop childbed fever." I stand and remove the letters out of me satchel and pile them on the desk in front of him. "These are some of the letters I've received from patients."

This seems to turn the five of them even more against me. There is noticeable rumbling behind hands and beards. Dr. Putnam speaks again. "Do you claim your process is superior to that of trained physicians?"

"No sir. I don't think that. I would welcome your training and an apprenticeship with any one of you." I look at them expectantly. There is no response. "However," I continue, "I've heard some physicians reject the use of chlorine as suggested by Austria's Dr. Semmelweis. I use it."

"Chlorine?" Dr. Putnam sputters, looking around at the other men, most of whom shake their heads in confusion.

"Yes, doctor. That's a precaution I choose, and the results speak for themselves, though I can't prove why. The most important point, though, is that I take cases certified physicians refuse. Because of that, I believe I save lives."

"And why do you think I would refuse a case?" Dr. Putnam says.

"Well, doctor, if you're willing to deliver a baby for a bag of potatoes, have at it."

That ends the meeting.

CHAPTER FIFTY

Can true love be destiny?

That night, as I lie on me couch reading by candlelight, me mind keeps repeating every word of that meeting. I'm proud of meself. I don't think the medical board will trouble me further. I'm jarred from me reverie by a knock on the door. It shocks me. None of me mothers are due this soon. Something bad may have happened. Jumping to me feet in me white nightgown, I throw the door open. "What's wrong?"

Daniel Kelly stands before me, his cap in his hands. "Nothing's wrong, Mary. I need to talk to you."

"But I'm not dressed."

He grins. "I've seen women in less. You look beautiful."

When I look down, me nipples are pointing against the white fabric. I cross me arms over me breasts.

"Mary, don't fret. You're covered from your chin to your feet."

He's right. Me white nightgown is as modest as any dress. Only *I* know that under it, there's nothing but skin. I pick up me slippers and wrap me shawl around me shoulders, then step out onto the porch. He closes the door behind me. He pauses a second as our shoulders brush together. "You smell good," he says.

"I took a bath this morning." I squeeze me eyes shut. *That's no business of his.*

He takes me hand. "Come, Mary. Sit down for a minute, won't you? No one's around. We won't be seen." He leads me to the little bench on the porch.

He sits so close that his thigh presses against mine. It feels made of steel. He doesn't let go of me hand as he angles himself face to face with me. Now, his left knee presses into me calf. *Am I daft or is he trembling?*

It's past midnight, and the gas light casts a gentle glow on him. His beautiful eyes look tired, and I have a strong desire to touch his face. *Stop it—he's not yours to touch. He loves another.* "I know what happened with Kam. About the murder. I know you know, too."

He nods. "And Kam told me what happened to you on the ship."

I jump to me feet, instantly furious. "He shouldn't have done that. That's no one's business but me own."

"But it is me business, Mary. Don't you know that?" Gently, he draws me back to sitting. "Anything that has happened to you or ever happens to you is me business."

"That's the silliest thing I've ever heard," I stammer.

"I understand why you're afraid of me. I understand why you'd be afraid of any man, but you must know I will never hurt you—in any way." He lifts me chin so that there's nowhere I can look except into his eyes.

We sit without words for a time, looking at each other. His fingers linger a caress on me neck. "Daniel," I finally say, "I made a decision long ago that I will not marry. Even before the ship."

He puts his hand on me shoulder. "And I made a decision long ago that you will marry me." He grins. "Now which of us do you think will win this fight?"

His smile is wide, beautiful, and totally confusing to me.

"But at Kam's party," I stammer, "when you spoke of some special woman you've met and that you are doing something to make yourself worthy of her, I thought . . ."

"That woman is you, Mary."

"But you said she was fair."

"She is." He runs his fingers through me hair and tucks it behind me ear. "The fairest girl in Boston. What happened to you on the ship did nothing to your soul. You are the most beautiful woman I've ever known—inside and out. Don't forget, Mary. I was on a coffin ship, too. I know what they were like." He pauses as if wondering whether to continue. Finally, he does. "I murdered on that ship."

"You murdered? And you continue to murder for Shiv McGraw?"

"That's not true. I've never murdered for Shiv, and I never will. Someday, you'll understand why I work for him, but not tonight. The murder I committed was a man who took a piece of bread from me mam on the ship. She was starving, and I knew the end was close for her. I stole a piece of bread from the cook's galley and, when the sailor saw it in her hands, he grabbed it away from her." His eyes fill with tears. "I put me hands around that sailor's throat and squeezed until he dropped the bread. I picked it up and gave it to her. When I turned back, I realized I'd broken his neck. Before me mother's eyes, I'd killed a man. She watched as I picked him up and threw him over the rail."

"Oh, Daniel, I'm sorry."

He shudders. "She was tossed the next morning. The bread hadn't come soon enough." The tears roll down his cheeks. "She was a sainted woman, me mam. Loved God and the Blessed Mother more than anyone I ever knew. I can never forget that the night before she died, she saw her son commit murder." He buries his face in his hands. As he lets go of me fingers, a loneliness comes over me deeper than I've ever felt.

I put me hand on his back and begin to caress him. I want to soothe this big man sobbing beside me on the bench. "Daniel, she understood. She knew it wasn't you that did it. She knew it was the craziness of the ship that drove you. Believe me, Daniel, she knew."

He straightens beside me. "I hope you're right. I didn't mean to tell you all that tonight. I just wanted to let you know that you aren't the only one with hell in their dreams." He clears his throat and turns again to face me. "I need to get back to me reason for coming here. As I told you at the party, I believe a man has to bring something worthy to a woman. For the past two years, I've been building a house; a house for us, Mary. It's not grand or fancy, but it's sturdy and warm. I want you to live there with me as me wife."

His wife? This can't be happening. "Daniel, I'm not sure I can be a wife."

"Well, you'd better get sure, Mary Boland. I know that you are me love and I am yours and that, stubborn as you are, I'm going to make us one."

He brings his lips down onto mine. For a moment, me head spins until I nearly faint, but then me arms go around his neck. He pulls us to our feet and presses himself against me. I feel him there hard and solid and think there's no way he can ever get close enough to me. I want more of him—his scent, his words, his love. The feelings coursing through me set me to weeping.

He pulls away, looking into me face with the dearest, most concerned look. "Mary, love, nothing will happen between us that you don't want as much as I do. I swear that."

I start to laugh and so does he, though I think he has no idea what has struck me funny. "It's not that I don't want you, Daniel. Oh God, no, it's not that. It's just that this is me first kiss, the first in all me life, and the wonder of it set me blubbering like a naif."

Smiling, he brings his mouth close again.

"I'm so grateful me first kiss came from you," I say, just before our lips touch again.

CHAPTER FIFTY-ONE

Snakes can hide in library stacks, too.

When I tell Kathleen about Daniel's proposal, she takes me in her arms and says, "Ah Mary, me child, you couldn't find a better man. But you are very young, and I fear marriage will distract you from the wonderful job you're doing with birthing. Whatever you decide, I'll stand beside you."

I look at me ring finger, left hand, and imagine a ring there. I imagine me last name as Kelly. I'd be Mary Kelly. The thought is exciting, but troubling. Not because I don't love Daniel. I know that I do. But I'm not sure I'm through being Mary Boland yet. I have so much work to do, and I'm just sixteen years old.

I'm no closer to a decision when the invitation arrives for the preview of the first public library to open in Boston. The distraction is more than welcome. I need time to think Men like Henry Wadsworth Longfellow and George Ticknor have worked long and hard to bring this library to Boston.

Kathleen is too tired to attend. That's a matter of great concern to me. She has served on the board to open this library and worked so hard to get the work done. I know if she could attend this preview, she'd be there. But she's just too tired.

So, I agree to take the girls. At ten minutes before two, Shannon and Molly are tugging at me skirt and jumping around like kittens on a hot sidewalk. "Let's go, Mary."

"Soon," I answer.

"Mary, I like the blue ribbon in your hair better than that white one." Molly waves a blue ribbon at me. "Here, change it."

Her eyes are innocent as an angel's, but I know this miniature of her mother is hoping Daniel will be at the opening. She's as big a matchmaker as ever existed in Ireland.

I pull the white ribbon from me hair and take the blue one from her sturdy fingertips. When I tie it into me hair, she says, "There now, that's ever so much better."

"The wagon's tied up in front for you, Mary," Tommy calls from behind the bar. "Take care of these girls, ya hear?"

"You can always rest sure of that, Tommy."

"Okay, off with ya then."

Shannon and Molly scramble up into the back of the wagon, and I climb into the front seat. As I bring down the whip, I look at the bench on the front porch and remember Daniel's kiss. As if reading me mind, Shannon says, "Will Daniel be there?"

"I don't know." I see his face—black hair falling onto his forehead, nearly reaching the thick eyebrows; his nose, long and straight—the only refined part of his visage; like a nose I've seen in Irish history books about kings and saints. But his jaw, covered with a dark shadow with a slight razor nick near its cleft chin, is not that of a saint or even a fine gentleman. His jaw looks like it belongs to one of the boxers advertised on posters at the gymnasium. The man is sinfully beautiful.

"So Mary," Molly says, startling me back to the moment. "What books will you choose?"

"I want a novel, I think." I've read me anatome book through three times. "I love Jane Austen, even though she's English. I've read of a book called *Sense and Sensibility*."

"What's it about?"

"Poor British aristocrats trying to marry off their daughters."

"Daniel's favorite book is *Moby Dick* by Herman Melville," Molly calls from the back of the wagon, leaning over so her face is right beside mine. "He told me so. It's about a one-legged seaman chasing a whale and the whale chasing him back."

For a second, Molly's description brings Seamus to mind, hobbling around on his peg just before he washed overboard. I shudder.

"Are you cold, Mary?" Molly asks.

"No, I'm fine. Probably just Satan planning where to dig me grave."

"Don't talk so sad, Mary," Shannon says, reaching up to play with me hair. When we get to the library, though, I stiffen and pull in the reins.

"What's wrong, Mary," Molly asks.

"That's Shiv McGraw's rig," I answer. "The one with the red fringe."

"Have you ridden in that carriage?" Shannon.

"Of course not, but everyone knows the bloody bastard's rig." I cover me mouth with me gloved hand. "Sorry, girls."

They giggle; bad language is hardly new to them, but they're not used to hearing it from me.

"Steer clear of him, girls," I whisper. "If he comes near you, come to me, wherever I am."

We pull up in front of the library, and there's Mr. Ticknor standing on the front porch shaking hands. Kathleen had introduced us to him once when he came in the pub. The girls and I greet him. Then the two of them run into the library and dash up the stairs to the children's room. I go to the downstairs room to select me books. I am thrilled to find *Sense and Sensibility* on the first shelf under the letter A. I begin to scan its pages. *Yes, I'll take this one,* I think to meself, tucking it under me arm.

I am lost in the beginning of a new book called *The Scarlet Letter* when a coldness comes round me shoulders like a shroud.

"Well, Mary Boland, ain't it?"

I turn to face him. He stands close, too close. The scar seems a deeper shade of purple than I remember. "Mr. McGraw."

"I saw you come in."

"I see."

"Rumor has it that someone in me employ has been dippin' in yer honey pot."

Words won't come. Does he mean what I think? Finally, I stammer, "I have no idea what you mean, Mr. McGraw, but I don't like your tone."

His smirk enrages me. "Playin' the grand lady, are ya? Well, Miss Fancy Pants, tell ya what, I'll just pick you up tonight when the pub closes. We'll get to know each other better. Why dither with an underling when you can spend time with the boss?" He runs a finger up me arm.

I brush it away. "Do not touch me."

"Look, Mary, I'll get ya one way or t'other. I always do."

Fury rumbles in me gut. "Not this time, Mr. McGraw. Not ever in this lifetime. Do I make meself clear?"

He backs away, his eyes flickering like a rattlesnake. "Well then, I guess I'll have a look at someone else, someone more agreeable." He walks away.

Shuddering, I finish me perusal and go to the front desk to check out me books, after which I look around for the girls. We need to get out of here.

They're not down here yet, so I run up the stairs to the children's room.

I grab Molly by the arm. "Choose your books, Molly. We're leaving."

She is startled but picks up the three books she had placed on a table. "Where's Shannon?"

Molly looks around. "She was standing right over there," she points.

I go to the spot and then around the shelves of books. "Shannon," I say, me voice rising. People turn to glare at me noisy intrusion on their browsing, but I don't care. "Shannon," I repeat, still more loudly. She doesn't answer.

A slow dread comes over me. *Mary, you're being silly,* I tell meself. *Shiv wouldn't. She's just a child. Of course he wouldn't. Besides, if he did, Tommy'd kill him. But Shiv's men would kill Tommy first.*

I strive to think rationally. "She must be in the outhouse." Grabbing Molly by the hand, I race back down the stairs. "Stay right here," I order her, running out the back door. "Shannon," I yell. There's no answer. I knock loudly on the door of the outhouse, screaming, "Shannon." Still, no answer.

Where is she? I hurry back into the library, trying to control the pounding of me heart. The sweet librarian still stands at the front desk. "Did you see the other young girl I came in with?" I ask, clutching Molly's hand. "Eleven, but looks older. Blonde, very pretty." For a second, me own description flashes me back to Ceili.

"Why yes, dear," the librarian says. "She left here just a minute ago with Mr. McGraw. He told me they were going to get candy. The child was so excited." Her brow furrows. "She told me he had gotten permission from her guardian."

As I pull Molly toward the wagon, Daniel appears, tugging on me sleeve. "Mary, I need to tell you something."

"Later, Daniel. I can't find Shannon."

"This'll take only a minute. It's important. About your father." He turns to Molly. "Wait in the wagon."

I stop in me tracks.

"You know I've been working for Shiv McGraw?"

I nod, dumbly.

"There's a reason for that. Kam knows why, but I swore him to secrecy. I wanted to learn if Shiv had anything to do with me father's death. The best way to do that was from the inside."

Numbly, I ask, "Did he?"

"Yes, he murdered me dad."

"I'm sorry, Daniel. Really." But he mentioned Da.

"Mary." He takes me shoulders into his hands as if to steady me. "Shiv murdered your father, too."

I cannot speak. I cannot breathe. Me world grinds to a hellish halt.

"I just learned for sure this morning. There was an eyewitness."

I shake me head. *No, no, no, no.*

"Shiv thought our fathers were trouble makers. They were talking to the Irish business owners about banding together against Shiv. Shiv's gang cornered both of them one night as they came home from jobs at the iron factory. Shiv agreed to a fair fight with your father, fists only. But when he realized he was going to lose, he pulled his switchblade from his right pants pocket. That's where he always has it. Your dad wrestled it away from him. He's the one who put that scar on Shiv's face."

I gasp. Me father was never a violent man, but he was strong.

"The others pinned your father's arms, and Shiv finished him off. Slit his throat. Me dad jumped in and tried to help. That's when Shiv got him."

"Are you certain, Daniel? Absolutely certain?"

"Beyond any doubt. Me witness saw the whole thing. I couldn't tell you until I knew for sure."

Tears blur me vision, and then I remember Shannon. There's no time for tears now. I run to the wagon, Daniel's voice calling after me. "Mary, Mary, let me help you."

No one can help me. This is something I will do alone. Daniel stands behind me staring helplessly as I bring the whip down on the horse's back.

CHAPTER FIFTY-TWO

A race against the devil . . .

I race like a madwoman around the streets of Boston looking for Shiv's rig. The galloping horse is pulling as fast as it can, but me whip spurs him on to greater speed. People crowd the streets doing last-minute Thanksgiving shopping, and I almost run them over. They raise their fists and scream at me, but I don't care. Me heart pounds to the beat of the horse's hooves. Da is dead. All that goodness—me safety, me memories, me family—all gone now.

Slowly, me tears turn cold, running rivulets of icy rage down me face. Me da is gone. Murdered by Shiv McGraw. The tears dry in the wind and me heart hardens. This is not the time for grieving. That will come later, when I'm alone. Now, I must get to Shannon before Shiv hurts her. *Remember, oh most gracious Virgin Mary,* I repeat the Memorare over and over.

At the confectionary store, the clerk says, "Yes indeed, Mr. McGraw brought in a darling young girl just a few moments ago. She asked for marzipan, but he wanted liquorice." She shakes her head in annoyance. I control me impulse to grab her by the throat and scream. I smile instead. "We were out of liquorice up front," she continues, "so I went back to the store room to see if we had some. When I returned, they were gone. He stiffed me."

"I want marzipan, too," Molly says.

Impatiently, I toss a coin on the counter and soon Molly is lost in sugary rapture.

He must have taken her to his house. As we climb into the wagon again, I say, "Molly, would you like to go to Peggy's house?" Peggy O'Neill is her best friend from school.

"Oh yes, Mary, but what about Shannon?"

"Ah, don't you worry, love. I'll find her quick as a wink and then we'll pick you up." She settles back in her seat. I'm surprised I can fool her.

At the O'Neill's, I control me trembling and smile as I ask Peggy's mother, "Is it all right if I leave Molly here for a while?"

"Of course it is, Mary. She's no trouble at all, at all. But where's Shannon?"

Me throat tightens. "I'm going to pick her up right now. Then, we'll be back for Molly."

As I ride toward Shiv's, me sorrow and fear are eclipsed by a fiercer emotion—fury. The power of the Banshee courses through me blood, strong as it was on the ship, and I welcome it this day. It will serve me well. It's clear as Waterford what I must do, comes to me all in one piece, each detail defined and definite.

Mr. Mendel looks up. "Mary, what brings you in today?"

"I need laudanum, quite a large dosage, for a friend of Kathleen's who's having problems with her husband. I'll need a month's supply."

He gets the drug. Then I notice silk stockings, and me plan picks up yet another detail. "When did these come in?" I ask.

"Oh, I bought a few pair from a vendor yesterday. He says

they're big in Europe, and I figured some of the ladies on the hill might buy them."

"I'll take a pair."

His eyebrows rise, but he wraps me purchases.

At the hardware store next door, I buy a stiletto.

"What's a lass like you want with a weapon like this?" the man behind the counter asks. "Mad at the boyfriend?"

"No, but I need to slaughter a pig for supper."

In less than an hour, I sit in front of Shiv's house. Now, I will have revenge.

CHAPTER FIFTY-THREE

Stalk the serpent in his nest, not in your own.

I pull the wagon to a halt, then climb down out of it and run into the shadows at the side of the immense yard. Hiding behind a shrub, I remove me rough, wool stockings and attach the silk ones to me garters. Tucking the dagger in the back of me skirt, I bury the wrappings under some leaves and snap the laudanum into me purse. Removing all the pins from me hair, I run me fingers through it and bite me lips. One pinch of me cheeks, and I'm ready.

Returning to Shiv's front porch, I take no pains to hide meself. A different girl answers the door this time. She must have seen all kinds standing on this porch as her expression registers no surprise. "Yes, miss?"

"I want to see Mr. McGraw."

"Who may I tell him is calling?"

"Mary Boland."

As I await her return, I feel no fear. Me resolve calms me senses, and I am certain of what must be done this day. What happened to Ceili will not happen to Shannon. A red curtain has descended over me brain, heavy and still. I welcome the return of the Banshee.

"Come in, Miss Boland," the girl says. "Mr. McGraw is in the drawing room."

She leads me through the gaudy foyer and down a hall to the closed door. She opens it, curtsies, and walks away.

Shiv stands, his smile beaming yellow and sinister as I walk in. "Mary, what a surprise to see you!"

Surprise, me ass. Forgive me, God. The bastard knew I'd come. He has Shannon.

I force a smile. "I've come to take Shannon back to Kathleen and Tommy. We're late." Me voice is even.

"I don't know what you mean." His eyebrows raise in mock confusion.

"Quit faffing with me. She's here, and we both know it."

He sits down and gestures me to a chair opposite him. "And if she is?"

"I'll stand." I hold me breath. "Has she been harmed?"

"Oh no, not a bit. She's with Agnes. They seem to know each other well."

I nod. "Let me see her."

"Ah no, I don't think so, Mary." He crosses his ankle over his calf, cocking his legs obscenely apart. "Like I told you, you're the one I want. But you playact like you're the Virgin Mary or somethin.'" He laughs. "Agnes tells me different."

I grit me teeth until they hurt. Shiv's venomous eyes glitter just as Seamus's did. I force me jaw to relax. "So, Shiv—what you're saying is that you'll release Shannon if I give you what you want?"

He smiles. "Smart lass."

Me mouth is bitter with bile. "How do I know you'll keep your word?"

He slaps his thigh. "Ha." His smile is slow and malevolent. "I don't think you have any other choice, Mary."

I study his hideous face. He lights a black cheroot and watches as the smoke drifts in a lazy swirl toward the ceiling.

"Very well," I say.

His face is the grinning mask of Satan himself.

"But I have terms." I lean toward him.

He raises his eyebrows. "A good whore always does."

Though the word makes me flinch, me resolve remains hard as steel. "You will dismiss all your servants from this house. That includes your bodyguards."

He shakes his head. "Oh now, Mary. You ask too much."

I lower me lashes and shrug me shoulders. "It'll be worth it, Shiv." From some place deep in me soul, I pull upon an instinct I never knew existed. I lift me skirts to me knees and run me hand down one leg. The silk of the stocking whispers softly as the stiletto presses into me buttocks. Slowly, I wet me lips with the tip of me tongue.

His eyes dart to me mouth. "And if I refuse your terms?"

"Then I'll walk out your front door, and you can have your way with a child. I promise you, though, she won't compare to me."

The glittering eyes flicker. The scar turns to a darker purple.

I slide down me skirt and get to me feet, then cross to him and bend down. Slowly, I trace the line of the scar with one finger as me other hand rests on his thigh.

His hands rise to grab me, but I jump away, waggling me forefinger at his face. "Oh no, Shiv, *me* terms, remember?"

"You bitch!"

I laugh and shrug me shoulders, never forgetting that Shannon is somewhere in this house, kidnapped by this monster who murdered me father.

"Maybe a bitch," I answer, returning to me chair, "but one worth the terms. I guess you'll just have to trust me."

He stands up. "Drink?"

"Sure."

He crosses to a liquor stand and uncorks a bottle. "This is Tullamore Dew whiskey from County Offaly. The best whiskey Ireland has ever made."

Tullamore? That's where Ceili came from. It's a sign from God that what I do is right.

He brings me a glass of the amber liquid. I sniff it and pour it down me throat, willing meself not to wince at the fiery taste. "It's good."

He looks surprised. "I like a girl what can handle her whiskey."

I run me finger around the rim of the glass. "Soon, you'll learn other things I can handle."

He stands before me. There's swelling between his legs. "Let's go upstairs *now*." Hunger invades his eyes.

I lift me skirts again and cross me legs. "Ah no, Shiv. Me terms have not been met."

I watch as a war rages in him. His body shows how much he wants me, but his mind clearly fears giving up his protection. "No, Mary, I canna do it."

"Very well, Mr. McGraw." I lower and smooth down me skirts. "I need complete privacy. If you won't grant that, I'll be on me way."

As I open the door to the drawing room, he calls out. "All right, you little witch. I think you've cast a spell on me or something. I'll tell them to leave."

Turning back from the door, I lift me chin. "Good. Don't worry, Shiv. It'll be worth your while."

When he leaves the room, I pour the laudanum into his whiskey glass and stir it with me finger. Licking me finger, I pray he'll never know the difference.

Let me prayer reach God's ears.

Chapter Fifty-Four

Better act the harlot than be one.

After mere minutes, he comes back into the room and drains his glass. He doesn't notice a thing and puts the empty glass on the side table.

Thank you, God.

As we go up the stairs, he grabs at me, but I push his hands away, taunting him with promises of things to come. I remember all that Agnes said about men and pray the strangest prayer I've ever prayed. *Please God, teach me the ways of seduction.* "Did you clear the house?" I ask.

"Yes, for God's sake. Yes." As he turns to open his bedroom door, I see Agnes stick her head out from a room down the hall. Her nod tells me that Shannon is in the room with her. The door whispers shut.

Shiv's bedroom is even more garish than the rest of his house. Everything in it is red and the ceiling has a mirror centered over the large bed, something I've never seen before, even in magazines. The spread on his bed is deeply scrawled and ornate, and paintings of nude women cover the walls. If me mission was less important, I might laugh at the silliness of the place. But silliness won't save Shannon. Only one person will leave this room alive.

He closes the door and advances toward me. He grabs me round the waist and tries to put wet lips on mine. I turn me head away. "Silly boy. I'll tell you when I want to be kissed."

He stands in the middle of the room, confusion and desire mixed in equal parts on his pale face.

"So, is everyone gone from the house?" I ask. "Yes, yes, for God's sake, girl. The only ones left here are Agnes and the kid."

"Good. Now, I want to look at you. Take off all your clothes and lie on the bed."

"For God's sake, Mary!" The scar pulsates. Is it anger or desire? That does not matter.

"Do it. It'll be worth your while if you follow me rules. With all the whores you've had, I guarantee no one has given you what you're going to get from me."

He begins to remove his shirt, pulling it up and off his body. His body is covered with a patchy blanket of black hair. I notice cigarette burns on his neck that look very old. For a moment, I feel pity for him, but bury that feeling quickly. He is larger than he seems in his black clothes—muscular and brawny. He stands before me, his arms reaching out to me.

I point to his pants.

He unbuckles the buckle on his belt and undoes his buttons. His pants drop to the ground. I hear the muffled metallic sound of a switchblade as it hits the floor. *The weapon that killed me da.*

This is the first time I've seen an adult man standing before me naked. In the sailors' cabin, me eyes were clamped shut. His purple member throbs between his legs. It strikes me how vulnerable he looks, his face fairly drooling with lust. *What a fool!*

"Now lie down," I order.

"Take off your clothes, too, Mary."

I slip out of me shoes. "Soon. First, lie down on your back."

"What'll you do to me?"

"Don't worry, Shiv. You'll like it." *At first.*

To me surprise, he follows me instructions. *Thank you, God.*

I stand up on the bed, me legs straddling his hips. He grabs for me. I smack his hands back. "Naughty boy. You'll not hurry this."

"Take off your clothes, Mary," he begs.

"I told you—soon."

His eyes begin to glimmer with suspicion. He must be distracted quickly. I begin to unbutton me blouse slowly. He reaches with long fingers, trying to touch me. Again, I slap his hands away from me. "I'll do it." When the blouse is open, I release it. A sheer camisole covers me breasts. His eyes bug out as he rises up, trying to grab at them. I laugh and jump away.

"Mary, for God's sake, you're driving me daft."

I tower above him. Slowly, I roll the silk stocking down me left leg and off me foot. If I didn't despise this man so much, I'd find him funny.

Next, I reach to me right side and hitch the skirt up to get the stocking. I slowly roll it down.

He tries to pull me down onto him, and I panic for a moment, fearful he'll feel the knife at me waist, but I jump away just in time.

"No, Shiv. First, I intend to pleasure you a bit. Put your arms up."

His pupils are growing large. The laudanum is taking effect. He obeys me order, and I tie his hands together with one of the stockings. He tries to reach for me again.

"Naughty, naughty. I told you—me way." I run the other stocking over his face, trying not to gag. I remember Shannon.

"Mary, please, please. I can't stand no more of this."

Lowering meself above his face, I reach behind me and pull the dagger from the waist of me skirt. Swiftly, I lift it over me head. Shiv is so dazed he hardly notices. But then, I see a moment of clarity in those black, black eyes.

When I bring the knife down onto his chest, he kicks. I am thrown off the bed. The stiletto only grazes his left side. I spring back up at him, ready to strike again.

A hand grabs me wrist. Frantic, I look back and see Daniel. He covers me hand holding the dagger.

Shiv's eyes glitter with fear. He gasps as Daniel's huge arm and me smaller one rise above him. The shining dagger hangs there for a long moment before we plunge it down into Shiv's hairy chest just beside his left nipple.

"Ah, God," Shiv moans.

"This is for Sean Boland," I growl. "Go to fuckin' hell where you belong."

"And for John Kelly," Daniel whispers. Then, he takes a pillow and presses it onto Shiv's face. Shiv's legs flail around the bed, trying to knock us away from him, but we both hold him firm. Finally, after what seems an eternity, he is still. Daniel lifts the pillow and closes the mad eyes.

"How'd you know I'd be here?" I gasp.

"Shut up, Mary. You haven't been out of me sight for a minute."

Daniel climbs off the bed and stands staring at me. "I must say, your act was mighty convincing." He looks down at me camisole and grins. "Now cover yourself."

Buttoning me blouse, I run to the room where I'd seen Agnes and throw open the door. Shannon is sitting on a bed as Agnes braids her long hair. "Mary," she cries, "what're you doing here?"

"Are you all right?" I pant.

"Of course I am. Mr. McGraw bought me candy and then invited me here to see Agnes again. I'm sorry I didn't tell you at the library, but I was afraid you'd say no."

I'm so relieved to see Shannon unharmed I don't scold her. I'll leave that for her mother.

Agnes cocks her head and raises her left eyebrow. "Is it done?" I nod.

"Good."

"Good?"

"Yeah, the bastard was trying to kick me out. I figured you'd finish him off—Banshee girl that you are. A client is setting me and the downstairs maid up in a house at the bottom of Beacon Hill. I'll be the Madam and split me profits with the old buzzard who's fronting me. 'Tis easy street I'll be living on from now on."

"So I've done you a favor?"

"Aye."

"Fine. Now you will return one to me."

CHAPTER FIFTY-FIVE

Revenge is sweet, escape is bliss.

I pull Shannon from Agnes's room but stop dead when I see rat face, the bodyguard, at the end of the hall. His back is turned to me. I push Shannon back into the room and close the door. "Shiv lied," I say to Agnes. "He told me he'd dismissed the bodyguards."

"And you believed him?" Agnes laughs. "Mary, you're such a naff. The house is probably crawling with them. Shiv never spoke a word of truth in his entire life."

"I've got to get her out of here," I try to think in spite of a panic that grows so quick it nearly blocks out me reason. Finally, I gain control. "Agnes, you must distract him."

Agnes grins and turns the doorknob. "Easy as pie." I watch her through a crack in the door as she strolls up to him. "Hi Charlie, how're keepin'?" She puts her hands on his shoulders and turns his back to me, then faces him, taunting him with her eyes. When she begins to rub herself against him, I hurry Shannon down the stairs and out of the house.

"You stay in this wagon, girl," I say with a swat to her backside as she climbs in. "Disobey me this time, and I'll blister your bottom." Me voice shakes with relief and delayed anger.

She crosses her heart and kisses her finger.

I leave her there and walk back in the front door. As I go back up the stairs, me brain works feverishly on a plan of escape. I vow this will be me last criminal act on earth. I've not the constitution for being a murderess. Though I must say I seem to do a pretty good job of it, when it is warranted.

On the landing, I find Agnes. She smiles and follows me. "I've taken care of Charlie," she says in a voice so dirty I nearly laugh.

But when I walk back into Shiv's room and see him lying there, naked except for the pillow on his face, me stomach threatens to empty itself onto the red carpet. The stiletto still protrudes from the hairy chest, sure proof that I indeed have killed and, remembering Seamus, that this is not the first time. Shaking off me guilt, I walk over to him and pull the knife out, then wiping the blood off on the bedspread, throw it on the sheet. It appears me constitution is cooler than I'd imagined.

Agnes stands with Daniel next to the bed. "All right," I say. "I'm going to pick up Molly and take her and Shannon home to Kathleen. While I do that, you two need to clean this up."

"Clean what up?" Agnes asks.

"Agnes, there's a dead man lying there, in case you hadn't noticed. He needs to be disposed of. Daniel can do that." I look at him, a question in me eyes.

He nods. "'Tis a big ocean."

I turn back to Agnes. "You must distract anyone Daniel encounters and cover for us with anyone left in the house."

"No problem," she answers. I can tell she's exhilarated by this criminal game.

"Agnes," Daniel says, his voice calm as a windless lake. "Where's Shiv's rig?"

She answers quickly. "Out back."

"And the horses?"

"Tied up back there, too."

"Good," he says. "It's only an hour 'til dark, and then I'll bundle him up in the bloody bedclothes and haul him to the wagon." He rubs his chin. "I'll be sure the knife goes with him," he says to me, then turns back to Agnes. "Do you know where they keep the sheets and spreads?"

"Yes, in the linen closet."

"Good. While I carry him out, you'll remake his bed."

She frowns. "Naahh, I'm not a maid after all."

This makes me so angry I want to slap her silly face. "Damn it, Agnes, you have to do it."

Her face drags down into a sullen frown. She nods. I think she's scared I'll really hit her.

Daniel turns to me. "It's lucky there's not too much blood."

"It's not luck. That's why I bought a stiletto. I read about them. The Italians use them because the victim doesn't bleed as much as with other daggers."

His mouth falls open. "Mary, you're a wonder, you are. I never want to cross you."

I smile for the first time. "Wise man." Sometimes, I wonder if maybe me da was right with his Celtic goddess and Banshee talk. This day, I frighten meself. How did I know with such certainty what had to happen to Shiv and how to do it? Every step was planned. I don't know if this monstrous ability came to me from heaven or hell, but I'm grateful for it. Shannon is safe.

We race toward the O'Neill's house at such a speed the horse is lathered when we arrive. Molly comes running as soon as she sees us pull up. "Where did you go, Shannon?"

Shannon gives me a sideways glance but doesn't answer her sister. She knows there'll be punishment. That'll be up to her parents when I tell them, and I surely will do that as soon as we're safe in the pub.

* * *

"You went to Shiv McGraw's house?" Kathleen screams at Shannon. "How many times have I told you never to go off with a stranger?"

"But he's not a stranger, Mam," Shannon answers. "I see him here regular."

Kathleen grabs her by the shoulders and gives her a good shake. "That's blather, and you know it. Go to your room. And don't let me see your face until tomorrow. There'll be no dinner for you tonight."

When the girls are upstairs, Kathleen turns to me and whispers. "Mary, how'd you get her out of there?"

Tommy has joined us in the kitchen. Seeing him leave his crowded bar on a Saturday shows me how worried he's been. "First of all, me da is gone. Shiv murdered him and Daniel's father the same night. Daniel told me at the library." Kathleen holds me long and close as I sob out the words.

Finally, I compose meself. "And I did a mortally dreadful thing," I begin me story. After the whole tale is out, Tommy sits before me, his jaw hanging open.

"Close yer mouth, Tommy," Kathleen orders. "You'll be catching flies if you're not careful."

"So, Shiv's dead?" Tommy says.

I nod. "As a doornail, and Daniel is slipping his body and the bloody bedclothes into the sea as we speak while Agnes cleans up the mess."

"Agnes is cleaning?" Kathleen says.

Again, I nod. "She protested, of course, but she knew I'd smack the face off her if she didn't help us."

Kathleen's eyes are wide with disbelief. "So, Mary, what you're telling us is that you seduced Shiv McGraw out of his clothes?"

"I had to. If he'd had that switchblade in his pocket, I'd have been done for."

"I don't know what to think," Kathleen says, shaking her head. "I want to scold you for doing a dreadful deed, but at the same time, I want to cheer. How can I want to cheer a murder?"

"I know," I answer her. "I feel exactly the same way, Kathleen. Mainly, though, I want to get to confession."

CHAPTER FIFTY-SIX

The sins of the father, the sins of the daughter.

"Bless me, Father, for I have sinned. It's been one week since me last confession."

"Go on, Mary," Father Ruzzo says from behind the sliding screen. There is no reason to pretend he doesn't know it's me. I'd pounded on the door of the rectory and demanded he open the confessional to me.

"Father, I committed a mortal sin this day."

I hear him rustle. He's sitting up straight. I can see his ear pressed to the sheer partition. "What was it?"

"I murdered Shiv McGraw in his bed today."

He gasps. The little curtain on the screen blows in at him. "Oh, dear God, I read about it in the Globe. They're still looking for the murderer, but not very hard I must say. Even the police hated the man."

"I had to, Father. I know the secret you kept; that he'd murdered me father. Today, he captured Shannon O'Halloran and hid her in his house. He told me he took her because I wouldn't, uh, service him."

He clears his throat. A slight scent of tomato sauce and garlic wafts through the screen. Me stomach growls in hunger. The confessional is dark and comforting, though the little wooden plank is hard under me knees. Finally, he speaks. "How did you murder him? He's never without that switchblade in his pocket."

I hesitate, but know I cannot hold back if I am to gain absolution. "First, I drugged him and teased him out of his clothes. I heard the switchblade clunk when his pants hit the floor."

There is a long silence. I think he's beginning to understand. "And then?" he says.

"I took off me blouse and silk stockings I'd bought."

Another gasp. "Silk stockings?"

"Yes, Father. I bought them at Mendel's. Oh, but I left on me camisole, Father," as though that covered much. I listen close to the screen, but hear no sound. "Once the laudanum started to work, I took the stiletto from me skirt band."

"Stiletto?"

"Yes, Father. It's less bloody than other daggers."

I see his head nod through the sheer partition. "And did you kill him then?"

"I tried, but he kicked me to the floor. Daniel Kelly grabbed the knife from me . . ."

"Daniel?"

"Yes, Father. He was hiding behind the door. He helped me finish the job."

"So I'll be seeing Daniel in the confessional next?"

"Yes, Father. I'm certain you will." And then I remember. "Father, another sin." I whisper, "I said the bad word—f-u-c-k."

Do I hear a chuckle?

"Are you sorry for this sin, Mary?" he says.

I don't answer. I can't lie in the confessional, and to be honest, I'm not one whit sorry.

"Do you promise never to kill again?"

Whew, he let me off the hook. "Oh yes, Father. I surely do promise that."

"Then make your Act of Contrition, girl," he says.

"Oh, me God, I am heartily sorry for having offended you," I begin.

I hear snatches of Latin words from behind the screen.

"*Ego te absolvo a peccatis tuis in nomine Patris, et Filii, et Spiritus Sancti. Amen.*"

As I rise to leave, Father Ruzzo tells me to kneel down. "Mary, you have great power in you. I've known that from the first time I met you. You've used that power in an evil way today, though you thought it was for a good cause."

Again, that word 'power.' What is he talking about?

He continues, "For your penance, I command you to use the gifts of strength God has given you for the good of others. Do you accept this penance?"

"Yes, Father. I do."

"Your sins are absolved." The screen slides shut.

CHAPTER FIFTY-SEVEN

God broke our heart to prove to us He only takes the best.

I finally break down that night with Kathleen. "I'm alone, Kathleen. An orphan. I have no family at all." I sob into her soft shoulder that night on me couch. She holds me tight and long.

"You'll never be alone, Mary, not as long as I draw breath. You are me child as much as Shannon and Molly are. You're me girl and always will be." And I realize her words are true. I guess sometimes God decides our family for us, and this wonderful woman is as much a mother to me as Mam was. I love her.

After she goes upstairs, I mull over Father's words long into the night. He said I'm strong, that I have a power that should be used for good. Others have said I'm strong, too. Mam called me laidir. She was right. A weak girl would not have survived the crossing from Ireland. Yes, I decide, I am a strong girl—woman—now, and I will use me strength for the good of mothers, as a midwife. I will not marry until I reach me goal.

It seemed had just fallen when a scream pierces the air. At first, I think I fell asleep and the scream is from one of me nightmares, but I'm wide awake when the second scream comes. It sounds so desperate it's enough to curdle me blood. At first, I can't figure where the screams are coming from. Then, I know. It's Kathleen, and it's the scream of labor. The clock chimes five.

Fear rips into me heart like scratching rat feet. She wasn't due until nearly Christmas, and Dr. Burroughs is in New Hampshire. When he told me his mother had passed unexpectedly, I didn't worry. I was certain Kathleen would go to term.

Tommy races down the steps. His face is ashen. "Mary, it's bad. Worse than with the girls. I can't help her. She won't go to the Lying-in Hospital. Says there's too much childbed fever there."

It's true. It's been like a plague lately. No one can figure out why. I remember Mr. Mendel's words about the doctors and their instruments. Maybe there's something we don't understand about sanitation of instruments.

"Should I fetch Dr. Burroughs to help you?" Tommy asks, putting on his jacket.

"He's away, Tommy. His mother died."

He stops in his tracks. I can see he's trying to get himself under control. "Is there anyone else can help you?"

"None of the other doctors in town will come to the South side. They've been stiffed too often." I force an air of confidence. "Don't worry, Tommy. I can handle this." *Please God, let that be true.*

I grab me shawl and wrap it over me nightgown. "When did the pain start?"

"Two hours ago. With the girls, things was different. Kathleen rode the pain like a champ, but not now. She's out of her head with it." He hesitates. "She didn't want me to bother you when her water broke last night."

"When did that happen?"

"Around midnight."

Five hours ago? I stuff down the fear rising in me throat. *A dry birth.* "She'll be all right, Tommy. I'll take care of her. You go on to Mr. Mendel's. He lives above the apothecary. He won't mind being wakened. Get me ether. I'm out of it."

Tommy nods, throws on his jacket and runs outside.

In their bedroom, I am overwhelmed by a fetid stink. Kathleen thrashes from side to side and her bed is covered in sweat. But this smell is more than perspiration. Has an infection started? I fall to me knees and pull a brimming chamber pot from under the bed. Shannon and Molly are in the room, all scared eyes and pinched mouths. They'd heard the scream, too.

"Where's me dad?" Shannon says.

"Mendel's, to get some ether."

"Will she be all right?" Molly asks.

"Yes, sure," I answer quickly. "One of you empty this pot!"

Shannon plugs her nose and backs away. "Ewww."

Molly pushes past her sister, hissing, "You're such a ninny, Shannon. Give it to me, Mary. I'll do it." Gingerly, she carries the pot out the door. I hear her footsteps go out the back door.

"Wash it out before you bring it back, Molly!" I yell.

The kerosene lamp burning on the table beside the bed also has a noxious smell to it. I light a candle beside the bed and say, "Shannon, take this lamp to the kitchen and bring me all the candles you can find. Make sure the lamp is turned off. Oh, and bring clean, cold water."

I turn me attention to the writhing creature on the bed. She looks nothing like Kathleen. Her face is crimson and she stares at me like I'm a ferocious eneme, not her best friend. Her mouth opens and closes, gulping for breath like a beached cod. The sight frightens me. In Ireland or in Boston, I've not seen a laboring woman in such distress.

When Shannon returns, I try to give Kathleen some of the water, but she flails and knocks them from me hand. Shannon begins to cry.

"She doesn't know what she's doing, Shannon. Clean the ice off the floor."

"It's starting again," Kathleen screams and convulses in a spasm that arches her back high off the bed. Her heels dig deep into the mattress. She screams until there's no breath left in her and then collapses onto her back.

"Shannon," I order, snapping the stunned girl to attention. "When your dad returns, bring me the ether. Along with clean cloths from me bag." I point to me black midwife's bag.

She nods, her eyes huge with terror. "Is she going to be all right, Mary? That time I went with you for Joan McBride's birthing, it wasn't like this."

"Yes, she'll be fine. What she doesn't need is to see you looking scared." I try to shoo her out of the room, but she stands like a statue, staring at her mother.

Molly comes back and places the clean chamber pot under the bed. Then, she grabs her sister by the arm. "Come on, Shannon. Let's go downstairs and wait for Dad."

"While you're down there, set the kettle to boiling. We'll need it for rags and me instruments."

Molly nods and I give her a look of gratitude. She's the one I can depend on—the solid-as-a-rock replica of her mother.

"Kathleen, love," I say, returning to the bedside. "Can you get up and walk with me a bit? I'll support you."

She turns her tear-stained face to me. "I can't walk."

"Yes, you can. Come on now. It'll help you."

Finally, she says, "I'll try."

But when she tries to get to her feet, the pain hits again and knocks her back onto the bed. Her screams are so severe they could tear the roof off the house.

Shannon peeks her head around the door jam again. "Mary, here's the ether." She sets it on the bedside table. "What's wrong with her?" Her eyes bulge with panic.

"Shannon, downstairs! There's nothing you can do here but get in the way." I don't want the poor thing anymore frightened than she already is, and this labor is a bad one. As she goes downstairs. The clock strikes eight.

"Kathleen, I need to examine you. Lie back, please." A quick probe shows that she is not progressing as she should. Her cervix is not dilating.

Her wild eyes stare up at me as she grabs onto me sleeve. "Something's wrong, isn't it, Mary?"

"No, of course not, Kathleen. This baby is a big one, though. Bet it's a boy."

She smiles for only a second and then is again engulfed in the agony of a contraction. I slip me fingers back inside her and shudder to realize that nothing is changing.

Sweat soaks the sheets, and her eyes dart around the room like she's looking for anyone, anything to stop the pain. "Help me. Please, help."

"I'm right here. You're doing fine. It'll be over soon." This is a lie, and I know it. It's time to use the ether. I pour a big amount of it onto the cloth and give Kathleen a moment of respite. She falls into a tortured sleep, waking when the pain attacks her body once again.

Nothing changes all morning, and afternoon brings little progress. On and on we go, me trying to encourage and Kathleen who remains convulsed in agony. When Tommy or the girls come into the room, I put on a calm face and reassure them. Then, I ask them to leave—except Molly.

At three o'clock, an examination of her belly confirms a fear that has nagged me for hours. I feel a hard, round mass up near her ribcage. The baby is breech. "Molly," I yell for the girl dozing at the bottom of her mother's bed, "I need your help."

Instantly, she is beside me. "What can I do?"

"The baby is upside down; it's called breech." I've done one such birth before, but Dr. Burroughs was with me. "I need to try and turn it. I want you to get down near your mam's stomach and help me."

She moves instantly, awaiting me instructions.

"First, I'm going to give your Mam some more ether. Then, I'll try to navigate the baby's head in a clockwise position to point down. You find what feels like feet and try to push them around and upward. We must be gentle and yet, push strongly together. Do you understand?"

She nods.

I give Kathleen another whiff of ether and look at Molly. "Now." I stand above Kathleen's face and find what feels to be a small round head. I grip me hands around it. "Turn," I say to Molly.

Like a woman twice her age, the girl follows me movements in the opposite direction. Kathleen moans, but Molly never takes her eyes off me hands, then exactly coordinates her fingers with them. We struggle together for over an hour until finally, a quick vaginal examination reveals the head is down.

"We did it, Molly! We did it!"

Were there time, we'd have hugged each other, but Molly quickly runs to get the wet cloths cooling on the window sill outside and starts to wash her mother's face. "Mam, you did so good. The baby's head is down now."

Kathleen smiles and raises her hand to Molly's face just before another contraction assails her.

By six o'clock, her cervix has fully dilated. "Kathleen, put your legs up and push," I say. "Molly, stay near her face, talk to her and keep her focused on pushing."

The girl again follows me instructions, and Kathleen tries with all her might to push the baby from her body, but she's exhausted and, though some progress is made, it's not enough.

"Molly," I say, trying to keep the panic from me voice. "Get the scalpel from me bag. Take it to the kitchen. Hold it by the handle with a hot pad and tongs. Lower it into the boiling water for several minutes. Be careful now. Don't burn yourself. Don't touch the blade. Bring it to me when you're done."

She nods and runs down the stairs. In minutes, she's back, holding the scalpel tight in the tongs. I take it and cut a small incision in Kathleen's perineum, a practice I avoid unless there is nothing else to be done. "Oh Mary, doesn't that hurt her terribly?" Molly says, her voice taut and trembling.

"She's past feeling anything there. This might help get it out of her."

But it doesn't help. Nothing helps.

When I put the stethoscope on Kathleen's chest, Molly says, "That looks like an ear trumpet."

What I hear terrifies me. Kathleen's heartbeat is irregular—sometimes rapid and other times, nonexistent. I must get this baby delivered.

"Kathleen, remember the breathing we practiced?" I say to her. "Tuck your chin now. Molly's got your legs. Now push."

And push she does, with all the might of her weakened body, but the baby won't come down.

She is so tired now. She closes her eyes and grips me hand. She looks at me with wild eyes as her hand leaves mine and flies up to clutch at her chest. Her mouth opens in a dreadful gasp and then, with a look of fearful panic, her eyes blur. I watch helplessly as life runs out of her.

"Open your eyes," I scream, pumping at her chest with me hands and putting me ear to her heart, willing it to beat. I take her wrist in me hand and search for a pulse. There is none. I pound at her chest again and check her pulse. There's no beating.

I make the decision.

"Mary, what's wrong?" Molly whispers, her face grey as ashes.

I grab the scalpel.

"What are you doing?" Molly screams.

"It's too late for your mother," I sigh, tears running down me cheeks and onto Kathleen. "We must try to save this baby now."

Molly collapses and begins kissing Kathleen's lifeless face.

Pausing for only a second, I stand above me dearest friend with the scalpel clenched in me fingers. I check her pulse one last time and find no beating.

I poke the scalpel into the flesh of her upper arm and get no response of pain. I cannot wait. Poising the blade over her swollen belly, I start to cut downward carefully. Tears flood me eyes, but I shake them away. I cannot allow me vision to be dulled.

Molly moans me name. I have no time to pay her mind.

When I have cut through all her flesh and muscle, the womb throbs before me. Gently, I make the cut. Blood and fluid rush out, and I see the baby inside. Quickly, I lift it out and wipe the fluid from its face. It is a boy. I hold him up by his feet, praying, and give him a giant wallop on his buttocks. He screams in outrage. Lying him back on the bed, I grab the twine and tie and cut the cord that attaches him to Kathleen, then knot it off at his navel. Molly doesn't move. The look of shock never leaves her face.

"Clean the boy up, Molly," I hand the infant to his sister and wrap the afterbirth in a sheet. Then, I carry it far from the house, crying from grief and defeat as I leave it for the pigs. Back upstairs, I gather up all the bloodied sheets and towels and take them to the wash tub. Before I leave the room, I kiss Kathleen and cover her with a clean blanket.

When it's done, I try to comfort Tommy and the girls as best I can with words, tea and hugging. Daniel comes in, his eyes swollen and red. Me own grief threatens to overwhelm me, but I cannot allow that until I am alone. Kathleen Halloran, me dearest friend, me second mother, is dead—her great heart stopped.

CHAPTER FIFTY-EIGHT

Do not stand by me grave and weep. I am not there.
I do not sleep.

Four days later, we bury her. We reached Kam, and he made it back for the funeral. The earth is not yet frozen, an ironic largess from a God I distrust. Kathleen's daughters sob as they each throw a handful of dirt onto the casket. Tommy seems numb, as if he's hostage to another place and time. His eyes are vacant and his mouth hangs slack. Kam cradles baby Sean in his arms, a child who will never know he has lost the sweetest mother in the world. And so have I, again.

Jim Burroughs, returned from New Hampshire, says he could have done no more than I did, but I'll never know. All that's sure is that Kathleen trusted me with her life, and I failed her.

A lovely colored woman arrives at the pub the next day. "I was here for the party for Kamua Okafor. Miss Kathleen was so kind to me. Word reached Joy Street about what happened here last night. You'll need milk for that baby, and I'm a wet nurse. How can I help?"

Her name is Miata, and she is a gift from heaven during this hellish time. She drapes the windows with black mourning cloth and takes over all the cooking for the family. She moves into my old room in the basement. "I'll stay as long as you need me," she says.

Miata is with us at the cemetery when we bury Kathleen. After the earth forms a perfect round mound atop Kathleen's casket, I turn to Father Ruzzo and ask him to walk with me from the grave. Clouds hide the sun, and tree branches stripped of their leaves are covered with crows, their beady eyes hungry and alert.

Father looks as thin as the branches, like a skeleton in his black robe, its white collar sticking away from his skinny neck. Though I saw him not long ago, I hadn't noticed how old he's grown. His hair is now thin and gray. A wisp of it blows back and forth like corn silk across his shiny head.

When we are a sufficient distance from the mourners, I sit on a tree stump and look up at him. "Why did you forbid Kathleen to prevent pregnancy? She was too old." Me voice is angry, but does not convey anything close to the fury I feel.

His head bows. "It was God's will, Mary. Some things are beyond the scope of human understanding. God simply decided to call Kathleen home."

"It was *not* God's will, Father," I say, me tone growing shriller as a torrent of rage rises in me. "It was because you told her she couldn't protect herself. If anyone is to blame this day, it's the Church."

His face crumples, and he shakes his head sadly. "There are rules, Mary. I have vowed to keep them. We must not take God's will into our hands."

He turns to walk away. "God wouldn't make such rules, Father. Men in Rome make them." I scream after him. "And they're about control, not compassion." I stand and shake me fist at his retreating back. "I vow in the name of Kathleen O'Halloran that I will protect women from your rules."

And then, as if he could read me mind, Kam is there. Just before I fall to the earth, he takes me quaking body into his arms and holds on firm.

Later, as Kam and I sit at the waterfront, our hearts numb and broken, he asks, "Did she suffer?"

I am muted by the memory of Kathleen's agony. Me nod is sufficient.

Kam cries as he did the night he learned of his father's death. Sobs roll up from his stomach and convulse his face. He tries to gulp them back, and I wrap me arms around his neck and hold on for dear life. He grabs onto me as if he's drowning.

After a time, Kam pulls himself loose. He again looks the quiet warrior, planning his next move. "We must do something to remember her."

I mumble in confusion. "Tommy's ordered a gravestone."

"No, something living. Something as big as Kathleen's heart. What would she want?"

It comes to me formed—all in one piece. Perhaps it's been hiding in the back of me brain all week, but now I'm sure. "I know what she'd want, Kam, a safe birthing center here in Boston. She showed me pictures of one in New York run by women. She wouldn't go to the Lying-in hospital, said it was full of death. A safe, clean place for women. That's what she'd want. I know it."

He turns to me. "Yes, and it will be called Kathleen's Haven."

Kathleen's Haven? Yes. This is me destiny. I've found it. I'll build a place where women can be cared for during their pregnancies, where they can be properly monitored, where births can be clean and compassionate.

* * *

The following Sunday, as I remove the black crepe from the mirrors and windows, Daniel arrives at the pub dressed in a suit. "Aren't you going to get dressed, Mary? We'll be late."

"Daniel, I don't want to go to Mass anymore."

He looks astonished. "But you must."

"No, I must not."

"What'll happen when we have a child? Will you not have him baptized?"

Me laugh comes from a gallows. "You're assuming it would be a boy?" I doubt I can conceive a baby. Me body was damaged by the sailors. "What if God makes me barren as punishment?"

"Mary, that's crazy. God doesn't work that way."

"How do you know how God works?" I hiss angrily. "Look what He did to Kathleen. I'll *not* go to Mass."

He shakes his head and turns away. As he climbs into the wagon, he does not wave goodbye.

I take the gold cross from around me neck and place it in the top drawer of me dresser. "I'm sorry, Mam. I can't wear it anymore."

CHAPTER FIFTY-NINE

May your pockets be filled with gold.

I walk into the bank where Kam made his deposit four years earlier. Though I've not been here since then, little has changed. There are more men wearing little peaked caps, and I think they all jump in their cages when they see me. Understandable since I'm the only woman in the place. Their astonished faces amuse me. Kam offered to accompany me on this visit, but I want to do this alone.

The folder with me plan for the birthing center is clutched firm in me hand. Looking at it, I realize it's stained with perspiration. Wiping me hand against me skirt, I tuck the folder under me arm. I look for the little man who opened Kam's account, but he's not here, so I pick the youngest of the caged men. He wears the same hat and starched shirt as the others, but he is the only one who doesn't turn his eyes away when I glance at him.

The place smells like enamel paint. It's the smell of new money—different than the library—the paper and ink scents are crisper here, less warming.

When I get to the front of the line, I say, "I wish to inquire about a business loan, sir." Me voice sounds firm, but me legs are shaky as willow branches.

The man's eyebrows arch. His mustache twitches on the left side of his mouth. "What kind of business?"

"A birthing hospital—it's a business sorely needed in South Boston."

He smoothes his moustache and begins to scratch under his cap with a pencil. "Needed, perhaps, but the Boston Lying-in Hospital is failing because of lack of funding. It soon will close. Did you know that?"

"Yes sir, I know that. That's why a birthing hospital is needed. And I will make sure we are well endowed; I have connections." I bite the inside of me cheek. *And who are your great connections, Miss Boland?*

His mouth quirks up in the tiniest of grins. Good. I picked the right one. "Well, Mrs.. . . ?"

"It's Miss Boland."

"Well, Miss Boland, I'm not authorized to grant business loans. I'll have to get you a manager. Give me just a minute, please."

When he returns, he is accompanied by a man who does not wear a peaked cap. Unlike the tellers in their black vests, this man wears a suit coat. "Miss Boland," the teller says, "this is our assistant manager."

"Let's sit down here," the man says, indicating a sofa in the corner of the bank. "I understand you're interested in a business loan."

I settle meself on the sofa. "Yes, I am."

"How old are you?"

"Nearly eighteen," I lie.

He shakes his head, then continues. "What do you have for collateral?"

Kam has coached me. "I have some money saved. I'll take residence in the birthing center to save on rent."

"Cash on hand?"

"A hundred dollars or so, Mr.. . . ?"

"Winslow, James Winslow." I can tell from his expression that he is patronizing me. Kam has said what to do when that happens.

"Would testimonials from nearly one-hundred women count as collateral?"

He begins to gather up his papers, a frown pulling down the side of his mouth. This is the moment Kam told me to watch for. "Mr. Winslow, though I'm not rich in collateral, I do have a friend who banks here. He's a partner in me idea."

"Who is your friend?"

"His name is Kamua Okafor."

Everything changes. The bemused look disappears from his face, and he leans in close to me. "He's your friend?"

"More than that really; he's like a brother." I reach into me folder. "He gave me this letter expressing his willingness to be me partner in this venture."

"Excuse me, Miss Boland. I'll be back in a moment."

And he is, but this time he has with him a distinguished looking gentleman with white hair. "Mrs. Kelly, this is Jonathan Morgan. He's President of The Massachusetts Bank."

The white haired man says, "James tells me you'd like a business loan."

"Yes sir, that's why I'm here."

"And your partner would be Kamua Okafor?"

"That is correct."

"Well, Miss Boland, we can best do business in me office."

As we enter the room, I try not to gape at the beautiful woods and upholsteries that adorn it. Everything looks elegant, but understated. Nothing is garish or ostentatious. *And this man knows of Kam?*

Has me brother amassed a fortune? You'd surely think so

from the way Mr. Morgan is behaving. Kam never told me he was rich. His suits are made of cashmere, and his top hat of the finest silk, but he never talks about money.

"Is Mr. Okafor willing to co-sign for your loan?" Mr. Morgan asks.

"Yes, he is. He indicates that in this letter." I hold it out for him to study.

"Hmmm," he says, a look of satisfaction on his face. "Then, the next step is to take a look at your plan."

The papers Kam and I put together are in the folder clenched under me arm. I open it onto his desk and push it toward him. "Look these over and, if you have any questions, I'll answer them. If I can't, Kam will."

He takes glasses from his jacket pocket and positions them near the tip of his aristocratic nose. He studies the papers, never uttering a sound. He punches some numbers into a metal machine next to his desk. It's the size of a meat locker. It whirs and cranks and obviously produces a result that pleases him, for he beams at me.

"Sir, what is that machine?"

"It's the Thomas Arithmometer, the only one in this country. I just got it last week. It adds, subtracts, multiplies, and divides." He looks around his office as though a spy might have snuck in. "Miss Boland, here's a little secret between you and me. I'm not good at arithmetic." He begins to laugh. "Not a good admission for a banker, eh?"

A laugh burbles up from me belly and out of me mouth. I think I'm going to like this man. He can't cipher. "Oh, thank you for telling me that, Mr. Morgan. I'm not much good at it either."

CHAPTER SIXTY

Death leaves a heartache no one can heal. Love leaves a memory
no one can steal.

Christmas, 1852, is a somber affair. "She always loved Christmas,"
Tommy says, his eyes hollow. Miata helps Molly and Shannon
make a coconut cake, but even as I rave at its beauty, I know
we are all thinking of the woman who always baked the cakes;
always enlivened the celebration with her laughter and heart.
The mother whose memory has formed me destiny.

Daniel offers me a Claddagh ring, but I can't accept it. He
is hurt and angry, but, much as I love him, I mustn't focus me
attention on anything but Kathleen's Haven. The good news is
I believe the bank will be with me on a loan when I find the
proper location.

I scour the south side of Boston for a suitable site. It's cold and
snowy and reminds me of the many weeks I searched for work
here; the weeks before I met Kathleen.

I'll know it when I see it. Mr. Morgan will have it inspected
once I find it. It must have at least four bedrooms and a large
kitchen which I'll divide into the examination and birthing

rooms. We'll need stoves in the kitchen and upstairs to keep mothers and infants warm during the harsh New England winter. I'll train interns in midwifery. Molly wants to be the first of them. Dr. Burroughs has already agreed to be our medical consultant. I'll make sure we have more than one medical doctor to contact in case of emergency.

Daniel has joined the Boston Police Department and, though he's still peeved at me, he keeps his eye open for signs of properties. As soon as a suitable house comes onto the market, I am at its front door. But most of the homes are dark inside, and I want sunlight streaming through Kathleen's Haven. It must be a cheery place. Most of all, it has to meet the budget I've agreed upon with the bank.

On a Tuesday morning in mid January, I walk to Dorchester Street where Daniel spotted a sale sign on a brownstone the day before. The instant I see it, I know this is the one. There are three stories, and each flight has windows on every side. When I walk around to the side and peep in a downstairs window, I see a large, sunny kitchen. The yard has enough room for five wagons. I can visualize exactly where we'll hang the sign on the front porch. I'll put rockers there, too, so families can come and relax while the mothers are being examined or are in labor. If I didn't know better, I'd swear the carvings on the wooden front door are smiling at me.

The front door opens. A cheery, white-haired woman says, "Come in now, you'll catch your death." She reminds me of Kathleen. When she lets me inside, me breath stops. It couldn't be more perfect had I designed it meself. "This house is filled with so much light," I tell her.

"Yes, dear," she answers. "It's a happy house. I've reared seven children here. It's always been a home filled with sun and joy."

"Why are you selling it?"

"It's time. Me oldest daughter in Waltham wants me to come help with her little ones. I love being around children."

That night, I say to Daniel, "This is the place. I can make it work. Will you help me with the remodeling?"

"Of course," he answers. He knows how important this is to our community, so he backs me plan though he's still angry. "I'll be your construction foreman. And there's plenty of boys on the force looking for extra money. I can put together a crew from them alone." I wish Kam were here for when we begin the remodeling, but he's off in New York again.

The owner accepts me written offer of four-thousand dollars. Another six hundred will pay for furniture and equipment. All I need is the final loan approval letter from Mr. Morgan. It finally arrives in early January, and I'm overjoyed.

But two days later, another letter arrives. An official looking mailing from the bank. I tear it open on the steps of the post office. The bank has nullified its approval.

I charge into Mr. Morgan's office, waving the letter in me hand. "Why was our loan rejected? The owner has accepted our offer. What changed?"

He looks down at his fingers and begins fiddling with his Arithometer again.

"I asked why the bank changed its mind, sir."

When he raises his eyes, they are different, cold. "Miss Boland," he begins. "It has become apparent that you are not qualified for a business loan. The officers of the Boston Medical Society claim you have no credentials to run a hospital. They say you are uneducated, and that your birthing center would be a danger to the women of Boston. Are they wrong?"

Though the 'uneducated' scratches at me belly, I bully the feeling away. "Yes, they are wrong. Dead wrong." I stand over him and slam me hand on his fancy desk. "I *am* qualified. You read the letters from me patients. None of those doctors have a mortality rate low as mine. They are jealous and they are wrong."

He sputters and turns red. "The doctors are concerned in case of emergency."

"But you know a physician will always be on call for such a situation. Jim Burroughs is lining up a backup doctor in case he's away. You know all that."

Me brain whirls with frustration. The Medical Society doctors won't treat poor women. Kathleen's Haven will save lives. I'm sure of it. I shake me head as tears of anger begin to trail down me cheeks.

"Ah now, Mary," Mr. Morgan says, rising from behind his desk and coming behind me. "Don't start with the waterworks." He pats me on the shoulder. "Those doctors are some of our biggest account holders. The Board is afraid they'll take their business elsewhere."

"Let them," I scream, smacking his hand from me shoulder. "For once in your life, do the right thing. I'll run a good business. It will save lives. Please, don't do this, Mr. Morgan."

His face crumples. "I'm afraid I have no choice, Mary. The Board of Directors has voted. I can't override them."

CHAPTER SIXTY-ONE

Destiny comes hard with empty pockets.

Daniel comes to the pub that night, and me bluster has dissolved into defeat. "It's time to quit," I tell him.

"You can't quit, Mary. You're the best midwife in Boston. Every day on me beat, I hear about how wonderful you are at birthing."

I shake me head. "I can't get a loan, Daniel. How can I buy and renovate the property without one? I'll still deliver their babies at home."

"But these women need education and early examination. You owe this to Kathleen. Perhaps she could have survived had a safe birthing center existed."

I shake me head. "No one knows that for sure."

"Marry me. I'll get the loan."

At those words, me anger erupts. "I'll not marry just to get a loan. And Kathleen would have died anyway. Her heart stopped. She shouldn't have been pregnant in the first place. The rules of the Church are what killed her."

"So, your answer is to blame the Church?" He shakes his head and stares deep into me eyes. "The one to blame is Tommy!"

I dart me eyes toward the bar. Tommy's not there. Thank God. I wouldn't want him to hear such words.

"The Church makes mistakes," Daniel murmurs in a softer voice, "but it does good as well. More people in Ireland would've starved had it not been for the church. It's a couples' obligation to use common sense in these matters. The Church takes hundreds of years to make changes. But St. Augustine's is a good community. And it's our community. I want you back there."

"When hell freezes over," I hiss.

He storms out the door. As soon as he's gone, though, I begin to think about what he said. Is he right? I knew Kathleen should have been more careful. I explained to her what I knew about protection, but she blindly followed ancient rules made by men. She who so believed in the strength of women. So strange.

But I do miss St. Augustine's. Me soul yearns for Communion. Is Daniel right? Have I been wrong to blame Father Ruzzo and the Church for Kathleen's death? She and Tommy chose to take a chance. It was her decision, and considering little Sean, she might make the same decision again.

But I do not want other Catholic women making decisions blindly. They need at least to be educated about their risks.

I decide to pay Father Ruzzo a visit the next afternoon.

The two of us sit in the tiny rectory living room. I pour us both a cup of tea. "I've missed you, Mary," he says, brushing the sparse hairs over his shiny head.

"I've missed you, too, Father, and the church." I say, taking a sip. "You've said I have a great destiny. I believe me work of midwifery must include advising women against dangerous pregnancies. Please tell me how I can reconcile such a belief with the Church?"

He scratches his head. "The church's rule against birth control is a man-made rule, Mary. Jesus never said anything about it. I find meself questioning the dictates of Rome sometimes." He inclines his head downward and wipes his eyes with a handkerchief. "Did you know I buried Mrs. O'Brien yesterday?"

"Martha O'Brien?"

"Yes."

When I learned Martha was expecting her ninth child, I worried about her. But her husband insisted she be taken to a doctor up on Beacon Hill, though he could ill afford the cost. Dr. Burroughs told me her physician was a hack and a lush. He used those very words. Said that all the degrees after his name didn't make him a good doctor when the whiskey took him over."

Father Ruzzo continues. "So now, here's Jack O'Brien left with nine children." He puts his head into his hands. "God doesn't want such things, and I know it. Sometimes lately," he lifts tormented eyes, "I wonder if I should remain a priest."

I lean across the desk and take his quivering hand. "Hush now, Father. You're a grand priest. You do so much good for the people here. You mustn't abandon your vocation."

His eyes are gentle as he grasps me hand. "And neither must you."

I leave his rectory and go to Kathleen's grave. Tears streaming down me face, I talk to the mound of dirt with the tiny tombstone at its head. "Ah, Kathleen, if only you were here to tell me what to do. I want to create a birthing house, but have lost the will to fight. Help me."

I feel a hand on me shoulder and look up into Molly's eyes; the image of her mam's. "Mary, stop crying. That's not going to get me mother's haven built. Get to it. It might help if you pray, so get yourself back to church." She's so like Kathleen, bossy and determined. That makes me laugh. I stand and grab her into a hug.

* * *

On the following Sunday, I put on me finest dress and climb into the wagon with Daniel. When we arrive at St. Augustine's, people surround me, greeting me back. Their warmth dispels all the guilt I feel as I approach the communion rail. As I take the host onto me tongue, I pray, "Jesus, please let me find a way to open Kathleen's Haven."

So it is that I return to me faith. If that return is loaded with a bit of hypocrisy, so be it. When I advise an at-risk woman about preventing conception, I will confess to God in the privacy of me bedroom. I shan't ask Father Ruzzo for absolution. The poor man has enough problems.

CHAPTER SIXTY-TWO

A scandal in the making...

Two days later, Kam arrives back from New York, looking like nothing short of an African prince. Sitting beside him is Imani, the beautiful girl I met at his party years ago. I'm surprised to see her. Kam hadn't written they were still keeping company. Did he pick her up at her house on Joy Street before he came here?

He wears a striped black coat which nips in to show his narrow waist. The jacket ends in a swallow tail in the back and has only one button in front. His trousers are black and slimmer than any I've seen in Boston. At his neck, a loosely tied black cravat falls casually at the front of an open-throated white silk shirt. As he steps from the wagon, I look down at his feet. "Kam, you're wearing spatter dashes?" I exclaim.

"Actually, Mary, they're called spats now. I bought them on our trip to New York. They're all the rage in England."

"Our?" I ask.

"Yes, Imani travels with me now, actually keeps the records of me sales." He doesn't bat an eye.

She travels with him? The colored people in Boston are nearly as straight laced as the Irish. Her family must wonder the same things I do in this moment. So, I ask the question. "Are you married?"

"No, not yet. But that will probably happen one of these days."

Adoration beams from her face. As she steps from the wagon, I notice that her bosom swells over the neckline of her gown. "It's good to see you again, Imani. Are you well?"

"Yes, Mary," She looks timid as a frightened deer, and I realize she's ashamed.

"Ah, don't be shy, Imani. Kam is me brother, so now, you're me sister. I shan't pass judgment on you."

Her head inclines down from the slender neck. "Thank you, Mary. That makes me feel better." She touches me shoulder gently. "I was so sad to hear about Kathleen."

I nod. The sound of her name still hurts.

"You're still working at O'Halloran's?" she asks.

"Sometimes, but mostly I work as a midwife."

Her eyes light. "Yes, Kam mentioned that." Then, she asks, "It's been a long trip. Would it be impertinent for me to ask to use your facility?"

"Of course not, Imani. It's in the backyard."

When she leaves, Kam and I sit down on the front porch rockers, knees touching. I study his face earnestly. I've missed him so much and can tell from his probing gaze that he's missed me, too. Finally, I ask the question that's deviled me. "Can it be, dear brother, that you are tinkering with Imani's heart? She obviously loves you."

He clears his throat and stares straight out at the street for what seems a long time, and then answers. "I love her, too, Mary, but me life has been so busy for the past few years. There's been no time for marriage."

"No time?" I want to continue, but our conversation stops as Imani returns. Kam excuses himself to go to the outhouse, seeming glad to get away from me questions. I invite her to sit with me on the porch.

Her dark eyes are large with excitement. "So, Mary, you birth babies?"

"I do."

"Do you also take care of mothers while they're awaiting childbirth?"

"Very good care, I believe."

"Are you able to tell if a woman is with child?"

"Yes, almost always." I look again at the swelling of her bosom. Dare I ask? Just as Kam comes back to the porch, Daniel's wagon pulls up in front.

"Kam," Daniel exclaims, grabbing him round the shoulders and clapping him on the back. "When did you arrive?"

"Just a few minutes ago."

Daniel grabs me into his arms and kisses me on the lips. "Hello, Miss Boland," he whispers and turns back to Kam. "This one won't marry me, Kam. Crazy eejit, aye?"

Kam darts me a skeptical look, and the men go inside, laughing and talking. As I begin to follow behind them, Imani tugs me sleeve. "Daniel!" I yell. "Tell Tommy to make you two a drink. We'll be in soon."

Imani and I return to the porch. She begins to stammer. "Uh, Mary, I've never been to a doctor, but I'm beginning to wonder if . . ."

I turn to face her. "If you're with child?"

She looks down at her boots. "Yes."

"You and Kam are living as husband and wife?" The question seems unnecessary, but I mustn't assume anything.

Her coffee-colored eyes turn liquid just before she casts them down. She doesn't speak but nods her head. I am flooded with anger at Kam for putting this lovely girl in such a position. "Does Kam know?" She shakes her head.

"Well, perhaps you're not expecting."

She looks hopeful but then shakes her head again. "I haven't had me monthly blood for eight weeks. Sometimes, I throw up in the morning. What else could cause that?"

"Are your breasts tender?" I ask.

"So tender I can hardly stand for my dress to rub against them."

I take her hands into mine. "Well, me new sister, I think I'm going to have a talk with Kam."

"Are you sure?" Kam says when I tell him that evening.

"Ninety-nine per cent sure," I answer. "So, what do you intend to do about it?"

"What can I do, Mabo?"

"Marry the girl, of course. She can't go back to Joy Street unmarried and carrying your baby. You said you love her."

"I do."

"Then why haven't you married her?"

He shrugs. "In Africa, men have many wives. Here, once you're married, that's it. Besides that, I've become quite successful these past few years. In me wildest dreams, I didn't expect to be this rich."

For the first time in me life, I don't like Kam. Finally, I speak. "And what does that have to do with being an honorable man?"

Finally, his eyes become those of the old Kam. The slave boy who turned me into the banshee and took care of me like a brother when we first arrived in Boston. "Absolutely nothing," he answers.

* * *

They schedule the wedding for two weeks later. We hurry things along; there's no time to waste. In the flurry of preparation, I do not tell Kam of the bank rejecting me loan. I don't want to spoil his wedding.

The manager of the Albion House on Beacon Hill is happy to take Kam's money from Daniel as a deposit on the reception room. It's only when he meets Kam and Imani he realizes he's booked a reception for a negro couple. Then, he turns white as an Irish baby's backside.

"Oh, now wait a minute here," he says. "I didn't know, errr, actually, I'd forgotten another booking for that very day." Frantically, he starts to thumb through his ledger. When he arrives at a page with scribbling all over it, he stops and points with his index finger. "See, the room was booked a month ago." I notice he has his hand covering the date at the bottom of the page.

"Let me see that page, sir," I say, me voice pleasant as I can make it. I lift his hand from the bottom of the calendar and see that it's one week before the date for Kam and Imani's reception. "Ah, look there. You have the wrong date. Just an oversight, I'm sure." I flip the pages to the next Saturday. "See? All you have scheduled for that day is the Okafor wedding."

Kam and Daniel have grins plastered all over faces. But those grins fade when the man says, "Well, actually, we're planning to be closed for renovations on that Saturday."

Daniel steps forward and stares down into the man's face. He wears his policeman's uniform and holds his hat in his left hand. He slams his right hand down on the calendar, but speaks quietly. "No, actually, you'll have to plan your renovations for the following week." He flips through the next seven pages. "See, you've not one thing planned then. It'll work out fine."

"But," the hotel manager stutters. He pulls Daniel away from us and walks him to a corner of the foyer. I follow behind them to listen. "You understand, Mr. Kelly, that an establishment like the Albion House must be careful about its reputation."

Daniel nods sympathetically. That makes me so angry I nearly jump between the two of them, but then, Daniel puts his hand on the manager's shoulder. "Yes, indeed, sir. I understand how important your reputation is. But think of what will happen to that reputation if I contact Robert Morris about settling this matter in court."

The veins in the manager's temples begin to pulsate. Everyone knows who Robert Morris is, The Boston Globe has written about him for weeks. He is a Negro lawyer who, in 1849, took the case of Sarah Roberts, a five-year-old, because her father didn't want his child traveling four miles to the black common school. Though the courts supported the segregation of schools initially, Morris is continuing his fight in the state legislature, and it looks like he'll win it.

"You'd actually get Robert Morris involved in this?" the manager asks.

"Only if I must," Daniel answers softly.

So, on January 10, 1853, Kamua Okafor marries Imani Owusu. The wedding is grand, and no one notices the slight swell of belly under the white dress.

CHAPTER SIXTY-THREE

The travel bug is tough to exterminate.

"How soon do you think the baby will arrive?" Kam asks.

"Sometime in June."

"Will Kathleen's Haven be ready? I want Imani to give birth there."

I must tell him the truth now. I'd spared him the bad news until after the wedding. "That's not going to happen, Kam."

His eyes turn dark, nearly glaring at me. "What?"

"The bank refused me loan."

He relaxes some. "I thought you meant because of her color."

I shake me head.

"Did you tell them I'd back the loan?"

"Of course, but the Medical Association put pressure on them to reject me. They say I'm not qualified." I sip me tea quietly. "Perhaps they're right."

"Why not, Mabo? Because you don't have a medical degree?"

"Because I don't even have a grade school education."

"Mabo, you're an excellent midwife."

I put down me tea cup and stare into his eyes. I have to make him understand. Kam thinks I can do anything, but not this time. "Kam, if I can't get the loan, I cannot buy the property."

He runs his hand across his jaw. "I need to stay off the road right now, but I miss it. Maybe I've just thought of a way to stay busy here in Boston."

I stare at him in silence. Finally, he speaks. "I can be your bank, Mabo." His voice is soft.

I am purely flabbergasted. Me words come out in a stammer. "What about your foundation?"

"I set that up months ago."

"Why didn't you tell me?"

"Didn't want to brag about it, but I was going to make another deposit at the bank this week. Instead, I'll buy and remodel the house for Kathleen."

So it is that plans change and dreams are fulfilled. He has two stipulations: One is that the Whistler portrait he commissioned for Kathleen hang in a prominent place in the birthing center. Of course. I would've done that anyway. His second requirement is right and proper, but troubling. He insists that colored and white women will be welcome at Kathleen's Haven.

I know the stink this will cause in the community, but the community is wrong. Kam is right. "Of course," I answer firmly. "And I'll pay you back someday, somehow."

He laughs. "Mabo, believe me, I know you pay your debts."

The next day, we go back to the house on Dorchester Street. Thank God, the sign is still there. Kam and I seal the deal in less than two hours. It is January 20, 1853, and we are ready to remodel.

CHAPTER SIXTY-FOUR

A dream is built with paint and mortar.

Kam, Daniel and three of Daniel's friends from the Sixth Ward start renovations. Our lives become a blur of plaster powder and sawdust. Walls tumble and the kitchen is expanded to house two delivery rooms. Upstairs, four large bedrooms are halved into eight sleeping areas. If a woman has no family to support her during her pregnancy, she can stay here until her delivery and for one week after. Wash tubs are placed next to the two wood stoves so that heated water can be available quickly for sanitizing the birthing areas and linens from the delivery tables.

Payment will be collected from those who can afford it. For the others, Kam's foundation will pay for care. Donations arrive from St. Augustine's and the Joy Street churches.

Shannon volunteers to cook food at the pub and deliver it daily to the site when it's ready. Tommy asks only to be reimbursed for the cost of the food. For the first time since Kathleen's death, he appears to have a reason for living. When Kam and I tell him that the birthing haven will be named for Kathleen, the grin on his now haggard face almost reminds me of when she was with him.

"Tommy, where's the portrait Kam had painted of Kathleen?" I ask.

"Down in the basement of the pub, Mary. I wanted to put it over the bar, but it seems far too grand there and, besides, I weep each time I look at it."

"It must have a place of honor in her birthing haven!"

His eyes mist. "Ah, Mary," he answers. "That'll be a grand place for it, now won't it?"

But as I stand here on a ladder, slathering yellow paint on an upstairs sleeping room, I worry that we'll meet our deadline for opening. Imani sits on a bed, near an open window keeping me company. She says the smell of the paint sickens her. I refuse to let her climb the ladder, so she helps by quilting a lemon and green comforter for the room.

"Imani, you may be the one resting under that quilt when your time comes," I say.

"Oh, Mary, do you think that would be proper?"

"Proper?"

Long lashes sweep down over coffee and cream cheekbones. "I mean, for a negress to birth her child here in the same house with white girls."

I climb down from the ladder and sit on the floor in front of her. "Imani, if it weren't for your husband, this birthing haven wouldn't exist. It's part of our agreement. Yes, it's proper." The bravado of me words belies a certain disquietude in me soul.

She smiles. "That's such a relief to me, Mary. There's no place on Joy Street like this. I'd feel so much safer here with you to help me."

I jump to me feet and climb back up me ladder. "Well, if I don't get back to me painting, we'll never get this place open. Are you feeling all right?"

"Wonderful." She stands and runs her hands over her stomach, then sits back down to her stitching. "I just have to watch how much I eat. I don't want to be a waddling fat lady after I deliver."

I laugh. "That's not going to happen, Imani. All your weight is baby weight. You'll be slim as ever in no time at all."

"When I look at how me belly sticks out, I doubt I'll ever be slim again," she laughs. Then her voice deepens, "Will you be with me for the entire birth, Mary?"

"Yes, you have me word on that. And guess what? You're the first to know this, but Molly, Kathleen's youngest, asked this morning if she could apprentice with me. So, she'll be with us as well."

Imani puts down her needle and claps her hands together. "Isn't that perfect? The O'Halloran's were the first white people in this town who welcomed me in their home. Now I'm going to have me first baby in Kathleen's Haven with her daughter there. These are good omens."

On the day we finish the renovation, we hang Kathleen's portrait in the foyer. Mr. Whistler has captured all her strength and humor in his painting. Her dress is a brilliant red. Her long brown hair cascades over one shoulder. She wears no jewelry except her gold wedding ring. She's laughing in the painting which is unusual enough, and Mr. Whistler, captured by her giant spirit, also placed a floured rolling pin in her right hand.

CHAPTER SIXTY-FIVE

As Tranquil as a Basking Shark . . .

I am awakened the next morning by a loud knocking on the pub door. Muffled male voices come from the porch. I hurry to put on me shawl. The men sound panicky so I race to the porch. "What is it?"

A patrol man named Murphy, stands next to Daniel. "Shall I tell her?"

"No, I will," Daniel answers. "Mary, come inside. I need to talk to you."

"What is it?" I nearly scream the words after he closes the door.

"It's Kathleen's Haven," he says.

"What about it?"

"Someone wrecked it last night. They used mallets and pick-axes. The damage is bad."

I struggle to understand. Who could have done such a thing? And why?

Daniel grabs me under the arms as me knees buckle. "Mary, I think it's because of Kam's involvement." He turns me toward our bedroom. "Now, get some clothes on. We'll see what the damages are."

I cannot believe me eyes. Every window on the first floor is smashed. The white picket fence is a pile of shattered wood. The sign with Kathleen's name on it has been torn down from above the front door and hacked to pieces. The pretty lace curtains the ladies of St. Augustine's crocheted for the windows have been torn to shreds and littered all over the front lawn. The front door hangs off its hinges. We walk into the reception room.

There on the lavender wall I see it—a black scrawl of hatred on Mr. Whistler's portrait. The paint is still wet. It says "Nigger Lover."

Daniel holds me as I begin to keen and wail. He says me words are, "Why, why, why?" I don't remember any of that, but I'm sure he speaks the truth.

When I wake again, Daniel is there in the pub. His eyes are red from weeping, too.

Kam comes later. "We'll fix it, Mary. I ran into ugly things like this on the road."

I shake me head. "What's the use?" Me despair is a black shroud over me hope. "They'll only do it again."

For two weeks I stay at the pub, venturing out only to birth Sally Lucas's baby. It's an easy delivery, but I leave it no happier than when I entered their house. I refuse to visit again the site that was Kathleen's Haven. Kam signs the police report and, after a few days, they catch three men who admit to the crime. When asked why they did it, the oldest one says, "We don't want no niggers birthing babies in the same house as whites."

"I don't understand it, Mary," Daniel says as we sit on the bench in front of the pub. "The investigator says the ringleader lost his wife in childbirth just last year because she couldn't afford a doctor." I turn away from him, but he takes me hand.

"Sweetheart, maybe it's time to throw in the towel. I'm worried about you."

I shake me head.

"Please, let's visit Father Ruzzo and get our Banns of marriage posted. We can live in the little house I built for us, and you can continue to birth babies as you did before."

For a moment, I want to say yes so much me heart hurts. But instead, I look up into his eyes, the eyes of this man I love. "I can't marry you, Daniel."

"But, Mary," he sputters, "Don't you love me?"

"I love you with all me heart. I'll never love another. But before I become Mary Kelly, I must fully be Mary Boland. I must be certain I've done everything in me power to accomplish me destiny."

He hangs his head and shakes it side to side. Then he speaks. "Am I not your destiny?"

"Perhaps someday, but not now."

He stands, turns on his heel and walks away.

CHAPTER SIXTY-SIX

Though a decision is rash, it may be right.

Two weeks have passed since I refused Daniel's proposal, and I haven't seen him once. He's not been at church or any of his usual haunts. I am so very sad and miss him terribly but do believe me decision is right, or at least, I think it is. As I lie slumbering this morning, I am awakened by Molly. "Mary, get up. Now!"

She sounds so like her mother it almost makes me smile, but I do not stir from the couch. If I don't move a muscle, maybe she'll go away.

But, no. She begins to shake me, somewhat violently. "Stop it, Molly. I'm tired," I snap at her.

"No, I won't stop. Get up. Get dressed. We've a meeting to attend."

How dare this child give me orders! I sit up, finally, and rub me eyes. "What meeting?"

"At the Haven. Let's go."

I fall back onto me pillow. "I want nothing to do with that place." I roll over so me back is turned to her.

She grabs me by the shoulders and forces me to face her.

Mad as this makes me, I am impressed by her strength. "You are coming with me. I'm going to heat the water. Then, you'll get up and into the tub. We only have an hour to get there."

Shaking me head, I struggle to me feet. *Why am I taking orders from an eight-year-old?* But Molly's determination is total, so when she tells me the water's warm, I shuffle toward the kitchen. When was the last time I bathed? I can't remember.

She pulls the nightgown over me head and points to the tub. No sense in arguing with her. I sink into the warmth.

With no warning, Molly pours a pitcher of heated water on me head. I sputter in protest, but she says, "Your hair's a mess, Mary. Wash it."

I obey, washing the dirt from me tangled mop of hair. "That's going to take a stiff brush," she murmurs, heading toward the door, "and I've got just the thing."

After a few moments, she returns to the room, hefting over her head a horse brush that looks like it could groom a porcupine. "This'll work. Come on, time to get out."

I want to remain in the calming warmth of the water, but again, I obey her. She wraps me in a towel and pushes me to sit down on a kitchen stool. Then she starts with the brush. "Owww. That hurts."

"It'll teach you not to wait so long 'til your next hair wash, Mary," she says, continuing to pull the brush through me matted hair.

Though I yell and complain through the brushing, she soldiers on. Finally, she stands back from me and says, "There, that'll have to do." She takes a ribbon from her pocket and ties me hair back from me face. "Now, get dressed." She pushes me toward the bedroom.

When I stand staring into me tiny chest of drawers, she pushes in front of me like a whirlwind. "Lord, Mary, how can it be so hard? You only have three choices." She pulls out me church dress and shawl. "Put this on."

When I'm dressed and shod to her satisfaction, she smiles and says, "Let's go."

She drives the wagon toward what was to be Kathleen's Haven, me sitting beside her like a sack of flour. When we arrive there, I'm surprised that standing in the cold on the front porch is a ragtag assembly of humanity. Heading up the group of twenty people are Father Ruzzo and, of all people, Agnes Dooley.

Chapter Sixty-Seven

Friendship is the thing that holds the world together.

Agnes wears a mink shawl. Whoring must indeed be a profit-able business. "What're you doing here, Agnes?" I exclaim.

She puffs herself up like a bird dampened by the rain. "I've a perfect right to be here."

Molly grins while I stutter and stammer, trying to recover meself. "Surely, you do, Agnes. It's just surprised, I am. I mean no offense to you."

Father Ruzzo steps in. "I'm sure Agnes takes no offense at your surprise, Mary. She wanted to be here."

I draw meself up to me full height, grateful for his diplomacy. "So, why are *all* of you here?" I wave around the porch, indi-cating the sea of smiling faces. I recognize most of them from Mass. And then, I am stopped by one face that stands out from the others. "Kam, I thought you were wrapping things up in New York. Is Imani all right?"

"Great, Mary," he answers, his grin joyous. "Getting bigger by the day. She's over the morning sickness and can't wait for the baby to come."

Molly beams with pleasure. "I'll be here to help Mary deliver it."

"That's nice," I murmur, still dazed.

Seeing the confusion in me face, Father Ruzzo steps up and takes me hands in his. "Mary, St. Augustine's has been deeply distressed by what happened here. It's important that our women have a safe birthing center. We want to repair it."

I shake me head. "What's the use of that, Father?" I ask. "They'll just do it again."

"And we'll just keep fixing it," Kam answers.

"We mustn't let ignorance win, Mary," Father Ruzzo continues. "The Haven is a good thing for South Boston. Everyone knows it. I don't know why there's evil in the world, but I do know it's the work of the devil and that we must continue to fight against him. God wants you to help this community with your haven."

A hand tugs on me sleeve. I turn to find Agnes. "Mary, can I have a word in private?"

We go to the side of the porch where no one can hear us.

"I know you're wondering why I'm part of this, Mary," she says. "A gentleman, Jeremiah Doggett, has asked me to be his wife." She actually blushes. "He has quite a lot of money. I figure using it to help restore Kathleen's Haven will go a long way to giving me a better reputation in this town."

"Do you love this Mr. Ryan, Agnes?"

She quirks one side of her mouth as though she'd never considered me question. "Well, he doesn't make me retch, and he's never beaten me, so is that what you call love?" She begins to laugh, and the sound is so merry I join right in with her. Before I know it, the two of us are standing there giggling our heads off. When she gets control of herself, she continues. "Lest you think I've become a saint or something, you should know I've a somewhat selfish motive in all this."

"Surprise, surprise," I say, me chest still bouncing with mirth.

"You see, I'm expecting again."

I raise me eyebrow in question.

"Yes, it's Jeremiah's. And this time, I'll keep it. I know you're a better birther than any doctor around here. I want to come to Kathleen's Haven when me time comes. And I'll be able to pay handsomely for the privilege."

I look down and detect a very slight swelling in her stomach. "That's grand, Agnes," I say, and mean it.

As I turn to go back to Father Ruzzo and Kam, I see a familiar hulking shape standing beside them. "Stash!" I'm so excited to see him I grab him in for a hug. "What're you doing here?"

"I heard about all the trouble those bastards gave you. It was in the paper enough. I want to help you rebuild The Haven."

"Oh, Stash, that's wonderful. Thank you so much."

"Well, there's another reason," he says, pulling a woman from behind him up to face me.

"Darya," I exclaim. From the restaurant where I had my first corned beef.

She grins and loops her arm through Stash's. "Me and Darya finally got married last year," he says. He pats her stomach. "She's expecting a little Stash or Sophie, so I want a safe place for her."

"Congratulations. Darya, come to O'Halloran's pub tomorrow and I'll examine you."

She nods gratefully. Father Ruzzo and Kam stand there in front of the sea of expectant faces on the porch. "What do you need from me to start the work?" I ask.

"Just your prayers, Mary," Father Ruzzo answers.

CHAPTER SIXTY-EIGHT

May God give you a rainbow after every storm.

March 17, 1853

The ribbon cutting is scheduled for two o'clock today, me seventeenth birthday. Tommy, the girls, and baby Sean have already left for the celebration. Miata will meet us there. She went back to Joy Street a month ago but still brings breast milk for baby Sean twice each week.

Kam and Imani will take me. I dress carefully in me green dress. It's hard to believe it was only one year ago that Kathleen pinned me into it. It still looks like new. I've saved it for special occasions. And this is indeed special, probably the most special occasion in me life so far.

Tonight, I will sleep in Kathleen's Haven. All four of its rooms will probably be filled with expectant mothers. One of them is colored. Tommy took me few belongings over with him earlier. Me four years of living here are ending.

As I gaze around O'Halloran's, every glance brings a memory. In the kitchen, I see Kathleen rolling out her pies and laughing her wonderful laugh. Behind the bar, there's Tommy pulling a draught and spooling out a great yarn. Clustered around the stove, I envision Kam and me and the girls, eyes wide as Kathleen teaches us lessons that will carry us throughout our lives. And the customers, ah the customers; happy and loud, telling their stories of the auld country and downing their Irish ales and whiskeys.

I've learned so much here in me first home in America. I've experienced love and grief and salvation in this place, and in some ways, I hate to leave it. But it's time for me new life, me true destiny.

After Kathleen passed, I worried Tommy would flounder, but he's astounded me with his instinct to survive. I guess he had little choice with Shannon, Molly, and little Sean to guide and provide for.

Shannon now bakes pies nearly as well as Kathleen did. And Molly is a whiz at making O'Halloran's famous scrappy beef sandwiches. Baby Sean bounces in his little chair behind the bar with Tommy, and if any customer comes near that baby with a cigar, they get a dose of swearing from Tommy that'd curl their hair, though most of them have little hair left.

All in all, life goes on pretty much as it did before the tragedy. We speak of Kathleen constantly. Every one of us has a story about the woman who was larger than life, and twice as loving. And just when I think we've exhausted every possible memory, someone brings back a gem from the past that we'd all forgotten for a moment or a day, and the laughter begins again. It is as though she's still here with us—well, almost—though when I recall her pain at the end, me eyes always fill. So, I try not to think of the pain, only the joy of loving her.

Last month, Tommy hired the widow Sullivan for wait-ressing, and watching the two of them together, I wonder if she's delivering on more than sandwiches.

At first I was scandalized and angry at him, but then I realized this is exactly what Kathleen would want. She couldn't bear for Tommy to remain lonely for long. Mamie Sullivan is good for O'Halloran's, and good for Tommy. Though she'll never compare to Kathleen with her lank, blonde hair and skinny frame. Ah, that sounds catty, doesn't it? Well, I guess I didn't learn all the lessons Kathleen had to teach. I've a perfect right to be jealous on her behalf, if I want to.

Molly will spend as much time as she can spare from school and this place with me. "If I want to get into a medical school someday, Mary, an apprenticeship at the birthing center may go a long way toward helping me."

I can't argue with her logic. Besides, she's every bit as stubborn as her mother was, so I don't quarrel with Molly about much of anything. Some battles are best left unfought.

There's one thing left to do. Me fingers tremble as I take Mam's gold cross from its hiding place in me pocket and fasten it around me neck. I saved this moment for today. It shines in the sunshine coming through the window and feels warm, nestled between me breasts. I've missed this cross just as I missed me church. It is right to wear it again because I now believe I'm worthy of it.

Kam and Imani arrive at exactly one thirty. As she climbs back into their carriage, I can't tell from behind that she's expecting. She's still so slender, but her belly is large. "I'm getting so uncomfortable, Mary. I want this baby now," she says as I settle in beside her.

"Be patient, Imani. I figure about ten more weeks." I run me fingers over her and am punched by a tiny wallop. "Oh, baby Okafor is feeling frisky today." I laugh and caress her belly again. "Behave yourself now. You'll be with us soon enough."

During the restoration of The Haven, I couldn't have asked for a better business partner than Kam. He's been there with me every day and has put his brain and muscle into its restoration.

He's investigating the possibility of selling his tonic by mail order. Isn't that crazy? I've never heard of such a thing. But I've learned never to doubt Kam's abilities when his intentions are set, and his intention now is to support the birthing center and other local charities and remain close to Imani.

Watching me friends from St. Augustine's working side-by-side with Stash and Miata and others from Kam's Joy Street community in this reparation has been a huge healing for me heart. If they can work together, coloreds and whites and Jews, for a common good, perhaps this weary world has a chance for a better future. I worry, though, about the rumblings of rebellion from slave owners in the South. So many puzzles left unsolved, but this is not a day for quandaries. This is a day for joy.

When we arrive, the haven looks even better than it did before the wrecking. A white band plays Irish music and alternates with a colored band playing Dixieland, the new jazz music from New Orleans. I notice that the band not playing claps and stomps to the beat of the other.

People dance in the street and on the sidewalk. One of the dancers looks familiar. I go up to him. "Tim?"

"Mary, we were in Boston visiting relatives and saw your picture. Lord, girl, you've done well for yerself, haven't ye?"

Suddenly, Moira appears beside him. "Mary, see I told you you'd turn out a great beauty, and you have!"

I grab them both in for an embrace. "But I'd never have grown up had you two not picked me up off the stones that day."

"Was Elizabeth kind to you?" Moira asks.

What sense is there in telling her the truth. "Yes, Moira, very kind. Thank you for introducing me to her."

Green banners fly from every lamp post, and streamers cascade across Dorchester Street. I find a shaded bench under a tree and sit down. Across the street, I see Agnes arm in arm with a portly gentleman whose mutton chops cover his cheeks. They are in deep conversation with Sam Mendel. An odd trio they make, and I can't begin to imagine what these three can find to talk about.

On the porch, Father Ruzzo and the Sisters from St. Augustine's serve punch and cookies alongside colored women wearing fancy hats. Father waves joyously when he sees me. He looks young again—almost like the man I met on the street four years ago.

But one face is missing, though I look everywhere for it—Daniel Kelly's.

Kam, who has followed me to me bench, says, "You look sad, Mabo?"

"I'm not—not really, Kam. I'm thrilled about what we've accomplished here. I can't wait to move in and get started. The rooms are full for tonight, and I have eight more women on a waiting list. Five of them are able to pay cash. This is beyond doubt the destiny I'm meant for, but . . ."

"But you gave up Daniel to get it."

Me heart sinks. "I guess I did. He wants marriage, and I have too much to do. Maybe someday, but not now."

"Trust, Mary. What's happening in your life is God's plan. If Daniel is part of that plan, it will happen someday."

His words console me, but what really perks me up is seeing a man from the Boston Globe taking pictures of the Haven and the crowd. "Do you think we'll get a picture in the paper?" I ask the photographer.

"On page one," he answers. "The publisher has promised to spring for the engraving. This is big news, Miss Boland. This whole rebuilding fits the spirit of independence that the Globe thrives on."

A drum rolls, I stand up, and the crowd gathers around the front porch. The mayor says a few words and cuts the red ribbon at the door and. Kathleen's Haven officially opens. The mood is so festive it feels like the Fourth of July. Though it's only March, I almost expect fireworks. And sure enough, they roar. Watching the rockets soar up into the air, I raise an eyebrow to Kam. "No point in cutting corners now," he says, grinning. "We can afford it."

I take Tommy's hand and escort him inside, and the first thing we see is Kathleen's portrait. There she is, strong and stalwart, rolling pin in hand, her face alive with laughter. I turn to Tommy and see his eyes are misty. "Ah, Mary, she'd be so proud, wouldn't she?"

Me eyes brim, too, and I put me arm around his shoulders. "Indeed she would, Tommy. Indeed she would."

The painting no longer has the black scrawl across her chest.

"How'd they get the paint off it?" Tommy says.

"Mr. Whistler did it. He was furious when he saw it and repainted over the black. Kam says it only took him two days."

Going back out into the sunshine, me heart fills to bursting with the glory of this historic day. As if on cue, the Irish band strikes up a jig. The rhythm pulsates up me body from me tapping toes to the top of me head, and I begin to move and bounce.

I then feel his presence. The crowd noise mutes in me ears as I turn slowly around. Daniel stands there. Me breath catches in me throat as he looks into me eyes. "You're here."

"Of course, I'm here." He reaches out his arms. "I couldn't miss this. May I have this dance, Miss Boland?"

"Oh, Daniel, I didn't think you'd come."

"Must admit I was mad as a hornet in the beginning, but then I decided that you're right."

Me heart catches. "You don't love me?"

"Mary, I will always love you. And I believe you'll always love me, too." He pulls me close to him. His chest is hard and his scent so intoxicating I want to stay there forever. But he pushes me away. "But you have things to do with your life, and so do I. I've been accepted by James Marsden for a law apprenticeship. I am going to become an attorney."

I jump away and look up into his eyes. "Isn't he an Englishman?"

"Now, don't be getting your pig-headed Irish up, girl. There are some good English people. Marsden is one of them."

"I suppose so. I've heard good things about him."

"And I'll use that law degree to help our people, Mary. The poor Irish here in Boston are getting banjaxed by the Massachusetts courts. Hanged for horse thievery where no horse existed, just because they're Irish."

I nod. "So, it's a lawyer you'll be, huh?"

He grins. "Yes. In four years."

"That's wonderful, Daniel."

"You know I want to be the first Irish mayor of Boston, don't you?"

"Yes, Kam told me that, but . . ."

"You didn't think I had the gumption? You're not the only one with a destiny, Mary Boland."

I laugh up into his beautiful blue eyes. "And guess what?" he says.

"What?"

"In four years, you'll be twenty-one. I'll be twenty-three. Good ages for marrying, don't you think? Kathleen's Haven will be established. Perhaps then, you'll have time for me."

"Perhaps I will indeed." I lower me eyes and sashay me bustle.

"No perhaps about it. Now, move your feet, girl. It's time you finished that dance you stiffed me out of last St. Paddy's Day. But brace yourself, you should know you're dancing with the dance champ of County Mayo."

"I'd love to dance with you, Daniel, but first, do you still have the Claddagh ring I refused at Christmas?"

He pats his chest pocket. "Right here."

I am so relieved. "I thought perhaps you'd returned it to the jeweler."

"It was me mam's ring. Not mine to return."

"And what does that ring mean, Daniel?"

"A promise to try. That's all. Just a promise to try."

He slips it on me finger. I take it from me left hand and put it on me right ring finger. "I'll try, but I can't make any vows yet."

"No vows required, Mary. We'll talk in four years. Now, though, let's dance."

He dances me like I've never been danced before. His arms feel strong and secure, and I relax the control of me body into his keeping. We stomp and whirl, and I think I've never been so happy before. Me gold cross flies out in front of me. The crowd encircling us claps and yells its encouragement. I see Kam and Imani and Tommy, Shannon, Molly, and Father Ruzzo. Every face that blurs by me is smiling—even Agnes's. There she is; I swear Kathleen's face is there, too. Grinning at me with the pride of a mother. Then, she's gone. Was I imagining?

But one thing I'm not imagining—on this day, this first day of destiny begun, one thing is certain—I am surely the best dancer in Boston. Well perhaps, the best *female* dancer in Boston. Daniel might be a wee bit better.

Acknowledgments

It does take a village to write a novel. All of these people have helped *Shanty Gold* to become the book it is.

Matthew Brenckle—Research coordinator for the U.S.S. Constitution Museum in Boston

Sister Judy Kappenman, Director of Irish Studies, Elms College in Chicopee, MA

Peter Clarke—owner of Brack Tours, Dublin, Ireland

Paddy Shields, manager of The Junction Irish Pub in South Boston, MA

Joe and Claire Williams, Castle Island, South Boston, MA

Queenstown Museum in Cobh, County Cork, Ireland

Cobh Historical Museum, County Cork, Ireland

Dermot Ryan, Kinsale, Ireland Heritage tours, County Cork, Ireland

Stacia Baker, M.D., for all medical questions related to the book

Pink Fire Writers: Susan Blexrud, Beth Robrecht, and Sallie Bissell for our invaluable critique sessions

Jim Puffer for his help on naval matters

Kennon Webber, The Poet of North Asheville, for editing suggestions

The Catholic Archives in Braintree, MA

ACKNOWLEDGMENTS

The Boston Harbormaster
The Boston Athaeneum
The Boston Public Library
Sallie Bissell, for editing assistance
Kaila Spencer, equine assistance
Matt Restivo, tour partner extraordinaire, on our many trips to Ireland and Boston
Father Edward Sheridan

ABOUT THE AUTHOR

Jeanne Charters is a veteran of the broadcast television industry. She was vice president of marketing for Viacom TV and opened her own broadcast ad agency, Charters Marketing.

Charters grew up believing she'd be a stay-at-home mom and live in her hometown in Ohio for the rest of her life. However, after four children and a divorce, Charters ended up in Albany, New York, where she met and married Matt Restivo, her husband of thirty-five years and counting. Charters and Restivo moved to Asheville, North Carolina, after retirement. Beyond her novels, she has also written for magazines and newspapers.

DAUGHTERS OF IRELAND

FROM OPEN ROAD MEDIA

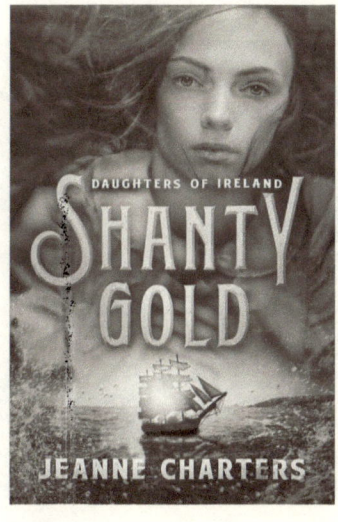

OPEN ROAD

INTEGRATED MEDIA

INTEGRATED MEDIA

Find a full list of our authors and
titles at www.openroadmedia.com

FOLLOW US
@OpenRoadMedia